The Emotional Evolution of Thomas Sanders

Steven A. Freeman

Abigail Smith

Hardcover ISBN: 978-1-961605-85-5

Library of Congress Control Number: 2026901173

KI Productions
Noblesville, IN

talesofcardinalcreek.com

This book is manufactured in the United States of America.

Editor: Janet Schwind
Cover Design: Ana Robino
Manuscript Overview: Rachel Hills

Prologue

The Cardinal Creek Character List

A cheat sheet I, Thomas Sanders, came up with to be sure that you, gentle reader, will get a factual description of the people in this book.

The Sanders Family:

Thomas Sanders - Does not like long walks on the beach or sharing anything (this covers a wide range of items from intimate feelings all the way to dessert). In fact, I'm not crazy about sharing my life through this book with the whole world, but here we are.

Bea Sanders - Intelligent, nurturing, witty, and quite deceased yet very opinionated wife. She's far more interesting to me than anyone else, living or otherwise, so I still spend a great deal of my time talking with her. Bea loved everyone, and I loved Bea terribly.

The Harper Family:

Wilma Harper - Wilma makes the most delectable pies I've ever tasted. I had to choose between a life with her conspiracy theories or a life without her pie. I think you know I made the right call. Wilma is supposed to also manage the diner's busy front end, but her full attention is usually spent on keeping her eyes peeled for the big juicy crime she's certain is being committed around every corner.

Scott Harper - Wilma's only child, unfortunately for him. He could use another sibling to share the burden of Wilma's smothering attention. On paper he's technically the owner of the Munch Box Diner, although Wilma forgets that a few hundred times a day. Rather than viewing Scott as her boss or son, she tends to treat him more as a resource for getting future grandbabies to spoil.

Dan Harper - Reverently referred to as Saint Dan by some of us in acknowledgement of his station in life as Wilma's husband. Dan uses words sparingly, probably because Wilma floods the world with enough for them both.

Maggie the Boxer - I don't know what words to use to accurately describe Maggie. I'd say first you should throw out everything you know about pets. Maggie is a dog in theory, but she's a whole lot more than four legs and an aggravating bark. Once you've cleared your mind of what a dog is supposed to do, then you can read the book to learn about her. I'd also recommend using hand sanitizer.

The Bistro Ladies:

Olive Denton - She's the co-owner of the Daily Drip Bistro and bakes cinnamon rolls so exquisite they've become a warm, gooey thorn in Wilma's side. Along with avoiding Wilma, Olive is also good at staying away from the local nut jobs and too much serious conversation.

Taffy Compton - Not to be confused with a popular candy of the same name, Taffy is the other co-owner of the bistro, Olive's life partner, and another all-around nice gal.

The Wild Cards:

Jordan Tackett - What can I say about this heavily tattooed man with dreadlocks hanging halfway to his ankles? He's Joe to his friends, pastor to his congregation, and a drug dealing hippie according to Wilma. I don't feel like anyone really knows Joe unless they've seen him in his overalls.

Jewels Tackett - Somewhere along the line, Jewels got the impression that kale and quinoa are not only healthy for humans but provide essential nutrients and should be eaten daily. Other than her outlandish eating and lying though, she's a terrific human being.

The Three Wise Men (it's really too bad sarcasm doesn't translate well in print):

Pastor Mike Briggs - Mike was one of Bea's closest friends, so out of respect for that relationship I won't tell you he tries (but fails miserably) to cheat at poker. He's simply too nice to pull off something nefarious. Together, Mike and Bea founded the Rapturous Finds Thrift Store to fund the town's women's shelter. He oversees the thrift shop, the women's shelter, and his church. (When it's presented like that, I suspect he cheats at poker because he doesn't have the time to learn how to play.)

Pastor Lee Calloway - Lee and I grew up as a good friends and I know him pretty well. It's hard for me to lump him in with the religious types because he's not like them at all. He's fair, in control, and respects everyone he meets. If it was up to me, I'd call that being a good human and leave the religious stuff out of it.

Pastor Vallen Walters - Val used to work for the Greatest Nutjob to ever live, Pastor Frank Norris, but that didn't last long. Val's not an evil authoritarian and Frank doesn't have a functioning heart, so obviously their relationship was doomed from the start.

A Singular Sensation:

Kenny Stambaugh - The almost always shirtless Kenny is the poster child for kindness and having a level head. He's also an expert beer drinker, an important part of Joe and Jewels's inner circle, and possibly the only person I know who isn't intimidated by Wilma.

People I trust enough to check my mail while I'm on vacation:

Rusty Burdine - Rusty has worn the same old disgusting baseball cap for more years than I can count. I would know since he sits across from me for three meals a day at the diner. He took over the Pit Stop and all its customers when his dad retired, so if you need an alignment or new brake pads you should head on over to his shop.

Ido Marchetti - Slightly chunky, always optimistic, and terrified of the bossy females in his huge Italian family, Ido is the proprietor of Ido's Market. He doesn't have that "big box store" energy, and that's why his is still the only grocery store in town. We don't appreciate retail shops where you can buy in bulk. No one needs twenty-six pounds of plain Greek yogurt all at one time.

Palmer Rawlings - He thinks Hollywood is divine, can quote every line from every movie I've never seen, and is the owner of the Starstruck Theater. Palmer sells concessions for a reasonable price, and I believe there's a lot of good things to be said for a man who values his customers above his profit margins.

The Langdon Family:

Sally Langdon - Sally will most likely end up running a successful business of her own in a few years because she is just that clever. Together, Sally and I can destroy a box of donuts in roughly the time it takes to watch a sitcom, so you can see why I think so highly of her.

Hart Langdon - When Hart walks into a room, you better be ready to play with toys, eat sticky snacks, make up unusual words, and giggle. For someone who hasn't even been alive five full years she sure has a way with humans. Well, and dogs, too.

Peggy Ackerman - Along with baking mouthwatering treats and being Sally's surrogate aunt, Peggy is also my neighbor from across the street. She made friends with Bea long before she did with me, but that's not unusual. Bea has that effect on people.

A group of two or more nutjobs is called a mistake:

Bob Frazier - Old Brimstone Bob is the numbers-hungry pastor of Cardinal Creek First Baptist Church. If your Aunt Joan's daughter's best friend from college who lives in Anchorage, Alaska, is looking for a new church, Bob would be able to smell their interest from across the country. He'd have you on one of those awkward phone calls where he's fishing around for information in under sixty seconds. If you have any advice on navigating life as his offspring, I'm sure his son Neil would appreciate it.

Frank Norris – I don't usually rank the nastiness of things, but I'd put Frank's demeanor at the top of the list well above nuclear waste, telemarketers, and gluten-free hamburger buns. I feel sad for the humans who attend Harmony Church because it feels like Frank's been their pastor for as long as the town has had a charter. If you're smart, you'll skip over any mention of him in this book.

The Liar's Bench:

Averitt Whitt - If you aren't familiar with the concept of what a Liar's Bench even is, I can help. It's a gathering of people who weave a tapestry of lies in and out of one or two true facts and then become outraged when their stories aren't believed. Since Averitt is the oldest living member of the storytelling fraternal, he fancies himself some kind of small-town royalty.

Harold Richardson - Harold is Averitt's sidekick in all things. Whether eating fried catfish or spicing up a story about the size of a watermelon, wherever you find Averitt you'll also find Harold.

That Nitwit:

Charlotte Davens - Gaudy. Fuchsia. Excessive. Baffled over the lack of valet parking at the drugstore. If she cuts a finger on one of her ridiculously sharp fake nails, glitter will spurt out and cover every surface of the room. I hustle myself in the opposite direction whenever I see her, and you'd be smart to do the same.

The Brothens Family:

Edda Mae Brothens - Back in the day, Wilma and Edda Mae were the best of friends. Not so much these days though. Currently, Wilma would love to figure out a legal way to blow Edda Mae off the map and out of her life.

Denise Brothens - Edda Mae's daughter. Probably a lovely person, but none of us around here would know because Wilma won't let anyone get close enough to find out.

Chapter 1

I'm having a fantastic morning at the Munch Box Diner. It's peaceful. It's quiet. It's exactly the way I want it to be.

Wilma's wandering through the last few lingering members of the breakfast crowd with a steaming hot carafe. My watch tells me it's almost nine. I toss down the last swallow of coffee before positioning my cup at the edge of the table. Since my morning routine is to have breakfast and complete a crossword by nine-thirty, give or take a few minutes, I'm right on track for one last cup before I go.

"Stuck?" she teases, glancing down at my crinkled newspaper. Her apron is covered in flour smears and a wayward length of auburn hair is swinging across her eyes. She's a powerhouse of a woman both mentally and physically, in spite of barely reaching five feet with shoes on.

"I am never stuck." I retort, smoothing out my paper.

"Right," she taunts. "The great Tommy Sanders knows everything."

"You're talking to the man who was awarded Crossword Master of Cardinal Creek last year." I arch my eyebrow at her.

She snorts. "Any old rooster with a pencil can do a crossword,

Tommy. You're crowing about a very commonplace achievement in a very commonplace town." She snaps the lid closed on the carafe and scoots my newly filled cup back over to me. "Try doing that puzzle in pen if you want something to crow about."

"Alright then, let's see if a yappy hen twenty years my junior can do any better." I flip my newspaper around toward her and jab at it with my pencil. "What's a four-letter word for 'should that be the case'?"

She scrunches up her nose and glances out the window into the parking lot to think, then gasps, "Hippies!"

I throw my head back and laugh. "Hippies? That's not a four-letter word."

She slams the carafe down and hurls herself across the bench seat, pressing her hands and nose to the window. She feverishly whispers, "Tommy! Tommy, get up here and look at this!"

Among other outrageous things I'll have to fill you in on later, Wilma's always imagined herself as a sort of honorary police officer who helps keep the ebb and flow of our small town honest, safe, and free from dangerous types.

I use the term "helps" very loosely, mind you.

I glance outside and grumble, "Wilma, for heaven's sake, I'm looking out the same set of windows as you. I can't see a single thing happening that's going to merit the amount of peace and quiet you're about to ruin for me."

"This is..." she squints for a better view and hisses again, "this is something serious! Get up here!"

I drop my pencil with an annoyed sigh and pull myself upright.

Standing next to a well-worn pickup truck at the back of the diner parking lot are two fine examples of what she would classify as Grade-A hippies. There's a skinny guy who looks to be in his mid-twenties with a bushy mustache, dreadlocks, and more of his skin tattooed than not. The other guy might be a bit older and is also heavily tattooed but gets bonus hippie points for being proudly shirtless.

I can't say we get a lot of tattooed, shirtless, dreadlocked people in Cardinal Creek—I'll give Wilma that much.

The dreadlocked man is holding a brown paper package that's suspiciously nondescript in its plainness. If there's one thing Wilma's learned from hours and hours of watching crime shows on television, it's that hippies deal their drugs in plain brown paper packages. And if there's anything Wilma despises more than a regular hippie, it's a drug dealing hippie.

"Drug deal!" she slaps my arm. "Gawd's nightgown!"

Did I also mention that Wilma thrives on a good old crisis?

Olive Denton, co-owner of the nearby Daily Drip Bistro, walks up to the hippies. Olive and her partner Taffy have had Wilma's wrath aimed at them since they dared to add cinnamon rolls to their menu. Wilma seems to think she's the only place in town that should sell cinnamon rolls.

Scott Harper, Wilma's only child and the technical owner of the Munch Box Diner, unknowingly gets caught up in his mom's web as he strolls past us. His dark auburn hair and green eyes came from his mom, but his calm, level-headed demeanor is all from his dad.

"Scott, get over here and look at this!" she practically yells, her ponytail swinging back and forth with her frantic movements.

"What is it, Ma?" Scott asks, leaning over her shoulder. I'm glad for the company. When Wilma gets going, it can sometimes take two or three of us to reel her back in.

Scott is just in time to see the dreadlocked guy trade Olive the mysterious package for an envelope. "Boy, oh, boy," Wilma says in a low voice. "You both saw that, didn't you? That definitely *was* a drug deal, and I should've known it would be with the likes of *them*!"

Olive shakes hands with the young man and off she goes, casually strolling back toward her coffee shop with the mysterious brown package tucked under one arm.

"I know you've got your reasons for disliking Olive and Taffy, but Ma, come on. You can't really think..." Scott starts to defend them, but his words get lost in her verbal volcanic eruption.

"I absolutely think that about them, Scott. I most certainly do!" she scoots backwards out of the booth. "You two are being gullible.

You don't have a mother's intuition, so you're just not wired to spot nefarious activities like I am." She holds her hand out to him. "Now give me your cell phone so I can get a picture of his license plate. I left mine at home." She snaps her fingers. "Hurry it up!"

He pats at his empty pockets. "I guess it's in the back,"

"How's it going to do me any good whatsoever if it's in the back?" she yells. Ordinarily you'd think the kind of ruckus that's been happening over the last few minutes would cause a few heads to turn, but most people are used to Wilma flying off about something or other pretty regularly. No one's even looking at us.

The shirtless man walks around to the other side of the truck while the dreadlocked man leans in the driver's side window to speak to a lady I hadn't noticed until now. He nods a couple of times at her before they turn to look in our direction, which gives them a clear view of the three of us staring back at them.

Surprisingly, an enormous grin sweeps across his face. He waves at us with a sociable flip of his hand like it's not odd at all to be stared at by total strangers from a diner window.

Wilma dives below the edge of the table, but Scott and I wave back at him with welcoming smiles of our own, like normal human beings.

"Are you crazy? Get down!" she hisses through clenched teeth. "It's bad enough *he* saw *our* faces, but he'll send a hit man after us if he thinks we saw *the drug deal*!"

"Ma, I seriously doubt a drug deal just happened or that guy would want to kill us. There's gotta be a perfectly logical explanation." Scott pats her on the shoulder consolingly.

"I better call the sheriff." She shrugs Scott's hand away and rushes off.

"So much for your calm morning," Scott chuckles. "Finish the crossword?"

I laugh with him. "What's a six-letter word for 'Wilma is once again off the rails?'"

"It's been a couple weeks since we've had any bomb threats or alleged shoplifting rings, so I reckon we're about due for some kind of upheaval," he answers dryly.

"Yeah, I guess it has."

"See you later, Thomas," he says and finds his way back to his grill.

My morning routine is ruined. I pick up my crossword and head for the door. I have a feeling this is just the beginning of a marathon upheaval.

Chapter 2

I look across the table at my dinner companion, Rusty Burdine, with unbridled agitation. He pushes up the bill of his grease-stained baseball cap and scratches at the close-cropped graying hair beneath. He grins at me, the dark skin around his laughing eyes crinkling with humor.

Wilma's standing at the end of our booth, hands on hips, ranting about the dangers of drug deals in the Midwest. "That's exactly why I told the sheriff we have to move fast on this case." She nods once, giddy with imagined authority, and adjusts the bandana around her neck.

It's a good thing for her she's taken on the role of the little sister I never had. Otherwise, I might've strangled her with that blasted bandana by now.

"Great. Problem solved," I wave her on. "Now can we eat in peace, Barney Fife?"

"So, according to you we should throw the baby out before we can run and walk?"

I usually get a kick out of the way she murders the English language, except days like today when she's in the middle of one of her imagined catastrophes. "That's not how the saying goes, Wilma," I say tiredly.

She sniffs disapprovingly. "I'll go talk to someone who genuinely cares about the integrity of our town." She struts away.

I roll my eyes at Rusty.

"If you thought this mess was going to spiral out of control, why didn't you go somewhere else for dinner?" Rusty asks. I've already filled him in on the terrible disturbance of my peace and quiet earlier.

"For starters, you know it's practically impossible to eat anywhere else in this town without Wilma finding out. You think I want to risk having to hear the disloyalty lecture on top of all this hippie hype?" I wave a hand at the plate in front of me. "You also know Tuesday night's my chicken fried steak night."

"Yeah, yeah, I know." He shakes his head. "The Code."

"That's right. The Code exists for a reason, and that reason is to keep me safe in a world of nut jobs." I shovel mashed potatoes dripping with sawmill gravy into my mouth and smile contentedly.

Rusty is the owner of Trusty Rusty's Pit Stop, the best (and only) car repair shop in town. We share widowhood, a mastery of sarcasm, and anywhere from eighteen to twenty-one meals a week here at the Munch Box. At sixty-three, he's younger than me by a few years, but still considers me ancient of days.

Scott emerges from the back and heads straight for us. "Mom's in rare form." He winces, rubbing his hands briskly over reddish beard stubble. "This is worse than the time she swore the mafia had set up shop in the back of the Masons' barn."

Rusty grimaces. "That was a rough week for sure."

"Dad is so sick of this hippie junk he went down to the feed barn to see if he can drum up any work," Scott says with a dry look. Dan Harper has been trying to retire from his lifelong handyman job for the last year, but every time he thinks he's ready to coast, Wilma gets caught up in a new obsession and he decides he needs a reason to be out of the diner for a few days.

"Olive and Taffy aren't drug dealers any more than the three of us are," I state the obvious. "We need to find a way to shut this down."

"I guess I could always lock her in the office," Scott suggests with a wry grin.

"You'd have to gag her. No one would be able to eat with the racket she'd make," Rusty says.

"True," Scott chuckles. "It would never work, anyway. Maggie would just let her out."

"Well, all I know is, I'm not gonna suffer through this for a whole week," I say firmly.

A small human from the booth behind us lets out an ear-splitting squeal. "Speak of the devil—Maggie must be making her rounds," Rusty predicts.

Maggie is a rotund boxer mix who showed up out of the blue one day a few years ago. Wilma went out to the dumpster with a bag of trash and came back inside with Maggie. As Dan tells it, Wilma was heard saying, "Maggie, what're you doing out here at this late hour? Come inside and get your dinner," as if she'd always known the dog. Within a couple of days, she and Wilma were wearing matching bandanas. Within a couple of months Wilma had her licensed as a therapy dog, legally giving her free reign inside the diner. She became an overnight sensation with the town, and now people expect to see her when they come in to eat.

Personally, I don't have anything against other people owning animals, but you won't ever catch a dog smelling up my house. Since Maggie is a permanent fixture at my favorite eating establishment, it benefits us both to coexist amicably, so that's where we've landed.

"Hey there, Mags," Rusty greets her. She lays her reddish-brown head on his leg, and he does his best to scratch every inch of her head, making sure to get underneath her yellow bandana because he says that's her favorite itchy spot. She rolls her giant brown eyes up at me and I know exactly what she's thinking.

"Don't look at me like that, Mutt." I warn her. "He's scratching you enough for the both of us."

"Don't pay attention to Mr. Grumpy Pants, Maggie. He's mad at your mom." Rusty fishes around in his front shirt pocket and produces a dog biscuit. "Here you go, sweetheart." Maggie licks his hand lovingly, does the same to Scott, shifts a comical side eye toward me and then disappears with the biscuit in her mouth.

"Here," I offer Rusty my travel size hand sanitizer.

"I've outlived my parents, several aunts and uncles, and Hildy. I'm pretty sure a few dog germs won't catapult me into a terminal illness," he says contemptuously.

"Scott?" I offer it to him, but he waves me off.

"I'm good," he says, "but thanks."

"Suit yourself." I tuck it back into my pocket.

Wilma comes to the cash register with a takeout bag. I watch with mild distaste as Pastor "Brimstone" Bob Frazier saunters up to the register. I've always been irritated with him, and it's got nothing to do with his slicked down hair or insistence on wearing a dress shirt and tie regardless of the day or time. It's his know it all, fanatic's take on religion that sours me.

Brimstone Bob, I like to call him when he's not listening.

"I hope he doesn't see us," I nod at Bob's back. "The agony of hearing about some upcoming Bible study he wants me to attend is all I need on top of today's insanity." Bob's one of the biggest religious nutjobs I know. Ever since I moved back to Cardinal Creek, he's been trying to reel me in like a first prize fish.

"If he tries to invite you to something, just douse him with your hand sanitizer," Scott suggests. "That should get your point across,"

"I'd buy it by the gallons if I thought it would repel weirdos," I say.

Wilma greets Bob with an abrupt, "I guess you've heard about the infiltration of our God-fearing town this morning." Usually, she keeps it short with him. She might not be an atheist like me, but she's never had an interest in being chatty with looneys. I'm a bit surprised at her, truthfully.

"Infiltration?" he asks, instantly engaged.

"Oh, yes, an infiltration of the very worst kind." She warms to her topic, leaning slightly toward him. "Thomas and I had our world turned upside down when two disgusting tattooed hippies sold drugs to that awful Olive from the bistro."

"Uh oh, she brought your name into it!" Rusty whispers.

"Scott, get over there and interrupt this!" I plead, but he shakes his head no.

"How do you know it was a drug deal?" Bob asks her.

"Well, Bob, they handed Olive a brown package and she handed them an envelope. In my experience that means drug deal," she replies haughtily.

Rusty pushes his empty plate away and leans back, grinning at me. "This is gettin' good."

"How can you be happy about this? Him getting involved will be the same as dumping gasoline on an already raging fire," I groan.

"So?"

"So... that's going to create more craziness and more obsessing and more general disruption of my routine," I grump.

Wilma continues with deep sincerity, "... and you know I've always had issues with them, anyway. Of course, anyone who would try and steal business right out from underneath me, a pillar of the community, would also deal drugs."

Bob shakes his head. "Unbelievable. Just unbelievable."

"Something's gotta be done. We can't stand idly by while our town is corrupted by the hippies and those..." she pauses to wiggle her eyebrows suggestively, "well, you-know-whats."

"Asians?" Bob guesses.

She clucks her tongue at his stupidity. "No, Bob, the bad thing."

"Lesbians?" he guesses.

"What? Gawd's nightgown, nobody cares about *that*," she rolls her eyes in dismay at his inability to read her mind. "I meant crooked businesswomen!"

He blinks in surprise. "Oh, well, I guess drug dealers come in all shapes and sizes."

"Oh, brother." I scoot out of the booth. "You two are cowards," I frown at Scott and Rusty.

"Good luck!" Rusty chuckles.

I stand next to Bob, digging deep for a shred of politeness to shroud my words in. "Evening, Bob. Wilma, cash Bob here out and ring me up, too. My treat." I toss some dollars on the counter and push his bag closer to him.

"Tommy, I was just telling Bob about—" she starts in, but I cut her off.

"You were heavily engaged in slander, something I'm pretty sure Bob's Bible frowns on," I say.

"You saw exactly what I saw—" Wilma protests, but I cut her off again.

"I did, so I feel completely justified in telling him that regardless of whatever we saw take place this morning, we can only be sure of what it *wasn't*. Olive has lived in this town her whole life, and Taffy for at least fifteen years. They're not drug users, drug dealers, shoplifters, car thieves, or guilty of any other crimes you can think of," I push his bag even closer to him. "Better get going while that's still warm, Bob."

For a split second he looks as if he's going to argue, but then he takes the bag from me and leaves without a word. Not before I see his calculating expression, though. Wilma's planted the seed in spite of my efforts.

Wilma fixes me with a steely emerald stare. "Tommy, you're really something else, you know it?"

Rusty and Scott laugh at the irony of a comment like this coming from the likes of her. "It can probably seem that way, I guess," I tell her and head to the door before anything else can happen.

If I know Wilma, tonight won't be the last we hear of this.

I need to get home and rest up for tomorrow.

Chapter 3

Sometimes Indiana weather is unpredictable, and we end up with snow gathering on the tulip blooms. Today's early April morning is warmer than usual, showcasing nice blue skies, fluffy white clouds, and the slightest breeze. I've been forced to finish my crossword on the park bench in the middle of the town square, so I'm glad Mother Nature's on my side.

I maneuver the newspaper around on my leg, searching for a place flat enough that I can make a few legible letters without the pencil poking a hole.

You might be wondering why I'm doing my crossword on a park bench.

I can sum it up with a six-letter word for *fiercely burning*. I can even use it in a sentence for you: Wilma's imagination was *ablaze* during breakfast.

Since I won't agree with her about the drug deal, she's added my own mental stability to the list of massive problems she has to solve. The straw that broke the camel's back was when she started talking to me about cognitive testing. I packed up my crossword and here I am.

I'm mulling over twelve down when I hear a piercing, horrible, nightmarish voice calling my name. Confound it, that nitwit Charlotte

Davens has spotted me. Much like old Brimstone Bob, Charlotte's been trying to reel me in too, but for a different reason. She wants me to lend my name and talents to her daughter's show choir.

I'm sure I don't have to tell you why there's no section of the Code that allows for my involvement with show choirs, teenagers, or their nitwit mothers.

I look straight into her brightly made-up eyes and turn away. I march with determination toward the diner, hopefully making it clear she shouldn't follow.

"Oh, Thomas!" she calls. "Thomas, can you hear me?" I pick up the pace a smidge.

"You're being awfully rude, dear," Bea says. Oh, sorry, let me introduce you—Bea's my late wife and tether to sanity. She also pops up from time to time to lecture me on being a better human.

"Yes, darling, I'm well aware of how rude I'm being. It takes an enormous amount of rudeness to get your point across to a nitwit," I bark.

"But, Thomas, wouldn't it be fun to get involved in music again? You've done nothing meaningful for the last five years but plunk out the occasional tune on your piano. Your talents are just wasting away," she nags from the afterlife.

"My talents are as brilliant today as they were fifty years ago. The important detail you're omitting is that they're *my* talents, not hers. She's trying to upset my routine and capitalize on my name." I argue back. "I'm not a cash cow, Bea."

Bea clucks her tongue at me. "There's nothing wrong with adding a little fun to your routine, you know."

"I have a lot of fun. I nap regularly and eat pie every day of my life. On occasion I play poker with the guys. I do my crosswords every morning." I flap my crumpled newspaper at the sky. "I have all kinds of fun."

"You're in a rut. We made the Code so you'd thrive, not drown yourself in all this mundane blah," she responds coolly.

A little over six years ago, Bea was diagnosed with stage four cancer. The doctors and specialists said we had a few months of get-up-and-go left without chemo, or maybe a year of pain and sickness with it. Bea was adamant about not spending her last days as a bald, weak, nauseated woman. We packed our bags, picked out five of our favorite places around the globe, and set off on the vacation of a lifetime.

In Greece it was easy to act like nothing was wrong. She wasn't feeling all that bad yet and our days were almost like normal. Her vibrant blue eyes were still alert, and her energy was as good as mine.

In Austria she hit a few rough spots, but we got some pain meds and that helped a lot.

In Hawaii she started to speculate on what life would look like... after. I didn't want to have these talks, but she had a way of being sweetly persistent.

"The thing is, dear, you are socially awkward. Painfully so," she'd said, squeezing my hand. "You really only have Rusty, and it's rare you've seen him more than a few times a year since Hildy passed."

"*You're* my friend," I had stated simply. "Besides, it's not exactly easy to make friends when you're a genius musician turned world-famous conductor who travels forty-three weeks out of the year."

"I blame myself. I should've made you retire the day you turned sixty," she sighed, mumbling more to herself than to me.

In Colorado, she had her first really bad spell and had to spend a few days in the hospital. Late one night with the lights dimmed and the nurses busy elsewhere, she gave me one of her stern looks. "It's time to talk now, my love. Seriously talk."

We were both terrified of her leaving me, but for completely different reasons.

I couldn't refuse her when she was like this, sickly and pale in a hospital bed. "Okay, let's talk," I brushed the hair away from her forehead, marveling at how stunning she was to me even now.

"I don't want you to be all alone," she said.

"I don't see how we can avoid that, honey," I said softly.

With a slight frown she pushed herself up into a sitting position. "I've been thinking. Let's skip out on New England and head straight to Cardinal Creek. You can make this hiatus permanent and announce your retirement. We'll pick out a sweet little house near the Munch Box and Rusty's shop. It'll be perfect."

I smiled at her dreamy look. "I've always wanted to go home when I retire."

"Yes, you have, and once we get the house straightened out, we'll create a Code." She patted my cheek. "With some tender loving care, you can have all kinds of good friends at home. The Code will be a set of guidelines, you know, to help you figure all of that out."

"We can try," I shrugged, "but there's no substitute for having you to talk to."

"Who says you have to stop talking to me?" she insisted. "Talk to me all the time if you want to."

And so, that's what we did. We bought a house. We started decorating, Bea calling out orders to painters and movers from her wheelchair. She had a vision in her mind of what she wanted the house to look like, starting in the kitchen and working her way toward our bedroom. She filled the sunroom with potted plants and got an antique upright piano for me.

She also created what she called Thomas Sanders' Code for Happy Living. She filled five sheets of paper, back and front, with a structured and thoroughly explained plan on how I was to go about living a full, rich life after she died.

I had her with me in person for over six months after we moved to Cardinal Creek. Five years later she's still here, in my head, and I'm still talking to her.

Although sometimes she gets going on a topic I'd rather not discuss, like today.

"Don't ignore me, Thomas Sanders," she says, pulling me out of my reverie. "I said the Code was meant to help you thrive, not settle into a rut."

I laugh fondly. "Yes, woman, I heard you. Your idea of thriving is different than mine, that's all. The Code's taken good care of me. There's nothing at all wrong with it or the way I live my life."

A quick glance over my shoulder reassures me I've lost the nitwit, so I feel safe to slow down in the parking lot of the Munch Box.

"The Code of today isn't at all like the Code we made five years ago," she points out.

"I may have tweaked it some," I say stubbornly, "but it works just fine."

Ido Marchetti, the jolly proprietor of Ido's Market, emerges from his car and heads my way. He's a bachelor by choice, dedicated mainly to his aging Italian mother, who doesn't speak more than fifteen English words, and his store. He makes time to play poker with us, though, and Wilma's determined to fix him up one of these days when she can find the right lady. He's carting a box of produce, something I'm sure Wilma coerced him into delivering. "In fact, here's a great example of how I've thrived," I tell Bea, motioning at Ido.

"Say what, now?" he asks.

"Bea says I'm not happy—" I start to explain, but she interrupts me.

"Thriving. You can be happy in a rut, but you can't be thriving in a rut," she corrects me.

"Oh, excuse me... Bea says I'm not *thriving*." I gesture broadly. "But I say I've got plenty of friends and a rich, full life, and you are proof of that."

He has a hearty, deep laugh. "Oh, sure, you're a regular social butterfly."

"That's not helping," I try to look wounded.

"Well, you do the same exact thing every day with the same exact people. You never go out, dress up, see the sights," he says, looking over my left shoulder to talk to Bea. "You're right, Bea. He's in a rut."

"Hah! That shows how much you know. She's over here," I point to my right side with my crumpled-up crossword. "And she's irritated with me because I won't give in to the demands of that trainwreck Charlotte Davens. Now I ask you, is it truly in my best interest to add Charlotte Davens to my list of friends?"

Ido scrunches his face up. "Ok, yeah, you've got her on that one. Nobody deserves that," he chuckles. "I'm gonna get this inside before Wilma loses her cool. She's all fired up over some hippie sighting, and I don't want to give her anything else to gripe about."

"I was standing right beside her for the alleged hippie sighting. I'll come by later and fill you in on what really happened," I salute him with mock solemness. "Be brave in there, soldier."

As soon as Ido walks away, Bea chastises me. "You misrepresented me, dear. I'm so happy you love Ido, Rusty, and Palmer. I just think you've got room in your heart for more than a handful of friends."

I wait until I'm in the car to answer her. "Love them? I don't love anyone, Bea, except you."

"Well, of course you do. You love the guys, and Wilma and her family, too."

"They're my friends, yes. I mean, I have to trust someone enough to get the mail and water all your flowers while I'm gone on vacations," I clarify. "But that's not the same as loving them."

She's clearly aghast at this logic. "Now you're being ridiculous. Tell me one vacation you've been on since we got here!" she demands.

"For all you know, I might be planning a trip next week," I say.

"I'm deceased, Thomas, not deaf. You haven't made any such travel plans."

I sigh. "I call a truce. No more serious talk tonight, okay?"

"Ok, truce," she says, but her tone suggests she's plotting against my version of the Code.

Chapter 4

Ido's Market is on the fringe of the downtown shopping area, about five blocks west of the town square. The chain groceries and big box stores have positioned themselves on the edges of Cardinal Creek, but we're all happy Ido's charming establishment has no competition inside town lines.

"Come on, Mutt, let's give this list to Ido and make him do the footwork," I tell Maggie, leading the way through the market. Wilma's sent us to pick up her produce order. Ordinarily I'd be aggravated at being asked to run errands for her, but not today.

Yes, you guessed it. Three days later she's still sounding off about the hippie to anyone who'll listen. One minute more and my ears would have started bleeding.

We follow the baritone rhythm of two familiar male voices through the canned soups, past dry cereals, and around endcaps of spring flowers to the produce. We spot Ido and Palmer Rawlings animatedly discussing something near the leafy greens. Although they're both in the earliest part of their fourth decade of life, Ido's shorter, darker Italian features create a sharp contrast to Palmer's leaner, blonder looks. "Thomas, tell this man that arugula is far superior to romaine," Ido huffs.

"I would imagine grass where the Mutt has done her business might taste better than arugula," I say. "No one should eat it on purpose."

"Finally, someone else with good taste!" Palmer exclaims.

"I should've known better than to ask him, huh Mags," Ido bends down to pet Maggie. "If it's not deep fried or covered in powdered sugar he won't even look at it."

Palmer snorts, tossing the head of romaine into his basket.

Palmer is the owner of our very own Starstruck Movie Theater. It's old and slightly tattered, but he stubbornly refuses to replace the worn velvety curtains and dark wood because he thinks they have so much character. Along with the auditorium he's got a couple of community rooms downstairs where people play games and such, and his modest, three-room apartment upstairs. He's not movie star rich by any means, but he says being an integral part of the local entertainment makes him feel like a billionaire.

Ten or twelve years ago he got some wild idea about moving to Hollywood. He wanted to mingle with his tribe while he was still young enough to raise heck, he told everyone. He put the Starstruck on the market and talked it up big for a few months. Offers poured in, but Palmer found a reason to turn them all down for a number of silly reasons. I wasn't in town as it all unfolded, but Rusty says he thinks Palmer realized he didn't actually want the Hollywood life and was just too embarrassed to admit he thought he did.

Eventually he stopped talking about moving and quietly took the Starstruck off the market. Rusty says that was about the same time he created a local theater group. This way he gets a taste of the stage without leaving home, and he's content with his choice.

Personally, I think he dodged a bullet. The big wide world is a nice place to visit, but I wouldn't want to live there again.

"I eat lettuce on occasion," I quip. "But arugula isn't lettuce. It's dark green wickedness."

"The best kind of lettuce, of course, is butter, but due to horrible negligence on Ido's part, there is no butter lettuce in the store," Palmer says.

"I'll talk to you, Maggie, since you're the only one here with any sense," Ido says, making a face at Palmer. "Your special order is on my desk if you want to go get it."

Maggie does the thing with her lips that Wilma says is a smile and trots off to the back. I've lived a long time with Maggie's out-of-the-ordinary behavior, but sometimes her grasp of the English language still catches me off guard. Ido chuckles. "She's more human than canine, isn't she?"

"At times, absolutely," I say.

"Makes me wonder what Wilma feeds her," Palmer laughs.

"Which reminds me, her highness needs today's produce order now rather than later. She sent us over to pick it up," I say, handing Ido Wilma's list. He looks it over, murmuring to himself.

Two ladies whose faces look slightly familiar but names I've never needed to know come to a standstill behind us, absently picking at a giant mound of baking potatoes. "There are signs, you know, that Pastor Bob says we can all be watching for," says lady number one, picking up a potato. "He says these drug dealers will linger around the high school and *that* coffee shop to try to get to the teens. I've already had a talk with my kids about interacting with strange, tattooed men."

I connect the dots immediately. "Oh, this is just fantastic," I say quietly to Ido and Palmer, tipping my head in the direction of the gossips.

"Imagine having to educate our children on something like this here in Cardinal Creek," says lady number two, who selects a potato of her own. "It's not like we live in a big city like Indianapolis or Chicago."

"It's awful." Lady number one glances around surreptitiously before saying in guarded tones, "Pastor says the drug dealers targeted the bistro as a selling location because the teens and college kids like to spend so much time there."

"I think we should send out an email to the ladies' group to spread Pastor Bob's warning. Good Christian parents will keep their kids from going to that place if they know what's going on there," lady number two suggests.

"That's an excellent idea," lady number one agrees. She looks over the spud in her hand and adds with a sneer, "Potatoes have so much starch."

"We rarely eat them," lady number two says, dropping hers back onto the pile.

Lady number one plops hers down, too, and rubs her hands together as if they're dirty. "You know, our church's population isn't the only one who needs to know about this. We really should get the warning to the other churches in the area—the churches that are on the right side, anyway."

"Another excellent idea," lady number two agrees as they walk away.

"Can you believe that?" Ido whistles. "I'm glad you told me what really happened."

"What's going on?" Palmer asks.

"Wilma told Bob there are some hippies dealing drugs in Cardinal Creek," Ido sums it up.

"*Bob?* She can barely stand him." Palmer is rightfully confused. "Why is she talking to him about anything?"

"Scott and I were there for the whole thing, and it wasn't a drug deal. I tried to diffuse the situation when she started blabbering to Old Brimstone, but apparently it didn't work," I say grouchily.

"What exactly was the whole thing?" Palmer wants to know. I start with the disruption of my crossword and sum it up with Wilma spouting off to Bob. "I don't know what's worse—Wilma's obsession over this or Bob spreading gossip under the guise of a sermon." I finish my rant, annoyed.

Ido rubs his chin. "I feel bad for Olive and Taffy."

"Same. Those girls aren't drug dealers. Or drug *users*, for that matter. We know them too well to believe a story like that," Palmer says.

We can't broadcast it to Wilma, but all of us, Rusty included, frequent the bistro. Mostly because their cinnamon rolls are actually a lot better than Wilma's, but we'd never let her know that's how we feel. It would crush her, which we'd never do intentionally.

Besides, she'd crush us, which we'd never intentionally bring on our own heads.

"From the sound of it, Bob's put a big target on the back of these so-called hippies. I almost feel sorrier for them," Ido says.

"We probably won't ever see them again," I predict. "In my book that makes them the lucky ones."

"Bob can be a real nasty guy when he wants to be," Ido continues his train of thought. "Maybe one of us should go over to the bistro and warn them about being the subject of Wilma's newest uprising,"

"Bob's not as bad as Frank Norris. I bet I get half a dozen complaints every month from his people." Palmer adds his two cents, referring to the perpetually angry pastor of Harmony Church. I've always marveled at the irony of the least harmonious human in town using that word to describe his business.

"Complaints about what?" Ido asks.

"They can find a sin behind just about any movie I show. It's incredible. Shoot, half the sins they talk about are things I've never even heard of!" he laughs.

"More proof that most of those religious types *are* nutjobs," I chime in. "That's one of the main reasons I don't believe in their fairy tale god."

Maggie strolls casually back toward us, a plastic bag hanging from her mouth. Palmer points at her, saying, "Oh, look, here's Maggie with a bag I can't see inside of. How do we know you didn't buy her some doggie drugs?"

Ido shushes him, joking. "Keep it down. If the wrong person finds out I'm dealing doggie drugs they might tell Wilma and Bob!"

"I'll give Wilma this the two guys did have a look about them that's different than what we're used to around here. Still, I'm sure whatever was in that bag wasn't worth ruining my life over," I say.

"Ruining *your* life?" Ido quips, amused.

"Sounds like all the gossip is about Olive and Taffy. How is it that this is ruining *your* life?" Palmer laughs.

"Like I said, if it disrupts my peace and quiet, it disrupts the Code. If the Code is disrupted, my life is ruined." I tap my forehead with a finger. "Think about it,"

They look at each other with astonishment.

"Oh brother," Palmer says with a snort.

"Such a travesty," Ido grins back at him.

"Okay, okay, enough of that. How about you get Wilma's order ready so I can get out of here. The merriment you're finding at my expense is overwhelming," I snap.

"He said merriment. Who uses the word merriment anymore?" Ido snickers, and they both start laughing again.

It's going to be another long day, I think.

Chapter 5

It's a rainy day, my arthritis has flared up, and I'm alone in the middle of a disaster. Rusty had to deal with a vehicular emergency beyond his nephew's capabilities, so I've been left to fend off Wilma's continuing rampage over the hippies all by myself.

Dan whooshes by me with plates of food, his suntanned face sporting a weak smile that says he's over the hectic lunch rush. Dan's ability to carry several plates at once, along with his steady composure, makes him a necessity for the diner's busiest times. He's the very definition of that old saying, "opposites attract." I've described Wilma, so it should be pretty clear that Dan's patiently steady.

Scott whips by on his dad's left side, stopping to grab my empty glass and whisper, "I love it when the place is full. Keeps Mom too busy to talk about my future wife or dangerous hippies!"

"Have you considered making up a fake girlfriend? It might switch her mental frequencies off the hippie and onto something else," I suggest.

Just then the door chime tinkles and who should walk in but the hippie himself! Scott and I exchange wide eyed glances. "No, somehow I don't think that will help," he says.

The hippie takes in the diner's retro design with childlike wonder, and I'd have to agree with him. Scott restored the place to the glory of its original turquoise walls and black and white checkered floors when he bought it, which is one of the reasons I've always gravitated here. The Munch Box and I are only a few years apart in age.

Scott puts my glass down, straightens up, and gives our visitor a welcoming smile. "Hey there. Can I help you?"

"Should I find a seat, or..." he looks around the overflowing diner for an open seat.

For the first time ever, I find my curiosity overpowering my need for peace and quiet. On a whim, I wave a hand at Rusty's vacant half of my booth, saying, "You're welcome to sit with me if you don't mind having lunch with an old man."

"Really? That's so cool of you," his impossibly gigantic grin grows so big it threatens to cover his ears. Up close and personal, I see he's tall and lanky. His hair is... well, you know what dreadlocks look like. His wet jacket comes off, and he wipes raindrops from his gold rimmed glasses with the shirt tail of his black and red flannel shirt.

"Thomas can lend you his menu. What can I bring you to drink?" Scott says.

"Their sweet tea is incredible," I volunteer.

"Sweet tea it is!" he nods at me, then holds his hand out to Scott, saying, "Thanks, man. I'm Jordan Tackett, but everybody calls me Joe."

"Scott Harper," he answers, giving Joe's hand a good shake. "Let me get your drinks while you look over the menu," he grabs my empty glass again and turns, giving me one last "holy cow" look.

"Thanks, Scott!" Joe calls after him before shoving his hand across the table at me. "Man, thanks again for the seat, Thomas..." he pauses, wanting my last name.

"Thomas Sanders, at your service," I give his hand a firm shake and then push my menu over to him. "And it's no trouble, Joe."

He asks what I'm having, drooling at my description of the open-faced roast beef sandwich, horseradish potato salad, and brown sugar crumb peach pie. He says he'll have exactly what I'm having if that's okay with me.

Scott returns with drinks and takes our orders, comically surprised when Joe asks for three different pieces of pie to go. "My wife had meetings today and couldn't come, so I promised to bring her something that would really, you know, capture the feeling of the diner," he explains.

"You nailed it, then. My mom's pies are one of the things we're best known for," Scott says.

"So, this is a family-owned gig?" Joe's eyes light up. "I'm all about small business."

"Scott's name is on the deed, but Wilma runs the show," I tell him.

"And my dad just tries to clean up after us both," Scott adds, tipping his head toward Dan who's rushing by with an armload of dirty dishes.

"This town has a charm, you know, that gets me right here," Joe flattens his palms against his chest and pats, up and down, like a heartbeat.

"Well, Thomas and I are glad you dropped by," Scott says warmly. "I'll go get your orders in," he taps the tabletop with his pad and heads off.

Joe asks me how many other locally owned businesses are in Cardinal Creek. I start with Ido's Market, Rusty's Pit Stop, and the Rapturous Finds Thrift Store. He's got questions about each one of them. How big is Ido's Market? Is Rusty a retired race car driver? Who came up with the brilliant name Rapturous Finds?

I think I've answered enough of his questions by now that it won't sound odd if I ask one of my own. "Indulge an old man's rudeness for a moment. Wasn't it you I saw in the parking lot last week with Olive Denton?"

He looks reflective for a few seconds before launching another face-wide smile. "Dude, you waved at us from the window!"

"I did," I smile.

"That's just bizarre. What are the chances of you seeing me last week and then being here today to share your seat with me?" He's delighted. His boyish attitude is kind of refreshing in light of my regular go-to stance of sarcasm.

"I eat two or three meals a day here, so I'd say the chances are pretty good," I chuckle. "I'm surprised you aren't eating at the bistro today, since you obviously know Olive."

His eyes light up again. "Oh, that! I've eaten there once, now that I know where it is, actually. She was nice enough to meet me in this parking lot for the first drop-off since I got lost that first day!"

"Drop-off?" for a split second I hear Wilma's voice smugly say, *I told you it was drugs.*

"Olive and Taffy are going to start using my coffee beans. Roasting has been a personal hobby of mine for a while, but I'm trying it out as a sort of side hustle to see if I can make any money at it."

"Coffee beans!" I say with amusement. "You're an entrepreneur, not a—" I stop myself from saying drug dealer, but just barely.

"Yeah, an entrepreneur," he grins.

Well, this is simply hysterical.

As if on cue, Wilma rushes up with what she probably thinks is food for me and Rusty. When she sees Joe sitting across from me she sucks in a deep breath, eyes bulging, and grabs at my arm. Scott arrives seconds behind her, breathless. He places a firm hand on both of her shoulders, smiling with all his teeth at Joe, saying, "Ma, I didn't realize you picked that order up for me."

"Scott, it's the dr—" she starts to say what neither of us want her to, so I grab the hand she has on my arm and give it a good squeeze.

"Joe!" Scott talks over her, and she hushes. "His name is Joe, Ma."

"Joe, this is Wilma Harper, Scott's mom and the town's finest pie maker," I say.

"Good to meet you, Wilma. My wife and I are in love with your place," Joe extends a hand to her. She brushes his fingertips with the barest of touches.

Scott turns her body away from our table and pushes her along, saying, "Sorry guys, we've got orders piling up back there like crazy. Gotta go!"

I can tell Joe's baffled by Scott's behavior.

"The lunch rush is always somewhat on the wacky side," I explain it away with a shrug.

For the next however long, Joe and I eat and talk, casually getting to know each other. We discover we both dislike sports and politics but love Thoreau and old black and white movies. There's a significant difference in our musical interests, but we come together in agreement that Dean, Sammy, and Frank are the only crooners that matter. He asks me all kinds of questions about my life and listens attentively to my answers. Oddly, I find myself telling him the truth, which I rarely do.

"Seriously, Thomas, I like this young man," Bea says. "He's got an old soul."

I've known all along he's not a dangerous drug dealer, but I'll admit I've always expected people who look like him to have terrible grammar and a lack of intelligence. The fact that he's good at both, not to mention friendly, has been a pleasant surprise.

I'll go even further—in fact, I think I like him. I'm going to have to redefine my concept of a hippie.

We're enjoying ourselves so much I don't even notice when Wilma walks up (wearing a pair of disposable gloves, I might add) until it's too late. She carefully pinches the rim of his mostly empty glass with two gloved fingers, scoots it onto her palm, and walks away.

Well, she's gone and collected his fingerprints.

"That was, uh," he gropes around, finally going with "interesting,"

"Like I said earlier, the lunch rush is always a little wacky," I cast a glance around for Scott, worried about what else she might do.

Joe doesn't seem to be offended. He devours the last bite of potato salad, savoring it with closed eyes. "I can handle a little wacky if it means I get to eat food like this and hang out with dudes like you."

"Do you think you'll be around more often, then, to sell coffee beans?" I return his smile.

"Yep, I will. The response this week has been great, so they've offered me a contract," he tells me with obvious pride.

"How about that." My smile quickly turns to a frown when I see Old Brimstone Bob come flitting through the diner directly toward us.

I can tell the precise moment he notices Joe. His nostrils flare and his footsteps take on intention. "Who is this?" he demands, stopping in front of us.

"Joe Tackett," poor unsuspecting guy that he is, stretches out a hand to him. Bob ignores it.

"Is this... *him*?" The question shoots at me like a bullet.

"Your cup of stupid runneth over, Bob," I remark dryly before telling my new friend, "Joe, this is Pastor Bob Frazier."

"Ah, another man of the cloth!" Joe, undisturbed by the snub, clasps his hands together and beams brightly at Bob.

"Another?" Bob asks.

"Yeah, you and me," he says to Bob. "I lead a small church on the east side of Indy."

"*You* are a pastor." Bob states it with a snort of harsh skepticism. "Isn't that rich,"

Maggie the dog pushes past Bob and jumps right up onto Joe, wiggling her oversized rump and licking his face like he's an old friend. He lets out a belly laugh and hugs Maggie.

Bob demands to know why Joe is here, but I don't think Joe can hear him over Maggie's slobbering kisses.

Scott rushes past and I jab an aggravated finger first at Bob then at the door. He picks up what I'm laying down and leads Bob by the elbow to the other end of the diner, speaking quietly. That's one crisis averted, and I allow myself a deep sigh of relief.

Unfortunately, another fiery eyed crisis rears her head. "Maggie, come away from there right now!"

Maggie looks over her shoulder at Wilma with her tongue lolling and rump wiggling even harder. Dan, who must've been trying to keep an eye on Wilma, hurries over to do damage control. He whistles at Maggie, and she runs to Wilma, who whisks her beloved dog away to the back.

"How's your meal today, gentlemen?" Dan asks, pretending everything's normal.

Although I don't see how it's remotely possible, Joe seems unaffected by the chaos of the last three minutes. In fact, he's positively radiant. He thrusts a hand at Dan, introducing himself with a smile. Dan shakes his hand and excuses himself, giving me a furtive glance as he departs.

I know, Dan. Me too.

"Man, what a great day. Great people, great food, great dog," Joe motions at me, "and great conversation! I love it here!"

Even as I give him a weak grin of my own, I make a mental note to stop on the way home for a bottle of aspirin. A big one. If he's going to be around town more often, I'm going to need it.

Strangely, I hope that he is, even if it is going to cost me.

Chapter 6

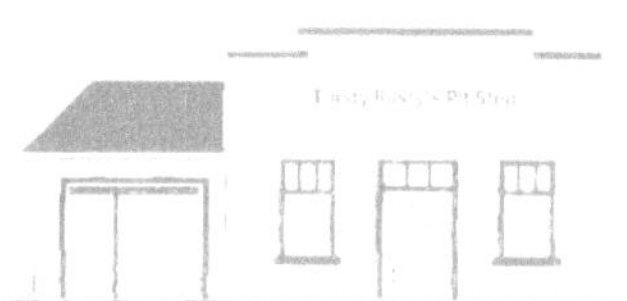

"I don't think she saw us," Palmer holds the door to the bistro open so Rusty and I can hurry inside. If Wilma happened to be in just the right spot by the diner's dumpster, we know she'd be able to look across the town square and see us. Since Joe showed up a few days ago, Wilma's drug dealing hippie rants have evolved from a steady downpour into an F5 twister. In all the years I've known Wilma, I've never wished for a mind-controlling zapper more than I have in the last couple of weeks.

Anyway, Olive asked us all to come over and try their new line of coffee, so here we are. Besides coffee sampling, we've been meaning to give them a head's up about the Brimstone and Wilma show.

Rusty leads the way to a table, and as I take a seat I notice Joe sitting nearby. He's with a pretty young lady and—hold onto your hats —Bob's son Neil.

"Well, well, guys. The plot just thickened so much Old Brimstone might choke on it," I direct their attention toward Joe.

A snort escapes Rusty. "I don't believe it."

"Of all the people to see together," Palmer shakes his head in disbelief. Of course, as soon as I could I told them both about my lunch with Joe. They'd been very entertained to learn the truth behind who Wilma's hippie really is. Pastor and entrepreneur weren't two words any of us would have guessed.

Taffy makes her way over with a tray of steaming hot coffee and cups. "Gentlemen," she greets us, patting my shoulder, "I've got a cream cheese pastry Bea would kill for," she tells me with a wink.

Not only are Olive and Taffy life and business partners, and Wilma's greatest source of competition, but they happen to be two of Bea's favorite townies.

"Oh yeah?" I grin. "She's killed for less."

"I have not!" Bea retorts.

"Bea says hello," I tell Taffy, smiling at the huffed indignation coming from my ethereal wife.

"I'm surprised you let Bea out of the house in such dire circumstances," Taffy widens her dark eyes with mock seriousness. "I hear there's been a drug dealing hippie loose in town."

We all laugh with a slight cringe of embarrassment. "We should have come sooner to fill you in. It's been a rough couple of weeks, I can tell you that," I say apologetically.

"He thinks it's rough because it's been days since Wilma let him finish a crossword before ten a.m.," Palmer tells her, sarcasm dripping from his words.

"It's a lot more than just the crossword," I reply briskly. "Wilma's draining me of my will to live."

"How ironic," Taffy remarks. "Joe's brought so much life into this place I'd almost be willing to fight Wilma for him. His roasts are delicious, but it's his personality that's the biggest hit. Our younger crowds can't get enough of him," she nods in Joe's direction. "That's the third time in two weeks he's hung out with Neil."

"Does he know he's been branded a drug dealing hippie?" Rusty asks.

"*I've* heard it from a few people, but I'm not sure he has yet," Taffy answers.

Our loud mouths get the attention of Joe. He waves dramatically at me and says something to the pretty young lady, who turns to look at us. I wave back, and the next thing I know they're standing in front of us. "Thomas, my favorite Cardinal Creek citizen!" He's sporting that face-wide grin while pumping my hand up and down so fast my head bobbles in unison.

"Hello, Joe, good to see you again," I return his grin. It's hard not to. "These are the two other citizens guaranteed to not be your favorite. Rusty Burdine and Palmer Rawlings, meet Joe Tackett." He shakes hands with both of them warmly.

"This gorgeous creature is my wife, Jewels," he side-hugs the young lady. She's dainty with long, dark, wavy hair and an intelligent gaze. The first thing I notice is she doesn't have a single tattoo.

"I've heard all about the ultra-cool Mr. Sanders. It's really good to finally meet you in person," Jewels say with genuine warmth, shaking my hand.

Suddenly I'm incredibly curious to see if Rusty and Palmer find Joe to be as intriguing as I do. There's no time like the better, as they say. I gesture to the empty seats around us, "Maybe you three would like to join us? We've got plenty of room."

They agree immediately. While they gather their things and Neil, Taffy tells us to help ourselves to a cup of what Joe calls "ridiculously decent brew" and goes back to the kitchen.

When we're alone, Palmer says in low tones, "That was an odd thing for you to do."

"Yeah, since when did the Code allow for coffee with strangers?" Rusty adds.

"I had lunch the other day with Joe, so he's not a stranger. I thought he was interesting and wondered if you two knuckleheads might not enjoy getting to know him, too," I whisper loudly. "This is obviously the perfect place since Wilma and Nutjob Bob aren't here to ruin it."

"Oh, so this is all for us, then," Palmer snickers to Rusty.

If Joe, Jewels, and Neil hadn't arrived at just this moment, I would've thrown a cup of ridiculously good brew at their ridiculously comical expressions. Instead, we introduce ourselves to Neil because, in spite of living in the same town for I don't know how many years, Joe's given us the only opportunity we've ever had to talk to him.

I'm happy to report he's nothing like his stiff-necked dad.

Joe is the same happy-go-lucky, animated ball of energy today that he was when he and I had lunch the day before. He conducts a conversation between this group of strangers the way I conduct an orchestra, and before I know it we're all laughing like old friends.

The Tacketts are thrilled to discover it's Palmer who owns the endearing little theater in town. He gleefully tells them all about his struggle to keep the interior true to its original design and a comprehensive list of all the activities he hosts besides movies, including the free night out for the ladies for the local women's shelter. "Sometimes an hour and a half of movie nonsense is exactly what those ladies are looking for," he says. When Jewels remarks on his generosity, he points a finger at me. "It's all because of Thomas. He's the money bags behind the whole thing."

All eyes turn to me. "Once again, you're wrong," I correct him. "It's all Bea."

Rusty leans toward Jewels and says in a conspiratorial low voice, "I know he's not much to look at, but our Thomas here is a filthy rich old man who uses his money for good."

"He's very good at making noises other people pay gobs of money to hear," Palmer adds.

"I do create exquisite music, and it's rude to discuss what I do with my gobs of money," I say dryly, uncomfortable with how this is going. I wanted them to talk to one another, but not about me!

"Joe mentioned you're an extremely gifted musician, but he left out the part about the gobs of money," Jewels laughs softly at my discomfort. "But don't worry, I won't tell a soul."

"Our famous world traveler would come home a few times a year with his wife Bea so she could see how the regular folks were living," Rusty continues in spite of my glare. "Bea fell in love with our little town, which turned out to be good for everyone."

"Bea met Mike Briggs and discovered his women's shelter was struggling to keep the lights on," Palmer picks up the storyline. "So, she burned a hole in Thomas's wallet to get the shelter back on track. Then she put her brilliant mind together with Mike's and created the Rapturous Finds Thrift Store as a way to help fund the shelter."

"I never knew you two were behind the thrift store," Neil says admiringly.

"Bea used our checkbook a lot of times to fund various adventures around here," I wave it off.

"Bea is a real humanitarian," Palmer says to the air beside me.

"Oh, Palmer, you dear, sweet man," Bea says warmly.

I hold up a hand to her, "He's not a dear sweet man *all* the time, and let's not forget how sweet I am for still writing these checks of yours every month now that you're not here to do it."

"Aww. Bea thinks I'm sweet," Palmer says to Rusty.

Joe, Jewels, and Neil are staring blankly at us. This wasn't how I wanted them to find out that the locals humor me while I talk to my dead wife.

Olive and Taffy come to check in on us. "Well, what's the verdict on the coffee?" Olive asks.

"Forget the coffee. Palmer talked to Bea in front of strangers, so now they think we're a little off in the head," Rusty says calmly. I roll my eyes, and Palmer laughs.

"All small towns have skeletons in the closet," Taffy tells the three confused faces, making Rusty and Palmer laugh even harder.

"I'm not a skeleton," Bea says indignantly.

"Bea says she's not a skeleton," I relay, laughing myself.

"You guys are making it weird," Olive scolds us. She and Taffy explain to the bewildered three about Bea, the Code, and my unwillingness to let her go. "It's really that simple. Thomas is the only one who can see and hear her, but we indulge him in this because Bea asked us to."

"That's so mystical, man," Joe marvels, eyes wide.

Jewels impulsively squeezes my hand affectionately. "That might be the most romantic thing I've ever heard, Thomas."

"It's like I said—isn't it, babe? This town has something special," Joe nudges her.

"So special," Jewels agrees.

"Aside from us," Rusty motions at the table, "what's so special about Cardinal Creek?"

"Obviously, yes, you all, but just everything else. There's such a sense, you know, of *love*, man." Joe has a dreamy look in his eyes. "Like the Munch Box Diner. That place has some deep character," he claps his hands together excitedly. "So much love and community around here."

I'm positive he has no idea why the native residents of Cardinal Creek erupt in laughter all over again at the idea of love being all around the diner.

I'm certainly not going to tell him.

Chapter 7

Apparently finding out I talk to my dead wife hasn't convinced the Tacketts that I'm a crazy old man, because I've run into Joe and Jewels again a few times since that afternoon at the bistro and they both seem sincerely happy to see me. The more I see them, the more I like them. Bea thinks it's fabulous, of course, that I'm making new friends. As I've told you, she's always been strongly opinionated when it comes to how I should be living my life.

I had a single Tackett sighting at the bistro, Joe flagging me down with grins and violent waving hands. He insisted I sit with him, and we ended up talking for almost an hour.

A couple of days ago I ran out of potato chips and stopped by Ido's to rectify the situation. I came upon Joe and Jewels in the snack aisle debating between a bag of roasted root vegetable chips and a bag of kale crispers. Jewels planted kisses on my cheek in spite of my best efforts to avoid them and then tried to tell me why I shouldn't be eating greasy, calorie laden potato chips. I distracted her with an introduction to Ido who (thankfully) chatted them up. I grabbed my chips and ran.

Yesterday I found Joe meandering around Rapturous Finds. He was with a shirtless, heavily tattooed man cradling a serving dish with a dainty pink flower print in one hand and sipping from the can of beer clutched in the other one. You might remember him as Wilma's other hippie. Turns out his name is Kenny Stambaugh, and he doesn't deal drugs, either.

It's a lot harder than you might think to *not* stare at a shirtless man's tattooed torso when it's covered with caricatures of voluptuous women. I had to force my eyes back to his more than once as he told me about buying the flowery dish for his elderly neighbor who collects this print.

I'll admit I had some concerning thoughts about his appearance in the first few seconds, but they disappeared by the time we parted ways. And let me stop you before you lecture me on how rude it is to judge a book by its cover. I've already caught heck from Bea, and I've already decided I like the guy. Underneath all the body art he's a caring, witty man, and if he's buying a serving dish for an old lady, he's gotta be thoughtful, too, I guess.

I'm with the Tacketts again today, but this time we planned our meeting. I mentioned the Liar's Bench once and they begged me to take them to see it. Apparently congregating, stubborn old men who get together for the sole purpose of one-upping each other isn't something that happens in the big city.

The Liar's Bench meets on the oversized porch of the Midwest Feed Barn. Averitt Whit and Harold Richardson are the ring leaders of the Bench. Averitt's got a good eight to ten years on me and is still sharp as a tack. Harold is a year or two older than Averitt, and now that they're both widowed, they've turned the Bench into their full-time occupations.

They're fussing over Jewels like they've never seen a pretty lady before and treating Joe like a neighbor. To get a step ahead of any gossip about alleged drug deals, I called Averitt last night and told him I'd be bringing the Tacketts by today. I knew Averitt and Harold would be eager to meet anyone Bob dislikes, since they've long agreed with me that Bob might be a bit too pompous for his own good. Averitt had a good laugh with me over the unlikely pairing of Bob and Wilma against Joe and said any enemy of Bob's is a friend of his.

Joe watches, fascinated, as Averitt produces a grungy pipe from one of his many pockets. Of the five men here, four are dressed in the standard attire of the Midwestern farmer: well-worn overalls. "I love these duds, man. Where can I get some for myself?" he asks.

"Well, right here at the Feed Barn, a' course," Averitt tells him. Joe throws a wink at Jewels, who shakes her head dubiously.

"Babe, think of all the stuff I could carry around with that many pockets," he bargains.

"I'm not sure you own that much stuff," she giggles.

Averitt waves his unlit pipe around to get everyone's attention. "I reckon we can start with you, Clem," he says to a weathered man about my age with a battered straw hat perched crookedly on his head.

"I'd like to open up with a situation that happened to me three days ago," Clem starts out with a touch of dramatic flair. "You all know my wife Shirl and how she loves that mangy cat of hers," he began.

The rest of us nod at him like we are expected to.

"Well, I was tryin' to close the garage door usin' the gadget," Clem says, referring to his garage door opener by making a clicking gesture with one thumb. "I no sooner had pushed the button when I noticed her dadgum cat perched up there on top. I ask you, what kind of plain stupid animal sleeps on top of an automatic garage door?"

Mumbles about a plain stupid animal are appropriately presented.

"Correct!" Clem threads a finger through each side of the straps on his overalls. "Well, naturally, I tried to stop the door, but it wasn't for any good. Not that I cared about the cat, mind you, but more that I cared about avoidin' the butt chewin' I'd get from Shirl if the cat got hurt."

"Oh sure," Averitt chimes in. "Women take their felines seriously." Averitt is known for his love of all animals no matter the species.

"The door kept moving down, and the stupid cat just kept clingin' on, riding the top as it closed. That cat ended up getting sandwiched between the top of the door and the frame." He pauses here for effect, then rephrases his statement to make sure we all got the full impact of what transpired. "Flattened like a pancake."

"No!" Harold gasps.

"Yes," replies Clem solemnly.

"Lordy," empathizes Averitt sadly.

I look over at the Tacketts and have to stifle a laugh at their equally horrified and captivated expressions. Jewels has her eyes covered with both hands, peeping at Clem through her fingers. Joe is shaking his head back and forth, silently mouthing the word no.

"Right quick I opened the garage door, hopin' against hope the stupid cat might still have a breath in it, but I was out of luck. It dropped from the top and fell, deader than a doornail, not a foot away. Pretty much six inches of its midsection, the place where all the workins are stored, was squashed. It wasn't moving, and it sure as heck wasn't breathing." He illustrates this by running his hands across his midsection.

There are sharp intakes of breath and exclamations all around.

"Did you bury it somewhere so she wouldn't find it?" Harold asks.

"Well, I'm not going to lie to ya, I considered hidin' the evidence to protect myself. After careful consideration though, I decided to rely on the one thing that might be able to save me from the wrath of Shirl: the power and compassion of The Almighty. I laid my hands upon the dead body, pleading for Him to have mercy on this poor servant who was in dire circumstances." He peers around at all of us intensely.

I think Jewels might be holding her breath. Joe's eyes are as big as saucers. For their sake, I hope this story has a believable happy ending. Maybe I didn't make it clear enough to them that the Liar's Bench is a place where the truth is often stretched. I'll have to make sure and do that when we leave.

"The poor servant? That's me, not the darned cat. I'm not the dummy that sleeps in a dangerous place—I'm just the dummy Shirl would hold responsible," Clem clarifies. I think he's stretching the story out a bit, enjoying the attention.

"Get on with it, won't ya?" Averitt demands. "What happened?"

"Well, I said amen and then waited. A minute later, maybe two, right before my eyes, its body filled with air, like a balloon bein' inflated. It jumped up, full o' life and madder than a wet hen!"

"No, not possible," cry a chorus of voices. Not from the Tacketts though. They are grinning again. It's easy to forget that they subscribe to all that business about an invisible god up in the clouds because they don't act like nutjobs.

"It WAS and IS possible!" Clem exclaims. "The stupid cat hissed at me as if I closed it in the garage door on purpose, then ran off to hide in the hedges behind the house. Stayed there till Shirl got home."

"So, the cat is still alive?" Harold asks, doubtful.

"Alive and well three days later. I called Shirl up to tell her what happened, leaving out the part about how stupid I think the cat is, of course. I ain't no dummy." He winks conspiratorially at Joe, who slaps his thighs and laughs. "She rushed home and right away took the cat to the vet."

"An actual veterinarian who said the cat wasn't really dead, right?" Harold nods to the group like he's got it all figured out.

Clem looks around slowly, letting the tension build like a good storyteller should.

"Well?" Harold gestures.

"Oh, the cat *was* dead, alright. The vet showed Shirl some marks on the x-ray that meant every single rib had been broken then healed up. There were scars on its organs and stuff, too. They were both just pert-near speechless, you know, since Shirl's had that cat since it was a few weeks old and it ain't never had nothin' broken or injured in its whole dadgum life!"

Various opinions, theories, and arguments are springing up all over the group. A suggestion arises that maybe Shirl should be consulted to verify the story. Someone else wonders if the vet might want to chime in. Clem is deeply offended by their doubts and offers up a suggestion of his own on what they could all do with themselves that I couldn't possibly repeat to you.

The discussion of the dead cat eventually loses steam. Other stories are told, but none of them are quite as interesting. A while later the Tacketts regretfully say they need to head out for another appointment. I can't help but smile as I watch Joe clap Clem on the back and Jewels lean into Averitt, shaking her head with laughter at something he says.

"What a great day," Joe exclaims as we walk to our cars.

"Yes, thank you so much, Thomas!" Jewels wraps her arms around my neck and kisses my cheek in a very invasive gesture of affection I didn't ask for.

I remove her from my personal space, but with a smile to soften the gesture. "Yes, well, you're welcome. Let's not get overly rambunctious over it."

She dissolves into giggles again, but I can't imagine why. I'm being completely serious, after all, about not being kissed so often.

Chapter 8

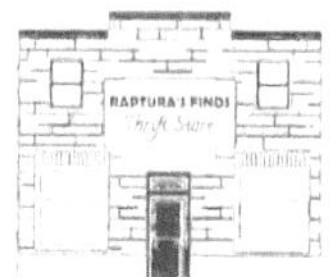

When Joe walks into the Munch Box today I feel myself form an honest smile. I've decided, much to the delight of my meddling wife, that Joe and Jewels are friends now. They aren't nutjobs in spite of believing in a make-believe sky god, and I don't have to clear it with anyone if I think they're worth my time.

Rusty and Palmer catch a glimpse of him a few seconds after I do, faces lit with astonishment.

"Will you *please* look at this," Palmer whistles.

"I can't think of any way to *stop* looking," Rusty laughs.

"What is it Wilma's teenage employees say?" I ask, then answer my own question. "I cannot *even* with this," I imitate their dramatic use of the phrase.

Joe knows right away what we're making eyes at and spins around so we can get a good look. He's bought himself a brand-new pair of denim overalls at the Feed Barn. "My dudes," he greets us, grinning ear to ear. "You can look, but please don't touch! I'd hate to get these babies dirty," he runs his hands lovingly down the sides of his torso, and we laugh even harder.

"I didn't think you were serious when you asked Averitt about his bibs," I chuckle.

Joe sidles into our booth looking very pleased with himself. "So? What do you think?" he tucks his thumbs into the shoulder straps the way he saw Clem do.

"Let me guess," Palmer lifts a finger, glancing up to the ceiling with pretend concentration. "Um, you're doing a stint with a traveling rodeo?"

Rusty pushes Palmer's hand down and titters, "No, that's not it. He's clearly just finished slopping the hogs!"

"These are okay guesses, but, come on guys, I think you can do better," Joe claps his hands together, turning to me. "Thomas?"

"Okay, you fell down and bonked your head good, waking up to think you're Averitt Whit." I play along.

He slyly reaches into the bib pocket and pulls out a pipe, flourishing it for us with a ta-dah! "As a matter of fact, Averitt helped me pick them out and even gave me one of his old pipes. He says it makes me look more natural."

The other two get wound up into another laughing fit. I shake my head. "I can't take much more of this hillbilly fashion hour. Are we eating lunch, or what?"

Joe flags down one of Wilma's younger servers who, of course, he knows by name. She takes our orders, promising to return promptly with drinks.

Joe and Palmer start talking about some movie I have no understanding of or interest in. It's kind of nice to have a younger person talk about pop culture with Palmer since Rusty and I prefer to stay in the dark ages of black and white sitcoms.

Rusty tells me about the newest crisis he has at the shop. I know he loves his nephew, but I'm pretty sure this is the third or fourth time the kid has messed up the billing for a customer. Rusty doesn't like to inconvenience his customers, even if it's accidental.

Maggie trots up to us and flops a half-chewed beef hide stick onto the seat next to Rusty with a loud harrumph. She throws a sad look at the rest of us before walking away with her head down.

"Do I want to know what that was all about?" I ask.

"She and I had a bet going over who would win the Cubs game last night. Turns out Miss Maggie is a sore loser when she has to pay up." He waggles the beef hide at me.

"If that's what you call winning, I think you might need your head examined," I look over the partially chewed stick with a grimace.

"Aww, well, it's not like she has money to bet with," he says. "I'll leave this here, anyway. It's enough to know I bested her. I don't need her chewie to be a winner."

"That's about as silly as Joe's overalls," I say. "How do you place a bet with a dog, anyway?"

"Very carefully," Rusty laughs at his own joke.

Wilma, always one step ahead of us, marches up with a tray full of drinks, sniffing at Joe. "Tampering with the youth of this town is punishable with jail time, you know," she says icily, handing glasses directly to the three of us but leaving Joe's on the edge of the table.

"Um," he falters, looking to me for guidance.

"Wilma, honestly," I scowl.

"And you three should know that playing with a horse of a different color can get you burned," she says over me, huffing away.

"Can I," Joe scrunches his face up as if he's deciding whether to share what he's thinking, then plunges ahead, "can I ask you dudes something and you promise to give me an honest answer?"

We say he can.

"Me and Scott and Dan are cool, but I feel like I can't get anywhere with Wilma. Have I done something, do you think, to make her mad?"

And all this time I've been hoping he wouldn't notice. How silly can one old man be?

"Wilma's just high strung," Palmer says dismissively, sliding me a glance.

"She's always going goofy over something," Rusty agrees. "It should wear off in a few more... weeks."

"It's more about her than it is about you," I say, adding, "When nobody buys into her side of the drama, she gets aggravated."

"So, I'm her drama?" He's been listening with a frown. "What is it I'm doing that is causing her drama?"

"Look, we'll tell you what's going on, but you have to promise to not hold it against us," I say.

"Or her," Palmer interjects, always fair-minded. "She's not a bad person; she's just, you know," he wiggles his fingers alongside his forehead.

"High strung, which can often be seen as loopy," I nod at Palmer in agreement.

"Wilma's good people. You could say she's our little sister, couldn't you, Thomas?" Rusty chuckles. "You know how a sister can be a big fat nuisance but you're protective of her anyway? She's got a gigantic personality that can scare some people away, but Thomas and I have a way with her."

Joe's bobbing his head up and down enthusiastically. "I love people with gigantic personalities. I *want* Wilma to like me, but no matter how nice I am to her it feels like she can't stand the sight of me. I just thought if I could figure out what I did wrong I could apologize for it. Make things right."

"Why do you like her so much? She's been a total snot the whole time you've been here," I say, surprised.

"Dude, I like everybody." He says it straightforwardly. "So, if you guys know something, I'd appreciate it if you would fill me in."

"It's like this, Joe... you guys jump in if I forget something." I start with her long feud with Olive and Taffy over the right to sell cinnamon rolls. Next, we explain her distrust of hippies, drugs, or any combination of the two. Finally, we delve into her obsession with cop shows and how she fancies herself to be an amateur detective.

Then we tell him how she rolled all that together into one huge assumption that he was selling drugs to Olive that fateful morning a few weeks ago.

There's a lot of laughing.

Our server comes back with plates of food, overhears what we're saying, and adds her own two cents. "Now that there's a drug dealing hippie on the loose," she laughs, handing Joe his plate, "we're getting the overprotective mother side of her she usually saves for Scott. If Joe's anywhere within fifty feet of the diner, she makes us pick a safety buddy." She indicates a young man behind the ice cream counter with a toss of her head. "Steve over there is supposed to be keeping an eye on me today in case you try anything nefarious."

"He looks extremely nefarious in these overalls," Rusty says, choking on his own laughter. It's impossible not to. My rib cage is starting to hurt, and Palmer and Joe are leaning into each other, giggling like schoolgirls.

"Need anything else?" the young lady asks, eyes wide. "A scale to weigh your drugs on maybe? I could get you one of hers from the back."

"Will it work on cocaine? Joe's thinking of expanding his business." Rusty asks. She shakes her head, laughing as she leaves us.

"Poor, poor Wilma," Joe says, pushing his glasses up to wipe his damp eyes.

"Poor Wilma?" I gasp. "More like poor everyone who comes in contact with Wilma."

"I mean poor Wilma's missed her calling. If someone could harness that imagination, just think of the brilliant books we could get out of it," he argues. "She'd write those murder mysteries set in restaurants, like Mashed Murder and Gravy, or Dinner Bell Death at the Munch Box Diner."

"She'd clearly be the main character, right?" Palmer adds, howling. "Diner Detective!"

"Peach Pie a la Murder," Rusty sniggers.

We spend a few minutes eating, the quiet punctuated with the occasional snort of laughter or loose giggle or another clever book title.

Joe's laughter finally boils down to a smile. "But listen… I gotta find a way to win her over. Any ideas?"

"You've got as much chance of winning her over as I do of getting a tattoo," I snort. "And I'm fairly certain Bea would come back from the grave to make sure that never happens."

"Is that a challenge?" Joe asks, eyes twinkling.

"She's in too deep now, Joe." Palmer says. "She's even drug Bob Frazier into this, for crying out loud. Half the town's tied to his church, and she'd never be able to live it down if she admitted to Bob she was wrong about you. That's a huge audience for Wilma to have to come clean in front of."

"So, the key to winning over the town is in winning over Wilma," Joe says thoughtfully. "Which I bet I can do."

"He's not listening to us," I say.

"It's not gonna happen, buddy," Rusty shakes his head. "Not with Wilma, and not with Bob's crew. Like Thomas said, why do you care?"

"I care about the relationships I'm missing out on. I can't let a little misguided assumption stand in the way of what could turn out to be many great friends," Joe says earnestly.

"Trust me, you don't want a relationship with Bob or his nutjob types," I shake my head emphatically.

He blinks at us, surprised. "Sure, I do! Passionate people like Bob make the best kind of friends."

"I guess that's a moot point. Wilma's mad because she wanted to catch a drug dealer and didn't get to. She's going to be salty about this for a long time," Palmer says.

"I'm feeling lucky," Joe says, grinning at us. "You guys want to turn this into a little bit of a wager?"

"I'm always interested in an easy win," Rusty says.

"What are the stakes?" Palmer asks.

"I don't want to start a fight with Bea," Joe looks mischievously at me. "But I think once she's my friend, Mr. Thomas Sanders will be getting his first tattoo."

Chapter 9

Joe called me late last night, voice exploding with anticipation, and asked me to meet him at the Munch Box today around ten. He's figured out how to win Wilma over, or so he thinks. I don't know what he's up to, but by the sound of his voice it's obvious he thinks he's cooked up something good.

Personally, I don't think he'll ever get Wilma to be his friend. I'll admit I'm getting curious to see what kind of a stunt he thinks will work, but still, I'm going to try to talk to him again before he does anything today. I want to make sure it won't hurt his feelings when she continues to reject him, which is the likeliest outcome.

I spot his rickety truck pulling into the parking lot and throw a quick look toward the door to the kitchen. Wilma's back there putting the finishing touches on the pies for today's lunch and dinner rush, so I should be able to get a few minutes alone with him.

The bell over the door jingles and Joe whooshes into the diner. I'm surprised to see he has a short legged, droopy eyed, floppy eared dog with him. He hoists the dog onto the bench seat across from me, scoots in next to it, and winks at me. "Mornin', Thomas. Ready for some fun?"

"Have you stolen a mutt to help you woo Wilma?" I ask. "That might be cheating."

He's feeling around in his overall pockets, slightly distracted. "What? Oh, uh, no I didn't steal him... ah, here it is," he wrestles out a metal badge. "This is Wigglesworth. He's lived with me and Jewels for about three years now. He's playing the part of my official police dog."

"If that's a police dog, I'm a circus clown," I retort, taking the badge when he offers it to me. I scrunch up my eyes to better see the small print, clicking my tongue at how real it looks. "And how did you come to have something like this in your possession?"

He's digging around in his pockets again, only half listening to me. "You know, Thomas, I can't imagine how I got by in life without overalls. I've got pockets for days. You can carry a ton of things around with you, but still have your hands free to do stuff," he produces three or four folded pieces of paper and places them on the table, lining them up into a neat pile next to the badge.

"What are you up to?" laughter bubbles up in me.

"I think it's obvious, buddy," he winks. "I'm going to win Wilma's heart by speaking her language."

The swinging door to the kitchen smashes open. We turn to see Wilma heading this way, eyes flashing and mouth tight. "Good gravy, that didn't take long. It's like she's got some kind of internal hippie radar," I say.

"Okay, here we go!" he says in low tones, then motions frantically for her to come to our table, even though that's what she's already doing. "Your job is to go along with me, okay, Thomas? And try to not look surprised."

At first she scowls at him, but as soon as she notices the dog her expression softens, and her pace quickens. He's laid his head on the table, ears spread out like napkins, eyes sad. I can't be sure, but I suspect she thinks she has to save the dog from the hippie.

He whispers seconds before she's within earshot, "Tattoo, here we come!"

Well, he's got a badge, which means this is something to do with cops, and he's got a dog—the only thing more important to her than cops. I might just be in trouble.

"What's going on here?" she demands, hands on hips, green eyes alert.

"Good morning, Wilma," his voice is uncharacteristically formal as he hands her the first folded paper from his pile. She puckers up her lips in distaste, and for a split second I think she's going to refuse to take it. Curiosity wins over distrust, and she snatches it out of his hand, reading through it quickly before putting it into her apron pocket.

He places one finger across his lips to indicate silence before handing her the second note. She reads this one, brows furrowed, before asking me in a barely audible voice, "Tommy, you know about this?"

"I do," I reply seriously. The second note joins the first one in her apron.

He scoots his fake badge across the table to her, saying, "Beautiful weather today, isn't it? I just love May." She picks up the badge, turning it around in her hands carefully as she considers it. She casts another questioning look at me, so I nod again, solemnly.

Her eyes are glowing. She's circling the bait like a ravenous fish, and it's clear to me that his plan is working when she answers him, imitating his formal style of speaking. "Yes, the weather has been perfect."

Joe takes a second badge out, angling it up so she can see it, then slides it back inside his bib pocket. He hands her the last folded note, not a trace of anything on his face she might find suspicious. He deserves an Oscar for this. She scans this one with a touch of eagerness, nodding to herself a couple of times, then slips it into her apron. Her eyes skip around between the dog, Joe, me, then back to the dog.

Shockingly, she smiles at Joe.

I mean, this development is about as shocking as shocking can get.

Joe recognizes he's on the brink of something big and goes in for the kill. He says in a voice so low it's practically a whisper, "Your town needs you, Wilma. The force needs you, and I need you. Will you help?"

She draws in a deep breath and answers, "Does a bear have its cake and eat it, too?"

He doesn't know if she means yes or no and looks to me for a translation. I've been playing along with him up till now so I might as well go all in.

"Congratulations, Joe." I whisper. "Looks like she's on board!"

He looks up into her face earnestly, whispering, "Thank you, honorary Detective Harper."

I choke back my laughter. It's outlandish to think he's walked in here with some ruse involving a dog and a badge and made friends with her. Right? This is Wilma we're dealing with.

Then again, I guess I've just answered my own question. It *is* Wilma we're dealing with. Wilma Harper loves a good crisis, and Joe has obviously just given her one she thinks is bigger than a drug dealing hippie.

Her eyes shine as she looks over the badge in her hand again. She places it into the pocket of her apron along with all her notes, pats it fondly, and smiles at him again.

A thought crosses my mind, and before this can get out of hand and cost me dearly, I ask, "Uh, Wilma, can I possibly get a slice of that spiced apple pie, please?"

She's mildly annoyed with me for changing the subject, I think, but Joe saves my hide.

"I'll be back in with, um, a new *order* in a day or two," he assures her with a sly look, which appeases her.

"Oh, alright Tommy," she says. "You want anything, Joe?"

"No ma'am, I'm all done here," he says, tossing me a broad smile. She may not get his double meaning, but I sure do.

She sashays away with a spring in her step.

As soon as she's gone, I roll my eyes at him. "Okay, okay, I played along with your dumb little game. The least you can do is fill me in on what it is I played along with."

He taps his temple with a finger. "I listened to what you guys said.

I told her she's the backbone of the community and the FBI needs her help. Wiggles here is a drug sniffing genius, I am his humble handler and an agent, and together we've tracked a drug dealer to this small, sleepy town. We've gone undercover at the bistro with the coffee bean story but are hitting dead-ends. That's where she comes in,"

"You are really something," I say.

"Can confirm," he gloats. "We will be friends before the bear eats it's cake," he laughs, adding, "or whatever it was she said."

"Yeah, if you're going to work a case with her, you're going to discover she's a real expert at words." I chuckle along with him.

He drapes his arms along the back of the bench seat, smug. "I think it's quaint when she says things like that."

"Quaint, huh," I shake my head.

"You know, I'd hoped it would work, but I had no idea it would go over so smoothly," he says. "Jewels isn't super thrilled with me, but I just couldn't think of any of other way."

"I know Wilma pretty well and this is probably the *only* way you could have made friends with her. I'm impressed you thought of it, truthfully." I laugh. "My only question for you is what will you do when she realizes this is a joke and tries to saw your head off with a dull knife?"

"By that time, it won't matter, because she'll have seen what a solid dude I am. I just need a way to spend enough time with her so my charming nature can get to work," he sounds so sure of himself. "We'll laugh about the whole thing over a nice meal. Dude, I bet she'll even help you pick out your tattoo."

"What makes you think I'll go through with it," I smirk.

"Oh, Thomas, Thomas, Thomas," he sighs. "The only thing I'm worried about is whether you'll go with full color or stick with a classic black and white."

Chapter 10

It's an ideal May afternoon. Perfect temps, the scent of lilac in the air, and no rain in sight.

Ordinarily I would be napping during this part of the afternoon, preferably on a lounge chair in my backyard. The Tacketts have asked me to join them at the diner for a late afternoon piece of pie, so as much as I'd like to be napping, I guess I'll enjoy pie in the middle of the day just a little bit more.

I can rearrange my own schedule for extra pie, you know. That's not the same as having my peace and quiet ruined.

"You have half an apple pie in the fridge," Bea teases me in a sing-song voice. "You're not skipping your nap for pie. You're skipping your nap for companionship!"

"Wow. Isn't that interesting," I say out loud to the diner in general. "Suddenly I've gone completely deaf."

It's none of Bea's business if I happen to think it's been two days too many since I've seen the Tacketts.

As if on cue, the bell chimes and they appear, laughing over something. "Hey, hey, my main man!" Joe claps me hard on the back and shakes my hand. He's swapped out his usual flannel for a thin tee shirt, but the overalls are still in place. I've never seen anyone in my whole life so obsessed over a piece of clothing.

Jewels wraps her arms tightly around me so she can force loud, smacking kisses on my cheek. I protest, naturally, but she laughs it off and scoots in next to me while Joe drops down across from us.

"Kenny's coming, too, but he's running a little late," Joe says.

"Oh, good," I reply. "I'll be glad to see him again," I say, and I actually mean it.

Wilma, who can always sense when there's something going on and she's not in the middle of it, drops whatever she's doing behind the ice cream counter and rushes over, excitedly waving a piece of paper at Joe. "Gawd's nightgown, it took you forever to come back! I've been gathering intel for two days but had no idea how..." she notices Jewels next to me and pulls up short, sliding the piece of paper back into her pocket.

"Good to see you again, Wilma!" he says, sounding as if he actually means it. It still strikes me as peculiar how much he likes her. "I've been dying to introduce you to my wife Jewels. Babe, this is Wilma Harper!"

Jewels pops up and gives Wilma a hug. She's got a real problem when it comes to keeping her hands to herself. "Oh, Wilma, I'm so glad to finally get the chance to meet you! Joe's told me all about you and the fantastic pies you make."

Wilma's confused look breaks into a generous smile and she hugs Jewels right back. "Wife? I had no idea. Aren't you just full of surprises, Joe,"

Joe nods, then holds one hand against his mouth and whispers, "She's not part of the operation, but she knows who is. Speaking of which, another detective will be joining us shortly. He got assigned an even crazier disguise than me." He tugs at a dreadlock hanging over his shoulder.

Wilma brightens up at this. "Oh, *great*, because I've got some good news and he will want to hear it too, I reckon." She thinks for a second, then asks, "How will I recognize him?"

"No shirt," he grimaces. "Never wears one,"

She nods sympathetically. "Being undercover isn't for the faint of heart."

"Uh, detective," I waggle a finger at her, "how about tea for everyone before we get started on official business?"

She looks at me with mild annoyance but goes to fetch the tea anyway. The internal battle between the need to "cop" and the need to "serve" is a very real thing for Wilma.

"For the record, Thomas Sanders, I do not approve of this silly prank you two are playing on poor Wilma," Jewels says critically. "I've already scolded Joe for it."

"I'm more interested in seeing Joe get himself out of the con than I am worried about Wilma's feelings being hurt," I counter. "Wilma's having the time of her life playing cops and robbers. Whether she forgives Joe or not, she'll still look back on these days fondly. You have my word on that."

"Babe, I told you," Joe takes her hand across the tabletop. "I need a way to get close to her. She'll see I'm a good dude and love me as much as I love her. After that, I can tell her the truth *and* have her as a friend," he nods insistently.

Jewels makes a disgusted face but let's the subject drop.

Joe asks me if I've seen the new juice bar Ido has going on over at the market, which I have not. Jewels visited the Rapturous Finds Thrift Store and wants to know if Bea had anything to do with the book exchange program, which she did. Joe retells a story about some of the kids in their church having a spicy food battle, which makes me simultaneously laugh and shudder.

A commotion just past Joe's shoulder catches my attention. I crack up as Kenny, who was on his way to our table, is intercepted by a zealous Wilma. "Looks like Detective Harper is delivering some sensitive information to Detective Kenny."

They follow my eyes, Joe laughing and Jewels groaning. "He doesn't know about our bet, but he'll handle it like a pro. Kenny has a way with people," Joe says with assurance.

Wilma's gesturing wildly with one hand and gripping his arm with the other. We watch with curiosity.

A few minutes later Wilma releases her hold on Kenny. She returns to the kitchen, and he finds his way to us, eyes bright with humor. There's a great deal of back thumping between him and Joe, high fives with Jewels, and a robust, "Hello again, Sanders" for me.

"So, uh, that red-headed chick gave me a list of names I should be, uh, what did she say…" Kenny lays a piece of paper on the table, and I recognize Wilma's handwriting. "Something about surveillance teams and suspicious people," he laughs.

"Edda Mae Brothens and family; all employees of the bistro; Sam (or Shawn) who goes to the hardware store too many times a week to be believable," Jewels reads aloud.

Laughingly I say, "Edda Mae is her long-time arch nemesis. If someone accused Edda Mae of heading up a group of Al Qaeda scoundrels, Wilma would break her neck trying to google the phone number for the CIA."

"Well, what about the bistro employees, or poor Sam or Shawn who simply needs a lot of DIY supplies?" Jewels protests.

"I'll tell her I'm looking into the list," Joe says easily. "Then in a couple of days I can report back that they all checked out as clean."

"This is getting too complicated," Jewels warns.

Kenny looks like he's reading a book that's missing a few chapters in the middle.

"I think you better explain to your FBI partner here what's going on," I say.

Joe laughs, apologizes, and explains the situation to him, starting with the morning my crossword puzzle got so horribly ruined.

"The risk is worth the payoff, huh?" Kenny observes. "I mean, if you want this chick to be your friend, far be it from me to stand in the way."

"I kinda told her your undercover disguise is to not wear a shirt," Joe admits somewhat sheepishly.

"Man, at least you gave me the good one. I can't believe you're still wearing these farmer rags," he flips the strap of Joe's overalls with a finger.

Wilma sends one of her servers over with warm peach cobbler and glasses of iced tea, and we fall into companionable silence marked by the occasional comment between bites.

Wilma finds her way back to us eventually, Maggie at her heels. The girthy girl pulls herself up onto the bench seat with me and Jewels, forcing me to shove down, and starts in on one of her slobber-filled licking sessions. To my horror, Jewels doesn't even try to stop her! By the look on her face, I'd say Maggie's immediate affection for Jewels impresses Wilma almost as much as Joe's fake badge. When it's time for the three of them to leave, Wilma tells Joe and Kenny to crack down on her suspect list and extracts a promise from Jewels to come back to the diner sooner rather than later.

As luck would have it, Old Brimstone strolls through the door on the east end of the diner just in time to catch a glimpse of Joe and Kenny's backsides as they walk out the door on the west end. His mouth drops open in shock and he makes a beeline for me and Wilma.

"What in heaven's name were they doing in here? It's bad enough that Joe character is in town all the time, but now he's bringing shirtless riffraff with him?" Bob starts fuming from ten feet away.

"What are you going on about?" Wilma asks coolly. It didn't occur to me that Joe's detective ruse would cause Wilma to revert back to her usual treatment of the barely tolerable Bob Frazier, but it's a nice realization.

"What am I talking about? That, that *hippie* and his druggie friends —that's what I'm talking about. Do you know I've caught Neil with that tattooed nightmare three times in as many weeks? It's an epidemic!" Bob splutters.

"Now, Bob, look," I start to say, but Wilma holds a hand up to me.

"Hang on just a second there," she squares off with Old Brimstone, hands on hips. "You know what, Bob, there's nothing in the Bible against hippies wanting to spend their money at privately owned eating establishments. His money pays my bills every bit as well as yours. And Neil is a grown man. Why, he's got to be at least twenty or twenty-one! He doesn't need your permission to talk to Joe." She shakes her head at him.

"But, but that guy is a *drug dealer*! *You* told me so *yourself*," Bob grunts in protest, shocked at her drastic change in attitude.

"And when have we ever had drug deals at the Munch Box Diner? I was misled and I'm not too proud to admit it. It's called being human. You should try it sometime." In an instant she swaps her corrective tone to the one she uses for running the restaurant, adding, "Are you here to pick up those pies? Come on over here and I'll get you rung up."

Bob takes his pies and leaves, mumbling about everyone losing their minds overnight.

"He's like that cousin nobody can stand who keeps showing up at family dinners," Wilma comments, wiping her hands on a dish towel.

"To be fair, you did switch the game up on him without any warning," I laugh.

"It was pretty funny, wasn't it?" she giggles.

I don't want a tattoo, but it was entertaining to see Bob have to go through that with Wilma.

Chapter 11

"But, you see, we are men. Men do not care about dust bunnies," I argue with Bea while I set the table.

"If you would just let that young lady come back and clean once a week, Thomas, we wouldn't have to keep having these little talks," she purrs critically.

"I put a candle in the guest bath. Isn't that enough?" I find a place for the last bowl of chips and survey my handiwork.

The monthly poker game is at my house, and I'm already regretting it. It's only slightly about the invasion of privacy, and mostly because if I don't do things to Bea's specifications, she carries on like I've committed the crime of the year.

"But, honey—" she starts.

"No, and I'll tell you something else..." a knock on the door saves me.

Mike, Val, and Lee are fierce poker players. They're also pastors. Weird, I know, that I'm playing poker with men who believe in that unseen tyrant, considering how nonsensical I find all that religious stuff. It's all Bea's fault, as usual. She accumulates friends like I do naps, and it just so happens that three of them were tolerable enough that I liked them, too. They are non-nutjobs, like Joe.

Lee Calloway and I are both men of a certain age who grew up just a few houses apart but didn't get acquainted until our fifties. He's alright as long as you don't get him started on shoes, which he's obsessed with, or snakes, which he detests. He'll bore you to tears with debates about both topics.

Vallen Walters, thirty or more years my junior, used to work for the king of the nutjobs, Frank Norris. Val left Frank's church because he couldn't get onboard with the scare tactics Frank tried to pass off as religion. That's reason enough to like the guy, in my opinion.

And Mike Briggs, simply put, is just a good guy. He takes care of people the way Bea used to, and that makes him good enough for me. He's also got the handsomest head of hair in the whole town, according to Wilma. She calls it pepper and paprika, although Rusty and I think she means salt and pepper.

When Bea and I moved here, these men were regular fixtures around the house. They kept Bea busy when she was able to be busy and held court around her when all she could do was huddle in a blanket. They made her laugh when they could and when she needed it, they prayed with her.

In those ways, they were good friends to me, too.

Ido, Rusty, and Palmer are the last to arrive. In the spirit of giving credit where credit is due, I should also tell you they spent their own fair share of time here, just like all three Harpers, Olive, and Taffy. Bea thinks I don't realize just how much these people did for us in her last months of life, but I do. Food was cooked, Bea was tended to, and in the end, the hardest decisions I couldn't handle were made for me.

I know who took care of things when I couldn't, and I appreciate them for it. Now that Bea's gone, I prefer to keep my emotions tidily confined within the boundaries of my Code, so I don't go on and on about it. All the same, I know what good friends they were to us both.

Speaking of boundaries... Rusty's hauling in a platter of Scott's burgers, which is great, but he's followed by the chubby Maggie, which is not so great. I raise my brows at him, but all I get in response is a handwritten note. It's from Wilma, who obviously thinks she can bully me via pen and ink. She and Dan had matters to attend to up in Indy, says the note, and Maggie preferred to stay with Rusty.

"Here," Ido thrusts a foil wrapped burger into my hands. "Put that in your mouth before you start griping."

We've slaughtered the burgers, made significant dents in the chips, and played at least five rousing hands of poker when a rapid knock on the door reminds me about the Tacketts. They called earlier this afternoon to ask if they could come by with some news that simply couldn't wait another day, according to Joe's exuberant voice.

"Hang on, fellas. I forgot to mention we're having company." I open the door, ushering in two humans and another canine I wasn't expecting.

"I'm not running a doggie daycare around here," I tell Jewels, who merely smiles tolerantly at me.

"Hello, dear Thomas," Jewels squeezes me so hard I lose my breath then manages to sneak a kiss onto my cheek while I'm incapacitated.

"Ugh," I detach myself from her laughingly and make a production of wiping off my cheek.

"My man," Joe pumps my hand excitedly. They both have shiny eyes and suspiciously happy grins.

"Joe," I greet him, motioning for them to come on in. "For those of you who don't know, this is Joe and Jewels Tackett," I say. Jewels gushes to Mike over how much she loves the thrift store even as she moves to give Rusty, Ido, and Palmer more of her suffocating hugs. Joe warmly shakes six sets of hands.

I sit down, moving my cards aside, and gesture to the table. "We ate all the burgers, but you're welcome to chips."

Joe shakes his head no. "We're too excited to eat," he says enthusiastically. "We've got news!"

"We've been dying all day to get over here and tell you," Jewels says breathlessly.

"Oh, I just bet they're pregnant!" Bea squeaks.

"Bea's so curious she's having a conniption. You better go ahead and spit it out before the three of you implode," I say.

"The Tacketts are moving to Cardinal Creek!" Joe exclaims, hands extended above his head like he's signaling a touchdown.

"In two weeks!" Jewels adds exuberantly.

The rest of us are speechless.

"Ta-dah!" Joe does jazz hands.

"How, er..." I clear my throat. "*What?*"

"When you know, you know. We just can't get enough of this place," Joe says emphatically.

"I got the idea about a month or so ago, and no matter how wild I kept telling myself it was, I couldn't shake it," Jewels says.

"Then, a couple of weeks ago, I told Jewels I wanted to move here, only to find out she'd been wanting the very same thing!" Their expressions suggest they just discovered life on Mars.

Rusty's jaw is hanging open in shock, Ido's bushy eyebrows are drawn together in confusion, and Palmer has cupped the left side of his face in his hand.

At least I'm not the only one who's astounded.

Bea squeals again, "This is *almost* as thrilling as a baby announcement!"

Lee recovers first. "By the look on your faces I can tell you're over the moon about this. Let me be the first to congratulate you."

"Absolutely! We always have room for more young people around here," Val says warmly as Mike adds his own, "of course we do" to it.

Rusty gains his wits, saying, "It's not like we aren't happy for you. You just took us by surprise."

"It's quite unexpected, but great news!" Palmer hurries to agree.

Ido's closest to them. He stands up, reaches out a hand, and bleats dramatically like the Italian man he is, "Welcome to town!"

"Thanks, Ido, thank you!" Joe shakes his hand, grinning.

"I don't understand. What about your life? You'd be giving up everything." I ask, aware that I'm the only one being less than welcoming.

"We aren't dying, dude, we're expanding. Who says we have to give one part of our life up for the other?" Joe replies logically.

"We're here half the time for one reason or another anyway. It wouldn't be much different if we live here and visit there," Jewels reasons.

"But it's such a huge decision," I try again, although the argument sounds weak to my own ears.

"Stop being such an old pooper, honey," Bea needles me. "For heaven's sake, you like having them around. Why wouldn't you want them to live here?"

"Like I said, when you know, you know," Joe adds. "We lived there until we finished what we started, and now it's time to move here and start something new. It's honestly not any deeper than that," he says, confident in his simplicity.

"You said two weeks," Lee says. "Does that mean you've found someone to take over your church?"

I lose interest right away when the pastor talk starts and my mind drifts to the real reason I'm hesitant about this move. I think back to Ido's Market and the ignorance those two nutjobs from Bob's church were spouting. I don't want Bob and the town to tear the Tacketts apart.

"That's sweet of you, dear," Bea assures me, "but they're smart, strong, mentally healthy people. I think you might be surprised at what they can manage in spite of your so-called nutjobs. If you like having them around as friends, imagine how much fun life would be if they were our neighbors!"

She's right about the neighbor part, at least. As I think about it, I realize I would, in fact, like it if they lived here in Cardinal Creek. I don't know if they would be happy here, and I'm not sure how long they'd be willing to put up with Bob's stupidity before he would drive them away. If I take Bob out of the picture, though, I know I'd love to have them move here.

I refocus on the present conversation in time to hear Palmer say, "The problem will be selling your house."

Joe's face lights up with joy. "Nope. Got a cash offer yesterday for a couple grand over our asking price."

"That's why we'll be moving in two weeks. The buyer's only stipulation was that they wanted into the house that soon," Jewels explains. "It's like God set the whole thing up!"

I roll my eyes. "Did God find you a house around here to buy while he was at it?"

"Well, no, but it'll all work out," Joe says smoothly.

"Seems like all the apartments have a no pet policy though," Jewels frowns. "We've been looking into renting a house anyway, because Wiggles is used to having a yard."

"Not a lot of homes for sale in our price range either," Joe remarks.

"Whereabouts are you looking?" Mike asks. "I can keep an eye open."

"We want to be close to the bistro, close to the diner, and close to Thomas, so anywhere around here would be lovely!" Jewels gestures vaguely to the front door.

The fact that they want to be close to me causes a little tweak of something pleasant to spark in my chest.

My house has three bedrooms upstairs, a den, a finished basement, and a fenced-in backyard, most of which I haven't used in ages. A huge, almost empty house is sitting right here in the area of town they want to live in. I sneak a glance at Bea, who's eyeballing me with hopeful speculation.

It's so annoying how she can read my mind like this.

"Since your invisible God got you into this then left you high and dry, I suppose the only decent thing to be done is for Bea and me to offer up our place to you," I say.

Rusty chokes on his drink, Ido and Palmer splutter out unintelligible words, and Lee spits an ice cube onto the table. I scowl, using a napkin to maneuver it back to him.

"Are you ill?" Val asks, reaching toward my forehead. I smack his hand away with a growl.

"Should I call 911?" Rusty pats his pockets for his cell.

"Cheese and crackers!" I slam my hand down on the table. "A man's home is his dang castle, and I'm the king around here. If I want to move them into my house I'll do so without listening to this rabble rousing."

"It's such a deviation from the Code, Thomas. I'm sure you can see how shocking this is," Mike says with a smile resembling Bea's.

"I don't appreciate your tone," I snap.

"What tone? I'm making an observation is all," his words are jumbled with laughter, which makes me even madder.

"You can all get out. The poker game is cancelled." I scoot my chair backwards and stand up, aggravation making my nostrils flare. "First it's 'Oh, Thomas is such a grouch. Don't talk to Thomas, he's a bully with a Code.' Then Thomas does something nice and you all act like I've gone mental!"

Apparently my irritation is their favorite flavor of amusement. They don't take me seriously at all. In fact, every last one of them starts laughing. Rusty stands up too, holding his stomach, and Lee wipes tears from his eyes.

"Oh, Thomas, ignore them! I'm so proud of you, honey!" Bea has tears too, but for different reasons, and that's all it takes to deflate my aggravated mindset.

I smile her way before turning to Joe and Jewels.

"Well? Do you have any better offers?" I ask them.

Jewels and Joe exchange looks. Then she closes the distance between us, links her arm through mine, and says with a smile, "I'd love to see our bedroom, please."

CHAPTER 12

The last day of May has crept up on me. Time isn't flying by, as the old people say, but the past two weeks didn't seem to take quite as long as I thought it would. It's only now that I'm realizing my days of solitude are gone, at least for a while.

"No, I'm not regretting it," I reassure Bea. "I was in full control of my faculties when I invited them to move in."

"I didn't say you are, dear," she smiles.

"Oh," I look around the kitchen.

"But I'm not regretting it either," she adds.

"Well, that's good," I say.

"It's not like they'll be living here forever. The few weeks they are with us will fly by, just like the old people say," she recycles my phrase with a grin.

"True," I nod.

"Something to think about in case you *do* start to regret your decision," she says.

But I won't. I don't alter the Code very often, and on the rare occasion I make a change it's always deliberate and exactly what I want.

"Come on, let's go make sure everything is ready," I tell her, leading the way down into the basement.

Bea sniffs the air approvingly. "Aren't you glad you used the baking soda?"

"Why I have to get the carpet even dirtier before I vacuum will always be a mystery," I say, flipping on the light switch. "Besides, the dog hasn't even slept here yet. I suspect the whole place will need a good sweep at least a couple of times a day once he's here."

"You are seriously exaggerating the hairiness of a dog," she snickers. "But I'm so excited you've finally agreed to get a pet!"

"*I don't* have a pet! Joe and Jewels have a pet," I correct her. A loud bang and a "Yo, roomie!" from the top of the stairs announce the Tacketts' arrival. "And don't you go saying anything to them about me getting one, either." I warn her.

"If only they *could* hear me," she sighs.

"Down here, Joe," I call out.

He trots down the stairs faster than I'll ever be able to again and engulfs me in a bear hug. I thump his back a couple of times before pushing him back into his own space. "Does the confounded hugging and kissing from you two ever stop?"

"Gotta share the love, man," he replies. "Kenny and Jewels are upstairs. She's unloading all the food and stuff first."

"I told you it wasn't necessary to bring groceries," I protest, but he protests louder.

"Dude, just... stop. Okay? Stop," he trots back up the stairs, ending the argument before I can really get it started. Dutifully I follow him up and say hello to Jewels, who's squatting in front of a mostly empty cabinet. Wigglesworth is on the floor next to her, sad eyes half closed. I guess dogs can sleep just about anywhere.

"Hello, Thomas, you dear, sweet man," Jewels' voice echoes from deep within the depths of the cabinet.

"Tell her I say welcome to the family!" Bea gushes.

"Bea says she's happy you're here," I lie, dampening down the emotionally charged wording to better suit me.

"Hello, Bea, and thank you! Joe and I are so excited to be a big, happy family with you and Thomas," Jewels calls out.

"It's like she read my mind," Bea says with wonderment. "Maybe I *can* talk to them, after all."

Rolling my eyes at her, I say, "I'll go out and see how Kenny's coming along," I hastily slip out the door and make my way to the moving truck. Kenny is there in all his shirtless glory, balancing a beer can on top of a large box. "Good to see you again, Kenny."

"You too, man," he says amicably. "Hey, I was just wondering about the lady that lives across the street there," he tosses his head in that direction.

"What about her?" I take a box from the back of the truck, and we start for the house.

"Looks like those trash cans of hers might be too much for her to manage," he says. "I saw her fight pretty hard to get them back to the garage, and they were empty. Imagine how hard it probably is when they're full and she has to drag them down here to the street," he gives me a meaningful look. "Just thought maybe someone might let her kids know she could use a helping hand once in a while."

"And?" I blink at him, confused at why we're discussing the woman across the street from me.

"And that someone should be you," he says directly.

"Nope, you're wrong about that," I shake my head firmly.

"How am I wrong?"

"I can't get involved." I inform him.

"Can't... or won't?" he squints suspiciously at me.

I squint back defiantly. "Can't."

"I'm gonna need you to explain," he says.

So, I patiently lay out the basics of how the Code protects my privacy and why I don't socialize with any of my neighbors. His dumbfounded expression begs for further explanation, so I try wording it in a different way. "Knowing the people who live in close proximity to this house would be bad for me. It starts out small like a casual wave as they check their mail. That's just a gateway gesture, you know. Soon it escalates to them actually believing it's perfectly okay to walk over to talk about the weather any time they see me outside. Once they start that, it's only a matter of time till they're knocking on your door. Invitations to cookouts, needing favors from you while they're on vacation, the whole nine yards."

Pausing at the door, he hefts his box against one hip and eyeballs me as he takes a drink. He lowers the can at me, saying, "I bet you're one lonely dude."

"Not at all," I counter, opening the door for him.

He scoffs at my denial, saying, "I still think she needs some help."

"Who?" I ask, momentarily forgetting the whole subject of this conversation to begin with.

"Dude," he huffs at me with exasperation, "the lady across the street!"

"Oh, uh, right," I gesture over to the house with one hand. "Knock yourself out."

"Maybe I will! What's her name?"

It's my turn to look at him in amazement. "How should I know? Haven't you been listening to my Code?"

He roars in mock disgust, pushing past me into the kitchen. "I don't know how you guys got invited to live with this hermit," he announces to Joe and Jewels.

"Hermit?" Jewels laughs.

"Ask him about this crazy Code he's got," he says and heads down the stairs.

Joe takes the box from me, grinning. "You know Kenny lives in our old neighborhood, by the church. He watches over every widow, elderly person, retired military vet, and single parent in a two-mile radius who might need a little extra attention. Remember how he was buying that pink bowl the other day for the lady who collects them? He's always finding ways to get someone groceries or arrange a car ride, or about a thousand other helpful things."

"Kenny's more of a pastor than Joe, really. Wouldn't you say so, babe?" Jewels says.

"Oh, hands down," he readily admits. "And kind of the opposite of the Code."

"What an angel," Bea says with admiration.

"I guess it's better than being a nutjob," I say to all three of them. "I'll go get another box."

Kenny reminds me a whole lot of Bea. It surprises me that someone who looks like Kenny would be like Bea, but I guess that's what I get for judging a book by its cover, isn't it?

The day passes by quickly, like all days tend to do when you're busy. When my stomach grumbles a bit too much, I look at my watch and am surprised to see it's well after five. We hold a brief meeting, and it's decided that Joe and Kenny will make a food run while Jewels and I wait for them on the porch. I settle down into a rocker while she finds a place on the steps.

"So, you're not much of a healthy eater, are you Thomas?" she asks, gazing up at me.

"I'm at that place in my life where I've decided it's fine to suit myself," I reply.

"But you're not worried about your health?"

"What—at this age?" I laugh. "Not really."

She frowns at me, puzzled. "I guess *I'll* have to worry about it for you then, because you're not all that old."

Her voice is thick with determination and reminds me so much of Bea I look around to see if she's here listening—and worse, agreeing.

Mike pulls into the drive and waves with a pleasant smile at Jewels first, then me. "Oh, I didn't know he was stopping by!" she says happily.

"Tomorrow's June first." I say. "He's here to pick up Bea's check."

"You mean *your* check, don'tcha?" she grins. I chuckle a bit but don't argue.

"Afternoon! I forgot about it being moving day," he says.

"That's all over with for the moment. We've segued into eating time." I motion at the empty rocker, adding, "Joe went out for some food. Have a seat with us if you can stay."

The two of them strike up a conversation about the thrift store while I go inside and get his check. Their voices carry in through the window and I can't help but smile. Jewels' vivacious affection and constant do-gooder attitude are more ways she reminds me of a young Bea.

By the time I make it back out to the porch they've worked themselves into a frenzy. "You didn't tell me she's a licensed counselor, Thomas," Mike says.

"I didn't know," I retort.

"How many times have I told you I need more help?" he admonishes, but I shrug. The touchy-feely stuff he talks about isn't anything I can help with, so it usually goes in one ear and out the other.

"I'm going to start taking shifts at the store and do some group therapy at the shelter," her eyes glow with brilliant rays of happiness.

"Well, what about that," I say.

"Isn't it fantastic, Thomas? I can pick up where Bea left off," she beams.

"Oh," I smile, and when she keeps looking at me expectantly, I add, "that's a great deal then." This seems to satisfy her, and she goes back to brainstorming ideas with Mike.

"Um, aren't you forgetting something?" Bea says.

"No, I am not," I reply, flicking the check in my hand.

"You're going to need to write a different check now, dear," she insists.

"Whatever for?" I ask.

"Because Mike has a new salary to pay, Thomas, and the amount we give him each month isn't going to cut it," she answers.

I look at Jewels' animated face as she talks.

I sigh.

I go back into the house and write a new check.

Chapter 13

"Have I mentioned how unnecessary this all is?" I grumble.

"About seventy million times," Joe replies with his usual good humor.

Jewels and Wigglesworth are on a play date with Wilma and Maggie at the dog park, while we men have been sent to Ido's Market. Jewels insisted that she absolutely *positively* had to have a few staples in the kitchen. I skimmed the list and immediately asked Joe if she's trying to kill me.

"Kale? Quinoa? *You* don't eat this mess, do you?" I ask.

"My man, you'd be surprised at what a dude can eat if it's got cheese sauce on it," he laughs.

"If you don't like it then *why* are you eating it?" I ask, puzzled.

His reply is quick but simple. "Because it makes her happy."

I realize I can relate to that.

We round a corner and practically run right into Mike, Val, and Lee.

"Whoa there," I pull up short. Joe greets them with hearty hugs and slaps on their backs, and they don't even seem to mind.

"Thank heavens you're here," Val says. "We've got to bring desserts to the quarterly ministerial meeting and we're out of ideas."

"For the safety of those eating, none of us should be cooking," Mike adds on with a scowl.

"We'd like our dessert to take some of the bitterness out of the sixty minutes the speaker has the floor, if you know what I mean," Lee smiles wryly.

"It's either Bob or Frank," I make a guess.

"Bob," there's a depth to the agony in Val's one word answer.

"Sounds like a dreary fiasco you'd be better off avoiding," I observe.

"It's like this," Lee replies, sending Joe a wink. "Sometimes it's better to go to those kinds of things so you can keep an eye on the undesirables."

"Meetings can be a drag," Joe agrees, carefully stepping around the inflammatory subject of Old Brimstone. "I do have an idea for your dessert dilemma though. You should get something from Wilma."

The three of them look at one another. Val smacks his forehead with his palm while Mike makes a disgusted face. "The obvious choice," Lee says with a laugh.

"Alright, fellas, shall we head to the diner then?" Val says.

Mike checks his watch. "If we hurry I've got time to have a quick piece of pie."

I sigh wistfully as I watch them leave. "I wish I was going with them for pie instead of buying grass and tree bark," I say glumly.

"You know she's trying to feed you healthy food because she loves you," Joe reasons.

"This is rabbit food," I flick the leafy greens he's tossed into the cart. "That's a twisted way to show love, even for you Christians."

Ido finds us in the grain aisle, me lamenting over the bird seed appearance of quinoa. "Here, why don't you start out with this instead," he plucks a box off the shelf.

"What's this?"

"Couscous," Joe mutters, checking out the box. "Good idea," he praises Ido. "You'll be eating quinoa in no time after you figure out how good this is, Thomas,"

"Highly unlikely," I moan.

"I just love a man with an open mind, don't you, Joe?" Ido laughs as he walks with us to the front of the store.

To my horror, Brimstone Bob and Frank Norris are heatedly arguing right in front of the checkout lanes. There isn't anything good about Bob, but if I had to say something minutely positive in his favor it would be that he's never hitched his wagon to Frank.

I grab hastily at Joe to stop him from getting any closer to the nutjobs, but my fingers glide right over the back of his blasted overalls. He walks up to them big as you please. I can't see his face, but I'd bet a pound of couscous he's got the volume on that outrageous grin of his turned up to max.

"Pastor Bob, good to see you again," he says warmly.

Bob and Frank pause their bickering and turn to look at him, four beady eyes widening in shock when they land on his hair and tattoos.

"What are you doing in town again?" Bob demands.

"Oh, I—" Joe starts to explain but Frank interrupts him, voice louder than necessary.

"What do you mean 'again'?" Frank thunders.

"He's been here a lot recently under suspicious circumstances," Bob's face has a nasty twist to it, like his glass of milk has gone sour.

"Suspicious how?" Frank asks.

"I roast and sell coffee beans statewide. At least, I hope to. The owners of the bistro were kind enough to give me a place to start out," Joe sums up.

"Your dealings in town are with the lesbians?" Frank growls, his expression as ugly as Bob's.

"I've had it on good authority you're selling something, but it wasn't coffee beans," Bob disputes. I roll my eyes at Ido, who rolls his eyes back at me. Dang it, Wilma!

Joe plunges his hands into the back pockets of his overalls as if he doesn't have a care in the world, responding calmly, "Yes, it's true, they are lesbians. But it's also true that they do purchase coffee beans, not drugs, from me."

"There's no place in this god-fearing town for people like them,"

Frank looks Joe up and down again, adding, "And certainly not for anyone who would defile God's temple in such a way."

"Joe, this is Frank Norris, another shining example of Cardinal Creek's fine religious leaders," I cut in. "And as religious leaders I'm sure they'll be delighted to know you've decided to follow in the footsteps of the lesbians and make Cardinal Creek your hometown, too," I gleefully drop this little bombshell and smile when their eyes bulge out.

"Impossible," Bob splutters.

"Oh, its possible alright. As a matter of fact, they're living with me. How's that sit with you wonderful men of God?" I give them both a triumphant smile. Joe pats me fondly on the arm in the same way Bea used to when she wanted me to hush.

Ido steps around us and asks them, "Can I help you two find anything else?" He's probably trying to diffuse the situation, but Frank is wound for sound now.

"Thomas Sanders," Frank asked, "what would your late wife say if she knew you were housing someone who looks like this?" Bea was especially good at getting along with everyone, but this hateful attitude is exactly why she never could make friends with the likes of him.

I glance at Joe. He shines his larger-than-life smile at me, and just like that I realize he and Bea are right, of course—I shouldn't let Frank get under my skin. "She'd scold me for letting them take the basement bedroom instead of the one upstairs with the fancy shower," I reply, adopting Joe's calm tones, although I can't stop myself from adding one tiny jab, just to see the look on his face. I know it's petty, but I'm old and it's a little on the exciting side to cause a stir. "Since he is a preacher and all. A *real* man of God."

Bob's already heard this information, but Frank's astonishment is quite satisfying. "Preacher?" he squeaks, surprise draining the strength from his intended growl.

"Okay, thanks buddy," Joe shifts his body forward slightly to put some space between me and the nutjobs, and I can't help but laugh because Bea would have done the same thing. "My wife and I led a small congregation for the last few years, but we aren't looking to start one here or anything," he tells them.

"Why are you always with a group when I see you then?" Bob asks suspiciously.

"I like hanging out with people," he replies with more of his natural ease. "If our talks turn toward spiritual topics that's just an added bonus."

"So, you *are* looking to start a church here then," Frank insists.

"Not exactly," Joe starts, but Bob jumps in front of him.

"If you're planning on any kind of ministry at all, you better come to the quarterly ministerial meeting. All the official pastors around town attend and it would be good for them to meet you," Bob spurts out.

I sense that Bob has an ulterior motive here, but before I can say anything Joe answers back with an overly enthusiastic, "That would be sweet!" I throw Ido another wide-eyed look. Why would Joe want to spend a second of his time with these wackos?

"This Friday, my church, ten a.m.," Bob says.

"Now, wait just a minute! I agreed to be a part of this quarterly meeting because I knew my presence would inspire others to be better shepherds, but I did *not* agree to you inviting this wolf in sheep's clothing to join us," Frank rails at Bob.

"I can invite anyone I want to as long as the meetings are held at my church," Bob rails back, and they plunge back into another one of their volcanic arguments.

With them focused on each other, it's easy for me to take Joe's right arm while Ido takes his left. We urgently steer him toward the door. "Just take my money and get us out of here," I say.

"We'll settle up another time," he suggests. "You two get going while you can."

"Good idea," I agree.

When we're safely in the car I breathe a sigh of relief. "What a bunch of hooey," I say. "You're not going to that stupid nutjob meeting, right?"

"I'm totally going," he laughs. "I'd love to rub elbows with all the town's churchy dudes at one time."

"But Joe, they're all morons!" I exclaim.

"Not Lee, or Mike, or Val," he answers.

"But you four will be the only good guys there!" I argue. "Besides, Bob just wants you to come so he can rip into you in front of his minions."

Joe pauses. Finally, he tilts his head slightly and sighs. "I've been getting glimpses of Bob through Neil's eyes. He's not the bad guy you think he is."

"I've known him for a long time, Joe," I say.

"You've known the grouchy, puffed out version of Bob. He's really more of a..." he hesitates, "he's just a concerned father who thinks I might get his son into trouble."

I throw Joe a sharp look. "For Pete's sake, why doesn't he just get to know you?"

"That's the goal, dude, but…" he exhales, "Like Averitt says, you catch more flies with honey. If I can do it with Wilma, I can do it with Bob."

"That's a disturbing thought," I smirk. "So, let's say you make friends with Old Brimstone. Surely you can't be interested in getting to know Frank?"

"Maybe." He laughs hard, asking, "Does he have any young adult kids I can make friends with?"

"Oh, brother."

Chapter 14

I let the door to the Rapturous Finds Thrift Store swing shut behind me. I see Jewels standing at the register, face aglow. "We got the beast onto the truck. Such an easy thing, too. Only three cracked femurs," I tease her.

A solid oak wardrobe that's been collecting dust for months, forgotten in the shadows of the thrift store, is now encased in blankets and secured by straps on the back of Joe's truck. Jewels spotted the beast the minute she started working for Mike and has since been insisting she needs to buy it.

"I have some Band-Aids," she teases right back.

"There's two empty bedrooms upstairs you're welcome to, you know, if you need more closet space," I offer, wiping sweat off my forehead. I can't see a reason for objecting to her bringing this massive thing home if she wants it, but I'm curious why she think she needs it.

"Oh, actually, I was thinking of putting it in one of the empty bedrooms upstairs if that's okay with you," she asks with a trace of apology in her voice.

"It's not going to bother me, but I still don't understand," I shrug, baffled. "If you don't need it, why even buy it?"

She shrugs back. "Don't know. I have this feeling it will come in handy someday."

The door opens wide to admit a bustling Maggie and Wilma, each carrying a bag of something to donate. They huff their way to us, and Wilma slings their bags up onto the counter, exhaling like she's just finished a full marathon. "Tommy, you could have helped us out."

"I had no idea you needed help," I reply.

"You know, Jewels, I was thinking," Wilma says, leaning in close, "Joe and the boys should buy their disguises here. Save the department some money."

Jewels' expression darkens for a few seconds, and she flicks her eyes toward me. I avert my gaze, aware that she's not thrilled with our little deception on Wilma. She mumbles, "I don't think the cost matters a lot."

"A penny saved is like two in the hand," Wilma argues.

"Pretty sure that's not how the saying goes, Wilma," I chuckle.

"You don't know everything," she sniffs.

The door opens again, this time for a young lady and a small human. The young lady looks like she's had happier days, but the small human runs straight for Jewels, thrilled. "Joey, Joey!"

I look around for Joe but realize she's talking to Jewels. "Hart, my little love," Jewels says excitedly, pulling the small human up into a hug. Then she waves at the young lady, who waves back with a reserved smile. "Sally, hello! It's so wonderful to see you!"

"It's stuffie day!" Hart announces, turning to look at Wilma. "I think your hair looks bootiful, like fireworks!"

Wilma touches her auburn hair with one hand. "Why, thank you, little lady."

"And look, mommy, a doggie!" she exclaims as Maggie presses her nose onto the little girl's cheek. A ball cap boasting a blue dog falls off her head and wavy brown hair tumbles out. "He has a pretty necklace, just like that lady," she observes, noticing Maggie and Wilma's matching bandanas.

Wilma's smiling down at her like she's just found a new pet.

"Sally, these are my dear friends, Wilma and Thomas. Friends, this is Sally and her daughter Hart," Jewels hands out adult introductions before squatting down to Hart's level and adding, "Hart, this is a girl doggie, and her name is Maggie."

"I love Maggie," Hart declares, wrapping her arms around Maggie's neck. The mutt shimmies her tush back and forth, obviously in love with the small human, too.

The young woman shakes our hands, her smile tired. She tucks her bobbed blonde hair behind one ear, lowering her gaze so most of the expression in her hazel eyes is hidden from us. I wonder if it's from trying to keep up with the small human all day. "Nice to meet you both," she says.

The small human marches up to me, leans her head back to look all the way up into my face, and says, "Down here, please."

Surprise overtakes me. I obey before I have a chance to think better of it, bending down on one knee like Jewels did. She scrutinizes my face for a few seconds before turning to her mother. "Mommy, look at this nice gramps."

The young woman gives me an apologetic look. I've felt this same way over Wilma's antics more times than I can count, so I get her discomfort. "I'm so sorry, Mister, um, Thomas," she reaches to pull Hart back.

"Drop the Mister. Just Thomas," I tell her before returning my gaze to the child. "What does *stuffie* mean?" I ask her.

"Mommy says if I poop in the potty for fifty days I getta stuffie on Friday," she answers. "So, I pooped in the potty!" she spreads her little arms wide.

"A stuffed animal," Sally explains to me before saying, "Five days, not fifty, and let's try to just say 'use the potty,' okay? No need to add the part about what you did in the potty," she corrects Hart with a grin.

She doesn't look tired when she talks to her daughter, I notice. She looks happy.

"But you told me everybody poops, Mommy. It's not a secwet," the tiny person turns back to me, asking, "You poop in the potty, Gramps?"

Amazed at the matter-of-fact way this diminutive dynamo discusses such a private matter, I laugh so hard I just about fall over. I have zero experience with children, but if they're all this funny I think I've been missing out.

Her mom does pull her back this time, mortified. I stand up, still laughing, choking out, "No, please, don't scold her. I haven't laughed like this in a long time. Besides, she's right. It's not a secret that we all do *that* in the potty."

Jewels and Wilma are laughing right along with me, and even Maggie barks a couple of times. The little girl scrunches her face up in confusion, not at all clear on what we're laughing about.

"What's so funny?" she demands, looking around at all of us.

"Adults always laugh when people talk about poop," Wilma tells her.

"Why don't we go find a stuffie, sweet pea," her mom tells her.

Maggie barks again, taking the child's shirt in her mouth. "Maggie will take her over to the toys," Wilma offers.

"Oh, I don't—" the young lady stutters.

"Your little gal's safer with Maggie than she would be with any human babysitter. Tell her, hon," Wilma encourages, nodding at Jewels.

Jewels smiles widely at the young woman. "It's only the next aisle over, so we'll be able to hear them if anything happens. But, yes, I've never met such a clever dog in my whole life. Maggie will guard Hart closely."

Hart doesn't wait for her mom to say yes or no, but takes hold of Maggie's bandana with a giggle, saying, "Fanks, Mommy and Joey." The round dog and the small human skip toward the toys, Wilma smiling proudly after them.

"Why does she call you Joey?" I ask Jewels.

"I'm not sure," Jewels chuckles.

Sally laughs too. "She's done that ever since she found out you had a husband, but I have no idea why."

"Well, it makes perfect sense to me," Wilma says, put out with our lack of understanding. "It's a combination of the two names, Joe and Jewels,"

Jewels giggles, asking, "But where does she get the 'ee' sound from?"

Wilma frowns at her. "The 'ee' sound is like killing two birds with two stones."

The door swings open again, admitting a sweaty Joe and Mike. "Oh, good, I was hoping you'd come back inside," Jewels greets them. "Sally, this is my husband Joe."

Joe smiles warmly at Sally without making any effort to give her a hug or even a handshake, which has to be the first time I've ever seen him refrain from the touchy-feely stuff. "I'm glad we finally get to meet. Jewels is crazy about you and Hart."

"Yeah, Jewels is kind of crazy about you, too," Sally smiles back at him, but with noticeable reserve.

"Good to see you, Sally," Mike smiles warmly at her, which she returns with only slight reserve. "I'm going to grab some waters, guys," he says before disappearing into the back offices.

We hear a shriek of delight and the pattering of feet as Maggie and Hart charge back to us. She has three stuffed animals crowded into the small space of her arms, her head bobbing above them like a rising moon. "I hope we see a lot more of this charming creature," Bea whispers in my ear. She's always lost her marbles where kids are concerned.

"Hey there," Sally laughs, catching hold of the speeding child.

Maggie trots up to Joe, who squats down to her level. Hart wiggles free from her mom's grasp and approaches Joe, showing him her treasures. "Hi. This is Beak, and Miss P, and Winnie," she recites, naming the stuffed animals.

"Oh, hi there," Joe pats each one on the head. "And what about you?"

"I'm Hart. Like a heart filled wiv love, but not the same letters," she replies. "Who are you?"

"I'm Joe. I'm married to Jewels," he answers, nodding at his wife.

"A nice man to match to Joey," she declares.

"She's very intuitive," Bea says warmly.

"Alright, well, which stuffie are we taking home today?" Sally asks. What follows is a round of glorious and masterful manipulation on the part of the small human. It's so intense, I am reminded of Wilma.

"Oh, Mommy, we can't leave any of them here! They'll be so sad because they're friends and friends never leave each other," Hart tells her with an unshakeable amount of sincerity.

"But we only agreed on one stuffie, remember?" Sally counters. "One stuffie every Friday."

"Well, these can be for the next free Fridays," Hart reasons.

Mike rejoins us just in time. "Mr. Mike, Winnie *and* Beak *and* Miss P want to go home with me," Hart informs him with what has to be a deliberate batting of her luminous eyes.

"They look like good friends," Mike agrees, smiling.

"Oh, they are!" Hart cheeps, hugging them tight.

Maggie eases up close to Sally and leans onto her legs, tilting her head back so she can stare up into Sally's face with her soulful eyes. Hart rests her back on Maggie, the two of them pouting pitifully.

Wilma groans. She's never told Maggie no, to my knowledge. "Oh, for goodness' sake, Mike, it's buy-one-stuffie-get-two-free today, isn't it?"

"No, that's okay," Sally begins to protest, but that's only because she doesn't know what Wilma's capable of.

"Nonsense. Pooping in the potty is a grand accomplishment," Wilma takes her own bandana off, puts it around the little girl's neck, and claps her hands happily. "Oh, my heavens, will you just look at these two!"

"Now I look like Maggie," Hart trills.

Sally throws her hands up in defeat. Wilma pats her shoulder affectionately, turning her and Jewels toward the register. "Maggie and I will pay for all three, Jewels."

While her mom is busy arguing about who should pay for the toys, Hart turns to me and Joe. "We should get ice cream soon."

Another hearty laugh explodes out of me. I've never met anyone like this small human.

Chapter 15

Wilma has taken a shine to Hart like nothing I've ever seen before. Joe says she's talked less and less about busting the drug ring in town and a lot more about trying to get Sally and Hart into the diner for a visit. This new obsession has also caused a spike in her meddling in her son Scott's current romances. She's doubled her efforts in finding him a future wife, which to her is just a means to an end—namely grandkids.

I can confirm the swapping of obsessions because she drags me into her matchmaking schemes at every meal. To show you how irritated I am at having my peace and quiet yet again ruined, I'll readily admit I jumped at the opportunity to take Maggie to the wretched dog park today because Wilma was too busy to do it herself.

I never imagined I'd choose an outing with the mutt over the chance to eat, but here I am.

Joe met me here with Wigglesworth because he thought it would take the edge off the whole dog park experience for me. I might allow Wiggles in my home and the occasional visit from Maggie, but that only works because neither of them are an example of what you'd call "common dogs." I'm not interested in mingling with the common types, and I've said as much to him several times.

Our two uncommon dogs are frolicking around the open play area like puppies while Joe and I recline on a shaded bench. I casually sip a bottle of water and stretch my legs out, sighing at the creaks from my knees.

"Has it been bad living with my Wiggles?" Joe asks, pulling Averitt's old corn cob pipe out of one of the many pockets in his overalls.

"I wouldn't say bad, no," I answer thoughtfully. "He's a lot cleaner than I thought he would be."

Joe chuckles, tapping his pipe against the bottom of one shoe. "Cool."

"Do you have plans of ever smoking that thing, or is it merely ornamental?" I ask.

"Nah, smoking grosses me out," he says with a goofy grin that makes me laugh. "I just like to fidget with it. Besides, right now I don't need another thing for people to hold against me."

"What do you mean by that?"

He gives me an odd look before answering. "Well, that lunch thing Bob Frazier invited me to come to didn't go super well," he sighs. "But I don't want you to get all worked up over it."

In a halting, careful way he tells me how Bob spoke to the group about being aware of "infiltrators" in town who might have ungodly intentions, warning them to keep a closer eye on their teens and young adults since they are more susceptible to bad influences. As awful as it sounds, it's obvious he's dumbing down what he tells me and is leaving the things out that will make me roar.

"I won't blow a gasket," I swear, holding up a hand. "But I will say that I actually forgot about it or else I would have tried again to talk you out of going," I remark dryly. "The last thing you need is to spend time with Bob and his type."

"Dude, you're not responsible for protecting me from Bob's nervousness," he laughs, tapping my arm with his pipe. "I can take a few verbal punches."

"Still... it's best to avoid religious nutjobs, Joe," I say, frowning at the audacity of Old Brimstone.

"Like I said the other day, Bob's not the nutjob you think he is. I mean, he's not too thrilled with me, but he has his reasons. It's like..." he pauses, then points to a fluffy white dog that's approaching Maggie. "Watch this," Joe tells me.

The white dog looks into Maggie's face for a few seconds, both of them wagging their tails slightly, before it walks behind Maggie and starts to smell her... well, her *back end.*

"That's disgusting," I flinch.

"To you it probably does seem disgusting, like the way you feel about Bob's behavior, but to the dogs it's perfectly normal. That's the way they decide if they can trust each other," Joe explains.

"By butt sniffing?" I ask incredulously.

"Yep, by butt sniffing." The white dog apparently likes what he smells because he and Maggie start playing. "Now that he's checked her out and found nothing alarming, that dog will recognize Maggie as a friend for life just by her smell," he grins at me. "And that's exactly what Bob's doing with me right now."

"Did he sniff your butt, Joe? Because if there was forced butt sniffing at that meeting, I'd have to say the nutjobs have formed themselves a cult," I ask with a straight face.

Joe laughs, and laughs, and laughs.

"Well? Was there?" I demand before breaking into laughter myself.

"Dude," he gasps, wiping a hand across his eyes, "You have to stop!"

"Just trying to get some clarity on how butt sniffing dogs and religious nutjobs go hand in hand," I defend myself, palms out.

He inhales deeply, a last little chuckle slipping out, before answering me. "You know very well I meant that Bob is trying to decide if I'm a friend or an enemy."

"Nothing is beyond belief where Old Brimstone is concerned," I shake my head, "not even butt sniffing."

"Seriously, buddy," he whacks me again with his trophy pipe, sounding like Bea. "Let me try to explain."

"Okay, I'm all ears. Explain away," I say. Sometimes, according to

Bea, it's important to listen to others when they're earnest, and he looks earnest.

"Bob loves his son Neil. He's feeling what a lot of parents feel when their kids start to get older and drift away. Neil's exploring God in ways that challenge his dad's viewpoints, and a lot of that exploring is being done with me. Mostly Bob's being so harsh because he's worried I might lead Neil away from God." Joe laughs again before adding, "It's *Bob* who's wondering if *I'm* the cult, not the other way around."

"That's crazy," I say.

"I don't hold up really well to Bob's idea of what a Christian should look like," he says.

"Not that I believe in the whole myth of a god myself," I explain, "but it seems idiotic to me to decide whether or not a man is a Christian based on the clothes he wears. You dress just like Averitt, for crying out loud, and Bob knows he's a Christian."

"True," Joe replies. "Bob's not so different from Wilma if you think about it. People don't trust what they don't understand. It's just how we are." He shrugs, not concerned over all this mistrust being aimed at him. He reaches down to scratch the white dog that's come closer to us.

"Maybe," I say. Wilma's problem with hippies and drugs isn't totally bonkers, after all. A small amount of concern over that is not only normal but probably also balanced.

"And here's another thing to think about," Joe adds. "If there's more than one dog in a family, one of them is always the alpha. The alpha is supposed to watch over the other dogs, keep them safe, and make sure they don't run astray. An alpha dog will even growl and show its teeth if it feels like there might be trouble for its pack. Wilma didn't trust me at first, so she growled and showed her teeth to make sure her town stayed safe," he says.

I study Maggie and Wiggles, who are completely at ease with the new dog.

If I'm being wholly honest, I know if you peel away all of Wilma's boisterous layers, what you're left with is a woman who protects those she loves. If she had the slightest notion someone might be out to steal Scott away from her and the diner, she'd be all over them faster than government money on a bad idea.

"Bob doesn't trust me either," he continues. "In their own ways, they both acted like an alpha dog would when their pack might be threatened. I won't fault Bob growling and showing his teeth when he's just trying to protect his son."

Weirdly, by using this butt-sniffing Wilma-crazy logic, I think I can see where Bob's coming from.

"I'll be darned," I say. "I think I just had an epiphany."

"You did?" he asks, voice cracking.

"Bob's still a nutjob, but I guess you've made your point," I admit with a wry grin. "I still don't like him or his tactics, but I can see where he's coming from. He's just like Wilma, and I know Wilma's real intentions are never bad."

Joe turns his most ridiculous grin to date on me. "Dude, that's beautiful,"

"It's not beautiful, it's logic. Stop assigning extra emotions to me," I chuckle. "And don't expect me to be Bob's pal or anything. I might see him in a slightly different light, but as far as I'm concerned, Bob and Frank and all their crazy minions can still stay away from me."

"Yeah, you're probably going to get your wish with Frank. I think it's gonna take a lot more work on my part to win him over than it'll take with Bob," he says.

"Uh oh," I say, "not sure I want to know what happened, but you better spill the beans anyway."

With a regretful sigh, he replies, "Let's just say he's thinking I'd be better off moving back to Indy and taking my shameful, wicked sins with me."

"Surely you can't try to explain that level of rudeness with butt-sniffing alpha dog talk," I snort.

"No, not so much," he sighs again.

"Well, chin up. You've got bigger problems to solve, like how to tell Wilma you're not really a cop." I stand up, wincing at the pull in my lower back.

His laugh is light. "Oh, I think she's forgotten all about that now. She and I have made friends and I'm off the hook, too. Double win for me!"

"If you say so," I laugh, too. "Having Wilma as an enemy is hard, but sometimes having her as a friend is even harder."

Chapter 16

Wilma's finally lost it. Since she's focused on Scott giving her a grandkid, I told you we were hoping she was going to drop the whole drug dealing hippie bit.

We let our guard down.

We underestimated her.

We realized our mistake a few minutes ago. Just as Joe and I were finishing up a nice afternoon snack of peach cobbler, a server brought us a note, explaining that Wilma instructed him to give it to us at two o'clock.

We opened the note, which says be at the bistro at two fifteen to see the drug dealing, cinnamon roll stealing, good for nothings finally get what they deserve. I glanced at my watch, saw that it was already a few minutes past two, and panicked. The bistro closes from two to four in the afternoon so Olive and Taffy can have a break, but I didn't know Wilma was aware of this. She must have chosen this time to do whatever it is she's going to do because the bistro would be empty.

Joe and I are now darting across the town square as fast as a man my age can dart, hoping against hope she's not done anything we can't undo without a court of law. Taffy and Olive are lovely women, but even lovely women get tired of nonsense after a while.

"Jewels isn't answering," Joe is out of breath. He's been trying to call Wilma, Jewels, and the bistro while we dart, but I don't know how he's managing the small buttons of a cell phone. Darting is a bumpy, jerky business.

"If we get out of this and everyone is still alive, it might be a bigger miracle than that virgin birth you believe in," I quip.

"Dude," he pants, too out of breath to reprimand me more than that.

We weave between people on the sidewalk as politely as we can, bursting through the door of the bistro like a couple of wild men, Joe leading the invasion. In sitcom fashion, Joe slams into a man dressed like a member of the secret service, and I slam into Joe. The man's reflective aviators hide his expression, but he raises his left wrist to his mouth and says calmly, "Copy that, southern belle. Agent Tackett has arrived. Commence Operation Storm Atlanta."

"Uh, hey there," Joe squeaks, throat dry.

I draw in a few deep breaths to steady myself and glance across the dining room. Olive and Taffy are all alone behind the counter, as shocked as we are.

"FBI! Taffy Compton and Olive Denton, raise your hands above your heads... now!" the man in the aviators yells. I look around frantically for Wilma, but I can't decide if it's to ask her for help or to ring her neck.

"No, sir, you don't understand," Joe starts to explain, but he's silenced as the agent simultaneously presents his open palm to Joe while pressing a finger to his ear. He tells Joe in a conspiratorial fashion that Task Force One is moving into sniper position as Task Force Two heads into the back of the bistro.

Circumventing the secret service guy, I address Olive and Taffy. "Ladies, are you okay?"

"No talking to the suspects, sir," the agent reprimands me.

"Thomas, you and Joe better make a break for it while you still can!" Olive yells.

Taffy dips below the counter and raises up with a shotgun aimed directly at us. "Guys, can you move out of the way, please?" she asks calmly. As long as I live, I will never forget the image she presents with one eye squeezed shut, one eye pressed to the sight of the gun, tongue sticking out between clenched lips.

"No, Taffy, no!" Joe yells, throwing his body between the agent and the gun.

A ruckus emerges from the back of the bistro. Wilma rushes in with a person wearing some kind of riot gear get-up, head to toe black with straps crisscrossing the torso and a shield that obscures their face. The person is taking calculated steps, like you see in the movies, gun balanced on one wrist, waving the barrel back and forth between the two bistro owners.

Maggie runs ahead of Wilma and the riot gear person, barking as she approaches the counter where Olive and Taffy are making a last stand. Wilma yells loudly, "I've always known you girls have been up to something horrible over here!"

Taffy swings her shotgun around, training it on Wilma. Olive grabs a pile of napkins from the counter and throws them at Wilma, yelling, "Your cinnamon rolls taste like dirty diapers!"

"Release that weapon!" the agent calls, taking a step or two toward the counter.

"Wilma, what in the name of all that's crazy is going on here?" I thunder, taking steps to stay equal with the agent.

"Justice, Tommy! Justice!" she shrieks, ushering her gun wielding partner toward the counter. "Get them both! Use excessive force if you have to!"

"Stop! It was all a joke, Wilma, I swear! I'm not a cop!" Joe rushes forward, hands raised, putting himself between Taffy's gun and Wilma. "It was just a joke, and nobody is selling drugs!"

Wilma raises both hands over her head, yelling, "Hold it!" We all freeze. "Repeat that!" she demands from Joe, hands going to her hips.

"It was a joke," he says hesitantly, looking embarrassed. "The guys said you like police shows, so I told you I was a cop to get you to like me. I didn't mean for anything bad to happen... I just wanted us to be friends."

"So, you're *not* a cop," she states, brows raised.

"No, I'm not."

"And there's no undercover operation."

He shakes his head no.

"You *and* Tommy lied to me," she says, frowning at me.

I smile weakly. "Lied is a strong word, don't you think?"

The person in riot gear drops their arms to their side, relaxing. Taffy does too, saying to Olive, "So, we aren't nefarious drug dealers?"

"We could be accused of dealing caffeine, I suppose," Olive says conversationally.

"I don't deal drugs, but I *do* have a decent used car I'd like to get off my hands if anyone's interested," the secret agent pulls off his aviators to reveal laughing brown eyes.

When the person in riot gear holsters their weapon and removes their helmet, Joe and I both utter in surprise, "Jewels?"

"Maybe we should take a look at this guy's car, babe, since my transmission is acting up," she makes this suggestion with an enormous grin.

Joe's mouth hangs wide open. I look at Wilma, then Jewels, astounded.

Olive and Taffy hurry to hug Wilma and Jewels, all of them giggling to one another. Maggie runs around in circles, barking at us all.

Wilma puts an arm around each of the Bistro owners with a triumphant smile. "Looks like the only thing that needed busted was a terrible prank."

"What is..." Joe turns to look at me, surprise stealing his voice. "What?"

I throw my hands up, just as surprised. "I believe we've been made fools of."

"I got suspicious of your policing skills a while back. I mean, seriously, an undercover cop moving into a civilian's house. Get real. And while I'm sure Kenny is a likeable man in spite of his bad taste in body art, he's no cop." Wilma says haughtily.

"She cornered me one day while you guys weren't around," Jewels admits, "and I spilled the beans. You know I haven't ever agreed with you guys pranking her anyway."

"Jewels and I had a nice talk," Wilma explains. "First she told me how hard you've been trying to impress me. Then she spent forever telling me how much she likes Olive and Taffy. I figured if Jewels thinks they're okay, they might be worth looking into, so we marched ourselves over here to get some things squared away."

Taffy picks up the story, smiling warmly at Wilma. "We were just as surprised as you'd think we would be when they walked in the door, but of course we were excited to end this feud. We sat down over a pot of Joe's coffee and tried to figure out what we could do to be friends."

"It all came down to a simple compromise over cinnamon rolls. We agreed to only serve cinnamon rolls for our Sunday brunch buffet," Olive smiles warmly at Wilma too.

"And I agreed to teach them how to make my biscuits and gravy that they can serve any day of the week they want to," Wilma finishes.

"See, babe?" Jewels loops her arms around her husband's neck, laughing as she squeezes him tight. "All it took was a little conversation."

"I should have listened to you all along," he agrees with a hangdog expression.

I remember the man in the aviators and turn to look at him, trying to place his face.

"Oh, I'm just a lowly service rep. I keep the diner's ovens in tip top shape," he laughs easily at my scrutiny. "She offered me pie if I joined in on this little, uh, charade," he swirls a finger around in a circle.

"Wilma Harper," I laugh, "You really got us good today."

"We came up with the idea together," she indicates Jewels, Taffy, and Olive with a broad gesture. "It's incredible what five women can pull off when they set their minds to it."

"Four women," I correct her.

She smirks in disgust, bending down to scratch Maggie's head. "I know you're not implying that Maggie is a man, are you, Tommy?"

Wilma's service rep takes his leave, telling her he'll drop by one day next week for his pie payment.

The rest of us gather around a table. Olive and Taffy bring out platters of dessert crepes and coffee. Joe helps Jewels out of the riot gear. Wilma pushes two chairs together so Maggie can sit with us. There's genuine, unforced friendliness between all the women. Wilma teases Joe, Olive teases Wilma, and Taffy teases me. I would never have guessed a day like this could exist.

"Ladies, I am truly sorry I created this mess, but I'm so stoked at the outcome," Joe says apologetically.

"We know how you can make it up to us," Wilma pipes up with a sly look at her three co-conspirators.

Joe grins, eager to redeem himself. "Lay it on me!"

"Be our assistant manager so we can take a few hours off now and then," Olive pleads, reaching across to grab his hand.

Wilma nods her approval. "We think it's a great idea."

"You've been talking about getting a job for a few weeks now," Jewels pats him. "Besides, I told them you would love to."

Joe smiles. "Well, looks like I got myself a job, Thomas."

Chapter 17

The calendar might say it's early June, but today's withering temps feel way more like early August. I watch Joe as he arranges a mismatched grouping of blankets, step stools, and lawn chairs into a circle, making sure to keep it all inside the shade of the trees.

"Tell me again about this drum circle," I say, handing him another blanket.

"Just hanging out, mostly, with a little music on the side," he tosses the last blanket down, admiring his work. He tucks his arms inside the front of his overalls and flaps the material in and out, laughing at my expression. "This gets the air flow going." To combat the unusual heat wave over the last few days, he's cut the pant legs off this pair for what he calls "superior ventilation purposes." The frayed edges fall mid shin, one slightly longer than the other, giving everyone a good look at his bare feet. I've never seen another human love to be barefooted as much as Joe.

"And you just... *drum*?" I ask, frowning. "No guitars or anything?"

He shakes his head, motioning for me to follow him back into the house. "It's simple drumming. Sweet. Soothing. Not like a marching band at a football game. You should come hang."

"No thanks." I make a face. "I said you could invite strangers into my home, but that doesn't mean I want anything to do with them."

"You're not the miserable old dude you hope people think you are, bud," he laughs.

"Just make sure nobody goes into my end of the house," I growl, making him laugh harder. "Past the kitchen is the no stranger zone."

We both sigh at the air-conditioned coolness of the house. "Oh, good, Kenny's here with the grub," Joe exclaims, hurrying to open the kitchen door. The shirtless man comes in with bags from the diner, the mutt on his heels.

"Hey, what's all this?" I demand, glaring at Maggie. She wiggles up to me and nudges my hand with her nose.

"Wilma said to bring her, so bring her I did," Kenny replies, depositing his food load onto the island with a thud.

Joe kneels down to say hi to Maggie and she douses his face with her slobbery tongue. Instinctively, I run my fingers over the travel sized hand sanitizer in my pocket. Wiggles, who has been even lazier than normal during this heat wave, appears at her side with newfound energy. The two of them romp away to the living room, the one place upstairs where a collection of canine paraphernalia has collected over the last few weeks.

"What's the news?" Kenny leans against the island, a freshly opened can of beer in one hand, scrutinizing me with an inquisitive eye.

"My house is being invaded by people who only play drums, so I'm escaping to my private sanctuary," I reply, his laughter following me as I retreat to my bedroom.

"Joe's right, you know," Bea says. I ease down into my recliner, prop my feet up, and search through the book for my place I left off.

"How's that?" I ask her, only half listening.

"You want everyone to think you're an old grump, but you're not," she says.

"My dear, I am exactly who I am and nothing more," I find the candy bar wrapper I used as a bookmark, settle back into the cushions, and lose myself in the story.

I can hear people arriving, their voices and laughter drifting down to my end of the house. I finish a chapter and a half before the sounds have all stopped and I know the house is once again empty. I mark my place and take a stroll back to the kitchen to see what types of things Kenny brought to eat.

I pile a plate high with cheesy sliders, coleslaw, and macadamia nut cookies. I'm trying to decide between milk or sweet tea when I notice a flurry of movement in my side yard. I open the screen door a foot and lean out, doing a double take when I realize Old Brimstone is standing on tiptoe, craning his neck to look over the privacy fence.

At first I'm understandably mad. What is this nutjob doing?

Bea says, "Butt sniffing, dear." Something causes me to pause, my brain playing a slideshow of Olive, Taffy, and Wilma's friendly faces from the last few days. If the diner and the Bistro can coexist, then I suppose there's a slim chance Bob and Joe could end up friends, too.

Suddenly, Bob in my side yard feels a lot more like a challenge than an intrusion.

Leaving my plate on the island, I grab two cookies off the tray and go out the door, practicing a friendly expression as I walk. I'm not used to looking at Bob without a scowl, so I hope you can see what an effort this is on my part. He's so intently focused on the drum circle that my voice startles him into smashing his forehead on the fence.

"Cookie?" I keep my voice light, holding out the cookies. He rubs the forming red mark on his forehead and surveys my outstretched hand suspiciously. "Wilma made them. They aren't poisoned, Bob."

He takes them from me awkwardly, mumbling something I don't quite catch.

"You can get to the backyard through the kitchen door," I offer.

"I don't, uh," he splutters, cheeks now almost as red as his forehead. At least he has the decency to look embarrassed.

"Listen, I'm not really sure what you're trying to do, but you can't stay out here like a peeping Tom. Either come in," I say, sweeping a hand toward the door, "or go home."

"That was too abrupt," Bea inserts quickly. "Remember, he's trying to decide if this is okay for Neil."

I can see some indignation mixed in with his embarrassment, so she's probably right. "I meant you're welcome to come inside so you can hear the drums better."

"I have no interest in joining their weird behavior," he snaps.

"They're just having fun," I shrug. "What's the big deal?"

"The big deal, Thomas, is that a strange man is back there teaching my son all sorts of oddball things, and I don't like it!" He raises his voice in frustration.

I sigh deeply. "You have something against drums?" I keep my tone light, but between you and me his butt sniffing is starting to irk me. I don't know how Bea and Joe stay calm when people act so stupid.

"You're supposed to be an educated man. How can you stand to have him live in your house, work in your town, and corrupt youthful minds when he looks like he does?" he pressures me defiantly before shoving a cookie ferociously into his mouth.

In spite of Bea's cautious expression, I laugh right in his face. I can't help myself. A grown man taking out his anger on a helpless cookie is funny, and I dare anyone to say it's not. He's not too pleased with me.

"I'm sorry for laughing," I wave my hands at his annoyance. "I mean, good grief, Bob, the guy might not dress like you, but that doesn't mean he's part of some brainwashing cult that's after the youth of Cardinal Creek!"

"How do you know?" he rails, small crumbs of cookie spraying out of his mouth. "How does anybody know what he's up to? He could be polluting their minds with all kinds of twisted ideas. Next thing we know, they'll all be covering their bodies in tattoos and worshipping the devil."

This time I manage to restrain my laugh to a small snort. "Oh, yes, I can see now that the man who loves every human he ever meets, led an inner-city church, and befriended me—a perpetual grump—is a devil worshipper."

"Those are EXACTLY the type of people you have to watch out for. The ones who sound good on paper are the ones who do the sneakiest kinds of damage," he says.

I look down at the flower bed, wondering what to say now. Joe's right about Bob being a concerned parent; that's easy to see.

"Tell you what, Bob. Anytime you want to stop guessing what's going on around here and actually get some facts, you say the word and I'll set up a nice peaceful meeting between you and Joe. If you'd get to know him, you'd see he's a good kid with good intentions."

Bob looks up to the sky, seeking answers from his invisible god, but apparently even the almighty dictator can't get through his impenetrable shield of judgmental scorn because he ends up shaking his head at me. "No, I don't think I want to sit down with the likes of him," he turns on his heel and leaves without another word.

Oh well. I tried. After this exchange, I'm pretty sure Joe and Bea are wasting their time on Bob. He's always been set in his ways, and whether or not he's a worried dad shouldn't get him off the hook. At least, I don't think so. He'd like Joe as much as we all do if he'd come down off his blasted soap box and get to know him.

Back to things that matter more than Bob's unwavering stubbornness, like my food.

"I can't believe he said those things about Joe," Bea sniffs.

I look over at her, intrigued. Could it be that I've finally opened her eyes to the real world? "Yeah, what a jerk,"

"He's so far off the mark, isn't he?" she goes on.

"So far," I agree.

"Judging someone when you only see them in passing is dangerous. I mean, who does he think he is, anyway?" she huffs and puffs, really getting into it now. "He's basing all his notions about Joe on what others tell him, or the few times he's seen Joe out in public, but not on any real conversations he's ever had with Joe."

I'm nodding along as we go back inside, half my mind on my plate of cookies and sliders and half my mind grateful she's finally seeing Bob for the nutjob he is. "He's got some nerve."

"You have every right to be defensive of Joe," Bea says. "Well, you're actually more protective than you are defensive," she adds thoughtfully.

"Darn right I do. I know Joe better than anyone in town," I take a bite of a slider. "Joe's a good man and I'll argue that with any man or woman."

"Thank goodness he has someone like you who isn't afraid to look out for him," she says warmly.

"Yep," I finish the slider and bite into a cookie.

She inhales deeply.

Sighs.

Smiles warmly.

"What?" I ask, suddenly feeling guarded.

"Oh, just mulling over how you and Bob are fussing over young men in the same fatherly way," she points out sweetly, eyes glinting with amusement. "I never realized just how much you two have in common, that's all."

Chapter 18

"This is getting to be silly," I complain to Maggie. She trots alongside me with her tongue lolling and tail nub wagging, not bothered whatsoever by my plight.

This will blow your mind—Olive and Taffy have rapidly become two of Wilma's most dedicated culinary students. Wilma sends them various bags and boxes of super-secret ingredients with handwritten instructions. They do their best to cook to her specifications and send the results back to her for critiquing. Somehow I've been deemed the errand boy in this arrangement and find myself ferrying deliveries between the two restaurants almost every day.

Yet again my routine is being routinely interrupted.

As we approach the bistro, I hear calls of "Can you spare a moment to talk about our savior" violating this gorgeous June afternoon. Frank Norris and some of his creeps have placed a booth strategically close to the Bistro. Based on their signs, today's target for persecution seems to be homosexuality. I refuse to repeat for you what the signs say, but you can take my word it's horrible.

With grueling tenacity, they're trying to summon a young woman with a child to their table. It isn't until she turns away while emphatically shaking her head that I hear a squeal from the small human. It's Sally and Hart.

"Gramps! I'm over here with my mommy!" yells the small human. I raise my free hand in greeting, but Maggie charges over to them with gusto. She covers Hart in slobbery licks while the child giggles.

"Good afternoon, Mr. Sand… uh, Thomas," Sally's slight smile at my warning finger does nothing to hide the ugly bruising around her neck and across one cheek, and I feel a twinge of something tight and hard in my stomach.

"It would be 'good' if certain people would stop shouting at us about stupid stuff," I remark, deciding to poke fun at Frank Norris rather than mention the emotional state she's in.

"Yeah, I've never really known anybody who likes that guy," she says in a low tone.

Hart pipes up, tugging at my arm. "Gramps, don't you think we should have some ice cream now? 'Member we made plans?"

"Did we?" I ask.

"Miss P just 'membered," she says intensely, stretching Miss P toward me. I'm pretty sure Miss P is one of the stuffies she got the day I met her.

"Hart, Thomas has things to do," her mom says gently.

"Mommy," she shakes her head as if her mother has just done the silliest of things imaginable. "His name is Gramps." Sally meets my eyes apologetically over her daughter's head.

Since my afternoon has already been turned upside down, I can't see what harm there would be in delaying my nap a little longer. I wink at her and say to Hart, "As a matter of fact, the mutt and I are on our way to have ice cream at the bistro right now. I guess we can get a table big enough for a Mommy, a Hart, a Gramps, a Miss P, and a stinky fat dog."

Hart cheers, Maggie wiggles her rump, and Sally laughs.

The bistro, which now stays open all day thanks to Joe's employment, is hopping. I'm glad to see Frank Norris's outlandish booth hasn't had a negative effect on their business. Sally and I situate ourselves around a table that seats six, Hart between us, as we discuss what flavors of ice cream are yummy and disgusting. Hart takes a firm stance that banilla is the best flavor and makes horrible faces at me when I extol the virtues of chocolate.

Olive comes over and introductions are made. Hart informs her that chocolate is "uh-sgusting" and that she "would never, ever eat that mess."

"Maybe you would like to try vanilla with sprinkles?" she asks Hart, and it makes me happy to see her indulge the child.

Hart dips her head as if she's listening to Miss P before grinning slyly at Olive. "I'll just have banilla, but Miss P would like strawberry with sprinkles." And just like that, Olive is as moon-eyed as Wilma for the small human.

Her mom starts to ask Hart to choose one flavor, but I speak up. "Four desserts is a small price to charge for making this delivery," I wink again at Sally, adding, "I'll have that chocolate ganache thing you made me the other day if you have any left. Sally, you should try some, too,"

"The ganache thing, as he calls it, is layers of devil's food cake and chocolate mousse with a ganache icing," Olive tells Sally, who says that sounds lovely.

"And, of course, I'm here to pick up something for Wilma," I say with a snort.

"You're getting free ice cream out of it, so drop the victim act in front of company," she orders me comically. "C'mon, Mags, Joe's got some treats in the back for you." Maggie trots off with her to the kitchen.

Hart fishes a notebook and crayons out of her mom's bag. "Gramps, I'll draw you a fuzzy spider," she informs me, tongue sticking out slightly between her lips in concentration.

"She's obsessed with bugs," Sally tells me. "Loves any and all of them."

"Cause they're my friends," Hart comments without looking up.

"Quite brave," I say.

Sally looks around admiringly. "It's nice in here. Jewels talks about it a lot, but this is our first time inside."

"Up until a few days ago, I used to have to sneak if I wanted to eat here, because if Wilma found out I was frequenting the bistro she'd have strung me up," I confide. At Sally's quizzical expression, I feel like I have to explain the history of Wilma and the bistro ladies, which takes a few minutes. She's got a lot of questions, naturally, so by the time Taffy brings our dishes of ice cream we've been lost down a bunny trail of Wilma stories.

I introduce Taffy, and Hart immediately draws a connection between the name of the human and her favorite candy.

"Fanks, Miss Laffy Taffy," Hart grins, positioning her bowls of ice cream in front of both her and Miss P. "I'm glad you and Eema made friends. Being friends with people is very 'portant, even if they argue sometimes." I am amazed. I didn't think the kid was even listening to us, let alone would understand the situation.

"Eema?" Taffy asks curiously.

"It's her nickname for Wilma," Sally supplies.

Taffy nods, then says, "I like that picture."

"Gramps needs it for his 'fridgedator," Hart's matter-of-fact attitude makes me smile.

"Gramps is her nickname for me," I tell Taffy, who raises a brow in surprise.

"Eema and Gramps, huh?" Taffy chuckles. "I bet Wilma's wild over that!"

"She's wild alright," Sally laughs in agreement.

Taffy laughs, nodding. "She is that, indeed. I've got to get busy, but let me know if you need anything" and disappears behind the counter.

"Wilma can be a lot, but ninety-nine percent of her wild ways are backed by good intentions," I say.

"Unless you happen to be her only offspring!" Sally says with a moan. "She's urgently fixated on finding him a wife."

"Yeah, she's really only after grandkids," I agree. "It's been worse since she met Hart."

"Hart is crazy about Maggie, so we end up at the diner at least once a day. I know Wilma loves to have us there, but she also pumps me for information," she giggles, and for a moment I see the girl she must have been a few years ago. "She's convinced I can give her a hand finding Scott a wife!" She drops her spoon into her dish and leans back, laughing, relaxing. "I'm all like, 'Uh, Wilma, don't you think Scott might want to marry someone *he* picks out?' But she says it's taking him too long."

"Yeah, that sounds about like Wilma," I shake my head.

"I love her though," she laughs. "She's hard not to love."

"Hey, hey, I heard there might be a little bunny out here who likes gummy bears," Joe sails around the counter with a small dish.

"Joey!" Hart yells, clapping her hands. "Me and Miss P *both* love gummy bears," she says, dropping her spoon into Miss P's now empty ice cream dish.

"I guess you guys can share then," he gives her the candy and moves to my seat, bowing at my companion. "Sally, good to see you again," he then thrusts his closed fist toward me with a greeting of "Dude."

"That is undignified," I push his hand away from me.

"A fist bump isn't undignified," he argues.

The door opens and Rusty and Palmer come in. Joe waves them over, slapping them both on the back. For what feels like the hundredth time in one day, I introduce Sally and Hart.

"You're the movie man," Hart points to Palmer. "I love your movie store so much!"

"Oh, you've been to my, uh, store before?" Palmer, the only one of us with any actual small human experience, immediately engages with her.

"Oh, sure, 'bout a million times," she flaps a hand at him.

Rusty sits between me and Sally, drilling me with a curious glance that I ignore. I'm sure he's dying to find out how I've ended up at this table today, but his curiosity will just have to wait.

"We have been to a few Tuesday Toon Days," Sally tags on, smiling a hello to them both.

"What's that?" I ask.

"Thomas only knows what things are if they're slathered in gravy or sugar," Rusty says to Sally.

"I happen to find a great deal of wisdom in a good Woody Woodpecker cartoon," I raise my chin, putting on airs. "Life lessons, if you will."

"Who's Woody Woodpecker?" Joe asks.

"He's a cartoon character from the fifties. Thomas also isn't what you'd call 'up to date' on pop culture," Palmer's grins. By the way Sally's laughing, I'd say she enjoys a little banter as much as we all do.

"Guys!" Hart yells, holding both her hands up in the air like a tiny referee. The entire group turns their attention to her. "His name is *Gramps,*" she says with authority. She crams another piece of candy into her mouth, eyeballing me with the perfect mixture of confidence and charisma. "Tell 'em, Gramps!"

"Oh, Thomas, isn't she a perfect little sweetie?" Bea's voice tinkles like bells.

I hold my hand out to the small human, and she puts a slightly sticky gummy bear into it. "You heard the lady," I plop the candy into my mouth. "Gramps is my name, candy is my game."

Hart giggles, repeating my words with a gleam in her eye, "Candy is my game, too!"

Chapter 19

I'm in a funk.

Bea and I are finally alone in our house for the first time in a minimum of a thousand days. That's how it feels, anyway. We're walking through newly decorated rooms to look at all the changes that've been made in the last few weeks.

"Feels good, doesn't it?" I'm talking about the peace, quiet, and solitude of an empty house, but she's got other ideas.

"A happy home!" Bea's excitement raises her voice half an octave higher than it needs to be.

Way back in the days when we were buying this house, Bea, and Wilma, and sometimes Taffy and Olive too when Wilma wasn't looking, spent hours and hours poring over websites to find just the right decorations our new small-town country house needed. At least, they did until Bea didn't have the energy for it anymore. Wilma took it upon herself to tell Jewels that Bea had passed away before she could finish covering every square inch of the house in yellow.

Jewels got sappy over the idea of finishing what Bea had started, and then Wilma suggested they take the whole teary-eyed discussion over to the ladies at the bistro. That's when the serious planning got started. Had these four women applied as much determination and elbow grease toward a matter that genuinely needed attention, such as world hunger or homelessness, they would be Nobel Peace Prize recipients.

Instead, they recruited three women from an interior design company who shared their burning desire to spend all my hard-earned riches. Seven women descended on my peace and quiet like a murder of crows on a field of sweet corn. I did make a few protests, but Wilma threw the phrase "in Bea's honor" at me like a hand grenade, and I caved.

The empty upstairs bedroom is in varying stages of having carpets cleaned, walls painted, and furniture added. Gauzy, floral curtains now adorn the windows, and a comfy new bed has been carefully placed near Jewels' heavy wardrobe.

Guess how many pillows can fit on a twin bed?

Five. The answer is five.

The empty family room got its share of their attention as well. A repurposed luggage chest is now serving time as a coffee table for the brand-new couch and overstuffed recliner. There are fancy do-dads on shelves and framed prints of trees, rivers, and birds on the walls.

There is yellow everywhere. They did up every inch of the guest bathroom in it, splashing some sage green here and there as an accent color. They put up a flowery shower curtain, hung more pictures of birds, and added jars and containers and candles on every flat surface they could find. They even put a shelf on the wall especially to hold glass do-dads.

I'm being told daily how much I love all these changes.

"Yes, five varieties of yellow feels like happiness," I sulk, inspecting one of the fancy knick-knacks. "Do you know how much they made me pay for this glass bird?"

"Don't pretend you're upset when you know very well you've loved indulging Jewels," Bea chides. "And when has money ever mattered to you, anyway?"

I run a finger down one wall, unable to find fault with the smooth paint and flawless trim job. "Mrs. Sanders, did it ever occur to you that it's the other way around?" I scoff. "Maybe I *wanted* to see this wall painted Buttercup Bliss and have simply manipulated the situation to suit my needs."

"Oh, so you want me to believe you Tom Sawyer-ed them into doing all this work?" she howls with laughter.

"Well, yes," I retort. "There has been painting, hasn't there, and not a single brushstroke came from my hand."

"Oh, darling Thomas, how you make me laugh," she guffaws.

"There's nothing funny about what's going on here," I protest.

"I'm just so happy to have our house full of life," she replies with a smile.

"More like strife," I retort. "But I'm happy if you're happy, I suppose," I sigh resignedly.

She spins around, clutching her hands to her chest. She's happy, alright.

Truthfully, I'm not upset about the remodeling. I, too, was disappointed that Bea didn't get a chance to finish her decorating plans.

It's just been a lot to handle, having seven women milling about from sunup to sundown, rooting me out of every room I try to sit in. It's made me antsy and uncomfortable.

Bea says this remodeling is an act of love on their part, and I can understand that.

It's not their love I'm bothered by.

It's my memories.

The smell of paint is stirring up a lot of them, and where there are memories there are feelings. You've heard that whole thing about how certain smells can take you back in time to a specific place? The house still smelled like fresh paint the day Bea died, so you can see why that's not a scent I relish.

"But Thomas, you are happy, aren't you?" she says seriously, looking into my face.

I sigh, wondering how to explain *what* I am. "On one hand I am, I think," I reply.

"Tell me about the other hand then," she says, giving me her full concentration.

I sigh again. "I've just been a little off lately," I flop down in the overstuffed recliner.

"How so?" she asks.

"I think I just miss my quiet time a little bit," I tell her.

"Do you hate having them live here?" she asks.

"Not really," I shake my head, then add, "No, I don't. I mean, they don't bother me. I can't hear them when they're downstairs, and they're gone so much it isn't like they're under my feet. Jewels has some strange ideas about what constitutes a good meal, but most of the time I can get around that by eating at the diner," I pause, not sure how to go on.

"You don't mind having roommates?" she asks.

"No, I don't," I answer firmly.

"And you're fond of them both. You've become good friends," she coaxes.

"Yes, they're my friends," I agree.

"So, you say you're off because you miss your quiet time, but you also say they aren't even home very often and not a nuisance when they are," she trains one of her looks on me, thoughtfully. "What's really wrong, sweetie?"

I look through the flowery drapes into the bright sunlit day outside, scrunching my face into a frown. "Bea, I just... you're the social one, honey, not me," I shake my head. "The truth is I'm uncomfortable with all of," I sweep a hand around the room, "*this*."

"The yellow?" she guesses.

"No."

"Nice furniture?" she guesses again.

"No," I say again, sadly.

"What are you uncomfortable with then?" she asks gently, but she already knows the answer. She knows everything about me.

"I'm uncomfortable with *them*," I finally admit. "All of them. I've got artwork hanging on the fridge from a kid that calls me Gramps, for Pete's sake. It's terrifying,"

"Hmm," she eases herself down onto the arm of the chair.

The desire to touch her is so intense I feel like I might choke on it.

I'd give every human in my life up for good if I could just have another day with my wife.

"Bea," I say weakly, "sometimes it hurts too much. You don't know what it's like for me to be here without you, because you've never had to live without me. I'm in over my head with these people, and I don't have you here to buffer all these feelings."

"You're terrified of how much you love them, and that's very normal for you. Can I make a few observations?" she pauses for a second, then goes on without giving me a chance to say no. "The ability to love and be happy about it isn't gone just because I am."

"It is though," I protest.

She begins to count on her fingers. "Honey, you have exactly the kind of love you need. It comes from Rusty, Palmer, Ido, and even the Harpers. It's there between you and Val, Mike, and Lee. You have it with Olive and Taffy."

"But I don't have *you*!" I say bluntly. "You were... *are* all I need."

"Trust me, you've got exactly what you need now, and it isn't me. I'm just what feels safe and familiar." She smiles at me gently before going on, "Look at it like this—you can't conduct an orchestra that's missing key players, right? It's the same with your heart. You can't get everything you need from just one or two people. Olive and Taffy might be your woodwind section, and let's say Palmer, Rusty, and Ido are your strings. But what if that's all you had?"

"Vivaldi wouldn't be Vivaldi," I say, but begrudgingly.

"Exactly. So, you need everyone, even Wilma. And especially Joe and Jewels," she says.

I smile feebly. "Wilma's definitely percussion."

"Oh, yes, completely," she giggles.

We sit in quiet contemplation for a few minutes.

It will hurt if I love these people and then they leave me for reasons I can't control, like Bea did. There's only enough room in my life for one Code and one ghost. The more people I let in, the more risk I take that I'll have to balance emotions that I'm just not equipped to deal with.

"What if the goal isn't to have an orchestra, though? Maybe I just want a small band, like only two people," I try again.

"You would never be content with a tiny band, babe. You need the whole group of them." She leans toward me a bit, whispering, "It can be scary, but it can also be wonderful."

I like to hear Rusty and Palmer laugh.

Wilma's annoying, but she also keeps me on my toes.

I think about how a small human called me Gramps and drew me a picture. I think about her mom's clever sense of humor.

Poker nights would be boring without the three non-nutjob pastors.

I remember the way life felt when the house was empty and colorless, and when no one was here to kiss my cheek and call me dude.

As hard as it is for me to admit, I know I like life like it is now a whole lot better.

"Okay, you win. I'll lighten up," I exhale loudly. "At least, I'll give it a try, although it's probably going to be the death of me."

I don't think I've ever seen her smile this big before. "I'm right here with you, dear. You're going to be just fine."

I wish I had her confidence.

Chapter 20

I reserve a special place in my heart for battered, buttery, deep-fried festival foods. Lucky for me, Cardinal Creek needs very little reason to hold a festival, giving me the chance to gorge myself five or six times a year. I weave my way through craft, clothing, and jewelry booths with minimal interest, even though Bea would have made those her first priority. I stop for a thorough inspection of the menu at every place that sells anything edible, and I usually manage to find at least one thing I can't live without.

This weekend the downtown square has been draped in red, white, and blue for the Fourth of July Extravaganza. I like to stop by on Friday night to have a few nibbles before returning on Saturday morning for a full-blown, day-long feast. Last night I dove into a lemon shake-up, an elephant ear, and two deep fried candy bars. Today I'm starting at the diner to get one of the specialty burgers Scott saves for days just like this.

Wilma never passes up an opportunity to capitalize on crowds. Scott says they make a killing during festivals, so he plays along. Besides, it would be easier to clothe every squirrel in Indiana than it would be to corral his mom. You've seen that for yourself. A few picnic tables, an outdoor grill, and Wilma's makeshift food prep table make up the patio area behind the diner where I find all the Harpers today.

"Hello, Harper family," I say.

Scott waves his spatula at me, and I wave back. A tin-canned sounding version of Wilma's voice says, "Welcome to the diner," and Maggie wiggles her rump at me.

Puzzled, I look at Dan, who shrugs, responding, "It was only a matter of time until she talked."

"Until *who* talked?" I ask.

"Maggie, of course," Wilma trumpets proudly.

"I'd like a treat, please," the tin canned voice says again, and I see now that there's a collection of circular buzzers, like the ones in game shows, lined up on a plastic tray. Maggie paws a buzzer and Wilma's voice crackles out again, happily, "I'd like a treat, please."

Wilma extracts a treat from her apron pocket and gives it to Maggie, who then pushes another button. "Thank you," says the tin canned voice.

"I..." I gawk in amazement.

"Cat got your tongue tied up, Tommy?" Wilma laughs at my astonishment. I'm so impressed, I can't even correct her misuse of the language.

"I guess you could say the dog does," I answer, which makes her giggle.

"Get yourself a burger, Thomas," Dan says, leaning back against the table.

"You read my mind, Dan," I turn toward the prep area but Wilma waves me off.

"Have a seat. I'll fix you up," Wilma says, and she does. The burger is loaded with mushrooms, a fried egg, and Scott's secret sauce. It's positively delicious.

Joe and Jewels pop around the corner, arms linked and smiles blazing, both on the way to their respective employers' booths for a shift. They're dropping Wigglesworth off to spend the day with Maggie, who promptly wows them with a tin-canned "Welcome to the diner."

"Miss Maggie, you are a wonder," Jewels says, scratching Maggie behind the ears. Wilma excitedly gushes out all the details of how Jewels can get her own set of buzzers to train Wiggles, but I don't think he likes the idea. He sighs exhaustedly and flops down on the ground, totally uninterested.

They take their conversation to the prep area, so I turn to Joe. "I was going to drop by your setup later. I haven't heard what the ladies have cooked up, but I figure it'll be good."

"Dude, we have some lemon cheesecake squares that'll knock your socks off," Joe replies.

Visions of sweet desserts are chased away as an excruciating voice like fingernails on a chalkboard reaches my ears. I cover my heart protectively with one hand, scowling. "Double darn."

"Is that the famous Thomas Sanders I see?" asks the terrible tragedy waiting to happen.

"Just ignore it and it might go away," I urge Joe.

Charlotte Davens is evidently such a nitwit she can't even be ignored like a regular human. "Thomas?" she asks again, inching closer to me.

Joe looks perplexed by my curious behavior and sends her an inviting grin.

I'll have to face her now, I suppose. "Carlotta," I turn toward her, once again pretending to get her name wrong.

A shrill sound blasts from her ruby red lips. "Oh, Thomas, you silly man, you know my name is Charlotte." She stops in front of me, looking over Joe with more than a little curiosity, when he speaks up first.

"Don't think we've met! I'm Joe Tackett," he extends a hand for her to shake, which she does cautiously.

"Charlotte Davens," she tells him coolly, eyes scanning the dreadlocks, tattoos, and overalls in one critical, evaluating glance.

"Care for a specialty burger today, Charlotte?" Dan asks with a slow drawl. This is only funny to me and him since Joe couldn't possibly know that Charlotte has never eaten at the diner.

"Uh, no thank you," she says with barely concealed disgust.

"You know where to find us if you change your mind," he tells her, standing up. "Thomas, see you later for the fireworks?"

"That's the plan," I reply.

"Good deal," he winks at me, says goodbye to Joe, and escapes into the diner's back door.

Charlotte douses me with her shark-toothed smile. "But, Thomas, I would just love to talk to you about the upcoming show choir performances for the county fair."

"I'm retired," I speak to an area below her hairline but above her left eye.

"Well, yes, I know, but the kids are really stellar this year! With a coach like you on board, they could get the attention of some important people," she fans a bejeweled hand with mock modesty, adding, "Of course Natalie stands out from the rest of the group."

"Who's Natalie?" Joe asks, bless his naïve heart.

Charlotte replies with unbridled enthusiasm. "Well, with all modesty I can say she's not only my daughter but the shining star of the show choir."

"Such modesty," I say quietly.

"What was that, Thomas?" Charlotte turns heavily made-up eyes back to me.

"Darling," Bea says quietly, and I can sense a good 'talking to' coming my way.

"Hmm?" I answer both her and Charlotte with a single murmur.

"Well-staffed orchestra," Bea's sing-song answer dwarfs Charlotte's words.

Ever since we had "the talk" and I agreed to give this whole be-friends-with-people idea of hers a try, she can't be satisfied with the addition of Sally and Hart only into my inner circle. She's been pestering me to look outside of my comfort zone for new friends, but she can't possibly mean this nitwit. The way I see it, Charlotte Davens is more like militarized zone material.

"Dude, that's straight up legit!" Joe flashes an award-winning smile at her. "Way cool! So, your daughter's show choir is going to perform at a fair?"

"Oh yes, our county fair, in three weeks," Charlotte chirps. "We placed high enough this year to catch the attention of several talent scouts and could potentially win Nationals next year with the right guidance," she takes another couple of steps closer to me, spinning her web. "I was hoping Thomas might be willing to coach them before the fair."

Joe clasps his hands together with glee and nods at us both. "What a terrific way to mentor some young musical minds, right Thomas?" He swears they can't actually see and hear Bea, but I'm telling you sometimes it's eerie how much the Tacketts sound just like her!

"That would be simply fantastic!" Charlotte practically yells, getting the attention of Jewels who drifts over to us.

"Hello," she says sweetly to the nitwit.

"Charlotte, this gorgeous creature is my wife Jewels," Joe says. Charlotte's smile for Jewels is nicer than the one she gave Joe. She must think she's found an ally in him and wants to capitalize on it by playing nice to his wife. "Her daughter's high school show choir is trying to get to Nationals next year, and our Thomas here is going to help them," Joe bypasses the daggers I'm throwing at him with my eyes.

"How exciting!' Jewels squeals, "And good for you, Thomas! Bea will be so proud when she hears."

"Oh, I'm quite certain she's heard," I snap. I look up, preparing to tell the nitwit in clear terms that I will not be helping any choirs this summer, but Palmer and Ido gallantly sweep in like the untimely fools they are and ruin my refusal.

I'll save you the trouble of hearing the whole wearisome conversation but suffice it to say that the lot of them are on a short list of people I'm mad at. The end result is that by the time the nitwit leaves in a cloud of nauseating perfume, I've not only been enlisted against my will but Palmer is apparently going to be a part of it, too.

"I was in show choir my whole high school career," Palmer tells me, ignoring my scowl. "It will be fun, I swear."

"It won't, and you can't convince me otherwise. And as for you two," I narrow my eyes at my roommates, "shame on you."

Jewels leans up to kiss my cheek, squealing again when I try to swat her away. "Gotta run, Thomas! See you later," she blows a kiss at Joe and scurries off, probably to torture an old lady trying to cross the street or something.

"Yeah, dudes, I gotta get going, too," Joe high fives Palmer and Ido, edges past me with a wide berth, says something in Wilma's ear that makes her laugh too loud, and disappears into the crowded streets.

I turn on Ido and Palmer, but they're ridiculously useless. "It will do you good," Ido assures me with a calm smile.

"Giving back to the community," Palmer also smiles.

"You're horrible friends," I tell them.

"Are we though?" Ido laughs.

"We're just doing what Bea wants," Palmer says, stretching his arms above his head. "Man, isn't it nice out today?"

"Do not change the subject," I snarl. "Of all the nitwits in the whole world, she's got to be the worst. What would make you think I'd willingly help her out? And Bea doesn't always need to get what she wants, either, for the record."

"Wilma, we're gonna need to get this man some pie, fast!" Ido laughingly calls to her.

She whirls around, frowning. "What's wrong now?"

"I've been betrayed, that's what," I tell her. "The Tacketts and these two buffoons are trying to force me to do something that could kill me."

She brings me a slab of her Peachy Keen pie, scrutinizing my face closely as she hands it over. "You look fine to me. Stop being such a big baby."

Wilma's tin-canned voice says, "Someone needs a potty break," much to the delight of the traitorous humans around me. Maggie wiggles her rump, and I sigh again.

The whole world is against me.

Chapter 21

I close the front door behind me, stopping briefly to right the gnome Jewels has placed precariously on the top step of the porch. She's gone hog-wild with flowers and yard décor, which tickles Bea. The last two days have been stormy, and the gnome has lost the battle with the wild winds more than once.

Thunder crashes out a rumbling, coming your way soon alert, and as I peer into the dark sky I rub my shoulder. Arthritis is for the birds. A banging across the street draws my gaze, and I see the pudgy form of my elderly neighbor struggling with her trash cans. My treacherous brain shows me a shirtless Kenny demanding to know why no one lends her a hand with the hard stuff.

"Darling," Bea says, "wouldn't it be nice if you helped her out?"

I'm about to deliver ten solid reasons why I shouldn't have to when a few fat raindrops splatter across my face. If I didn't know better, I'd swear Bea made that happen to guilt me into doing her bidding.

She's got to be less awful than the nitwit, I reason. I rush down the drive, across the street, and take hold of the handles. "Allow me," I say to her startled face. A surprised "oh!" slips out of her as I pull the cans past her and hustle them up to the door of her garage. She's waddling down the drive after me, hands shielding her eyes from the pattering raindrops. She motions for me to follow her up onto her porch, so I do.

"How very kind of you, Mr. Sanders," she says, robustly patting my arm.

"You have me at a disadvantage, it seems," I say. "I don't know your name,"

"Peggy Ackerman," she replies, pushing strands of snow-white hair out of her eyes. "I'm a big fan, by the way. I've followed your career since you first left town."

"Is that right?" I fix a smile on my face. Now she'll ask me for an autograph and expect to have friendly chit-chat at the mailbox, darn my luck. I knew this was a bad idea.

"Oh yes, it is. I'm so proud to come from the same small town as you. I was thrilled when you and your dear, sweet wife moved in across the street. I met her once, you know, way back when she first opened the thrift store. She was the loveliest woman," she looks as if she wants to say something more but changes the subject abruptly instead. "Mr. Sanders, do you like sweet potato pie?"

I'm thrown aback by this. "Uh, yes, I do," I reply hesitantly.

"Well, you go about your day then, and later this evening I will have a homemade sweet potato pie waiting for you." She gives me a grandmotherly smile, although she's most likely close to my age, and disappears into her house.

"Now, wasn't that easy as pie," Bea giggles, pleased with her play on words. The drive to the diner is insufferable with her giddiness over my encounter with Peggy.

At least I'll get a sweet potato pie out of it.

The Munch Box is busy as expected for a middle of the week lunchtime. Wilma stops me as soon as I walk inside, furious with Edda Mae Brothens. "Tommy, she walked right past us, right out there on our sidewalk," she complains angrily, pointing to the parking lot.

"Well, Wilma, she was probably coming from the town hall or something," I say, surveying the room for a place to sit. Play time with Peggy put me behind schedule and now the diner is almost full. I see

Val shrugging out of his raincoat and set a course for his table, Wilma following along with more details about the horrid Edda Mae.

"Vallen," I raise my hand.

"Hey, Thomas!" he says.

I plop down in the booth opposite him, looking up into Wilma's fiery face. "How about a Frisco melt with fries, Wilma?"

"Fine, but don't you think for one minute I'm going to let her waltz around on my property without consequences," she huffs, then switches gears to ask Val, "What can I get you, hon?"

With a smile he says, "What Thomas is having sounds good."

"I swear, I don't know how Wilma and Edda Mae haven't killed each other yet," I say when she's gone. "Thanks for letting me invade your space."

"Your intrusion is by far the nicest one I've had all day," he says wearily.

"Oh yeah?" I ask. He tells me how Frank Norris barged into his church office in a rage, accusing Val of stealing teaching materials from him.

"Teaching materials?" I scoff. "Doesn't everyone have access to the same Bible? How do you copyright that?"

"You'd be surprised at the things people think they have a right to," he replies sullenly.

"We have a right to run him and Bob out of town," I say with a smirk.

He rubs a hand across his face before saying, "One of them, anyway."

My jaw drops. "You can't be serious."

He studies me briefly. "Have I ever told you what actually happened when Frank threw me out of his church last year?"

"Wilma filled me in, although I'm not sure how accurate her version of the story was," I chuckle.

"Frank and I had been butting heads for months over my issues with his doctrine. I wish like everything I'd never taken the position with him in the first place," he says. "I was consumed with the need to come home and his was the first job offer I got."

"I remember," I nod, although truthfully, I'd forgotten all about his time as a youth pastor in southern Indiana. He'd moved back a few months before me and Bea, and everything surrounding that whole time gets a bit blurry.

"After Frank fired me, I was a mess emotionally," he says. "Not from being fired, but from months of tension and fighting with him."

"I'm sick just thinking about it," I say.

"So, there I was, jobless, feeling war-torn, struggling to even understand what it was I had been through and where I needed to go from there. A couple days later I was at the park trying to pray. It wasn't going well, Thomas," he grins. "Bob Frazier comes along and changes my life."

"Did he give you a million bucks?"

"In a way," he smiles. "He told me he'd heard about what happened between me and Frank, and it didn't sit well with him. He's never gotten along with Frank, you know."

"They're both hard to like, but they *are* always at odds with each other," I agree.

"There are degrees of nutjob, to use your phrase," he chuckles. "Bob's not even in Frank's category. He arranged for me to meet with a pastoral counselor, and that saved my sanity. A few weeks later, a small group of people who left Frank's church because I was let go approached me about forming a new congregation. I was overwhelmed with the idea of it, but once again Bob stepped in to help. He gave us space to meet in in his building temporarily, then he took me to his bank and co-signed for us to get a loan."

"He did not," I'm flabbergasted.

"Yes sir, he sure did. He found us a small building in our price range and gave us furniture and other stuff so we could start having services right away," he smiles at my astonishment.

"I don't know what to say," I shake my head. "I mean, I believe you, but surely you can see why this is a hard story for me to swallow."

"He's odd, I know," he agrees, "But all this help came from his heart, totally unsolicited, and he didn't ask for a thing in return, except for me to keep quiet about it. Bea and Mike overheard me on the phone with him at your house, but otherwise I've never told a soul. I made them swear not to tell, and to my knowledge they haven't," he says, then with total seriousness adds, "and you can't either."

"No one would believe me if I did," I say.

"Maybe not," he shrugs.

"Why all the secrecy? I'm used to nutjobs shouting from the rooftops when they do something good," I ask.

"Bob thinks I'm too liberal in my beliefs and doesn't want to be grouped in with me," he explains.

"What?" I scoff. This sounds a lot more like the Bob I know.

"I know it sounds hypocritical, but you have to consider the world we come from. Pastors are held to much higher standards than everyone else. My friendship with Olive and Taffy is enough to blacklist me in a lot of churches. Bob can't be caught between two different schools of thought, or he'll lose all credibility with his congregation."

"So, he wanted to do a good thing, but had to do it in secret because it goes against a specific twist on the gospel?" I ask, incredulously.

"I'm not defending doctrine, here, Thomas. I'm defending a human being. A dad. A fellow man. Our neighbor," he says. "As it stands, our tiny church has now tripled in size, opened our own daycare, and contribute to Mike's shelter both financially and with volunteers, and we owe it all to Bob. I just think it's important for you to see him through my eyes for a minute."

I glance up as a server brings our food. We thank him and dig in.

"Alright, so Bob did a good deed, and I'm not supposed to be too mad that he doesn't want anyone to know," I snort at this logic. "What's so important about *me* knowing?"

He chews thoughtfully before answering. "I was at the bistro the other day and Joe asked my opinion on dealing with Bob. He told me about Bob showing up at your house because Neil was there, and how you tried to get him to come in and talk to Joe so he could get to know him."

"Yeah, and the jerk said no way," I point my fork at him. "Can't do anything about him being stubborn."

"He did say no that time, but there's always a chance he might say yes if you keep trying. I was touched that you tried to reason with him, and I don't want you to think it was a waste of time," he says with sincerity.

It's my turn to study him. "Have you been talking to Bea?"

He laughs good naturedly. "You know we can't see or hear her."

"Okay, but let's just get this straight—you're not suggesting *I* can do anything about Bob, are you?" I demand. "Once bitten, twice shy, as the saying goes. I'll never waste that much effort on him again."

"Never say never, old man," Val wiggles his eyebrows at me.

"Old man, is it?" I laugh, glad the serious conversation has ran its course. "It was this old man that took you for about seven bucks at the last poker game."

"Funny, I'd have thought Bea would have told you," he smirks.

"Told me what?"

"We let you win at least one hand a night just to keep you coming back! You're easy money, old man." When he cackles with laughter, he reminds me of Wilma.

Chapter 22

The county fair refreshes my summer like ice cubes in a tall glass of tea. The three days we spend on the fourth of July is a mere teaser for the grandeur of the twenty days of county fair.

We've been at it for five days now and I've taken up the same routine I've used in years past with a couple of minor, albeit unwanted, adjustments.

You know how I like my routines.

I still start my days at the Munch Box, which are blissfully calm and quiet in the absence of Wilma. Don't you worry, I still see plenty of her. I'm usually over at the fairgrounds by nine-thirty or ten where I fiddle around at the antique car show until lunchtime. I let Rusty think it's because I want to hang out with him, but it's mostly because this building has the best buttered popcorn in the fairgrounds. Averitt, Harold, and a few others from the Liar's Bench hold court here at times, so there's plenty for me to do when Rusty gets caught up in carburetor talk with some grizzled mechanic buddy of his.

Around lunchtime I visit the main strip where they sell all the tenderloins, turkey legs, and burgers with donuts for buns. Bea takes one look at my plate and compares me to the blue-ribboned nine-hundred-pound hog, which is unreasonable and unfounded. I point out that my metabolism is doing fine seeing as how I'm still the same willowy hundred and eighty some pounds I've been since my days of brown hair and boundless energy.

Wilma sells pie by the slice or whole shebang. She's located inside one of the air-conditioned buildings, so I like to drop by there in the afternoons when the temps are at their hottest. This year her usual zest for making the big bucks has taken a back seat to her relentless pursuit of the perfect daughter-in-law. She's already set him up on a couple of blind dates, Scott told me. He's had to make awkward phone calls explaining to these poor ladies that no, he's not married but also no, he's not going to let his mom pick his wife out for him at the county fair. I don't linger too long after I've had my pie and cooled off some for fear of being enlisted to help her with one of these schemes.

This year's variance to the routine has been the blasted show choir stage. Palmer has dedicated himself two hundred percent to it, but he still drags me over there at least once a day because he says my presence motivates the kids.

Between us, it's the copious amounts of junk food I bring that motivates them, not my vast musical skills. I asked Joe what kids these days like to snack on, and he told me about an energy drink that's popular. I tried one, and I'm fairly certain straight ammonia might taste better. Still, when I figured out Charlotte disapproved of the kids having this stuff, I marched over to Ido's and ordered enough cases to last them for the whole fair. I added a variety of candy and chips to the order, and that's how I became an instant hero to my young show choir charges.

I'm hoping this will teach Charlotte that it's just not worth it to bully me into things in the future.

Secretly, when she's not been anywhere near the stage, there have been a couple of times when the kids talked me into sitting down at the piano. I played some of my more popular compositions and even managed to astonish them with a few pop songs that made them break out in spontaneous dancing.

They showcased their individual talents for me, and I was surprised at how very good their voices were. We didn't cover anything from the show choir list, because that's too much like rule following for my taste. I took a page from Joe's notebook and let them be silly, and they loved it.

In the meantime, I can't figure out what it is that's keeping Palmer so mesmerized by this show choir business. He can't play a musical instrument, and he can't carry a tune. I know it's not the glittery nitwit that's captivated his attention, so it must be the kids. Like I said, they aren't that bad if you catch them alone.

As soon as I can manage it every day, I ditch the show choir stage for Olive and Taffy's food truck. There's a good amount of snacky places to stop on the way if the mood hits me, but mainly I'm interested in getting to the shaded patch of land directly behind the truck. They've constructed a sanctuary of sorts with fans and fancy reclining lawn chairs, and it fits nicely into my routine to catch forty winks about this time of day.

Wiggles and Maggie are usually napping here, too, but there's not much I can do about that. The three of us lounge around like royalty while the rest of the fair whizzes by, and the break from a hot and humid day is always welcome.

"My main man," Joe greets me, coming out of the food truck just as I take a seat. A youngster I don't recognize is in the serving window helping the line of at least ten people. Olive and Taffy are doing great this year, now that Wilma's on their side.

"I thought your shift was over already," I say, slipping my shoes and socks off. I wiggle my toes in the coolness of the grass with a sigh.

"Neil's on his way," Joe answers, then remarks, "Dude, why are you so stubborn? I've told you ten times how much cooler you would be if you weren't wearing socks in this heat."

"Go out in public with those fake shoes on? No thanks," I protest. He keeps threatening to buy me a pair of crocs, and I keep threatening to throw him out of my house if he does. I've seen how silly his feet look in the pair he wears and I'm not having it.

Neil rushes up, sweaty and out of breath. "I am so sorry, Joe," he starts throwing apologies from fifteen feet away.

"No worries, bud. It's not that serious," Joe plops down in a chair beside me, flapping the material of his overalls to fan himself.

"It's my dad again," Neil shakes his head, adding, "Hey, Mr. Sanders, how's it going?"

"What's up with your dad?" I can't help but ask.

"Oh, he's got this thing about me hanging out with Joe," he says, discreetly rolling his eyes towards the other side of the street. I glance casually that way and can't believe who's lurking around.

Well, then again, I guess I can since I've caught Old Brimstone in this exact same position before. Bob, partially hidden by a phone pole, is watching us.

"I hate all this tension," Joe says sadly.

"Same," Neil says with exasperation. "I told him I was just helping them out for the county fair. He's got it in his head I'm going to give up college to sell coffee for Olive and Taffy."

"Poor old Bob," I snort sarcastically. "First the long-haired guy with tattoos stole his son's heart, and now a gay couple wants to steal his son's future!"

"Dude," Joe says with as much disapproval as he is capable of, which isn't much. He's really too nice to get cranky with me.

Neil chuckles, too, rubbing his chin. "You can't quote me on this, but in everyday life my dad's not the same guy people get on Sunday mornings."

What a curious thing to say, especially on the heels of my chat with Val. "Okay, I won't quote you," I say, "but I would love for you to elaborate."

"Only that he doesn't think Olive and Taffy are horrible for the same reasons as everyone else in his church," he replies. "Or, like Pastor Norris does."

"Horrible for being gay, you mean?" I ask. I'd always thought Bob and Frank were on the same side where all the usual Christian complaints are concerned.

"Dad's way more worked up over things like human trafficking and domestic violence than he is the queer community," Neil says.

"So, all this spy stuff is because he doesn't want you to spend time at the bistro with Joe?"

"I told you so," Joe answers for him. "He's not a bad guy—just a protective father, like I said."

"Yeah, he's worried Joe might be part of a cult," Neil says with a small laugh. "I've been hanging out at the bistro since my high school days and he's never complained before, so it's not Olive and Taffy he's upset with."

"Why don't we call him over here right now then," I suggest.

"One of these days he's gonna realize I'm a good dude and then it's gonna be..." Joe slides one palm along the other one with a whistle, "smooth sailing all the way, baby! But today's probably not that day. If we force the issue before he's ready, we'll just make things worse than they are."

I consider this. I still think Bob is outlandish, but the whole idea of not forcing him to do something until he's ready strikes a chord with me. I don't much care for that kind of thing myself.

"So, you guys don't want me to start waving at him then?" I chuckle.

"Definitely not," they laugh.

"Alright, I'll leave it up to you two to handle Bob's delicate sensibilities." I stretch my long legs forward and lean back, folding my hands across my stomach. "I am going to have to ask you to hold it down, though. You're interrupting the naps of three very deserving citizens."

They take themselves into the food truck and I let the sound of the fair drift over me, concerns of Old Brimstone fading away.

Chapter 23

Today is exactly the kind of day you want to have when you're at a county fair. The sky is blue, the breeze is gentle, and the temps are kind. Prime conditions for eating heavily breaded foods.

The best way to make sure nothing gets overlooked at the fair is to use their maps. I've got mine spread out over a picnic table, circles made around places I think I might like to hit this afternoon. A shadow falls across my map as Jewels slides in next to me on the bench seat with a heavy sigh.

"Hi there, kiddo," I say. "Care to join me for a day of feasting?"

"Can't. I'm covering the booth for Mike in a few minutes," she says quietly.

I turn to get a better look at her downcast face, realizing with a start this is the first time she hasn't tried to assault me with kisses and hugs since we met.

Something must be terribly wrong. "Is... everything ok?" I ask hesitantly.

She turns red-rimmed eyes toward me and with alarm I see she's been crying. Tears are absolutely against the Code. "Obviously I'm not allowed to talk about the clients I work with, so let's just say I'm upset about someone who showed up at the shelter again last night for the third time in two months," she says, voice weighted with gloom.

I look helplessly across the table at Bea. "Give her a hug, honey," she instructs me.

"I'm sorry you're upset," I say, compromising with a low-contact pat on the arm.

"It's just so hard sometimes. The kind of work I do, I mean," Jewels sniffs, covering my hand with hers. "I try to see the other side of things, try to find the good in everyone, but a lot of times it feels like there's no good to be seen. It's beyond me how anyone can intentionally hurt their spouse, or children." She sniffs again, and her next words come out angrily. "Today I've stopped looking for the good and started thinking about what I could do with a baseball bat."

"Whoa," a nervous laugh slips out of me, shocked to hear Jewels talk like this.

She matches my laugh with a clipped hard one of her own. "I know, I know. Not exactly compassionate," she pulls a tissue out and dabs it across her nose. "I don't mean it, really. I just wish I could convince her to take Hart and leave the situation for good."

My eyes dart away. She obviously doesn't realize she just slipped up and used a name. "Well, I don't know what to say, Jewels, other than I'm pretty sure your client is glad you care so much about her."

She smiles up at me, placing a slightly damp palm against my cheek. "Thanks, Thomas. That's sweet," she maneuvers herself out of the bench seat. "I've got to go wash my face before my shift. Come see me later if you have time," she grins and a little of her sadness slips away. "I've got my eye on a gorgeous clock that would go beautifully in the guest bedroom."

"Wait, where did I put that..." I search my shirt pocket. "Oh, that's right, I left all my interest in clocks at home. Too bad."

She chuckles at me, blowing her nose again as she walks away.

"The poor dears," Bea says sadly. "I feel bad for all three of them."

"Yeah," I mumble, unable to get out any other words. I quietly stuff my map into a pocket and head out for the tenderloin stand.

I wish I could say something better to Jewels, but I'm clueless. I do better with actions, like writing that check every month for Mike.

The thought of Sally and little Hart living in a home with an abusive man makes hard knots form in my stomach. The tenderloin line is in front of me, but suddenly I decide to ditch the heavy food and skip ahead to dessert.

Oddly enough, that's where I find Sally and Hart.

"Well, hello you two," I say with a rush of something that feels a whole lot better than that hard knot.

Sally turns toward me, her bruises looking fresh and tender. "Hello yourself," she says, not quite meeting my eyes.

"Gramps!" Hart cries, reaching up to me. I bend down to her level and five seconds later I'm upright again, her small form attached to me like a spider monkey to a banana tree. It's not entirely unpleasant. "I want to have a sneaker and a funny cake, but mommy says both is too 'spensive and I have to pick just one," she pouts.

I cast a confused look at Sally, who automatically translates, "Deep-fried snickers and funnel cake."

"Ah, that sounds like a really hard choice," I tell Hart sympathetically.

"It's making my brain hurt," she taps her forehead solemnly.

"As it so happens, I was just thinking about getting three sneakers and three funny cakes, but there's a problem," I reply, matching her solemn tone. "That's so much food I would need the help of at least two other people to eat it all."

A look of astonishment crosses her features as she does the math, "Me and mommy are two people! We could help you!"

"Oh, no, Mr. Sanders, you can't keep buying us stuff all the time," Sally protests.

I raise an eyebrow at her with as much cocky indignation as I can muster. "Who said anything about buying it? I was going to trade Maggie for it."

She laughs out loud once—a short, accidental snort of a sound—looks surprised at herself, and then laughs again, this one a little easier. "Wilma wouldn't like that,"

"Gramps! You can't trade doggies for food! You have to use money!" Hart sniggers. "Do you have any money?"

"Oh, money, is it? Yes, I do have money," I reply.

"Good," Hart says.

"I would really like it if you eat with me. What do you say, Sally?" I ask without any fanfare.

"Come on, Sally," Hart says sincerely, and her mom explodes with genuine laughter.

"Alright," she gives in, and Hart and I both say hooray.

"Have you seen the baby goats yet?" Hart asks me. Inwardly I groan. I make a point of staying out of the animal barns because they stink to the high heavens.

"Uh, no, I haven't."

"Lucky you found us, then," she says. "We're going there next, and you can come with us."

I stay noncommittal on the small hope she might forget.

Feeding Sally and Hart foods that are near and dear to my heart brings me a sense of contentment I didn't know I could feel. Everyone knows kids will gorge themselves on sugary stuff, but Sally's obvious love for my favorite obsession is icing on the cake, so to speak.

We eat slowly, savoring every gooey bite, Hart chittering about this and that. Once, over ice cream at the bistro, I happily discovered Sally has a quirky, sarcastic slant to her personality, but today I find out she's got an intelligent head on her shoulders to boot. She's a numbers person who had dreams of going to college for business finance, something she wistfully says she still hopes to get around to.

She's done her homework on me, managing to draw me into a lengthy ten minutes of talk about my career. She tells me how remarkable I am without sounding like a glory-seeking nitwit, asking thoughtful questions about some of my less popular compositions. I'm impressed, and that's hard to do.

We share a good laugh over Joe and his overalls, although she's much more of a fan of them than I am. She thinks it adds quirkiness to his already explosive personality, and I guess I can't argue with that.

She tells me how her parents died in a boating accident when she was only thirteen, so she spent her teen years bouncing between an elderly aunt and that aunt's best friend, equally elderly.

"Aunt Belinda passed away just a few months after I graduated, but I still see her best friend from time to time. It's harder to get over there with, well..." she drifts off, and I assume it has something to do with her disagreeable marriage.

"I guess it's better to have an honorary aunt than no aunt at all," I say.

"It is. She's wonderful. Of course, I heard all about it when she met Mrs. Sanders. Your wife made a huge impression on Aunt Peggy," she says, and then laughs all over herself. "I just realized my Aunt Peggy lives across the street from you, but I didn't put that together until just now! Seriously, what is wrong with me?"

"Small world," I muse, smiling. I don't know why it surprises me to find out that Bea would have some random connection to Sally and Hart.

"What was Mrs. Sanders like?" she asks me.

I find myself talking freely about Bea, which isn't something I ever do with strangers. It sort of happens without me noticing, actually.

"Mommy," Hart pipes in, "I need to go potty real bad," and I watch after them as they scurry off to the bathroom.

Bea takes our moment alone to sigh heavily. "It turns my stomach just thinking about those sweet girls living like they do."

"I hate it," I say truthfully.

They rush back, Hart full of baby goat talk. My hopes of avoiding the smells are dashed. I'm not so sure I could ever tell this small human no.

Sally's phone rings. By the look on her face, I don't need three guesses to figure out who the caller is. She turns her back to us, but her hushed, appeasing words make it clear the caller isn't happy about something.

"I think she's talking to my daddy," Hart tells me, and I didn't know so much sadness and disappointment could be crammed into a little kid's words.

"We have to get home now," Sally says, mechanically gathering all our trash into one heap. She tosses Hart's sippy cup into her bag and scoops the child into her arms. All the light has gone out of her expression. "What do we say to Thomas, Hart?"

"I'm sorry we didn't get to see the baby goats, Gramps," Hart says quietly.

Inspiration unexpectedly floods me. "Would you be free to see them tomorrow, maybe?" I ask Sally.

She looks into her daughter's hopeful face before nodding. "We could, but it would have to be after three."

"That's the best time to see them, I hear," I answer cheerfully.

"Yippee!" Hart seems happy, and that makes me happy.

"We'll meet you at the goat barn at three-thirty, okay?" Sally asks.

"See you then," I nod, and then they are gone.

"Those poor dears," Bea says again.

"I feel…" I don't know how I feel exactly.

"I know, Thomas," Bea says lovingly, sadly. "I know."

Chapter 24

I survived the baby goats, along with the cows, alpacas, and pigs. It wasn't as bad as listening to Wilma try to coerce young women into dating Scott sight unseen—but close. I did teach Hart to say "olfactory assault." Later, when she used it appropriately after passing gas, well, I guess it made trekking through the smelly animal barns worth it.

By the time we got to Wilma for pie, Hart was getting sleepy. My stomach was still making grouchy sounds, so Wilma offered to keep Hart for an air-conditioned nap while her mom and I went in search of sustenance. Sally tucked Hart into a lawn chair with Wilma's tablet, a blanket, and Miss P. Maggie perched at the child's side like a guard at Buckingham Palace, and we were dismissed.

"I'd love to have a tenderloin and a giant, juicy ear of corn," Sally says as we stand in line. She isn't nearly as downcast today over her idiot husband, thank goodness, and didn't even fight me when I told her I was paying. "If that's not too expensive for a big shot like you, that is," she adds teasingly.

"If you can eat it, I can pay for it," I say, adding with fake menace, "but tell anyone I was nice to you and I'll have to kill you."

"Throw in an ice-cold soda and my lips are sealed," she bargains.

"You got it," I chuckle.

Bea had to talk me out of another funk last night because I developed a bad case of panicky doubt. After their hurried exit yesterday, I couldn't stop flipping back and forth between wanting to see them again and wanting to run away fast. Emotionally draining situations do that to me. I don't think I knew what I was going to do until this afternoon rolled around and I found myself hurrying to the baby goat barn.

"Let's sit over there, under that canopy." I take the two platters of food while she grabs our drinks and gesture with my head toward a few empty seats at a shaded group of picnic tables.

"Oh, look, Thomas!" Sally says excitedly, drawing my attention to a sign. Harold, Averitt, and a few of the other guys are holding a Liar's Bench at the edge of the seating area, right where we've landed. "Jewels told me all about the time you took her and Joe to one of their shows."

"It's a show alright," I laugh at her description. We luck into seats close enough so she can see and hear everything. I point at the guy who's talking, "That's Jed Anderson. His stories are usually a little off color, just so you know."

"Perfect!" she says.

Averitt catches my eye and nods hello. I nod back.

Jed launches into his story, and the crowd quiets down just a fraction. "So, ya see, these two young fellas who share an apartment, Dale and Evan, had a dog situation. Evan is asked to keep his parents' dog Squeak overnight. Normally that would be fine, except for Dale's dog, Buddy, who also lives in the apartment. The two fellas agree they'll need to keep the dogs separated, because Buddy might be a little squirt terrier that weighs less than fifteen pounds, but he wants to fight every dog he meets."

"It's the little ones you gotta watch out for," Averitt nods.

"Trouble is, Buddy heard Evan's car before Dale did, and that was *not* a good thing," Jed sighs with premonition. "Did I mention Squeak is a ninety-pound black lab?"

"Oh, no," Sally whispers, absently wiping at the corner of her mouth.

"Evan assumed the terrier would be in his crate, so he let Squeak run right into the house. Buddy came tearin' down the hall, barking like there was a terrorist invasion. He leaped right at Squeak, teeth bared and snarling, gaining air and altitude like a furry little Michael Jordan, and latched right onto Squeak's ear!" he tells us.

A round of gasps circulates through the audience.

"The terrier was dangling like a heavy earring from the poor lab's ear," Jed yanks down on one of his own earlobes, demonstrating. "Dale flew into the room wild eyed, grabbing at the flailing body of his terrier. Evan tried to get a grip on the lab, but it wasn't easy. He was thrashing around, trying anything he could think of to get his ear free!"

"They should have gotten a bucket of water," Harold suggests.

"That's for dogs having intimate relations, not for dogs having a squabble," Averitt corrects Harold.

"Oh," Harold says thoughtfully. "Huh."

"The lab slammed Buddy into the side of the cabinet a time or two, but not intentionally. He was more like a bucking bronco than a dog at this point. Evan told me that the next couple of minutes happened in slow motion for him, you know like when they say your life passes before your eyes?" Sally nods, engrossed in the story. "Evan found himself nose to nose with a totally cross-eyed Buddy!"

The crowd makes a collective sound of astonishment, and Jed nods sympathetically.

"Evan had to yell to be heard over the racket coming from the dogs. He finally got Dale to notice Buddy's crossed eyes, which sent Dale into a tizzy! They scuffled around the kitchen for a bit longer, Dale desperately trying to get his dog to let go and Evan trying to keep his dog from banging them all into the cabinets again. It was something else."

Sally glances at me, "Is this going to have a terrible ending?"

I shrug, because it's really hard to guess what Jed might say next.

"Well, Dale finally decided his stubborn dog wasn't going to let go, so he yelled out 'I'm going in!' like some kind of maniacal warrior on the battlefield. He raised his right hand above his head, pointer finger extended, and jabbed it dart-like into the, uh, posterior cavity of his dog's, uh, backside," Jed demonstrates for us with his finger.

"Wait, he put his fingers *where*?" Harold asks.

"Apparently Dale read on the internet that this is the quickest way to break up a dog fight," Jed says. "Through the back door."

"He reviewed the dog's plumbing," Averitt interjects.

"He got up close and personal," Harold parlays.

"He took a short cut through the poop chute," Averitt banters.

"Well, whatever you want to call it, it worked beautifully. Buddy let go of Squeak's ear and Dale was able to grab him. Squeak flew past Evan and straight to the door, clearly wanting nothing to do with the tiny lunatic dog. Evan took him straight back to the car."

The crowd issues a sigh of relief.

"Here's the clincher though," Jed leans forward a bit, pausing to give his next words an added bit of zip. "Evan went back inside to see if Buddy was okay, and what he found amazed him. Buddy's eyes were now *uncrossed*!" Jed raises his hands in the air victoriously.

"Uncrossed?" Averitt asks. "Just like that?"

"The way they have it figured is that the force of the finger as it, uh, entered the cavity, forced his eyes back to their normal places," Jed explains.

With a snort of derision Hank Freidman, who is almost always a "be seen but not heard" kind of guy, slaps a palm on the tabletop. "Hogwash!"

Jed looks him over with a glint in his eye. This kind of challenge is, after all, the very heartbeat of the Liar's Bench. "Question, Hank?"

Hank holds his hands out wide, far away from each other. "The rectum is in no way connected to the eyeballs. Putting your fingers... *there*... wouldn't have any effect on the dog's eyes... *here*!" he wiggles the first finger on each hand.

Sally looks at me, brows raised. "Good point."

"It is," I chuckle.

"Is any of this true?" she whispers.

"The only truth you can be sure of is the men of the Liar's Bench love to argue," I say.

Jed is laughing hard as he replies to something Hank said, "Sure, but where would the wires come from?"

"That's exactly my point!" Hank exhales with agitation.

"They read his mail in braille," Harold pipes up.

"They caboozled the old keister," Averitt winks.

Harold pauses for a few seconds, thinking, before firing back at Averitt with, "He re-routed the circuits from the bottom up."

Averitt wobbles a hand in the air with a so-so motion. "Not your best one."

Harold thinks again before yelling, "He got a one-finger discount prostate exam!"

Averitt smiles around the end of his pipe.

I stack our trash into one neat pile and stand up. "Well, young lady, have you seen enough? I was thinking about walking down to that fudge and taffy place to see if they have any butter pecan in yet."

"I could go for some banana taffy," Sally says, rising too.

We walk slowly, wavering off the path a bit so I can toss the trash into a can. The sun isn't overhead anymore, and a nice breeze is making things feel cooler than they probably are. We pass the butterfly garden and a hot-tub salesman in companionable silence, something I like a lot. There's no need to talk all the time, I've always thought.

Eventually, Sally breaks the silence. "Honestly, a finger in the, you know," she sniggers. "So, so funny."

"He got a backstage pass," I say, imitating Averitt.

"He gave him the finger," she adds on.

"He got an exit interview," I grin.

She wobbles her hand at me in the so-so way Averitt did to Harold, and we both laugh harder.

"I guess I don't care so much if it was all true or not," she says.

"That's what I've always told Bea. There's nothing like a well told story."

"Yeah," she agrees, falling silent again for a few minutes. "Hey, Thomas?"

I look over at her flushed, happy smile. "What?"

"Thanks a bunch for today. I really needed a day out," she says with so much sincerity it makes my heart jump a little. Then her eyes dance to a place on my right and the moment is gone. "Ooh, look! Pineapple whip!"

I'm glad she's distracted, because I don't quite know how to respond to her. "I think maybe you needed it, too," Bea says softly.

Maybe.

CHAPTER 25

It is hot. Blazing hot. The dogs and I are taking a break in the tented area behind the bistro's food truck. Not only am I cooking from the inside out like a slow roast, but for the first time ever, the county fair feels a little on the dull side.

Bea says I'm missing someone small and loud and fond of baby goats.

I slurp the remainder of my chocolate milkshake with no real enthusiasm, sighing at the blandness of the day. Maggie and Wigglesworth are asleep on their gel filled cooling mats, and I wonder absently what it would be like to have one for myself. I let my bored mind run rampant with imaginings of how I could use a gel mat to cool down in this lawn chair, and that distracts me for a few minutes.

I hear a slight thump behind me. Oh yes, I forgot to tell you about *him*. I'm not totally without entertainment, although it's not what I would've chosen if given a choice. Old Brimstone has been slinking around for about fifteen minutes, his flushed red face glowing with sweat, his beady eyes darting back and forth between the food truck's back door and window.

When I got here, Joe and Neil greeted me with very poor imitations of Italian accents. They wanted me to call them Mario and Luigi, and the young lady who's working with them Peach. I don't get the joke, but everyone else seems to. The customers have been guffawing along with Joe and Neil.

This, of course, is what drew Bob's attention. It's like he can't stand for Neil to have fun.

He moves closer for a better view, trips over a small bucket, and flails into the tent pole with a poorly muffled "Oomph," his cover blown.

"Hey there, Bob. Feeling a little off balance today, are we?" I say smoothly, casually taking another sip.

Bob rights himself, brushing imaginary dirt from his pants, and looks around the tent pole at me. "Thomas," he says, his face a portrait of misery. I scrutinize his sad disposition for a few seconds, and I don't know how, but the darndest thing happens.

I feel a miniscule amount of something for him that's totally unlike the usual aggravation and annoyance that his presence typically causes in me.

I think it might be sympathy.

For a split second I remember Val trying to convince me that Bob was worth another chance. I think over the things Joe and Neil talked about the other day, especially how Joe wants to make peace.

Maybe I *should* do something. Maybe the time is right.

If I'm successful, we could put an end to Bob's paranoia, and I could regain a lot of the peace and quiet I've lost. It's mostly the idea of having order again, and just a little bit of feeling sorry for Bob, that makes me act.

I'm not one for taking part in big emotional scenes, but I would describe myself as practical. So, in a practical way, I say, "Bob, this nonsense needs to stop. You're worrying yourself into a frenzy over nothing, and I think today is the day to call it quits."

He studies me, eyes narrowed, before saying, "It's not nonsense."

"But it is. You're ill-informed, so you think Joe is the worst thing that's happened to Neil." I stand up, motioning for him to come fully into the tent, which he surprisingly does. "What you need is a good old-fashioned dose of reality." I take the three short steps to the back door of the truck, poke my head in, and ask the two men of interest to come out.

Bob starts to object, but I override him. "Listen, we're going to settle all of this right now. Bob, Joe isn't a scheming lunatic who moved to town with the sole purpose of corrupting your son. He's just a guy who wants to be friends with everyone he meets. I'm constantly being told what a great dad you are, and how you're always sneaking around like this because you're worried about Neil's well-being. So, today would be a great time for a dad to sit down with his son and listen." I turn to Joe and Neil, who are clearly baffled at my behavior. "Go ahead. Tell him the stuff, you know," I gesture encouragingly. "The butt sniffing stuff."

"Uh, well, that's not exactly—" Joe stammers, laughing at me.

"The... what?" Bob asks.

"The thing preachers do," I explain to Bob. "How you're always butt sniffing because you think Joe is dangerous, but it seems to me you're not sniffing correctly if you still think Joe's a bad man."

"Okay, okay, how about we sit down and start over, maybe from the top," Joe suggests, shaking his head at me. Neil's guardedly watching his dad like he might spontaneously combust while Bob's watching me like I've gone off the deep end.

"Five minutes," I say to Bob, motioning to a chair. "Please, Bob, sit down and have a normal conversation with them for five minutes."

Remarkably, he sits. I'm not sure which one of us is the most surprised by this.

Maybe Bob himself, judging by the astonished look on his face.

"Do you want to start, or should Neil?" Joe asks Bob.

"Why don't I go get us some cold drinks," I say. "I don't need to be a part of this," I disappear into the truck.

The young lady whose name definitely isn't Peach has two customers ahead of me. I wait patiently, taking the chance to look over the baked treats in delicate glass dishes waiting to be purchased.

"Hey there, Mr. Sanders," she finishes up with her last customer and turns to me. "What can I get for you?"

"Four lemonades, and maybe one of these cookies with the gooey looking red stuff on top," I answer, trying not to visibly drool. "By the way, I know your name isn't Peach, but I don't know what it is."

She cackles, handing me a pair of tongs and motioning to the cookie. "Those guys and their obsession with video games. It's ridiculous. My name is Evie."

"Thanks, Evie," I say, taking the tongs. Having solved the issue of Bob, the greatest challenge I will face for the rest of the day is choosing the cookie that has the most gooey red stuff.

I pay with my debit card, and she gives me the four lemonades in a drink carrier. I tuck my cookie in between the plastic cups and tell Evie to have a wonderful afternoon.

Assuming they've had ample time to get all the emotional stuff out of the way by now, I step lightly down from the truck... and right into a hellish scene from my nightmares. Worse than spending time watching Palmer and Charlotte Davens giggle over show choir songs. Worse than Wilma's matchmaking schemes. Worse than a day with no pie.

My old man's heart almost gives out on me.

The three of them are crying. I'm talking cheeks drenched in tears, shirt tails pulled up to wipe noses, voices cracked with emotion.

"Yes, I know, and I'm just... sorry, I really am," Bob sobs.

"I'm sorry too, Dad," Neil sobs back, draping one of his arms around the back of Bob's neck.

"What are you sorry about?" Bob wails. "I'm the one making mistakes here, not you."

"I'm sorry for..." Neil looks up at me, a small sob escaping him again, before saying, "I'm sorry I don't have guts like Mr. Sanders! I wish I could have started this conversation weeks ago, but I was too afraid!"

Now all three of them have their wet faces turned up to me, smiling. A nervous twitch flutters through me. "Dude, I'm so grateful for you," Joe says, rising to his feet. The others follow suit and before I have a chance to scream for help, I'm being patted and thanked and shown more affection than one man should have to endure.

"Knock this off right now!" I yelp, trying to look as stern as I can.

"I agree with them, Thomas," Bob says, hand on my shoulder. "You made me do what I was too embarrassed to even think of, and I will always be grateful."

I thrust the tray of drinks into his hands in order to get him to stop touching me and take a step backwards, putting a couple of feet between us. "I didn't do anything! If you've finally come to your senses, then that's on you."

Neil sniffles, swipes his eyes with the back of his hand, and smiles at me warmly. "Seriously, though, Mr. Sanders, thanks so much for getting my dad to talk."

He doesn't touch me, so I reward him with a quick nod and a very, very brief smile. "That's fine, Neil. Glad to have some semblance of peace and quiet reinstated around here."

Bob snuffles, clears his throat, and snuffles again. "I guess I owe you a huge apology, Joe," he looks at the ground, shamefaced.

"Apology accepted, my man. In fact, you have a lot of wisdom and fatherly love, and I'd appreciate any guidance you might want to throw my way, especially once Jewels and I start a family," Joe says warmly. "I hope to be a loving dad just like you one of these days."

"After the way I've acted I don't know about that, but I wouldn't turn down a cup of coffee with you at some point," Bob laughs. "In the spirit of getting to know one another."

"Anytime, dude. Anytime," Joe agrees.

"Well, glad that's over and all behind us now," I clap my hands together briskly, ready to not talk about emotions anymore for the next hundred years.

"I do have one question, Mr. Sanders," Neil says with a barely concealed laugh. "What was it you were saying about my dad smelling butts?"

Bob laughs too, adding, "Oh yeah, what *did* you say about that?"

"Joe told me that," I bluster, "about how the dogs smell each other's butts, you know, to see if the other dog is nice or not."

"I don't see the connection," Bob says, but he's still smiling.

"These two dogs here," I motion at Maggie and Wiggles, who are awake now and watching us with curiosity, "they do that when they meet a new dog. They butt sniff, you see, to check out the dog, see what he's made of."

"You mean, to smell what the dog ate last?" Bob asks, smile widening.

"No, not like that. The way their butt smells can tell, uh..." I pause, looking at Joe with exasperation. "Tell them."

He shoves his hands deep into his overall pockets and rocks back on his heels. "You've got this, dude."

"It's like a science lesson," Neil chuckles.

"Joe said you were sniffing around him to see what kind of a man he is, like how the dogs sniff back there," I motion behind me.

"I was out of control, but I don't remember sniffing anyone's, uh..." Bob looks at my backside.

I quickly turn my backside away so he can't see it, and they laugh. Maggie jumps to her feet, barking, and rushes behind me.

"Oh, she wants to see what kind of man you are!" Joe says, laughter making his voice high.

I mean, I can see the humor in this situation. I can. I just wish it was about someone other than me.

"Alright, alright," I slam my backside down into my chair and put an end to that.

Chapter 26

I drove to the fairgrounds this morning under suspicious gray skies. My bones ache the way only an impending thunderstorm can make them ache, so there's that. There are only three days left of the county fair, so I would say we've been lucky this year if this is our first day of substantial rain. Maybe I should have seen the gray skies as a warning, because nothing has gone according to plan all day.

I wasted almost a whole hour dealing with Palmer and that nitwit Charlotte Davens. One of their leads for today's show choir performance came down with strep and they're treating it like a statewide crisis. Instead of enjoying my normal routine, I was offering perfectly good solutions that were promptly shot down.

You ever wonder what it would be like to live in a world where Charlotte Davens has laryngitis? I've imagined such a place, and it's blissfully quiet.

Then, just when I escaped the clutches of the nitwit and made it inside the dairy barn, Bob discovered me. In his newfound role as "friend of Joe," he's also determined to prove to me he's turned over a new leaf. He's been after me for three days to spend time with him, but I want no part of it. Bea, who is of course over the moon about the whole plot twist, says Bob wants to establish some kind of relationship with me that's not based on him recruiting me to his church and that I should cut him some slack.

Truthfully, I'm glad he's being nicer now, and if he's genuinely having a change of heart then more power to him. I simply have no desire whatsoever to have one of "those" conversations with him where we discuss our feelings. Jewels says he's turning into a regular lovebug, and I don't like the sound of that at all. I just wish we could move forward from here as if I didn't have anything to do with him and Joe making friends.

I agreed to a milkshake with him on the understanding that there would be no touchy-feely talk. He readily said that would be fine, so we sat together for an entire thirty minutes, and he kept his word. I won't say it was terrible, because it wasn't. I will say I'm feeling shocked at having spent time with him, period.

I finally left Bob in the dairy barn, using the excuse of having lunch plans, which was true. I caught up with Ido and Rusty for lunch, but by then it had already started to drizzle enough to make things damp and uncomfortable. We made quick business of our barbeque sandwiches, standing upright around the table because all the seats were wet, and hustled over to Wilma's building for the tastiness of her pie and the dryness of her roof.

After two hours of steady, very wet rain, I decided it was officially time to go home.

Somehow I got roped into bringing Maggie and Wiggles with me, although I did put up a decent fuss. Wilma's mind doesn't work like everyone else's. I think I might have mentioned that a time or two. See, I think the person who owns the dogs should be the one to drive them around town. However, masses of people are seeking shelter inside her building, and they're buying pie, so she thinks it's my duty to take care of the dogs for her so she can make a small fortune.

I didn't win the argument.

The dogs and I got to my house a couple hours ago and collectively decided it was the perfect time to nap. I situated myself on the couch with a blanket, they flopped down unceremoniously on the floor, and off to sleep we went.

An unusually long crash of thunder rattles the windows, startling me awake. Maggie and Wiggles jump up, alert. "Good gravy," I mumble, trying to gather my wits. I extract myself from the tousled blankets and stand, a little frazzled.

It's dark inside the house. Middle of the night dark.

The dogs are looking through the sliding glass door into the backyard. The sky has morphed from the regular rainy gray of before to a more menacing batch of low hanging charcoal gray clouds. I can barely see to check my watch, expecting it to be at least seven thirty or after by the degree of darkness shrouding the room. I turn on the lamp by the couch, illuminating my watch, and am shocked that it's barely four in the afternoon.

My cell phone rings, which startles me all over again. I don't get many calls at all, especially on the cell phone. The sound of the ringing comes from the basket of odds and ends on the kitchen island. "Hello?" I answer, my sleep-heavy voice croaking.

"Hey, it's Joe. Wilma wanted me to check on you guys. Everything okay up there?" His voice is raised, but I can still hardly hear him over the roaring in the background.

"We've been asleep, but yes, we're all alive and well," I reply, glancing out the small window over the kitchen sink. The trees are blowing wildly, their leaves turned upside down.

"Good to hear! We're most definitely getting drenched down here, man. The wind is crazy! People are running and yelling and trying to get stuff covered up. It's a madhouse!" He raises his voice even more. That explains the racket I can hear on the phone.

"That's not good for anyone at the fair. The thunder here is a little obnoxious, but I don't think it's even raining yet," I reply loudly so he can hear me. "It is awfully dark though. I had no idea it was still afternoon."

"Yeah, the sky over your way looks kind of crazy, Thomas. You should check the news, just to be safe," he yells. "We're packing up down here and should be home in an hour or so."

I glance at the dogs. Maggie and Wiggles are watching the sky, and that makes me uneasy. "Okay, I'll get the TV turned on," I promise Joe. "You guys be safe trying to get everything closed up."

"Alright, man. See you in a few." He disconnects.

I search for the remote and turn on the TV. The weatherman is excitedly gesturing up and down a map that's centered directly above downtown Cardinal Creek. It doesn't take long to determine that something unpleasant is brewing itself up in awfully close proximity to me when I see the line of red, orange, and yellow headed our way.

"...rotating funnel clouds. Please move to an interior room or basement as soon as possible and stay away from any windows!" the weatherman is showing a little more enthusiasm about this mess than I think he should be. He's probably tucked safely away in an area of the map that's got no red, orange, or yellow anywhere near it.

In the distance the high-pitched drone of the tornado sirens go off, and I roll my eyes upward. "Well, this is just fantastic," I say sarcastically to Bea. "I've lived all this time, desperate to see a tornado. Looks like my dreams will be coming true!"

"Better get the flashlight out of the kitchen, dear," she says with more nervousness in her voice than I care to hear.

Chapter 27

There's another crack of thunder, this one so intense I can feel it jangle around in my chest. Maggie races through the house, barking, and plants her feet on the closed front door. I follow her and open up, thinking maybe Joe and Jewels are out there. I yelp with surprise as the wind whips the screen door from my hands. It bangs violently against the house, breaking free from its spring, and flaps again and again like it's nothing more substantial than a flimsy piece of paper.

Maggie pushes past me onto the porch, barking furiously. I step out, thinking I need to try to save the screen door, but she takes my pants leg in her mouth, tugs a bit, then barks at Peggy Ackerman's house. I know she's barking because I can see her mouth moving, but I can only hear the faintest snippet of it. She tugs again at my pants, then barks again in Peggy's direction.

Behind me, Wiggles is pacing, but I don't think he'll follow us onto the porch. I peer across the street, trying to spot what Maggie sees, but between the darkness of the day and stuff blowing around, I can barely see fifteen feet in front of my face.

She tugs at my pants one more time and then gallops down the steps and into the yard. The gnome that Jewels so lovingly placed on the porch steps has fallen to the ground, shattered, and I know she'll be sad. Maggie turns around halfway through the yard, making more soundless barks at me.

I know I have to follow her. Maggie might be a dog, but she's smarter than most humans I run up against and I'm not going to deny it. Something must be wrong with Peggy, and I might be the only one around to help.

"This is not going to be a nice casual stroll," Bea urges nervously. "Stay aware of your surroundings."

I have to stop twice to center myself against the force of the wind, but Maggie stays a few steps ahead of me, slicing through it like a stocky brown torpedo with a low center of gravity.

It takes us quite a while to cross my yard and step onto the sidewalk. There's a sharp pain in my heel, and I look down to see that my feet are covered only in argyle socks. "Well, that's like taking a knife to a gunfight," I tell Bea, but my words are carried up and away. A rogue trash can powered by the untamed wind bumps and rolls down the sidewalk toward us, forcing Maggie and I to hurry into the street to avoid a collision.

The tornado sirens are screaming into the noise of the storm and I'm not ashamed to say it's making me edgy. Something in the nearby distance is banging open and shut, open and shut. There's not a single moving car in sight, and no humans either.

Just me, a dog, and the howling wind.

I wouldn't be a bit surprised right now if Rod Serling popped out of the darkness and started to narrate my situation. "Imagine, if you will, a shoeless moron in his seventies and a fat little dog, facing off against a tornado, somewhere in the Twilight Zone."

"Now isn't the time for your brand of dark humor, Thomas. Get going, Bea warns me, and she's right. I store that one away to tell the fellas later and touch Maggie's head to let her know I'm ready. We force our way across the street and through Peggy's short yard, Maggie reaching her a good while before I can.

Peggy's hanging (or draped like a rag doll, more like it) out of the driver's side door of her car, one leg and foot still trapped inside. She's obviously unconscious. Maggie's licking the poor woman's face, and I think about telling her to stop, but my guess is that an unconscious woman isn't any more concerned with Maggie's germs than a dead woman would be, so either way it doesn't matter. I kneel down and take a fast visual inventory of my neighbor.

Her eyes are closed, her mouth is slightly open, and her skin is an unearthly pale in the dreary light of the storm. I grimace at the blood flowing freely from a deep gash across her forehead, feeling alarmed at how bright and serious it looks matted in the short, curly fluff of her white hair. I don't technically know how to check for a pulse, but I lay my fingers against her throat like I've seen them do in the movies and am overjoyed to find that she feels warm. I watch her chest for a few seconds and, sure enough, I can see it slowly rise and fall.

A surge of hope rushes through me. "She's alive!" I exclaim out loud. Maggie bumps me excitedly with her head.

I look around, wondering who can help, but see absolutely no signs of life. I imagine everyone around is either down at the fairgrounds or hiding away in their bathrooms.

At this exact moment a nearby tree loses its battle with the wind and a medium sized limb with several jutting branches skids across the top of the car and smashes right into my shoulder. If it had been much bigger or hit much higher, I might've joined Peggy in an unconscious heap. In fact, it's now that I notice this limb's larger, heavier cousin lying on the other side of Peggy, which explains the gash on her head.

It's clear that I need to get her inside the house as soon as possible, and I'm going to have to do it alone.

I know it's not polite to discuss a woman's weight, but Peggy looks to me like she might be working as a part time taste tester at the local donut shop. I reach under her neck and try to lift her girth out of the car, failing miserably. Her head lolls around unconsciously, briefly flopping against my chest a couple of times before coming to rest, blood seeping into my shirt. "Oh, uh, yeah… I won't be able to pick her up, that's for sure," I tell Maggie and Bea.

"Look, there on the passenger seat, Thomas," Bea says excitedly. I gently lower Peggy's head to the ground and raise up on my knees so I can see into the car, spotting her raincoat and purse. "Maybe you could use that to drag her," Bea says.

I grab the raincoat and try to fit it around her body. I can't get it beneath her like a stretcher, and I don't see any good in putting it on her backwards like a strait jacket. I try a second time to shove it beneath her, but she's heavy and I can't see where this will get me.

Maggie takes the raincoat's belt between her teeth and pulls hard, the whites of her eyes showing with the effort. A lightbulb goes off and I think I catch her idea. "Good girl, Maggie," I yell. I turn the lifeless body so that she's resting as flat as she can be on her back. I pull the belt the rest of the way out of its restraining loops and slip it underneath Peggy's upper back and through each armpit. When I stand at her head, I can pull up on each side of the belt and turn myself into a human winch. I can use this method to hoist her upper torso up, and if I'm lucky, drag her to the house.

She's still heavy—don't get me wrong—but at least we're moving in the right direction. We have to cross over half the paved drive and down at least ten or twelve feet of sidewalk to get to the porch, which is going to present its own set of problems with its two concrete steps to conquer.

"We can worry about the porch when we get there. Okay, girls, let's go," I say to Maggie and Bea. I begin the long and difficult process of yanking Peggy's unconscious form to the safety of her house, two blessedly precious inches at a time.

Maggie runs in circles around us, pushing against my legs in support. Within minutes, every muscle in my body is straining in ways they haven't strained in years, and I feel a few uncomfortable crackles run up and down through the bones in my back. My eyes burn from the grit caked in them, and the inside of my mouth is coated with the same filth. I've managed to move Peggy all of a whopping three feet, maybe, when it crosses my mind that I might have bitten off more than I can chew.

I look down into Peggy's face, noticing that her forehead wound seems to be aggravated into overdrive. Two dark trails of blood have been freely flowing, one into the white hair on top of her head and one down the side of her face and onto her neck and the collar of her blouse. I worry about what that means. "The skin on the head bleeds more freely because it's thinner there. It's more important to get her into the house than it is to fuss with this right now!" Bea reassures me. I take her word for it and throw myself into my work with a grunt and a groan.

Maggie must sense my failing level of energy because she grabs hold of the material of Peggy's pants and pulls each time I do. I can't decide if I'm desperate for help or crazy from fatigue, but it seems like our combined efforts actually make things a little easier.

I have no idea how many minutes it takes for us to get her to the porch, but I do know it involves many furtive glances into the dark sky, several pauses to clear out my eyes and catch my breath, and Maggie repositioning herself twice because Peggy's pants rip under the pressure of her sharp teeth. I fall onto the porch steps, panting, and look over my patient. I'm worried about knocking her head around too much or breaking her back while I drag her up and over the unforgiving concrete steps.

I decide the best route will be to shove against her rather than dragging her, hopefully rolling her up the steps like I would a large rug. A very large, frumpy, dead weight rug. Not very ladylike, but I guess it's best to save her anyway I can right now and apologize later for putting my hands in places where they ordinarily wouldn't go.

I take a quick second to catch my breath, pulling my shirt tail up to wipe my eyes again. I had no idea being in a tornado could be such a messy affair. Lightning flashes around us, casting shadows in weird places. I wince as another crack of thunder rips through the air, this one vibrating in my teeth. If what they say is true about the time between lightning and thunder being an indication of how close a storm is, then this storm is just about ready to knock on our front door.

The constant whine of the siren wavers haltingly for a few seconds, like a toy with a dying battery, and then fizzles out completely. An image of a tornado reaching down to rip the telephone pole straight up out of the ground flashes through my mind. "Better the pole than you, Sanders," I tell myself. "Get on with it."

I scoot-roll Peggy up as close to the bottom step as I can and begin to shove from behind, the muscles in my back complaining loudly. Maggie positions herself behind Peggy's short, stubby legs, using her forehead to keep them from dropping backwards. It takes me four or five "full steam ahead" pushes with both hands and one shoulder until finally I am rewarded with Peggy's torso resting on the porch.

It wasn't pretty, but it did the trick.

With no warning, the gusting wind stops tearing through our neighborhood. One second, it's braying in my ears and beating against my body, and then abruptly, nothing. The sudden quiet is more alarming than the deafening wind. I look down at my hands pressed against Peggy's back, the bottom falling out of my stomach at the green hue my skin has taken on from the changing light around me.

Everyone living in the Midwest knows what a greenish-yellow sky means.

Chapter 28

I look at Peggy's front door, and for the first time it occurs to me that it's more than likely locked. Making sure she isn't going to roll backwards, I crawl around her and fling the screen door open, swearing out loud when the doorknob refuses to be turned.

"I need a key," I tell Maggie, as if stating the obvious will produce a miracle.

You'd think I would have learned by this time that Maggie *is* a miracle.

She darts down the porch steps and races to the car, returning in under thirty seconds with Peggy's purse in her mouth. Like I've seen her do a hundred times with a toy, Maggie violently shakes the purse side to side, dumping a jumble of contents onto the porch. A key ring skitters across the mess and lands by my foot.

"You're one heck of a dog, Maggie Harper," I say with the utmost sincerity. "I don't know where I'd be without you right now."

I begin thrusting each key into the lock, swearing again when I can't find a match. After three false starts, the fourth key slides right in, triggers the lock, and the door swings gloriously open.

I prop the screen door ajar with a flowerpot, and Maggie disappears inside the house. "Probably getting the first aid kit so she can stitch Peggy up," I tell Bea. I can hear the strain in my own voice and realize just how ill-suited I am for this kind of activity.

I scurry back over to Peggy, momentarily distracted, when I hear a hard pinging sound on the metal porch roof. Instinctively I duck, then chide myself for being such a scaredy cat. "Twisters don't ping, so whatever that is, it's not the twister," I say to no one in particular. I reach down for Peggy's feet and cry out as something drives into the back of my head. More pings from the porch roof and hail the size of quarters start to pelt and bounce all around me.

Okay, this might not be the arrival of the actual tornado, but any seasoned Midwesterner also knows it's still a bad sign.

The hail throws me into a full panic, and I forget about my tired body. I swing Peggy's limp legs around toward the steps, run back to her head and reposition the belt, and give a mighty heave. I topple over backwards onto my own rear end, but not without getting Peggy's body a record-breaking six inches closer to the open doorway. Five more grunting pulls like that, and I have her body safely inside the house.

I double her up like a folding chair and roll her fully into the entryway, shove the door closed with my foot, and collapse next to her. Right away I notice how much quieter it is with the door shut. The hail was almost louder than the wind.

I'm out of breath and feel at least two hundred years old. My head is pounding, I'm sweating profusely, and every inch of my body is overwhelmingly weary. Peggy isn't doing much better than me. I see how much blood has smeared along behind us with a dull sort of alarm. If it wasn't for the obvious storm damage, I'd be getting an attorney right about now with this scene looking damningly bad from a homicide perspective. I check the rise and fall of her chest again, and my brain tells me her breathing is shallower than it was earlier. "Fabulous. I've killed her with my efforts to save her," I say blearily to Bea.

"The phone, dear. Find the phone and call 911," my dearly departed gently reminds me.

"Right. The phone." I hurl myself to my feet and shuffle down the hall and into a formal living room, looking around for the elusive device. I've stood on her porch a couple of times to talk, and to get baked treats, but I've never been inside. Navigating in the unfamiliar darkness is going to slow me down. Maggie appears in an open doorway, barking, and gratefully I follow her.

I find myself in the kitchen, and I'll be darned if she's not standing beneath a wall mounted phone. "Good work, Maggie. Good work." I praise her, ripping the cordless handset off the wall.

I press the talk button, frowning. No dial tone. I flip a light switch, swearing yet again. No electricity.

"Think, Thomas. Think." I hold my throbbing head between both hands. "I didn't see a cell phone in the purse, so she probably doesn't have one, what do you think?" I look down at Maggie, halfway expecting her to have Peggy's cell in her mouth. She's watching me anxiously but doesn't have what we need. "The power and landlines are most likely out at home, too, but I do have a cell phone, and I know it's charged up because I just used the thing." I head back towards the front door. "I mean, we have to get an ambulance here, so we have to get to a phone. It's that simple," I reason through the situation out loud. "We have to go back home for the cell."

I grab a brightly colored throw from a couch I pass and put it over Peggy's legs. "Peggy, if you can hear me, I want you to know I'm sorry for touching you in certain places, but it couldn't be helped. I'm going home to get my cell phone so I can call an ambulance to come get you," I tell her, speaking loudly. I check for the rise and fall of her chest and let out a sigh of relief, happy to see even this meager evidence that she's still with me.

"She'll be alright. It looks worse than it is," Bea reassures me again as I worry over the head wound that just will not stop bleeding. "You really can't do anything more than what you've already done, even if she is worse than she looks. You just need to call for an ambulance now."

"Okay, yes, you're right. Come on, Maggie, let's go." We step out onto the porch, closing the door behind us, and I gasp in shock at how much of the ground has been covered with hail in such a short time.

The yellow-green hue of the sky has taken on a scary neon quality and the air smells funny to me, almost like a dryer sheet.

What a weird thought to have in the middle of a tornado… that the air smells like a dryer sheet. The wind has picked up again, and now that I'm back outside, I hear the steady chugging of a freight train. "That's not a freight train, is it," I state more than ask Bea with dread.

"Hurry!" Bea yells. I shield the top of my head with my arms as we leave the safety of the porch to plunge ourselves into the pounding hail. I fix my gaze straight ahead to my own front door and tell myself it's nothing more than walking across the street. The hail covered ground is a lot harder than one might think to walk on, especially with no shoes, and I slip and fall to my knees a few times before even getting out of Peggy's yard. The sidewalk is an icy mess too, as is the street, and the hail on the smooth asphalt feels like marbles beneath my stockinged feet.

Maggie gets in front of me, looks backward beyond Peggy's house, and lets loose with a frenzy of barking. I risk taking a precious second to look in the same direction, and the bottom falls out of my stomach again.

I've never seen a tornado in real life, and my overworked brain latches onto the unimportant detail of how much darker the long funnel part of it is compared to the main cloud. All within a few seconds it snakes its way down to disappear behind a row of rooftops, climbs back up into the main cloud, then rockets back down to the ground with ferocious speed. It's in the vicinity of the town square, I gauge, which is only seven blocks away from us.

It's a disturbing, tremendously terrifying thing to be pummeled by hail while staring up at what could easily be your death. I'm paralyzed momentarily with the awesomeness of it all.

And then, with no warning, sheets of rain join the hail, the coldness of the water on my skin making me gasp.

Maggie bumps into the back of my legs with her head, urging me to stop gawking and get back to the house.

We skate-hop across the street and start up through my yard, my shirt whipping against me like the sails of a pirate ship. I slip and fall hard, flat onto my face this time, forehead banging into something sharp, nose and chin sinking into mounds of golf ball sized hail and wet, cold grass.

Good gravy, I'm spent. I lay here, too tired to move, and feel myself start to shiver. I'm going to close my eyes for just a minute, I think, too tired to even speak out loud to Bea.

Chapter 29

Maggie nudges me awake. She's pushing her muzzle into my face and neck and shoulder over and over again. Bea yells at me to get up, get up, get up!

I open my eyes, and for a few seconds I can't figure out why I'm so cold and wet. My hands clench beneath me and come away with ice and grass, which shouldn't be on my bed. But my bed shouldn't be cold and wet either.

Is it raining?

Where the heck *am* I?

I search around and find an ounce or two of strength deep inside. I use it to pull myself up to my knees, confused by how hard it is to do something so simple. Maggie presses her face into mine, and what's going on suddenly dawns on me.

I remember Peggy, and the blood, and the mission I'm on.

I don't even spare the tornado another glance. If it's about to bear down on me, I don't want to see it. I heave and shove and get myself onto my feet, and Maggie and I trudge slowly the rest of the way to my house.

"We need to get Maggie some steaks," I mumble to Bea. "Don't let me forget."

I stumble up to the steps of the porch and pause at the bottom, breathing deeply. Rain batters my face and drenches my eyes, but I can see that the screen door is still banging and smashing back and forth. Maggie pauses next to me, body pressed into mine, warily watching to make sure I don't pass out again. I run my hand across her wet head, grateful she's here. I don't even care that she's a dog.

Trash flies through the air around us, huge chunks, unidentifiable, smashing into anything in the way. Trees bend and bow almost to the ground, and thousands of leaves flutter around us, having been ripped off their limbs. A mailbox and its jaggedly broken wooden post skitter across my yard and right past me onto the porch, smashing into my shoulder with a red-hot searing pain. The name Pierce has been painted on the side, along with bluebirds.

Maggie prods me and my bogged-down brain whips into action yet again. I drag myself up the steps and manage to stand, using the railing as a crutch. I fall more than walk to the door and reach for the doorknob, relief flooding my brain as the latch clicks and the door opens.

I know actually getting inside the house doesn't guarantee the tornado won't get me, but all the same I feel like a little kid who pulls the covers over their head so they'll be safe from the monster hiding underneath the bed.

And then everything goes black.

Chapter 30

A wet, firm thing pushes into my cheek, ear, hair.

My arm moves, then my head, then a leg.

Things hurt.

My entire body hurts.

I don't want to move anymore, but the wet, firm thing keeps making me.

Chapter 31

"I'm calling 911!" a distant voice cuts through the blackness.

"Thomas!" a teary voice cries, this one close. "Thomas, can you hear me?"

Where's Bea? Why isn't Bea dealing with all these people.

"Here, let's do this," someone says with authority, and my head is shifted a little bit.

Pain thrashes around in my brain like water droplets in hot oil.

"Oh no! No, no, no!" the teary voice wails shrilly. "There's blood back here!"

Another voice, this one deeper, says hopefully, "Look, he's waking up I think!"

My eyes flutter, open, then close again.

Eyelids are such heavy things.

The distant voice says, "Yes, we need an ambulance! Two-five-seven Cottonwood Avenue. Thomas Sanders has been badly hurt." A pause, and then desperately, loudly, "No, but he's covered in blood and he's unconscious!"

A bossy voice commands, "Let me have that phone, hon." A pause, and then, "Who's speaking? Keith, this is Wilma Harper. You get someone over here to help Thomas or I'll personally see to it that your mama tans your hide." Another pause, and then, "The whole town's been hit by a tornado, Keith. You have to start rescuing people somewhere and I'm telling you you're going to start with Thomas Sanders!"

Chapter 32

"Wake up, Thomas. Wake up and look at me," the teary voice pleads, making me feel a little sad. Something soft touches my face.

I'm drained.

Every ounce of energy I had has been depleted.

Why do they want me to wake up when I'm so tired?

What I really want to do is sink back into the quiet I was just in before these loud, intruding voices stirred me awake. "Come on now, sweetie, you need to open your eyes. You've rested long enough," Bea instructs gently.

"That will do," the bossy voice says, adding, "he's sending paramedics in an SUV. All the ambulances are out, and I didn't want to wait."

Why does the bossy voice have to speak so loudly?

Someone takes my hand in theirs, and I can feel warm, wet skin pressed against my fingers.

A furry feeling touches my other hand. Maybe a blanket, or something.

That loud voice is still talking. It's interrupting my peace and quiet, and I feel annoyed about this. I'm definitely awake now, thanks to all this racket.

"Say something, Thomas, so they know you're not brain dead," Bea orders me, the gentleness of before replaced with a firmness I don't dare ignore.

"Too loud," I whisper, my voice rusty and unrecognizable, even to me.

"What? Hey, he just said something!" the deeper voice announces, then closer to my head he says, "Say again, buddy. We're all ears."

I clear my throat a little, notice bits of gritty stuff coating my mouth and tongue, and scowl at the disgustingness of it. "Talking… too loud."

Nervous, jittery laughter erupts on all sides around me. "Gawd's nightgown, if he's complaining, he's not going to die." The bossy voice says, and I recognize the bossy voice as Wilma.

Chapter 33

"Oh, thank God!" The teary voice starts to genuinely cry now, and I realize it is attached to the hand that's holding mine, which is attached to Jewels.

Now what on earth could be making Jewels cry like this?

"Is…Joe…hurt?" I manage to croak.

"I'm right here, Thomas," he says with tenderness. "I'm fine."

A soft, warm, wet something is bathing my arm. Maggie's slobbery tongue comes to mind, but I can't find the strength to reach for my hand sanitizer.

"You're starting to remember names, and that's great!" Bea says. "Now open up those baby blues, Thomas."

It takes gigantic effort on my part, but I do accomplish this with a painful moan. "There he is!" Joe says with amazement, his face hovering directly above mine, his dreadlocks tapping against my cheeks. Clockwise in a circle along with Joe are the upset and concerned faces of Wilma, Jewels, and Maggie.

I clear my throat again, sputter out a pathetic cough, and ask, "Can I have a drink?"

"You want whiskey? Or bourbon?" Wilma asks humorously.

"Wilma! My goodness…" Jewels rolls her eyes at Wilma and her face disappears from the circle above me, hopefully to fetch cold water. The urge to clean my sickeningly dirty mouth out has swiftly become overpoweringly important.

"Dude, you had us all scared," Joe tells me, and I don't care for the seriousness in his voice. I don't know what he's talking about, but I want him back to his usually lighthearted self.

"You sure did a silly thing going outside when it was so dangerous, Tommy," Wilma says, seriousness creeping into her voice now, too.

"Dangerous from what?" I ask, still foggy about what we're all doing down here on the floor.

"From the tornado, Thomas. Don't you remember?" Joe says, eyes bright with urgency. "A tornado blasted its way across town, right over our street!"

And just like that I remember the whole, dreadful, grueling afternoon.

Chapter 34

"I'm fine. I swear," I push up off the couch pillows with a grunt, cursing the uselessness of my left arm. The sling they shoved it into is driving me crazy, along with everything else.

"You're a lot of things, but fine isn't one of them," Rusty wisecracks.

"Let me tell you something," I point at him, but the quick movement makes angry muscles scream. I yank my arm back to my chest with a scowl. My face must say it all, because his voice softens.

"I get it, Thomas," he says. "It stinks. The whole day stinks." He takes another pillow from the end of the couch and eases it behind me. "You know, you should be focused on the good things that came out of today. The hospital said shock and exposure would have for sure killed your neighbor long before that gash on her head. You're her hero."

At the mention of Peggy and her family, my grouchiness dries up. "Yeah," I look away, momentarily out of words.

I don't feel like a hero at all.

"You ready for that pain pill?" he asks.

"I guess that's probably a good idea," I agree.

He goes to the kitchen and my mind races over the events of the last few hours for the millionth time.

From what they can figure out, just when I was opening my door a piece of vinyl siding blew across the porch and into my head. I was already in bad shape by that time, so I don't imagine it took much to knock me out. My body fell forward, half of me inside the house and half of me still on the porch.

Maggie, that incredible mutt, pulled me all the way inside the house. She even shoved my legs out of the way and pushed the door closed, which probably kept us both safe from more harm. When Joe, Jewels, and Wilma arrived, we're guessing maybe thirty minutes later, Maggie was lying beside me with her head on my chest, Wiggles on duty by my head.

That dog is more of a hero than I am. I'll personally see to it that she gets a month of filet mignon for her efforts today.

Once I was lucid, I told them about Peggy. Joe and Jewels sprinted over there, calling Wilma a few minutes later to say that she was unconscious, but at least alive. They stayed with her while Wilma and Maggie watched over me.

When young Keith finally got here, Wilma put something worse than the fear of God into him. I was adamant that he shouldn't lay a finger on me until he'd tended to Peggy, but Wilma had other ideas. For the first time in recorded history, when I genuinely begged Wilma to let me have my way about something, she listened.

Well, she compromised.

"You can have your cake both ways, Tommy," she'd said, eyes blazing. I guessed by that fractured phrase she meant we could come to an agreement, so we bartered. I allowed Keith to tape, bandage, glue, wrap, and secure any part of my body with a cut or bruise, and in return Wilma let Peggy take my place in his SUV.

At Wilma's insistence, Keith called us after a doctor had taken a look at Peggy. She had started to come to on the drive to the hospital, dizzy and disoriented, but according to Keith that was to be expected. She's now safely tucked into a hospital bed with an IV and a team of nurses. She'll need some time to recoup but should make it out of the whole thing just fine.

During the time Peggy and I were being seen to, Joe and Jewels had been on their phones calling everyone they could think of. A lot of the calls went unanswered, including the one to Sally. Joe pointed out that some cell towers were most likely down so we shouldn't assume the worst, which does sound logical. I guess we should just be grateful the Tacketts and the Harpers have working cells.

Rusty got ahold of Joe on his way to my house, desperate for news of me. He'd tried to call my cell and landline from the fairgrounds, and when I didn't answer either one, he got in his truck and drove as fast as the littered streets would allow.

Since I was refusing to let anyone take me to the hospital, Wilma had ordered Rusty to swing by her house to pick up some illegal drugs and come this way. Well, illegal in the sense that they were prescribed for Dan a couple months ago when he banged up one knee, but now I'm going to take them. Also ironic, considering it's Wilma. She told me in clear Wilma fashion that I would be taking these pain pills as instructed or she'd drag me by my sling to the hospital herself.

Once Rusty was here to babysit me, Wilma, Joe, Jewels, and Maggie loaded up what supplies they could find, like blankets and water bottles and whatever odds and ends the medicine cabinet held. They were meeting Dan and Scott at the diner to start forming groups of people. When I asked what the groups of people would do, Joe had smiled that hopelessly optimistic smile of his and replied, "Same thing you did, my man. Whatever it takes."

We haven't heard anything from them yet, but they've only been gone for a couple of hours.

Rusty brings me a cold glass of water and two pills. He sits down in the lazy boy, props his feet up, and sighs. "You ever see a tornado up close and personal before today?" he asks, leaning his head back and clasping his hands over his chest.

I lean back, too, stuffing the corner end of a pillow into the back of my neck. "No, never."

We sit quietly for a minute or two, and I'm a bit jealous of Wiggles' light snores. My racing mind won't shut up long enough for me to relax like that.

"My parents and I were in one a long, long time ago, back when all this was farmland," he says.

"I remember stories of that one," I say. "I was away at summer camp that year."

"You were already a prodigy by then," he recalls.

"I came out of the womb a prodigy," I reply.

"Uh huh," he closes his eyes, stretching his legs. "That's your take on it, anyway."

We sit quietly again. We've always been good at companionable silence.

I reposition my hips, grunting with pain.

Rusty's cell buzzes. "Hey," he says, listening for a few seconds, then directs a whisper to me that it's Palmer. He had been at the fairgrounds along with just about everyone else when the tornado hit, so we've known he was physically fine, but it's still good to hear his voice. "Hey, Palmer, I'm gonna put you on speaker so Thomas can hear, too."

"Hey, Thomas, I ran into Joe and Jewels. How are you feeling?" his strained and tired voice floats out of the phone.

"I'm tough. In a few days I won't even remember I had any trouble at all," I assure him. "Tell us about the town. We're stuck in here with no idea what's going on everywhere else."

"I heard one Red Cross worker say there were two tornados actually. Thomas, the one you faced was the biggest, longest lasting, and most damaging. The smaller one veered off to the east of downtown and mostly got houses, where the bigger one got more buildings and so on because it cut across the town square. But you know, any damage is too much," he hesitates, and now Rusty frowns at me. We're both wondering how bad the rest of his news is going to be.

"It sure is," I say just to fill the silence.

He draws in a shaky breath, then marches through a list of things he's seen. "Ido's got leaves and limbs, and just gobs of stuff all over his property. Can't even tell what it all is, really, but no harm done to the store. He said to tell you guys he's glad you're not dead, by the way."

Rusty laughs. "We can say the same about him."

"Alright, so the big tornado slammed diagonally right through the town square and kept on going as far as your house, we know. I'm not sure where it finally stopped. The diner lost the north wall, parts of the roof and a few windows. The town hall is in really bad shape. Rapturous Finds took a few hits, but I'd say it got the least damage out of that strip of businesses there. Every other building around the square is bad. Real bad. It's hard to see very well, you know, because the light is fading." He pauses. "My theater and apartment, the bistro, and that little art studio... are mostly gone," his voice trails off.

"Palmer," Rusty says gently.

Palmer draws in another shaky breath. "I needed to remodel anyway, you know? Those velvety curtains were so outdated," he exhales loudly, fighting to stay in control. "I feel so bad for poor Olive and Taffy, and all the others. And the people who are homeless now, you guys. There are so many people with nowhere to sleep."

"Hey, listen," Rusty rubs a hand over his face. "Here's what you're going to do. You've been out in this enough for one night, so you're gonna get back in your car and get your whiny rear end over to my house. The back door's unlocked, there's food in the fridge, and the spare bedroom is clean and ready for a guest. Just go on in." He looks me over, adding, "I'm going to hang out with this old geezer until he's ready to go to bed, and then I'll be home."

There's a few seconds of sniffles before he answers, voice thick. "Thanks, Rusty."

"Or come over here and watch a movie with us," I say. "You can still sleep at Rusty's house though. I don't let whiners stay overnight," I add with just the right amount of sting. I'm rewarded with half a laugh, and that's alright by me.

"If it's all the same, I think I'm ready to call it a night." He clears his throat, adding, "I sure am glad you guys are okay."

"Right back atcha, buddy. Go get some rest," Rusty says and disconnects.

"He's got insurance," I say. "The girls do too, right?"

Rusty nods slowly. "And as cliché as it sounds, I don't care half as much about their buildings as I do their bodies. Buildings we can fix. Bodies, well, you know," he sizes me up with a tired smile. "I reckon we both know how hard it is to fix a body after losing Hildy and Bea." He dabs at his eyes, clears his throat, and busies himself with the basket on the coffee table, hiding his face. "Why can't you keep the clicker out in plain view like everybody else, Thomas?" he grunts, tossing the random contents of the basket out onto the table until he locates the remote.

I reply accordingly to hide the fact that I see his tears. "I didn't get the memo telling me where you want me to keep it."

He turns the TV on, passing over the local news reports before stopping on his favorite old sitcom about people stranded on an island.

The laugh tracks become background noise and my thoughts drift to the things Rusty said.

Drywall, bricks, and baseboards *are* all just things that can be replaced. Palmer is sad, but he's not hurt. In fact, just about every one of the people I spend time with have ended up safe.

Rusty's cackling at the slapstick antics on the show. I look him over, noticing for the first time how laugh lines and wrinkles have etched themselves into his dark skin. The wiry black hair of his younger days has somehow turned salt and pepper gray. I've never realized until now how much he's changed since we met as kids.

"It's an illuminating thought, isn't it, Thomas, when you realize so much of what you value is fine. In a way, it makes today a little less awful, doesn't it," Bea says softly.

"Yes, I would agree with that," I answer.

Rusty turns his head when I speak, staring at the concentrated gaze I have aimed at him. "What?" he demands.

I smile. Of course, I'd never tell him the truth about what I've been thinking. "Bea says she thinks you've put on a few pounds."

"She did not say that!" He sits up straighter, pressing his hands against his stomach. "I'm fit as a fiddle."

"I've seen my fair share of fiddles, old man," I chuckle, leaving the rest of my sentence to his imagination.

If someone could just get in touch with Sally, I think I'd be able to completely relax.

Chapter 35

I was already awake when daylight washed over Cardinal Creek this morning, revealing a bright, clear blue sky. It also illuminated the destruction. I'm not easily upset, but the sight of my yard torn to shreds wasn't exactly an easy thing to see.

Determined to not sit around and have my joints stiffen up, I made Rusty swear that he and Palmer would pick me up on their way downtown. I might not be helpful, but I still want to see what's going on. Joe and Jewels never came home last night, but I suspect I'll find them around town hall since Palmer saw the Red Cross setting up stations there.

I fed Wigglesworth and left with the guys.

To say the roads are barely passable is an understatement. We had to turn around once because Evergreen Street was completely blocked by a garden shed with a tree rammed through it. It took us over half an hour to make the five-minute drive from my house to the diner.

Seeing it in this condition is hard. We crookedly park the car at the edge of the rubbish covered parking lot by Joe's truck and Wilma's SUV. We have to carefully pick our way over tree limbs, leaves, and a lot of unidentifiable wreckage to get to our destination, my injuries adding to our slow speed. We come out of the alley and into the town square, and the sight stops us dead in our tracks.

"It's like a scene from a disaster movie," Palmer says.

Rusty's sharp intake of breath matches my own feelings. I wasn't prepared for this...

As Palmer told us last night, there's not much left of the four strips of businesses that make up the boundaries of the town square. The town hall building itself is a mess, and the lush green lawn has disappeared under a carpet of tents, tables, emergency vehicles, and people.

So many people.

We walk into the fray, mouths open and eyes wide with shock.

"Heavens," Bea whispers.

The people are dirty and bedraggled, wearily standing in lines to get help with locating missing loved ones, housing assistance, food and water, and clothes. I spot Jewels at a table just a few yards away. "I'll catch up, guys. I'm going to check in with her," I tell them, pointing to Jewels.

When she looks up from the clipboard she's writing on and sees me, her sunshiny smile turns cloudy. "What on earth are you doing here?" she barks, handing her clipboard to the girl next to her. "Thomas Sanders, I swear, like I don't have enough to worry about!" She grabs me in a gentle but firm embrace, holding both sides of my face in her hands so she can look me over. "Your color is good. How are you? And don't hand me a pile of lies either!"

Her concern is touching, and for once not even annoying. "I'm in pain, but I suspect I will live. Wilma's drugs help a lot," I pat her affectionately, more than glad to see her and a little concerned about how tired she looks. "Where's Joe?"

She cycles through a huge amount of information and details in a few breathy sentences. Joe, Wilma, Dan, Scott, and so many others have spent all last night and this morning joining forces with Red Cross teams for recovery and rescue. The number of injured rises by the hour, she says, as well as the amount of homeless people stumbling around among the tents. Phones and electricity are out in over half the town. Sadly, there have even been three death reports from the trailer park on the northern edge of town, right where the largest tornado started.

"Isn't that where Sally and Hart live?" I ask, panic forming in my chest.

She exhales in relief. "Her husband had them at some stupid party up in Indy when the tornado hit. They got back late to find their entire trailer gone. No clothes, toys, nothing except the few items from the diaper bag. That jerk took one look at their ruined life and went into a rage," she chokes up.

I swear under my breath, instantly seeing red. "Hart?" I bite the question out.

"She hid from him," Jewels wipes her face. "She watched it all happen, so that's bad enough, but he didn't get to her.

I look up into the sky, wondering for all I'm worth how people like Sally's husband are allowed to exist. "I'll call the sheriff right now."

"No need. He said he was sick of being tied down, so he left. This time for good, she thinks, because he was headed to Arizona where some loser friend of his lives."

"Good riddance to that piece of—" I don't finish, but I'm pretty sure Jewels has been thinking the same about him, too. I look around at all the tents. "So, they're here somewhere?"

She nods, indicating a tent a few feet away. "I'm keeping them close. The shelter is full already, so I need to figure out what to do with them. As soon as things calm down I'll help her file for divorce, and she can finally be free for real."

"That's good, Jewels." I nod, mumbling, "Good thinking."

"Honey, I have an idea," Bea says.

"For once, I'm way ahead of you," I tell her. Jewels cocks her head curiously, so I explain. "Bea's had an idea, but for once I thought of it first," I smile. "What do you say we move them into those newly decorated rooms at the house?"

This time she starts crying in earnest. "Oh, Thomas!"

"I don't mean to be rude, Jewels, but there's no time for that. It's not only that I hate this crying stuff, but I just want to get them out of that tent and take them home," I pat her gently on the arm. "Okay?"

She nods, wipes her face again, and throws her arms around my neck. It hurts a whole lot, but I let it happen anyway. I hug her back with my good arm, making her gasp. "Thomas Sanders, you sweet, sweet old man, did you just hug me?"

"No, I did not," I snap. "I was losing my balance from your very badly timed embrace and had to steady myself."

She giggles, hiccups once, giggles again, and turns to say something to the gal at the table. We trudge through sad people to a sadder, well-worn tent. I see them right away. They're sitting on a sparse cot, feet folded up beneath legs, facing one another. Hart has Miss P clutched tightly against her chest and an open book lay across Sally's lap, unread.

The fresh black eye and angry red marks up and down Sally's arms and neck are worse than the other times. Hart's usually animated face is long and drawn. They both look weary.

It grips me right in the gut.

I hate everything about this.

Hart notices me first, jumping to her feet with a little cry and reaching for me. I slide my bad arm out of the darned sling and take her. She lays heavily against me, whispering in my ear, "The tomato broke our house, Gramps."

I feel a lot of emotions. And it's scary. Real scary.

I pull myself together because I know my level of scary doesn't compare to Hart's.

"I heard about that," I answer her, trying to keep my voice steady. Sally looks up at me with red rimmed, hollow eyes—no doubt in shock.

"Honey, we've got something to talk to you about," Jewels says, sitting down on the cot and taking Sally's hands in her own. "Thomas wants you and Hart to come stay with us."

"I don't—" Sally stutters, looking at Jewels, up to me, then back to Jewels, not understanding. "What?"

"You and Hart are welcome to come stay with us," Jewels says. "At Thomas' house."

She looks up at me again, blankly. I wonder for a second if that damnable husband of hers might have finally knocked all the sense out of her. "There's a bedroom and everything you can have," I say gently.

"Honey, look at me for a second," Jewels says, and Sally slowly turns back her way. "I think you're tired, and kind of in shock maybe, so it's probably hard to think. I understand, and it's okay. You can let us do the thinking for you right now, and tomorrow or the next day you'll feel better. For now, all you have to do is come home with us."

"Stay at your house." She repeats weakly, looking from Jewels back to me as understanding claws its way through her brain fog. Then she breaks into huge, gasping, gut-wrenching sobs that go on for long, grueling minutes.

Hart clenches me tighter but says nothing. That's okay with me. I don't know what to say either.

Eventually Sally's cries subside to a few whimpers. She stands up, swaying a bit, stammering, "I guess I thought maybe we could stay with Aunt Peggy, but I don't even know if she's okay."

The realization dawns on both Jewels and me at the same time that Sally doesn't know about my adventures with Peggy. I tell Sally a very abridged, loose version of what happened, leaving out as many of the terrifying details as I can. "The hospital says she's going to be back to baking in a few weeks. She's probably not ready for house guests, though, so you'd be better off to just come on home with us."

She sighs, shaking her head, still crying a little bit. "You just go around saving people all the time, don't you?"

"Absolutely not," I deny. "Never, in fact. It's not in the Code."

She looks me up and down, the tiniest gleam of the real Sally sparking in her eyes. "Sure, if you say so, Mr. Sanders." She brushes a finger against some of my bandages, frowning as she really notices how badly I'm hurt.

"Mommy, his name is Gramps!" Hart's muffled voice complains, and I pat her back.

"That's right, Hart. Get it right next time, will ya," I say to Sally. "Now come on. Let's find my chauffeurs and get the heck out of here."

Carrying Hart in my condition is possibly the hardest physical thing I've ever done, including hauling an unconscious Peggy to safety. We find Palmer and Rusty, but I let Jewels do the talking. If I speak now, they'll all know how much pain I'm in and try to take the small human from me, and neither one of us are ready for that yet.

Sally's pensive on the ride home, but at least the crying has dried up. She smiles a lot at me, and Hart, who is balanced on my lap. I hope it's because she knows she's safe now and will never be abused by a man again. Not as long as I'm around.

Chapter 36

I ease myself out of bed, so thirsty I feel like I could down a gallon of water. I glance at the clock, noting dryly that a mere twenty-four hours ago I was racing a tornado in my socks.

I head down the hall to the kitchen, slowly, muscles and bones on fire.

"You're feeling a lot worse," Bea observes.

"I overdid it this morning, I'll admit it," I tell her. "I just need a good meal."

"Or an exam by a doctor," she mumbles.

"Don't start, honey, okay?" I say tiredly. "You know how hard it is for me to go to those places."

When Rusty and Palmer dropped me, Sally, and Hart off earlier today I was bone weary. It was all I could do to drag myself to my room and collapse onto the bed. I gave Sally extremely firm orders to eat, rest, play, and do whatever they wanted to do with a promise of swift and angry retaliation if I find out she disobeyed. I wanted her to feel at home, but I didn't have the energy to stay awake and make sure she did.

Hart had cheered up considerably once she realized she was going to live with us, which had helped Sally to relax a bit more. There will be hard moments ahead for them both, I suppose, but for now I feel like the odds are pretty good they'll eventually be alright.

I hear male voices as I hobble into the kitchen, laughing inwardly at the sight of Old Brimstone and Joe hunkered together over a map. Joe leaps out of his chair and throws his arms around me, carefully, but enthusiastically. "Thomas, dude, you are *the man*!"

"There certainly have been rumors that I am *a* man," I laugh, "but no conclusive evidence that shows I am *the* man," I hold as still as possible, so he won't know how much pain he's causing, rolling my eyes at Bob. He shakes his head with sympathy, and I swear it makes him look like a regular human.

"Don't be coy. You know what you're doing for Sally and little Hart is amazing," Joe insists, finally releasing me.

I slump down at the table, exhaling heavily. "No, amazing would be an icy cold glass of water," I tell him. "And maybe a couple of Wilma's famous pills?"

"You got it," he bellows, swinging into action.

"Are Sally and Hart managing okay?" I ask. "Where are they?"

"Asleep downstairs," Joe says. "They took showers, turned on some cartoons, and zonked out on our couch."

"I was thinking they should take Bea's suite. What do you think?" I suggest.

"They can have the basement if they want it," he offers.

"I figured it might be faster and easier to not move you and Jewels," I smile wryly.

"Probably true," he hands me a glass of water and two pain pills, which I greedily swallow.

"Thomas, it's good to see you up and about," Bob says with genuine warmth. "Quite a couple of days we've had."

"You can say that again. How are your people doing?"

"It's hard to tell. Phones and power are down here and there, so no one has a good idea yet of how bad it all is. The Red Cross thinks it could be another day or two before we get some comprehensive figures," he answers.

"There's a lot of bad, but there's also a lot of good," Joe chimes in.

"Check this out. Maggie's helped find, like, how many, Bob? Over thirty people I think it was?"

"Someone said her human count was up to forty-one when I left about an hour ago," Bob answers. "Watching her and Wilma work is nothing short of miraculous."

After the way Maggie helped me yesterday with Peggy, I would believe it if they told me she has been rebuilding the diner with her own two paws. At this point I'd likely vote for Maggie to be president. "What have they been up to?"

"They walk up and down every street, pausing in front of each house or building. Maggie does a quick inspection, and if she thinks someone might be inside she tells Wilma. They have a whole system using Maggie's talk buttons, so she can actually answer questions. The Red Cross guys and volunteers from town follow along with them and prioritize houses depending on what Maggie says is going on," Joe sits down with us again, admiration in his voice. "Wilma says the pooch hasn't been wrong one time."

I shake my head in awe. "That's really something. Who could have imagined a talking rescue dog would save the day."

Joe elbows Bob with a laugh. "I bet Balaam's donkey would've liked to have a few of those buttons, too,"

Bob throws his head back and out comes an honest to goodness belly laugh. I didn't know he was capable of anything that might be linked to humor. "Balaam would have gotten the message faster maybe," Bob hoots.

"I probably won't care, but what are you guys talking about?" I ask.

"Oh, sorry, dude," Joe cracks up. "Pastor humor. It's a great story from the Old Testament about a talking donkey that saves his owner's butt."

"Oh, you're talking about fairy tales again," I tease him.

He laughs along but says, "Sure, sure, I get it. Maggie talks, and you're down with that being reality, but if it comes out of the Bible it's probably a fairytale."

I drain my glass and hand it back to him for more. "Well, I can see Maggie with my own eyes."

"Doubting Thomas," Bob quips, laughing almost as hard at this as he did the other joke I didn't get.

I narrow my eyes at Joe, who can't stop his own laughter. "A dude named Thomas who needed tangible proof to believe in Jesus," he supplies.

"Naturally," I scowl.

"Maggie does seem like a fairytale," Bob says to me. "Or some kind of an animal pied piper. Along with a bunch of humans, she's also alerted rescuers to almost a hundred misplaced pets."

"I didn't even think about animals," I admit.

"We finally had to force her and Wilma to go home, eat, and rest. This one, too," Bob says, indicating Joe with a nod of his head. "We have rotating teams of volunteers working with the Red Cross, so there's still a rescue effort going on, but the A team needed a break."

"Yeah, I'm good now. A hot shower and a two-hour nap fixed me up," Joe says, and I believe him. Him and Hart share the same boundless exuberance. "Jewels is still asleep, but I bet she'll be up soon."

"What's all this then?" I ask, motioning at their map.

"We're trying to get some kind of organized list of who's missing or unaccounted for and which houses have been checked," Joe explains, turning the map so I can see red marks. "And trying to decide where to go next. We're going to head down to Tulip and Daisy I think," he looks questioningly at Bob.

"Right, to meet up with a group from my congregation," Bob confirms.

"Your church people are going to meet up with Joe?" I ask, amazed.

Bob's face flushes. "Yeah, I haven't exactly had a chance to speak to the church as a whole yet since, you know, the big reconciliation," he laughs self-consciously. "I've had to do some creative explaining in light of this, but I'll be making a public apology and setting things right as soon as I get the chance."

"Dude, I keep telling you that's not necessary. We're cool." Joe pats his shoulder. "You just lead by example, man. No big public speeches are needed."

"If the speech is made in *my* church, how would you stop me?" Bob asks with a teasing tone, and remarkably, Joe bursts into laughter.

I never thought I'd see the day Bob Frazier would be sitting at my kitchen table, teasing Joe Tackett. Not in a million years.

"Before you two start holding hands and singing Kumbaya, how about one of you rustle me up a sandwich. I'm starving, but I'm also too old and banged up to do anything but go sit in front of the television and rot my brain," I say.

Joe howls. "We'll do you one better. Some ladies from Bob's church went over to Clarksville and bought a ton of food to divvy up between us rescuers. All we need to do is heat it up. I've got lasagna, burgers, and a pound of gourmet mac and cheese I grabbed with Hart in mind." He winks.

"Is that so?" impressed yet again, I look at Bob approvingly, but he shrugs.

"I'm trying to get things right," he says with so much humiliation it makes him seem like a human for the second time today. I could get used to this.

"Bob," I say, injecting every available ounce of sincerity I can find into my words, "I am proud of you."

He looks down at the table, but he's smiling.

Such weird times we are in.

Voices float up from the stairs, the basement door pops open, and a small human wearing an adult-sized tee shirt explodes into the kitchen. She scans the room and makes a beeline for me, flopping onto my lap with about as much grace as a baby seal. Pain courses through me, but it's almost worth it to see the sorrow from this morning has left her face.

"Gramps! Did you know there's a whole 'nother house if you go frew that door?" Wonderment makes her eyes bright. Is it possible she doesn't know what a basement is?

"What, you mean like with a yard and fence and driveway?" I ask incredulously.

"No!" she busts a gut. "Like with rooms and furniture and a tv!"

"Oh, yes, I think Joe told me about that," I nod sincerely.

Sally emerges into the kitchen looking clean and refreshed. "Hey, everyone," she greets us before gently removing Hart from my lap. "Little love, remember what I said about sitting on Gramps? We have to be careful with him because he's got so many ouchies from helping Auntie Peg."

Hart cocks her head to one side, scrutinizing the evidence of my battles yesterday. "He doesn't look so good, does he?" she reaches up to softly touch the bandage above my left eye. "You better get some candy, Gramps. That'll help."

"This is exactly why I moved them in here," I tell Joe and Bob. "So, I would have some allies to eat decent food with!"

Chapter 37

The high-pitched squeal Hart reserves for Wiggles and Maggie echoes down the hall and into my bedroom. "She loves those dogs," I say to Bea.

"Of course she does," Bea answers. "They love her, too."

When I told Sally I wanted them to use Bea's Suite, it took fifteen minutes to explain why we call it that. Sally made all kinds of favorable noises over the decor, so Jewels launched into a long, long explanation of the whys and whats of the decorating process.

I wandered off with Hart, whose only comment about the bathroom was to ask where I keep the tubby time toys. We decided the bed was perfect for jumping, laughing when all the silly pillows tumbled to the floor. She collected most of the figurines and do-dads from the family room and held a meeting with them on the steamer trunk turned coffee table.

"We need to get these two shopping," I tell Bea, thinking I should add bathtub toys to the growing list.

I've already made Sally start a list of things they have to have, like a car seat and so on. She tried to argue with me about buying her more stuff, saying there were all kinds of charities she could go to, but

I eventually wore her down. I think I've picked up a few tricks on manipulation over the years from Wilma.

"If you'd have told me six months ago that we'd have a house full of people, I'd have laughed in your face and called you crazy," I chuckle.

"Yes, you would have," Bea agrees, "but I'm really happy with a house full of people. The question is, are *you* happy about it?"

I think about this.

Sally and Hart are safe. There's no more abusive man in their lives. They aren't homeless, they have plenty of food, and I mean to see to it that their future is secure.

"Yes, I am happy," I tell her. And I'm serious.

I inch my foot into a slipper, wincing as a sharp pain shoots down my leg. I pick the arm sling up, hold onto it for a few seconds, then drop it back onto the bed with a hostile flip. I hate this stupid thing.

"Wonder what might happen if you actually followed doctor's orders?" Bea asks reprovingly.

"Hah!" I exclaim, "that kid Wilma bamboozled into treating me was an EMT. I haven't received any doctor's orders; therefore, I don't have any doctor's orders to follow."

I decide a piping hot cup of coffee is going to fix what ails me and head to the kitchen. Once again, I am filled with gratefulness that our house has electricity. A strong cup of coffee first thing in the morning is hard to live without.

The girls are milling around in the kitchen, Sally making toast and Jewels talking on her cell. I pull a chair out from the table, holding onto the back of it for support, and look across the room at Hart. She's wallowing around on the floor with Wiggles, her small form drowning in one of Jewels' tee shirts.

"Morning, Gramps," Sally says. "Coffee?" Hart can't control the whole town, but she's made sure anyone who frequents this house calls me Gramps.

"You've read Gramps' mind," I say.

Sally's brows draw together as I cautiously get myself into the kitchen chair. "When she's off the phone, I want to talk to you ladies about getting some shopping done today," I say.

"O-k-a-y," Sally says, drawing the word out. She brings me a hot cup of coffee, a glass of water, and the last of Wilma's illegal drugs.

"Thanks," I say, throwing the pills down with a sigh of relief.

Jewels ends her call and joins us at the table, dropping a kiss on my forehead as she passes. "Joe says hi. He's over at the apartments just north of the town hall with a group that's trying to salvage stuff."

"Stuff?" I ask, absently rubbing my tender shoulder.

"Yeah, a lot of people are finding things they can keep with just a little cleaning up, so that's great," she replies, face clouding over with concern. She looks at Sally, who gives her a subtle nod, although she's really bad at being subtle because I see the whole exchange.

I sense I better change the subject. "So, how's about we get started on that shopping list today?"

"Exactly how much pain are you in?" Sally demands, bypassing my words with finality.

"As I was saying about the shopping," I start again, "I think you should head into Indy or something. Maybe hit a mall?"

Sally rolls her eyes knowingly at Jewels. "Avoidance. Just like I said."

"Hart is running around in adult tee shirts," I point out.

"You're moving way too carefully to be feeling as good as you say you are," Jewels says. "We think you need to be seen by a doctor today. One of us can take you."

"We should have taken him yesterday," Sally tells her.

"I don't have a doctor, so that's not going to happen," I shake my head sternly. "Along with clothes, Hart will need toys and books and other things small humans think about."

Sally roars, "No doctor? For Pete's sake, Thomas, how do you not have a doctor at your age?"

"That's no problem. We'll just take him to the ER. That might be best, now that I think of it, because he might need x-rays," Jewels says to Sally.

"He holds his lower back a lot when he's trying to stand up," Sally tells her with an emphatic nod. "An x-ray might be a good idea,"

I look in amazement at these two women who are speaking about me as if I'm *not* sitting right here with them. "And *you* need your *own* clothes," I speak louder, aiming my words at Sally.

"What are your plans for the day?" Jewels asks Sally. "I'm due at the Red Cross in about two hours."

"Hart and I can take him," Sally instantly volunteers.

I wave my hands at them both, cringing at the effort. "Hello! I'm sitting right here!"

"You see that?" Jewels clucks her tongue with disapproval at me but continues speaking only to Sally. "He can't even raise his arm without making a face, and he's not wearing his sling *again*!"

"I am not going to any hospital," I say firmly.

There's a knock, and the back door swings open. A shirtless, smiling Kenny comes in. "Hey hey, gals and guys."

"Kenny!" Jewels greets him warmly. "Have you met Sally yet?"

"What's shakin'," he says to Sally, coming to stand by me.

"Good to see you," I greet him. "How about a cup of coffee?"

"No thanks, man. I'm on my way to see if Joe needs anything, but I heard about how you wrestled a tornado and wanted to see for myself if you're okay," he's looking at me like I'm one of the elderly people he keeps tabs on.

"As a matter of fact, he's in bad shape but stubbornly won't admit to it," Jewels says. I glare at her, and she makes a face at me. "We were just discussing how to arrange his trip to the ER today when you came in."

He surveys my blacks and blues before taking their side. "You do look pretty banged up, brother. You'll be glad you went."

"I'm fine. There's nothing a doctor can prescribe that would be better than a few days of peace and quiet," I tell him irritably.

"Why don't you stand up then and show Kenny how easy it is for you to effortlessly glide around the house," Sally challenges me.

"I will not," I say, busily rearranging the things on the table.

Hart gallops into the kitchen and throws herself onto my lap. To say this awakens millions of angry nerve receptors is a gross understatement. I draw in a sharp breath and flatten both my hands on the tabletop. "Gramps, this man isn't wearing a shirt," she tells me, oblivious to my pain.

However, Sally and Jewels aren't oblivious. Sally pulls Hart onto her lap and introduces her to Kenny, but Jewels covers one of my hands with her own. She looks at me pleadingly, and I nod. "I will go," I say quietly, "but I have a condition."

"Let's hear it," she says.

"I want them to go do some serious shopping. I mean it. I'll have Rusty take me to the hospital and I will even have a darned x-ray, but I want to come home to a house full of their new things," I tell her.

"You have a deal," she eagerly agrees, then announces out loud to Sally, "Okay, if you and Hart go on a shopping trip, he's agreed to let Rusty come take him to the ER."

"Truly?" Sally asks me. "Because you're really starting to worry us."

"Truly," I reply. "But you don't come home unless you've spent a small fortune, is that clear? And get this child some toys. Whatever she thinks is fun."

She scrunches up her forehead and I can tell she's going to start talking about bargains and charity again. "I mean, we can always find..."

"No deal unless you do it my way," I say flatly. "Copious amounts of clothes and toys. And don't forget to pick up bath toys. She was talking about having toys for the tub."

She leans toward me, touching my arm. "I'll find a way to say thank you for all of this," she agrees, but she's still as stubborn as I am. "I'll try to pay you back."

I grimace. "Please don't. The money isn't doing me any good and doesn't matter anymore without Bea here to spend it."

"But Thomas..." she hesitates, so I talk over her.

"I'm being completely serious for once. You want to make me happy, you go shopping."

She smiles, likely still a little uncomfortable with the idea of spending more of my riches but nods in agreement anyway.

"I'm going right past the hospital, so I'll drop you off," Kenny offers.

Rusty is called and arrangements are made for Kenny to deliver me to him at the doors of the ER. Hart showers me with more painful hugs at the mention of getting Miss P a playmate. Sally tucks the keys to my car and my credit card into her pocket and I pat her on the head like a good little girl.

Everyone is happy except me.

"They don't understand about the hospital," Bea says. "You could try talking to them about your feelings, you know."

"That's what you're here for," I say.

CHAPTER 38

Smells are funny things. They can be good. Great, even.

Smells can also be every bit as bad as they are good. They can transport you right back in time to a place when nothing was right, like how the fresh paint in my house only reminded me of losing Bea.

"Let's get this over with as fast as we can," I say to Rusty. "I hate the smell of a hospital."

"Keep your shirt on," he says. He thinks it's hilarious that Kenny rarely wears a shirt and hasn't stopped cracking jokes about it since I got dropped off.

He's found a wheelchair for me. I'm simultaneously glad I don't have to walk but angry that I can't. "Just don't dilly dally. It's like torture being in here," I say, grasping the armrests.

We check in at the desk and are given a mountain of paperwork with about a hundred dumb questions to answer, which only adds to the foulness of my attitude. I snap several times at him as he fills them out, but he doesn't bat an eye at me. His patience irks me, too, and then I start to feel guilty about taking my frustrations out on him.

I know I won't feel better until I get out of this cursed building, and I tell him as much when he comes back from the check-in desk.

It's the closest thing to an apology I can muster up. Besides, he's always been good at knowing what I'm thinking.

"Come on, old man," he says, grabbing the handles of my wheelchair. "Let's go for a walk."

"I don't want to go for a walk!" I exclaim in surprise. "What if they call my name while we're gone?"

"They won't. Because you're not in critical condition you've been shoved way down on the list. They said it's going to be at least two hours, if not three," he stops in front of the elevator and punches the button.

"Well, I guess that's fair," I grumble, "but I still don't want to walk around."

When the elevator opens, he says, "While we're in here, I'm going to talk and you're going to listen," he pushes me inside and the door closes. "When we get off the elevator we won't speak of it again."

"I don't need a lecture, Rusty," I say.

He pushes the button for the fourth floor. "You and I have spent way too many hard, terrible days in this hospital watching our wives die. If anyone gets why you hate hospitals, it would be me."

I grunt in acknowledgement. He's right, of course.

"Today, I want you to see that not every visit to a hospital is going to end up in tragedy. I'm taking you upstairs to see that neighbor of yours because what's happening with her is good. Time to stop letting the past steal all your fun, buddy boy. You've got too much of a good thing going to be afraid." The bell dings, the doors open, and he wheels me out into the hallway. "And that's the last thing I'll say about it."

True to his word, he doesn't say anything else as he pushes me to Peggy Ackerman's room. The door is halfway open, so Rusty pokes his head inside to ask if she is up for a visit. "You better get yourself in here so I can put a face to your voice," comes her reply, loud and clear.

He turns to look at me, saying, "I won't force you. Come in if you want to," and disappears inside the room.

It doesn't take long to figure out that Rusty, Sally, and Peggy have been talking quite a bit amongst themselves on the phone over the last three days. Their comfortable, familiar manner with one another quickly gets under my skin. It only takes a couple of big belly laughs from Peggy for me to realize I want to be in there, too.

For one thing, I did save this woman's life. I should be the one making her laugh, if you ask me.

And I knew her long before Rusty. For heaven's sake, I'm the one who's talked to her at least six times in person, and he hasn't even met her before today!

And wasn't it *my* idea to send Joe over to handle her trash cans every week! Rusty sure wasn't worried about her household chores.

It's very irritating, actually, listening to them yuk it up like long lost pals.

I cough once, heaving myself out of the wheelchair, and push into the room, awkwardly saying, "Uh, hello again, Peggy."

She's almost as pale as the white sheets she's wrapped in. There's a bandage across her forehead and wires disappearing into her hospital gown. However, when she sees me enter the room, her face lights up with pleasure and she yells, "Thomas Sanders, you're here!"

"Not by choice," I laugh, then clarify, "what I mean is, I was kind of forced by that wayward niece of yours to come let a doctor take a look at me." I throw a smirk at Rusty, who looks too pleased with my presence in the room for my liking. "So, I told this one we should come see how you're holding up while we wait."

"Oh, yeah, that's exactly how it happened," Rusty chuckles.

She reaches out with a hand, but when I move to shake it, she pulls me in for a hug. "You're, uh, surprisingly strong for such a small, old woman," I detangle myself from her, trying not to react to the pain her hug is causing. She pushes a lock of snowy white hair aside and wipes at a tear.

"I have so much to be grateful for, Thomas, because of you," she's violently patting my hand now, which jostles little aching jolts up to my shoulder. "I'm happy I'm not dead, but what I can't thank you enough for is taking such good care of Sally and Hart! Imagine my surprise when she calls me to tell me they're safe, and away from that poor excuse for a man, and living across the street from me with the famous Thomas Sanders." She beams at me and Rusty. "You know, I've thought long and hard about hiring a thug to make that creep go away permanently," she says with a wicked little laugh.

"I'm glad the tornado got the job done for you then," I say, amused at the image of this sweet little old lady in a transaction with some street thug.

"But Thomas, what a small world we live in!" she says.

"There have been some interesting twists," I admit.

She gestures to Rusty. "And, what a good friend you've got in this one."

I look him over, and he smiles innocently at me. "That's what he keeps telling me," I say.

She is right about him being a good friend though.

Rusty asks her, "When are you busting out of this joint?"

"The one with the white coat says I can go home as soon as my blood pressure behaves," she says.

We stay with her for another few minutes, talking about what's happening in the town. When her eyes start to look tired, Rusty gives me a knowing nod that I return. "Miss Peggy, we're going to head off in search of coffee, but we'll keep tabs on you," he tells her. "Can't wait to chauffeur you home."

She takes my hands in hers one more time, squeezing them tight. "A thousand pies wouldn't be enough to say thanks."

"We can start with one a week and go from there," I suggest, and she laughs softly, sinking back into her pillows. I think we wore her out.

I shuffle out to the wheelchair, plopping down into it with a sigh. "I'll say it, but only in private and only once," I tell Rusty.

"Say what?" he asks, wheeling me back to the elevator.

"It was smart to bring me up here to see her. You were right about good things happening at the hospital." I admit. "Not often are you right, but today, you were."

He laughs, pushing me into the elevator. "Can I get this in writing?"

"No, you can't." I answer. "Just be glad I said anything at all."

"Did seeing her cheer you up?" he asks.

I tilt my head, thinking about it as the elevator takes us down to the cafeteria. "I think seeing her was a reality check I needed to have. I get what you're trying to tell me, although I still don't like hospitals."

"That's alright then," he touches my shoulder softly. "I don't expect you to change overnight. I just want you to get that fear under control."

The cafeteria is busy but not crowded. As soon as the savory smells reach my nose, I realize how hungry I've gotten. "You suppose we have time to eat?"

Rusty glances at his watch. "Yeah, we've only been gone for about forty minutes."

"I wonder if the food's any good," I say, peering up at the menu board.

"Well, lookie here," a voice says. We turn to find Averitt and Harold standing in line behind us.

"What are you two doing here?" I ask, looking them over for injuries. As far as I can tell, they don't have any.

"It's Thursday," Averitt says by way of explanation.

"What's Thursday got to do with it?" I ask, puzzled.

"I don't like baked spaghetti all that much," Harold says, eyes twinkling. "Not the way I like catfish anyways."

"And I don't much care for pizza like I do catfish," Averitt says, shooting Harold a wink.

I look up at Rusty. "What are they talking about?"

He shakes his head. "Don't know."

"We've got the Bench on Monday and Wednesday, you see, so it has to be Thursday," Harold says reasonably.

"Can't do Tuesday," Averitt says, fiddling with his pipe. "Harold doesn't like baked spaghetti."

"Friday won't work since Averitt don't like pizza," Harold says patiently, like he's talking to a child.

"Let me try to get some sense out of them," Rusty repositions his baseball cap, asking, "Averitt, Harold, are you here today to eat in the cafeteria?"

Averitt points his pipe at Rusty. "This one's thinking clearly."

"And what are you here to eat exactly?" Rusty asks.

"The catfish, nat'rally," Harold answers. "Best thing this cafeteria fixes all week long."

"That's what we've been saying," Averitt replies smoothly. "They serve it every Thursday, so that's the day we come."

I exhale loudly. "For the love of Pete."

Harold laughs, saying, "Aww, come on, Thomas, we were just having some fun with you."

"It's been a little too serious around town these last few days," Averitt says. "'Bout time somebody made a joke or two."

I look up into their wrinkled faces, humor rooting out my aggravation. "You know, fellas, I think I'd agree with you on that."

Harold lays a hand on my shoulder, saying, "We heard all about your heroics with that neighbor of yours. Averitt 'n' me would consider it a pleasure to buy a guy like you a catfish meal."

"Will you listen to that?" I exclaim, giving Rusty a meaningful stare. "Someone's finally showing me a little respect."

"When have I been disrespectful to you?" he laughs dubiously.

"Only every time you open your mouth!" I say.

"You can pay for your own meal," Averitt tells Rusty dryly.

That's how we end up eating the catfish lunch special at the hospital on a Thursday.

Chapter 39

"Puppy?" I repeat after Wilma.

"Yep! I was as shocked as you when she jumped into the creek, which was more like a small river at that time, and came out with Mable," she says proudly.

Until today, I've only seen Wilma for a few minutes here and there since the tornado. She's been talking non-stop for almost two hours, desperately trying to make up for lost time. It will probably surprise you as much as it does me that I'm not all that bothered by it.

"You named her Mable?" I chuckle. "I guess it goes along well with Maggie, since you'll be keeping her."

She hands me two folded shirts to add to my box. "No, I didn't give her that name. It's always been Mable," she informs me. "And although I'd be happy to live with another dog, Maggie says Mable will live with someone else once she's healthy again," she replies, shaking out her empty trash bag. "Well, that's it for this one. Why don't you walk over there and tell them we need more."

"Alrighty," I say amicably.

Ever since my visit to the ER a couple days ago, the dictator-driven females in my life have seen to it that I'm not allowed to do anything for myself. (Aside from things you do in the bathroom, I should add. I had to draw a line somewhere!) I didn't end up in a cast, but I do have some bruised ribs, strained muscles, and various other small injuries. The doctor said I need rest and physical therapy, and of course Rusty blabbered that to everyone. That's what led to the babysitting.

I just couldn't sit around for another whole day. I'm growing moss on my appendages from all the inactivity. I insisted on coming to town with the Tacketts this morning. For twenty minutes they lectured me on the perils of overdoing it, as if I'm not the one who feels all the aches and pains. Joe threatened to bring me home and chain me to the couch if I exert myself, and Jewels would only relent if I promised to stay close to Wilma all day.

Mike has a big event going on this afternoon and desperately needs volunteers, which I think helped my cause. Donations of clothes, toys, and household items have flooded in from so many sources he can hardly keep up with the sorting. There are stations set up all around the grassy area in front of the thrift store, some of them sorting through items and some of them giving the sorted items away.

Jewels deposited me at a station with Wilma, issuing the strictest orders that I'm only allowed to deliver the occasional message between tables if I need to stretch my legs. "If I catch you picking up one of these boxes, Thomas, you'll be going home for the day. Understood?" she'd said with so much intensity I was too scared to tease her about it.

The joke's on her anyway. I couldn't pick up one of these boxes if Peggy Ackerman's life depended on it. They may not realize it, but I *am* taking my recovery seriously now, mainly because I'm sick of hurting.

Mike's situated at a table with Jewels. "We've finished with all the bags we had," I report.

"How are you feeling?" Jewels touches my forehead.

I swat her hand away with a snort. "Tornado fighting doesn't give you a fever, Jewels."

"Here. Sit down for a minute and rest," Mike taps an empty chair next to him.

"I'm not tired," I insist, but take a seat all the same.

A tired-looking middle-aged woman approaches us, and Jewels jumps into servant mode.

With Jewels distracted, Mike asks me in hushed tones, "How are you for real?"

"I think I'm in a reasonable amount of pain considering what I've been through, but it was a lot harder for me to sit around the house like an invalid than it was for me to help Wilma sort clothes," I answer truthfully.

"You'll do the right thing and go home if you get too tired, right?" he asks, and I nod in agreement. "Good enough for me. Sally and Jewels are worried sick about you, but if they see you use some common sense they'll lighten up on the bodyguard detail."

"Is that what they're calling it?" I laugh.

"Yeah, they think your body needs guarded from your stubbornness," he laughs along with me.

"Message received," I give him a little salute. "I'll exercise good judgement."

Another family comes up to the table, taking Mike's attention off me. I look around, pursing my lips in disappointment at the condition of the buildings. The thrift store fared really well compared to others, Palmer's theater got the worst, and it sounds like the bistro falls somewhere in the middle.

Speaking of the bistro, Olive and Taffy are winding their way through the crowds toward us. They see me at the same time and start frantically waving. "Look at you!" Olive squeals, moving to hug me.

"Yes, I know, black and blue *are* my colors," I bat my lashes at them.

Taffy leans in to plant a kiss on my cheek. "Do you ever stop making jokes?"

"That would be dull, wouldn't it? Tell me about the bistro. What's going on there?"

"It could certainly be a whole lot worse, so we aren't complaining," Olive says.

"Well, we are complaining a little," Taffy says glumly. "But only to ourselves."

"Did you know our whole strip mall is owned by the same man?" Olive says. When I shake my head no, she continues, "We found out he's in the market to sell. It's just too much for him to deal with all the insurance and damages and all. I know it's only four stores, but that could be a nice investment for us if we could manage it."

"You'd own the bistro and be landladies?" I smile. "That's an excellent way to build up a nest egg."

"We're still in the early stages, you know, talking with the bank and all that painful stuff," Olive smiles faintly, looking off to the right. "And trying to deal with other painful things," she murmurs more to herself than to us.

Taffy follows her gaze and frowns. "Oh, terrific. Exactly what we need."

Frank Norris and his nutjob lackeys are walking around the crowded town square, stuffing flyers into the hands of people. They look to me like they're in the mood for a fight.

"What's he doing?" I ask.

"He's on a mission," Olive says venomously, her sunny features replaced with a dark storm of emotions. She reaches into a pocket, pulls out a wrinkled sheet of paper, and hands it to me wordlessly.

I scan it briefly and my own face grows dark. "A march for pureness?"

"Yeah," Olive says bitterly. "Gotta cleanse this town, or else God might do something worse to us. You'll see that the tornado was a warning for us to get our act together, if you read further down."

Joe emerges from the crowd with an overflowing box, setting it down with a thump on the ground next to my chair. "Have you seen this garbage?" I ask, shoving the paper at him.

He glances around at our faces, takes the flyer, and reads. He doesn't adopt our anger, but he does look concerned. "Wow," he breathes out, eyes flickering to Olive and Taffy. "Lots of sins to account for around here, huh."

"He's lost his nutjob mind, Joe," I say hotly.

"Let's see here... tattoos, homosexuality, and... oh, I knew he wasn't super thrilled with me, or you guys," he nods at the girls, "But I had no idea he doesn't like *you*, Thomas."

"What are you talking about?" I demand. "My name better not be on that paper."

Joe frowns, rubbing his palm across his cheek. "Yep, although you're not as high on the list as we are. See?" he holds the flyer down for me to read, pointing to one word close to the bottom.

"Gluttony!" I read aloud.

Believe it or not, first Taffy and then Olive start to laugh. It only takes me a few seconds to realize he's flipped the mood on an ugly situation in typical positive Joe Tackett style, and knowing that makes me laugh, too.

"Who else made it on the list?" Olive asks.

"Hmm," he runs a finger down the paper. "Oh, I know! Who do we know that's a busybody!"

"Wilma!" we laugh together.

"What?" she says from behind us. The fact that she walks up at this precise moment makes us laugh even harder, but it just sets her off. "Here I am thinking you fell down or hurt yourself so I better come see what I can do to help, and I find you over here having yourself a little party. You know there's work to be done, don't you?" she lectures me.

"Uh oh, now we can add 'lazy' to gluttony!" Taffy howls.

Joe scans the paper, delighted when he finds laziness. "We've got ourselves a record holder! Thomas wins with two!"

I've laughed enough to make my ribcage sing, so I wave my hands at them. "You have to stop..."

"What in the name of Rhett Butler is going on here?" Wilma asks crankily, hands on hips. The absurdity of it all hurls me into another bout of painful laughing.

Joe, still snorting, drapes his arm around her shoulders. "Oh, Wilma, you beautiful creature. We're laughing at Frank Norris, not you. He's handing these out today," he holds the paper at an angle she can see.

She studies the paper for a minute, murmuring to herself an occasional, "for the love of..." and "lascivious behavior? What the heck does that mean?" before she finishes and pushes his hand and the flyer away. "Frank did this?"

"He did," Olive tells her.

"Well, isn't he a big fat swine trampling on pearls nobody even threw to him," she says huffily.

This wakes up the laughter in Joe, Olive and Taffy all over again, and I get the feeling they understand more of what she said than I do. "I assume you don't approve of Frank's antics if you're calling him a pig?" I ask, grinning.

Wilma, giggling, pats my hand affectionately. "Tommy, I think Frank is a first class nutjob who wants to smash all the good things this town has to offer." She gathers the girls into a fierce group hug, adding, "Don't you two give that buffoon another thought."

"I wish he would just leave everyone alone," Olive says.

"Or at least keep his toxic views to himself," Wilma suggests.

I look at Joe. He's watching Frank again, his expression sober. "I don't have the feeling he's going to do either of those things," he says softly.

Chapter 40

It's a cloudy, dismally gray day. Not a tornado kind of gray, though, just to be clear about that. A black, stormy sky might have kept me at home. The inside of your house doesn't seem dull at all when there might be a tornado outside.

The light gray skies of this morning didn't stop me from coming back to the town square to help Mike. We didn't come close to giving away all the donated supplies we had yesterday, and from what Jewels could tell there are plenty more people who still need things, so we came back bright and early.

Well, as much as Jewels will let me be back at it, anyway. I'm still under strict orders to take it easy. I'd never admit such things to Wilma, or Jewels, or Sally, but I'm running out of steam a lot faster right now than normal. Yesterday I was happy to get out of the house for a while, but between you, me, Bea, and the curtains, I don't think I've ever been so glad to get back in my bed.

For the first time since the night of the tornado, the rescue groups have called it quits. They think they've searched every house and building in the path of destruction, and all the names on the list of missing persons have been crossed off. The Red Cross and sheriff's office have issued a collective statement. Injuries are in the hundreds, but the death toll is still below twenty with hopes of it staying there. I've been more than lucky to not know anyone who died, and I'm grateful. I've had enough of this emotional stuff to last two lifetimes.

They're estimating property damages to be in the millions and the town cleanup might take months. I'm starting to see more groups of people out working in yards and streets, neighbor helping neighbor. It's heartwarming, really, and I'm not even being sarcastic.

Most of the regular gang have split themselves into groups between helping here with Mike's project or going over to the Harpers' to see exactly what needs to be done to get the diner open again. There's been some talk of Olive and Taffy bringing their food truck over for a Munch Box/Bistro combination, a way they can both make some money. Wilma's very excited because she's always dreamt of having her own ice cream truck.

"What about this thing?" Ido asks, holding up an unidentifiable contraption.

I glance over at it. "I have no idea what that is."

"Maybe a baby bottle warmer?" Palmer proposes.

"It's a bottle *sterilizer*. Huge difference," Rusty corrects him.

Palmer makes a face at him, gently tossing the contraption into a box with bottles. "Thanks, Mary Poppins."

"He's right," Sally chimes in. "That's a sterilizer, and it gets way, way hotter than a bottle warmer, so there is a huge difference."

"Whose side are you on?" Palmer asks with mock indignation.

"The right side, obviously," she barks back, laughing at his dramatic face.

Maggie, Wiggles, and Hart are playing on a blanket behind our table. Hart raises her head long enough to say, "My mommy's always right," drawing more laughs.

"So, Sally, what's it like to live in the same house as the famous Thomas Sanders? Tell us all the weird things he does when he thinks no one is looking," Rusty says.

"Finally, an interesting topic," Ido mumbles.

"He's stricken with bouts of flatulence that will burn the bark off a petrified tree," she replies smoothly, as if she was expecting the question.

"This man? He threw a fit when I accidentally let one slip out at the poker game last month!" Rusty roars accusingly.

"She's full of nonsense," I defend myself with an easy smile.

"Is that so?" she scoffs. "Explain then how I was awakened in the middle of the night by a rumble so loud I could feel the vibrations in my chest."

"That was the small human who sleeps with you," I answer, unruffled.

"I guess I can tell them about..." she says behind her hand, "*the other thing*."

Palmer hands me a stack of clothes. "She's about to spill the beans, Mr. Sanders."

I put the clothes into my box with a calm smile. "There are no beans. I am beanless."

Sally raises a critical brow, saying, "Oh, they already know about your teddy bear pajamas?"

Hart's head pops up over the tabletop like a meerkat. "Gramps, I never sawed your teddy bear jammies."

Amid the laughter, I see Rusty admiringly elbow Sally, who smiles back at him. "She needs more kind men in her life," Bea observes approvingly.

Joe and Bob amble up, arms bursting with more bags. "Friends," Joe greets us cheerily. "I'd say this might be the last of the clothes."

"Joey!" Hart screams. Joe grabs her up and twirls her around in his arms in a maneuver he calls "baby airplane."

"Hi, everyone," Bob says, dropping his bags with a thump. "Mike, sorry I haven't caught up with you before now. How'd your congregation fare? Your building?"

Mike's surprise at Bob's genuine concern couldn't be more palpable if it was displayed on a gold-plated tray. "Uh, hey there, Bob. I've got several families with injuries, but nothing fatal. As you can see, the store isn't bad, and the shelter wasn't in the line of damage at all, but the church isn't going to be usable for a long time."

"No fatalities is great," Bob says, nodding soberly. "I heard Val's building took a beating, too."

"It did," Mike replies. "So weird how tornados act, isn't it? Val's church was just about ruined while Lee's church only had some mild roof damage, but they're just a couple blocks apart."

"Yeah, I've been hearing some incredible stories," Ido says. "Lisa Pyle was showing pictures around the store the other day. The morning after the tornado they found a vacuum, a bicycle frame, and eighteen dead fish on the roof of their barn. Well, the fish were on the roof, but the vacuum was in the hayloft and the bike frame was inserted in the barn wall, like a 3D sculpture or something."

"That is simply fascinating," Sally says, eyes wide.

"The twister picked up Herschel Weller's old Ford that hasn't run in years and put it down inside Sam Dalton's used car lot," Rusty laughs. "Course, it wasn't ideal. The nice little Chevy that's underneath it won't be worth selling anymore, what with its hood and roof crushed in by the weight of the Ford."

"I guess I would believe just about anything," I say. "And if I never have another opportunity to hear anything else like this for the rest of my life, I would be over the moon about it."

"I'll drink to that," Joe upends a bottle of water, draining it in one long gulp.

"Well, uh, Mike," Bob says a little hesitantly, "I've been thinking..."

"What's up?" Mike asks cautiously.

"My building isn't hurt at all, which of course you probably know since your women's shelter is nearby and that part of town was completely missed." He falters nervously for a few seconds, and I swear everyone leans in closer to hear what he might say next.

"Sure, that's right. We were both lucky there," Mike says.

Bob exhales, looking around at all the expectant faces. "I was just thinking that maybe you and Val might want to use my building until you're back on your feet again. We could divide up the weekend, take turns using the facilities, maybe even get a basketball league started," he hesitates, smiling sheepishly. "Well, the Lord has blessed us with a bigger facility than we really need."

I've told Mike about Bob's transformation, but I don't think it really made sense to him until just now. It did take me a long time to see the good side of Old Brimstone, after all. Mike waits to answer just long enough to make it awkward before breaking into a giant smile. "Bob, that's just the nicest thing I've heard all day," he reaches out for Bob's hand. "I will absolutely take you up on that offer, and I'll call Val later today and talk to him."

Bob releases the breath he's been holding and vigorously shakes hands with Mike. "No need! I'll call him myself."

Joe's grinning so wide I'm afraid his cheeks are going to pop his ears right off his head. "Community, man. Sweet, sweet community."

"It's been amazing, hasn't it, to see how everyone helps everyone else," Sally says.

"Almost everyone anyway," Palmer says, pulling one of Frank's flyers out of a pocket. "I've seen about a thousand of these things all over town. Makes me sick."

Most of us recognize what he's holding, but Bob and Ido move closer to read it. "I do wish there was some way to calm him down," Rusty says. "He's getting on everyone's nerves with all this."

"Unfortunately, he's not breaking any laws so there's not really much that can be done," Palmer adds. "I might have mentioned it to the sheriff, and that's what he said."

"Wilma says maybe he'll stop getting in our faces if we ignore him," Sally says, writing on the side of her box with a sharpie.

"That's never worked with Wilma," I laugh.

Bob finishes reading and looks at Joe, frowning.

"Yeah, dark, isn't it," Joe says sadly.

"Things like this are," Bob looks embarrassed. "Wow."

"Wow is right," Sally says. "I'm taking this over to the men's table. Hart, you want to come with me?"

The small human comes around to my chair and takes hold of my shirt collar. She's been working hard on not jostling me, although she does forget from time to time. "I'll just stay here and keep an eye on Gramps."

"What's that supposed to mean?" I ask gruffly, poking her in the belly.

"Eema says you don't act like an old man should," she replies in that confident way little people have that makes us all bubble over with laughter.

"I've got to get going actually. Lots of plans to be made! I'll walk that way with you," Bob offers, saying goodbye to the rest of us.

Once they're gone and Hart has returned to her toys and Maggie, Joe slaps his hands on the tabletop. "Well? What do you guys think of *that*!" He lays a whole year's worth of emphasis on *that*.

"My mind is about as blown as it can be," Mike confesses.

"I won't say I told you so," Joe says before bellowing, "But I told you so! He's a great guy, isn't he?"

"You tell them I was always in Bob's corner," Bea insists.

"You were never in Bob's corner," I refute with a snort.

"What's that?" Mike asks.

"I'm hungry. Big surprise from the glutton, I know," I say. "Who's got food?"

CHAPTER 41

This is the first closeup look I've had at the diner since the tornado. In spite of the broken windows shrouded in plastic and the checkered floor being littered with storm residue, physically standing inside still feels as comfortable to me as my favorite pair of slippers.

The Harpers and their peppy band of volunteers worked for two days to clear the parking lot and deal with the building's exterior issues, which Scott happily reports weren't as bad as they had initially thought. It might be a couple of weeks before they can open the inside for business, he thinks, but he's in better shape than most.

"Tommy, just think how green with envy Edda Mae's going to be when she hears about my famous Maggie!" Wilma stacks another trash bag on the pile by my seat as she scurries by. I've been given hot soapy water and several tubs of silverware and cooking utensils to clean. She says if I'm going to hang around, I need to be useful but won't let me do anything she deems "physically out of bounds."

Life in Indiana, a very popular morning show, has caught wind of Maggie's involvement in all the rescue efforts. They contacted Wilma, asking if they could come out to the Munch Box tomorrow to do a whole feel-good piece on her. Give the people something positive in light of the last week, they said.

Now, I need you to pause with me here and just think about what this means. Wilma Harper, attention seeker and glory hog, is going to be interviewed about her beloved Maggie for a television program that airs in thousands of homes. For her, this might be the next best thing to uncovering a criminal mastermind's plot to overthrow the president. Attention on Maggie is still attention on Wilma, after all.

Thank goodness the interview is tomorrow. If I had to navigate more than twenty-four hours of television star Wilma, I might end up in the hospital with Peggy.

"You'll really show her this time," I play along because it's just easier.

"I've got to figure out what bandanas we're going to wear," she says, more to herself than me.

Activity in the parking lot catches my eye. "Joe and Kenny are here with the food truck," she squints through the flapping sheets of plastic with a gasp, and rushes outside.

Scott comes cautiously into the dining room, asking, "Did Mom go somewhere?"

"She's outside with Joe and Kenny looking at the food truck." I answer, standing up. My aches and pains are slightly less awful today, but if I sit for too long I get stiff.

"Cool. I'm going out to the dumpster, so tell her I'll be right back if she asks," he says with a peculiar expression.

"Alright," I nod, clueless about why he'd tell either of us he's going to the dumpster.

Wilma, Joe, and Kenny come inside, all three of them talking at once. "Walking tacos would be good," Joe says, looking at Kenny.

"Yeah, with corn chips," Kenny adds, waving at me.

"And we've got Scott's grill, too," Wilma's saying.

"Hey there, Sanders," Kenny looks me over. "You still look like you just walked out of a car crash."

I tap his naked, tattooed chest with a spatula, saying, "And you still look like a painted carnival worker."

"Fair enough," he laughs.

"Boys, can you grab these bags and help me take them out back," Wilma says, motioning to the group of trash bags. "Not you, Tommy," she barks when I reach for one.

"Okay, okay, calm down," I chuckle. "I can at least open the door." I lead the way, propping the door open with my good shoulder and blinking in the bright sunshine.

"Gawd's nightgown!" Wilma shrieks. She'd been right behind me, but now she's shooting down the stairs with her hands in the air. Joe and Kenny drop their bags, and the three of us run after her, assuming there's a rabid bear attacking someone by the way she's carrying on.

Standing just ten feet away, only partially hidden by the shed and dumpster, is Scott Harper with a dark-haired woman wrapped in his arms, her lips attached to his. As we converge on them like a wild-eyed band of lunatics, Scott releases the lady, and they turn toward us.

I see the reason Wilma feels the need to shriek.

Scott is kissing Denise Brothens.

Edda Mae's daughter.

His mom's arch nemesis.

Wilma's gesturing wildly, saying things like, "Is Edda Mae blackmailing you?" and "Are you trying to send me to an early grave, son?"

Poor Denise looks horrified, and Scott looks like a kid whose mom just caught him with his hand in the cookie jar. I feel a touch on my shoulder, relieved to see Dan. "Good gravy," I say, eyes wide. "The unthinkable has happened!"

"Stay close. I might need back up," he says with a grimace.

He places himself just slightly between her and the kids, saying, "Alright, let's get a deep breath here."

"Dan, he's kissing the wrong woman!" Wilma wails at him. Denise covers her mouth with one hand, which sends Wilma into another round of hysterics. I spot the engagement ring just as Wilma cries out, "Michael Scott Harper, what is that on her hand?!"

"Mom!" Scott roars loudly, commanding the situation with an

authority I didn't realize anyone could muster up with Wilma. He definitely has no intention of letting go of the cookie, I guess.

She blinks rapidly a time or two, then says, "What?"

"Stop yelling so we can talk," he pleads, and then with more patience than she probably deserves, adds, "please."

"Babe, let's calm down and hear what they have to say," Dan says soothingly, placing his hands on her shoulders.

"We've wanted to tell you for a long time," Scott says.

"A long time?" Wilma repeats, although to her credit she's lowered her voice an octave. "Exactly how long have you been sneaking around behind our backs?"

Scott smiles warmly at Denise as he answers, "Seventeen months, three weeks, and five days."

"Unbelievable," Wilma throws her hands up again.

Joe clears his throat. "We're like flies on a wall here. Anybody want to let us in on what's happening?"

"I guess you wouldn't have met," Scott laughs dryly, making introductions. Denise smiles haltingly at all of us except Wilma. I expect she's terrified to make eye contact with the fiery redheaded monstrosity in front of her.

Joe grabs Denise in a one-armed hug, pounding Scott on the shoulder with the other hand. "Denise! So good to meet you! And congratulations, too!"

"Hey hey, Scott's fee-AHN-say," Kenny shakes her hand.

"Traitor," Wilma snaps at Joe. "Don't tell me you approve of this horrible betrayal."

"You're being kinda harsh, don't you think?" Joe says.

"Hang back, cowboy. I got this," Kenny lays a hand against Joe's chest as if to hold him off. "Miss Wilma, I've got a few questions."

Joe and I exchange humorous looks, overwhelmingly curious to see Kenny try to corral Wilma.

"I suppose you want to know what Edda Mae's done to my boy, too. She's holding something over his head, I just know it," Wilma says.

Kenny's brows draw together. "Who?"

"My greatest enemy, that's who!" she asserts, jabbing an accusing finger toward Denise, "and this one's mother."

He scrutinizes her for a few seconds, puzzled. "Why in the heck would I care about Denise's mother?"

"Because, Kenneth," Wilma splutters, clearly baffled that she has to explain this to him. "Because they are related. Mother and daughter."

He laughs, but not like he thinks she's funny. More like he thinks she's crazy.

Which, to be fair, sometimes she is.

"First of all, your boy ain't marrying the mama, and the daughter definitely ain't responsible for whatever it is the mama did to make you mad," he says with such firm wisdom Wilma actually snaps her mouth shut. "Now, what's the one thing you've been trying to do all summer?"

She blinks a couple times before answering, "Find a wife for Scott. But it has to be a suitable wife, not the daughter of a treacherous—"

"Stop!" he cuts her off sharply. "She's suitable if Scott says she's suitable. It will be Scott she lives her life with, builds a home with, pays the bills with, so it's Scott who has to choose her, not you."

Wilma looks to Dan for help. "I agree with him, babe," Dan tells her steadily.

"So, you wanted Scott to find a wife, and now he has one. Super," Kenny smiles pleasantly at her. "Okay, dude, I'm gonna put you in the hot seat for a minute, if that's cool," he asks Scott.

Scott chuckles, "It's cool. Go for it."

"Are you and this little lady planning on having children at some point in your married lives?" he asks, brow arched.

"We sure are," Scott smiles down at Denise, who answers with a bright smile of her own.

Kenny holds his hands out to Wilma as if he's giving her a precious gift. "So, all you've wanted is for Scott to get married and to have kids so you can be a Grammie, and that's exactly what you've got."

Wilma sniffs, begrudgingly nodding her head once at this logic.

"Dude, are you happy?" he asks Scott.

"Deliriously," Scott answers.

"Little lady?" he asks Denise.

"Fairy tale happy ending happy," she replies.

"Dan?" Kenny asks.

"If Scott's happy, I'm happy," Dan says.

Kenny beams at Wilma, pleased with his own logic. "So, Wilma dear, I can't see any reason why you shouldn't be dancing a happy little Grammie dance right about now. Seems to me like the entire Hooper family got what it wanted."

"Harper," Joe corrects him, grinning.

"Whatever," Kenny dismisses his error.

Wilma sighs heavily, running her fingers through her ponytail. "If I'm nice to you, do I have to be nice to *her,* too?" she asks Denise.

"I doubt she'll want to be nice to you any more than you want to be nice to her," Denise answers. "But I'd love it if you and I could get to be friends."

Wilma considers this for a few seconds. "Does Edda Mae know about," she gestures at them, "this?"

"Not yet. Truthfully, we planned to tell you first," Denise says.

This obviously strokes the right part of Wilma's ego, because she offers a half smile. It's brief though, as she thinks of something else. She narrows her eyes at Denise again. "How do you feel about dogs?"

"I have two pitties—a girl named Riley and a boy named Hunter," Denise answers.

"Like Riley Hunter from the cop show *Homicide Hunter*?" Wilma gasps, delight illuminating her features.

"Exactly like Riley Hunter," Denise confirms.

Wilma grabs Denise by one hand, pulling her toward the back door. "Let me make you a glass of sweet tea and we can talk about last week's episode. I think Holly's neighbor is going to end up involved in nefarious dealings."

Denise follows along, casting a surprised glance at us before disappearing into the diner.

"I think I might be in shock. Did that..." Scott looks around, baffled, "did that really just happen?"

"You don't know the great service you've just done us all, young man," Dan says to Kenny. "Around here, you eat free from now on."

"Nah, dude, it's all good. She just needed things explained in plain English, that's all."

"I'm still super confused. Why does Wilma have such hard feelings for Edda Mae?" Joe asks.

Dan, Scott, and I laugh long and hard at this. "They were best friends all through school, right up until their senior year. Something happened to cause a huge fight, and they haven't spoken a civil word since," Dan explains.

"The real kicker though?" Scott says through laughter, "the super funny thing about the entire ordeal is that Mom can't remember what they fought about."

Chapter 42

Sally takes the seat belt from my good hand and pulls it across my chest, snapping it into the lock. "There ya go, Gramps."

Right now, we're headed to the Munch Box for Wilma and Maggie's fifteen minutes of fame, Sally at the wheel. I've decided to give in to the constant pampering because it's a lot more work to assert my independence than it is to be spoiled. My aches and pains are diminishing, but slowly, so I handed the car over to Sally.

It's been eight days since the storm. The power is back on, the cell phone towers have been replaced, and all the people who were homeless now have a place to at least stay, if not a permanent home. Most of the streets have been cleared and traffic is moving smoothly, more or less. The setup Wilma and the bistro ladies have with the food truck is one of only four damaged businesses that have been able to reopen, but the town celebrates every small thing.

Sally and Hart have settled in at my house. True to her word, the day I went to the hospital she bought enough clothes, toys, and equipment to start a small daycare. I've had to move baby dolls and building blocks from every surface of the couch before I can sit down, but it's fine. Having the small human around has kept me laughing.

Peggy's being released tomorrow or the next day. I assumed she might want Sally and Hart to live with her, but Sally asked me if I would mind if they stayed put at my place. She didn't offer up an explanation, and I certainly didn't want to open that emotional can of worms.

I told her they can stay as long as they can stand me and left it at that.

"Will Mable be there today?" Hart asks from the massive piece of equipment that dominates my back seat. This so-called car seat looks like something out of a space shuttle.

"Yep, that's the plan," Sally replies. Hart likes a lot of things, but she's particularly excited about the puppy Maggie pulled out of the creek.

"Look at this crowd," I gawk at the people gathered in the busy diner parking lot. I think the hundred or so who showed up today is an encouraging sign of the town's resilience.

The food truck is parked to the north of the diner. Joe's handing food through the open window, Olive and Taffy are behind him cooking, and a shirtless Kenny is leaning against the side door smiling. He salutes me with his can of beer, and I tip my baseball cap at him. Old Brimstone and Neil are standing near Kenny, both of them smiling and happy.

Dan, Scott, and Denise are huddled together in front of the diner, Denise holding a squirmy, fat puppy. This must be the famous Mable everyone is so thrilled with. Wilma is slightly in front of her family, preening for the camera operator, her face glowing bright enough to give the hot sun a run for its money.

Sally loads Hart and all her necessary things into a little red wagon and we trudge through the gravel toward the edge of the crowd where Rusty, Ido, Palmer, and Val are standing. "Have we missed anything?" I ask.

Ido looks at his watch. "Should start in a few minutes."

"I don't know if they understand what they're getting themselves into by putting Wilma on live TV," Rusty kids.

"Once bitten, twice shy," Sally's soft laugh takes the sting out of her words.

"I think they look sweet," Val says. Wilma and Maggie are wearing mustard-colored bandanas, but the red superhero cape draped around the mutt's neck takes the cake.

Mike and Lee push through the still growing crowd to get to us, shaking hands all around. Stories of the most recent recovery and clean up are shared.

"We're going to get started on the wiring in the theater tomorrow," Palmer says. Much like everyone else, he's spent all his time helping others and ignoring his own problems. "The insurance company is dragging its feet, so Rusty and I are just going to dig in."

"Anything to get him out of my house," Rusty says.

"I'm a blessing and you know it," Palmer laughs. "Without me there you'd starve." Among other things, it turns out, Palmer happens to be an excellent cook.

"Funny how we both seem to be getting fed very well in spite of the diner being out of commission," I say to Rusty, flashing Sally an amused smile. With her living at my house, I have plenty of things to eat that don't involve Jewels' disgusting quinoa or kale.

"Hey, I think they're starting," Lee points. The reporter's microphone is poised between his face and Wilma's. I can barely hear him over the murmuring of the crowd, but I don't need anyone to tell me how Wilma's doing.

The camera operator turns to the crowd and holds a finger to her lips, and the crowd quiets down considerably. The interview starts with the reporter asking Wilma about how Maggie came to live with her and Dan, and Wilma explains how Maggie showed up one day at her door. He asks Wilma another question I can't quite make out. Wilma says something to Maggie, and she hops into action. I hadn't noticed it before, but Wilma's got Maggie's talking buttons set up on a short stand. Maggie slaps a paw down on a button and the crowd goes wild at whatever she says.

"I can't hear a thing," Sally whispers to me.

"Go up closer." I suggest. "Hart is fine here with me."

"You sure?" she asks, and I give her a little shove. She tells Hart where she's going before worming her way to the front.

"When the TV people leave, can I play with Maggie and Mable?" Hart wants to know.

"Oh, I imagine we can work that out," I tell her.

She returns to her toys, and I go back to watching Wilma, but because I can only hear bits and pieces of what's being said, my mind wanders to what I might be having for lunch. I heard rumors of Scott firing up his grill after the interview, so maybe a burger is in my future. Joe explained the whole concept of a walking taco, the food truck's newest menu addition, but I'm not convinced I want to eat something out of a corn chip bag. What I could really go for is a nice big slice of Wilma's peach cobbler with a dollop of vanilla bean ice cream.

I'm pulled back into reality by a disturbance on the lawn just past the south side of the diner parking lot. I can't quite make out who all is involved, but there's no mistaking the sour face and stern stance of Frank Norris.

That nutjob better not spoil Wilma's big day.

"Don't look now, but Mr. Plays Well With Others is here," I say quietly to the guys.

"I was hoping we'd have one stinkin' day without him," Rusty growls.

"Maybe we should go see what he's doing," Val says. Mike and Lee think it's a good idea and go with him to Frank's side of the parking lot.

"How much longer will Maggie's interview last, do you think?" Palmer asks.

"Another ten minutes maybe?" I guess. "Let's hope they finish before Frank gets out a bullhorn."

The three non-nutjob preachers return grim faced. "It's more of the usual stuff. God's wrath and the sins of the nations," Mike grunts. "At least he's not too close to the fun."

"Maybe I should go see him in private. Try to talk him out of doing all this protesting and marching," Lee reasons. "I'm older, after all, so maybe he'll show me a little respect."

I disagree. "If you ask me, you'd just be spinning your wheels."

The crowd in front of us erupts in cheers and clapping. I look up to see Dan smiling, Wilma hugging Maggie, and Maggie's rear wiggling hard enough to almost knock Wilma over. Scott and Denise are waving one of the puppy's paws at the crowd.

The reporter has turned his back to them and is speaking directly to the camera, which sure looks like a sign-off to me.

"The Lord has a message for you today!" Frank booms, and sure enough, he's using his bull horn. "If we turn away from the raging sin in our town, He will bless us. If we continue on like we are, the destruction of the tornado will only be the beginning."

"I'm getting Hart out of here," I say.

"Let me help you," Palmer takes the handle of the wagon and we head to the opposite side of the parking lot toward the food truck.

Rusty pulls his cell phone out, dials, then begins speaking to what could only be the sheriff. "Can't you make him stop? Say he's inciting a riot or being a public nuisance or anything to get him to be quiet? He's ruining everyone's fun," he pauses to listen before saying, "Thanks Ryan. We appreciate it."

"Well?" I ask.

"He's going to at least make him put the bullhorn away," he says. "As long as he's on public land and he's not doing anything wrong, he can't shut him down," he shakes his head in displeasure.

The Harpers and their canines have moved to the food truck where the crowd is gathering around them like an impromptu street party. Wilma's living it up, shaking hands and talking to a long line of people who want to have their picture taken with Maggie. We deliver Hart to Sally, who's chatting it up with Denise.

Frank's still droning on but I'm glad to see that, in spite of the bullhorn, no one is paying much attention to him. In fact, his group of minions looks smaller than usual today.

Palmer snaps his finger. "I have a great idea," he disappears into the food truck, and a minute later cheery music blasts out of its speakers, dwarfing the sound of Frank's voice down to a light murmur.

Palmer returns to me and Rusty, grinning proudly. "Nice work, eh?"

"Well done," Rusty claps him on the shoulder.

"Lemonade and cookies for everyone!" Olive calls out from the food truck window, and the crowd cheers again.

Joe hops down from the truck with a tray, throwing me a Joe Tackett grin and a cookie. "Community, man. I love it."

"To community," I say, biting into a sugar cookie.

Chapter 43

"Look, how about I slip you a twenty and we can just part ways as friends," I grunt as the physical therapist mauls my arm.

"Mr. Sanders, I'm far more concerned with Mrs. Tackett's wrath than I am a bribe from you," the young man says dryly.

"Yes, that's what you keep saying, but I am the boss of myself, you see," I tell him. He stretches my injured arm up above my head, which does happen to feel incredible, but he doesn't need to hear that.

"You might think you're the boss of you," he says, rotating my arm around like a windmill, "but I know Mrs. Tackett is the boss of *me*, and I'm just following orders."

Sally strolls in through the back door with Hart in her arms. "Hey, Gramps!"

My torturer greets Sally with far more enthusiasm than he's ever shown me. "Hi, Sally!"

"Oh, hey," she answers superficially without mirroring any of his enthusiasm. He doesn't stand a chance.

Hart wriggles free from her mom and rushes to me. "Gramps, you ready to play now?"

"Sure am, kid," I pull Hart onto my lap. "You can see yourself out, right?" I say pleasantly to my torturer. He exhales with annoyance but has gotten to know me well enough in the last three weeks to realize that Hart takes precedence over all else. He packs up, throws a last longing look at Sally, and makes his exit.

"Time for a snacky-snack?" Hart suggests.

"What would you like?" Sally asks.

"Gramps can get it for me," Hart insists.

"We've got this," I say, noticing Sally pluck at her dress shirt. "You go get changed before those fancy school clothes give you hives."

She pulls at her collar with a scowl. "Well, that would be nice, actually. Thank you."

I carry Hart to the countertop by the fridge. "How was your big day with Ido?"

A couple of weeks ago, Sally started taking classes in an accelerated business program. She has class on Tuesday and Thursday mornings for a couple hours, and Ido usually keeps Hart busy at his grocery store.

"He's cheeky," she replies, quoting our favorite cartoon featuring a family of dogs from Australia. Cheeky is the latest phrase she and I have been overusing, much to her mom's chagrin.

"Why is he cheeky?" I ask, holding up an applesauce pouch and a container of blueberries for her inspection.

"Cause he made me eat broccoli before I could have ice cream," she complains. "You better tell him that's not how we do it."

"Oof," I reply, "that *is* cheeky." She taps the blueberries, so the applesauce goes back into the fridge. "I could have a word with him," I say seriously.

"What word would it be?" she asks.

"Flippity-floppity?" I suggest.

"Gramps," she giggles. "That's two words!"

"When it's my day to have you, we'll eat our ice cream first. How's that?" I offer, carrying her and her blueberries to the family room. We settle down on the couch and I turn on our dog cartoon.

Rusty asked me a couple of weeks ago if I thought Sally would want a job at his shop handling the front desk. I told him she didn't need one and he accused me of holding her back. It's not that I want her to hide away, but it's only been four or five weeks since the tornado. I don't want her getting overwhelmed.

She walked in on our argument, slightly miffed at the way we were planning her future without consulting her. The end of that discussion found her enrolling in business school, which had been her dream, and working part time for Rusty, which she said would be an excellent experience. I only got my way on two points—that she would allow me to pay for her school and that Hart would not be going to daycare. I insisted Hart's too young and valuable to be shuffled off to an institution when there's so many of us who can look after her. We've arranged a nice little system where she's entertained, and—let's face it—spoiled, by me, Wilma, and whoever else is free.

Sally, dressed in comfy clothes, joins us in front of the TV, sitting in the La-Z- Boy. She taps a finger against the side of her cell phone nervously.

"Something wrong?" I ask.

She glances at her phone, avoiding eye contact with me. "Uh, no, nothing."

"There's some leftover meatloaf if you're hungry," I say.

The way she answers is curious, not to mention suspicious. "Wilma just messaged me. She's coming over."

I examine her expression closely. Something's up, and I bet you a hundred bucks I won't like it.

As if she'd been just outside waiting to hear her name, there's one brief knock on the kitchen door before it swings open, and Wilma explodes through it. She's clutching a pink gym bag, and Maggie trots in after her carrying a tiny pink dog bed. Lastly, the puppy waddles in.

"Eema! You finally brought Mable!" Hart screams, rushing to the dogs.

Wiggles, who had been peacefully napping in his bed, jumps up and joins the party. The small human sits on the floor and the puppy launches herself into Hart's lap.

Wilma places the little pink bed down next to the recently vacated big one and then starts unloading the bag onto the coffee table. "This is her night-night blankie. I'd keep track of it or else you'll have a rough time getting her to sleep."

"Wilma," her name pours out of me like lava, "what do you think you're doing?"

She keeps unpacking, explaining each item as she goes. "These are her favorite treats, and this is her kibble. Half a cup in the morning and again in the late afternoon."

"I don't need these things or this information though, Wilma," I start putting the items back in the bag, "because she isn't staying here today."

"No, she's not staying here *today*, Tommy," Wilma agrees, unpacking each item again.

I look at Sally, who is studying her fingernails like a pirate would a treasure map. She's in on this, obviously.

"Okay, let's stop taking all this junk out then," I say, shoving the kibble back in.

"You're going to need it, Tommy," Wilma says patiently, "because she's staying here *forever*."

My mouth is open, but I can't come up with any words that can be said in front of Hart.

"Now, darling, before you fly off the handle, why don't you take a few seconds to think about this," Bea says. "Hart obviously loves the puppy. Why not let her stay to make Hart happy?"

I look down at the small human wallowing among the three dogs. She's a very, very happy small human right now. "Because I don't cohabitate with animals, Bea. That's why," I say, but with a touch less conviction.

"I figured Bea would be on our side," Wilma says smugly. "She's the goose that's good for the gander, I always say."

"There is no goose, gander, or baby dogs. That's the Code," I answer her automatically, but I'm losing steam fast.

How hard could a small dog be? After all, the child has turned out to be pretty easy, and Wiggles isn't all that terrible either.

"You want to tell Hart what the Code says?" Wilma asks sweetly, playing dirty.

"As a matter of fact, I do not," I reply.

Hart hears her name and looks up. "What did you say, Eema?"

"I think Gramps wants to talk to you, hon," Wilma says.

She hops up, barely able to balance the puppy in her arms, and comes to me. I kneel down to her level, and she places the wriggling pup in my arms. Mable leans against my chest and peers up at me with oversized brown eyes.

"I'm pretty sure Maggie taught you how to be manipulative like this," I tell the pup.

She isn't horrific to look at, I decide, with her brindle stripes and big eyes.

Hart drapes an arm around my neck and presses her face up against my ear. "She's perfect, Gramps," she whispers.

"She's alright," I concede. "But don't you think she should live at Wilma's house where she'll have Maggie to look after her?"

Hart cocks her head to one side. "No, Gramps, cause Maggie said she belongs here with you."

"But see, Hart, here's the thing," I hesitate, simply unable to finish my sentence. Her hopeful expression is really getting to me.

The kitchen door opens again, and this time Rusty and Peggy come in. I make a mental note to lock the doors from now on. "Right on time," Rusty says, gravitating to the puppy.

"Oh, will you look at this little sweetie pie," Peggy swoops down in a surprisingly agile movement to sit on the floor with me and Hart. The puppy stretches a paw out towards her, and she shakes it. "What a smart little girl, yes you are."

"Wait a doggone minute here," I say, narrowing my eyes at Rusty. "You two knew about this?"

"I mean, it's all everyone's talked about since Maggie pulled her out of the creek," Rusty replies, a tad flippantly.

"What do you mean everyone?" I ask.

"I mean all of us have known since Maggie told Wilma," he answers.

"Wonder why no one thought to tell me. Any ideas, Sally?" I ask.

The traitor sneaks a glance at me quickly, then hurls out of the La-Z-Boy to hide behind Wilma.

"Gramps," Hart says, placing her tiny hands on my face so she can turn it towards her own, "sometimes we gots to do fings that are hard. It's okay. Me and Mommy will be right here to teach you how to take care of Mable."

"I know how to take care of a dog," I say indignantly, although I don't really.

"Good boy!" she says, patting my head with a gush of laughter.

I give up. I've altered the Code before, so I suppose I can do it again.

Hart has a way with me I can't explain.

Or escape.

"Okay, Mable, let's get you a water dish," I say, my words a dim background noise against everyone else's cheers.

And that's how I got a dog.

Chapter 44

The air is crisp this afternoon. The trees are changing colors, leaves are falling, and Halloween decorations have cropped up all over the downtown area. Even Palmer is decorating the front of his theater, in spite of it having only two solid walls left.

Rusty's high up on a ladder, fishing things down from what used to be Palmer's apartment. A lot of it is ruined, but occasionally Palmer finds something he can salvage. Mable suspiciously sniffs the plastic black cat he's pulled from a storage tote Rusty unearthed earlier.

"People are excited to do something normal," Palmer observes. "It is October first, after all. The rest of the year is all about the holidays."

I smile at Mable's antics. Practicing her best stealth moves, she slowly places the cat's tail in her mouth before rolling her eyes around to see if I'm watching her. "Do you think that's a good idea?" I address her.

She considers my question for a few seconds before letting go of the cat and leaning against my leg. Wilma says she does this to show how much she trusts me, but I think she's trained me to dispense treats. She leans, I produce. "Do you need a treat?" I dig around in my pocket for her gravy coated milk bone.

"Oh good," Palmer points past me. "Reinforcements have arrived."

A robust looking Joe and Kenny are rounding the corner.

"Thanks for coming out today," Palmer says, shaking hands with them.

"Totally happy to help," Joe says.

"You're looking spry," Kenny greets me, leaning down to high five Mable.

"Feeling pretty good these days," I say.

"You guys want to trade me spots?" Rusty calls down. "I've been wanting to take a look at the wiring in the back of the building."

While Joe and Kenny take over for Rusty, Palmer checks his buzzing cell phone, shooting me the signal for "be right back" as he hurries out of earshot.

"I'm curious about a phone call he can't take in front of me," I remark to Rusty.

"Absolutely none of your business," he grins at me, switching on a flashlight. "I'm heading to the back of the theater. If I'm not out in fifteen minutes, send help."

"Afraid of the dark, are you?" I joke. "Hart can go with you if you need your hand held."

Palmer finishes his call and comes back, smiling brightly. "Why is Hart holding hands with Rusty?"

"I'll tell you if you tell me who was on the phone," I bargain, but Old Brimstone ruins this chance for me by coming out of the Thrift Store.

"Hey, Bob!" Palmer waves him down.

"Afternoon," Bob leans down to scratch Mable behind the ears. "Thomas, I still do a double take when I see you with Mable," he adds with a little laugh.

"Yeah, me too," I laugh with him.

Joe and Kenny bring more storage containers out to us, calling out hellos when they see Bob. "Pastor," Joe greets him. Bob side hugs Joe and shakes hands with Kenny.

Rusty emerges from the dark depths of the theater, wiping dust off his face with his sleeve. "It's gonna be some work, but I'm pleasantly surprised. The bones of the building seem to be decently strong."

"Finally, a little good news!" Palmer says.

Frank Norris and a band of his idiots appear at the end of the sidewalk, signs hefted above their heads.

"Oh, crud," Rusty says. "I forgot about this ignorant march of his."

"Ugh," Palmer says. "Just when I thought my luck was improving."

Frank's spewing more of his doom and gloom opinions into his bullhorn, claiming the town is being punished for harboring evil. He uses the words *tattoos, homosexuals*, and *deviants* about ten times in half a minute.

"There can't be more than fifteen people with him," Joe remarks. "He's losing supporters."

"I think we should have a word with him," Kenny says, probably thinking Frank might be as easy to reason with as Wilma was.

Joe clicks his tongue, shaking his head slowly. "He's not much on friendly debates, bud."

"There's always a first time for everything. Right, pastor?" Kenny says, clapping Bob lightly on the shoulder. "After a healthy conversation, you sure came around."

Bob sighs. "You're so right, Kenneth. Someone *should* talk to him, and his people. And I think it should be me."

"Are you sure about this?" Joe and I ask at the same time.

"I think I'm the most likely to get through to him out of everyone," he says firmly. "And something needs to be said."

Frank and his nutjobs are two storefronts away from us. Bob stands in the middle of the sidewalk with his hands held out, signaling Frank to stop.

Frank lowers the bullhorn, glaring at Bob. "Move out of the way."

"Now Frank, I just want to talk," Bob says evenly. "We need to find ways to connect the town, not divide it. What good have your speeches and protests done?"

"Said like a true backslider," Frank snorts with contempt. "God is angry with this town and you know it."

"Oh, I agree God's angry about a few things," Bob says to Frank, then turns his attention to the people with him. "Evan, wasn't your house demolished by the tornado? According to Frank, that means you've angered God. How do you explain that?"

"I don't, uh, necessarily..." Evan stammers, looking to Frank for help but getting none.

"So, which is it?" Bob asks again. "Did you have some bad luck, or is God highlighting your sin?"

Evan lowers his eyes and I'll be darned if he doesn't look confused.

Bob continues on. "Chris and Amy, is that you? Didn't Joe and Kenny here help you cut up and clear away the tree that smashed through your garage roof?" he says with disappointment. "So, they can do physical labor for you if they have tattoos, but those same tattoos make them not good enough to live in your town?"

Chris and Amy visibly blanch, averting their eyes to Joe and Kenny with embarrassment.

Frank snarls, "Tread lightly, Bob. If you don't get on the right side of scripture, the Lord will open the earth and swallow you up along with all these sinners," he flicks a hand toward us.

"Frank, that's just hateful, and ridiculous, and so far from God's heart," Bob says, then raises his voice to address the whole group. "In fact, all the ways you've been spreading hate and fear isn't godly at all. Why, the very ones you're condemning have been selflessly serving the community! The ladies who own the bistro provided free food for hundreds of people that whole first week after the tornado. Did any of you put that on one of your signs?"

"They're sinning against God with their homosexual lifestyles," Frank roars.

"They showed love and kindness when tragedy struck. They helped total strangers out of the goodness of their hearts, and they sure didn't exclude anyone from eating just because they were different," Bob challenges, a tinge of anger making his words sharp. "They did exactly what Jesus would have wanted them to do. They did what any decent human would have done. They made it about relationship and love, not obedience and blame. "

"Listen to yourself," Frank hisses, narrowing his beady eyes at us. "You sound like one of them."

"I'm glad you think so! I'd never have the guts to face my maker if I didn't," Bob exclaims. "Jesus loved people. He didn't bully them, he didn't harass them, and he didn't turn them away even if they were disappointing him. The thief on the cross next to him had as much of his heart as the best-behaved disciple did." Bob pulls Joe into the middle of the sidewalk next to him, leaving an arm around his shoulders. "That concept never occurred to me until I heard this guy saying it. This guy, with his tattoos and crazy long hair, has showed me more about love, more about the real heart of Jesus, than any resource I've ever counted on."

I didn't know Bob had all this floating around in that brain of his, but I'm proud that he does. I scan the faces of Frank's followers to see how they feel about Bob's words, surprised to see quite a few stunned expressions.

"Bob's winning them over," I say quietly to Rusty and Palmer. "I don't have to be a Christian to recognize repentance when I see it."

"He really pulled on the old heartstrings, didn't he," Palmer says.

A man and woman step around Frank and come close to Joe. "We, uh..." the man starts, stops, shakes his head. "Sorry," he mumbles.

Joe touches their arms, saying softly, "Thanks, man."

Another lady, this one older than me, joins the couple, silently gazing at him with teary eyes. Joe folds her into his arms and she genuinely starts to cry. Chris and Amy leave the nutjobs, apology written all over their faces. Three more people push past Frank to get to Joe, then another few, and then another. Before long all but two of Frank's nutjobs have defected in a mass mutiny.

Someone grabs Kenny by the hand and drags him into the middle of the circle so they can drench him in their apologies, too. He winks at me, and I bet you he isn't shocked at all that this mass defection is happening. It was his idea, after all.

"Do not be deceived!" Frank bleats, but they aren't listening to him anymore.

"Frank, come on. No one's asking you to embrace things you don't believe in, but we all need to come together and get this town back on its feet. All we're asking is that you be a part of the healing," Bob says gently. "Lord knows we can use all the help we can get."

"Please, Pastor Norris," one of his defectors begs, laying a hand on his arm. "It's enough." Voices of his own nutjobs go up in agreement, urging Frank to call a truce.

It's a real moment of truth for Frank. He's switching his gaze between Joe and Kenny. No words are forming yet on his lips—maybe for the first time ever.

"Has Bob just talked sense into Frank Norris?" I whisper to Rusty and Palmer.

"Hell must be freezing over," Palmer quips.

"And they say miracles don't happen anymore," Rusty chuckles.

Joe takes a step toward Frank, extending his hand. "What do you say, Pastor Norris? Can we sit down over a cup of coffee and talk things out?"

Frank's upper lip curls with distaste. "I can't and won't be swayed by these flowery words. You're leading this town down a hellish path, boy," he bites out.

"Frank!" Bob exhales, anger back in his voice.

It was too good to be true.

Frank's done listening. "I've tried to save you, tried to steer you all clear of the sins and degradation, and what do I get in return? Betrayal! Abandonment!" He clutches his sign to his chest as if shielding himself from harm. "I can do no good among these hardened hearts. I'm moving away and this town can wallow in its own filth." He looks around as if expecting us to beg him to stay, but no one does. "Do you hear me? I'm moving out of Cardinal Creek," he bellows.

Bob throws his hands up in the air, turning to me, Rusty, and Palmer in astonishment. Frank's always been a sour, disagreeable thug, but poor Bob really tried hard with him. He's upset that Frank won't be friends.

"Sometimes the butt sniffers turn into butt biters," I shrug. "You gave him every chance to be friends."

"I guess you're right," Bob's smile is bittersweet.

Frank and his two remaining nutjob minions storm off the way they came, thankfully in silence. The crowd he leaves behind are in various stages of emotional upheaval, all centered around Bob, Joe, and Kenny. I've never seen so much crying and carrying on in my whole life. I'm glad Bob did what he did, but all this touchy-feely stuff is starting to make my skin crawl.

Bea sighs wistfully. "Oh, Thomas, isn't this lovely!"

"I knew you'd show up once the waterworks started," I tease her.

"I do love to see relationships heal," she replies easily.

"Like my grandmama would say—we've done had ourselves church," Rusty laughs.

"Church?" I scoff. "I thought Bob just told Frank off."

Rusty pushes his dirty cap off his forehead with a laugh. "You have the weirdest way of looking at things, Thomas."

"Well, whatever you call what just happened, I'm glad I was around to see it." I pick Mable up, saying, "All this hugging and kissing is creeping us out, so we're going to the food truck for some lunch."

Chapter 45

As I've said before, Cardinal Creek doesn't need much encouragement to put on a festival. We've had several pieces of good news this week, and Wilma says we need to celebrate all the little victories. Wilma used her status as the town's switchboard to organize a mini block party.

Frank Norris did leave town, by the way, and that's a victory in my book. True to his fit throwing declarations, he had his house up for sale two days after the great confrontation and no one has seen him in at least five days. It's been quite nice. His leaving is good news, but Bea says we can't have a party to celebrate a man's failure to build healthy relationships.

That's okay though, because lots of other good things have happened.

My personal favorite piece of good news is that the diner is opening today. It's been a long few weeks without it, and I've missed my routine of crosswords and twenty-some weekly meals with Rusty. We've been sneaking inside for a sandwich here, a piece of pie there, but it's a big deal to me that my regular routine is about to be reinstated.

On Monday a hair salon, the hardware store, and Rapturous Finds will join the diner in opening for business as well. Mike could've had the thrift store open a couple of weeks ago, Jewels says, but he's been tied up in solving housing issues for the many people who are still without a permanent home. Bea made sure I sent the shelter extra funds to keep it going while the thrift store was out of commission, freeing him up to do what he does best. A few extra dollars wasn't a big deal to me, but getting out of hotels and into permanent housing *was* a big deal for the people Mike devoted his time to.

The bistro isn't ready to open just yet, but Olive and Taffy still have something to celebrate. They closed the deal with the bank and now hold the deed to the strip of businesses around the bistro.

The warmth of the day is another reason to celebrate, I guess. The skies are blue and the colder fall temps haven't quite found us yet, making this the perfect Saturday for the town to spend the afternoon goofing off.

Wilma's been able to arrange something for just about every age. A local bluegrass band is playing outside the bistro, a hayride is circling the town square, pumpkin spice and apple cider themed drinks are everywhere, and of course the smell of Scott's delectable burgers fills the air.

There's a roped off area featuring a ball pit, face painting, and bouncy house for the enjoyment of small humans. Maggie, Mabel and I are stationed here with Hart while Sally and Jewels check out the block party. The screams and squeals of happy children blended with live music and chatting voices makes a nice background noise for a relaxed afternoon. I watch as Hart's head and shoulders rhythmically rise and fall above the side of the bouncy house, wondering what could possibly be so entertaining about bouncing. She sees me watching and waves, so I hold up Miss P's furry arm and wave back.

Bea smiles. "I bet some people would say it's silly to decorate for Halloween and have a block party when half the town is still in ruins, but I think it's terrific. It really lifts the spirits, doesn't it?"

"I'd say it feels more normal around here today than it has in weeks," I agree.

Rusty and Palmer appear with their lawn seats, late by two hours.

Rusty's obsessed with the work on the theater. He's been late to everything lately because we can't get him to put his tools down for five minutes.

"I thought we'd find you holed up at a table two feet from Scott's grill, not sitting here playing with stuffed animals," Rusty says.

"It's people like you that ruin it for the rest of us stuffed animal lovers," I respond, pulling the rabbit close to caress my cheek. He laughs at me and settles into his chair, producing treats for the dogs.

"Stop that. You look creepy," Palmer says, giving me a handful of brochures. "Help me decide on new flooring."

I scan the brochures and hold one up that depicts a shiny, polished hardwood. "I vote for this."

"Interesting," he says, eyes half closed to hide his real thoughts. "That's the one Charlotte picked, too."

"The nitwit?" I ask, surprised. "What's she got to do with the flooring?"

Rusty chuckles, leaning back in his seat. "Yeah, Palmer, tell Tommy Boy here what Charlotte has to do with all this."

"I can't believe you spent so much time with us at the fair and haven't figured it out yet, actually," he says, taking his brochures back. "Before I go any further, I want to make it clear that I will entertain jokes and teasing when it's just us three, but any other time you're just going to have to restrain yourself," he warns me. "Especially if she's around."

Icy cold fingers of dawning realization grab my heart, squeezing tight. Visions of glittery nails and neon pink lipstick scutter through my mind like roaches at midnight. I can practically smell the cloud of nauseating perfume that constantly envelopes her.

Palmer is dating that nitwit, Charlotte Davens.

I almost wish I believed in God so I could call on him for help.

"Quick, we've got to get him to a hospital," I tell an amused Rusty. "Shock therapy should help, or maybe a lobotomy. Whatever we have to do to get him straightened out!"

"He's happy with her," Rusty shrugs. "There's nothing to be done."

"But her clothes are garish, she smells like window cleaner, and the sound of her voice is worse than fingernails on a chalkboard," I lament.

Palmer holds his arms open wide. "That's it, get it all out."

"She's outrageously flashy, Palmer! She wears stage worthy amounts of makeup just to check the mailbox. She has no sense of humor at all!" I tick off her offenses with my fingers.

"What else?" he asks, nodding.

"What do you mean what else?" I ask, astonished. "Isn't that enough?"

He smiles pleasantly. "I just want you to have a chance to get it out of your system."

"And then what?" I ask.

"Then I'm going to tell you that I really, truly like her. That goes for her daughter, too. In a few months I could see myself really loving her. In a year or so I could see myself marrying her." He leans back like Rusty, serene and collected. "That's what."

"I see. You *truly* like her, do you?" I ask.

He nods. "Truly."

Cheese and crackers.

"She won't interfere with poker night?" I ask.

"Nope. She won't interfere with anything. I swear." He crosses his heart.

"I won't do anything else with the show choir just because she's dating you," I warn.

He holds his hands palms out in surrender. "Obviously."

"No teasing at all?" I ask regrettably. "Not even just a little bit?"

He chuckles. "Maybe just a little, but never where she can hear you."

"My jokes would just go over her head anyway," I grin.

He rolls his eyes, but he still laughs along with Rusty.

"Cheer up," Rusty says. "We might get another grandkid out of this."

"Grandkid? We aren't his parents, Rusty," I balk. "Besides, I can barely keep up with this ball of energy," I wave again at Hart, who is howling "Helllooooo, Graaaamps!" from the top of the bouncy house slide.

"Hart could use a playmate," Rusty wiggles an eyebrow suggestively at Palmer.

"Denise and Scott can go first on that one," Palmer guffaws.

I chuckle, looking out across the square at all the people having fun. It's hard to be too upset, after all, when I'm so close to getting my peace and quiet back. I mean, sure, a few things are going to be different now if he dates her, but it won't have any effect on our daily routines.

We all know how important those daily routines are.

"Fine. Date the nitwit if she makes you happy," I say nonchalantly.

Joe and Ido are strolling casually our way, toting bags of popcorn. "You guys have to try this," Joe hands a bag to me. "It's candy apple flavored."

"Don't be fooled by the word apple," Ido teases me, "It's not healthy at all."

"Let me see this," I toss a couple pieces in my mouth, eyes popping in surprise. "Hey, no kidding, this is delicious," I say, handing the bag to Rusty. Joe produces a bag of chocolate covered pretzels with orange and black sprinkles from the bib pocket of his overalls.

"Are you going to wear those overalls in the winter?" Palmer asks Joe.

"Dude," Joe thoughtfully puts a pretzel in his mouth, chewing for a second before answering. "I'm gonna wear these overalls for the rest of my life!"

Hart flies down the slide, pops up, and runs to us. "Hi Joey!" she screams.

He picks her up with a grin. "Hi, Squish."

"Gramps says the bouncy house is in-san-awary," she tells him. "But I just fink it's fun."

Joe looks to me for clarification. "Unsanitary," I supply wryly.

"Oh, well, most things that are fun *are* unsanitary," he quips, tossing her into the air. She screams, he catches her, and she's off to the bouncy house again.

"You see? According to this pastor, fun things are unsanitary... like dating nitwits," I tell Palmer. Joe laughs hardest though.

"Dude, you just now found out about that?" he taps my arm affectionately. "Oh, Thomas."

"I'm the last to know about everything because I'm the only one who isn't nosy," I retaliate.

The argument dies as Wilma, Sally, Jewels, and Denise, arms loaded with treats, find us. Hart shoots down the slide and runs to her mom, who hands her apple slices and caramel dip. Wilma sets up bowls of food for the dogs, and I claim a warm foil wrapped burger from a bag.

"Seriously, this is a fantastic day," Jewels says happily, plopping into Joe's lap.

"The best!" Joe grins around a mouthful of pumpkin cupcake.

"Here's to the bright future of Cardinal Creek!" Rusty says, holding his burger out like a wine glass.

"And getting the town back in business!" Ido says, the only one of us who actually has a drink. He lifts his spiced apple cider in salute.

"To fancy remodels!" Palmer adds, touching his burger to Rusty's.

"To deep fried foods," Sally giggles, waving her half-eaten corndog at me.

"To regular routines!" I chime in, touching her corndog with my burger.

"To healthy grandbabies!" Wilma says with a pointed look at Denise.

"And patient mothers-in-law," Denise fires back.

Chapter 46

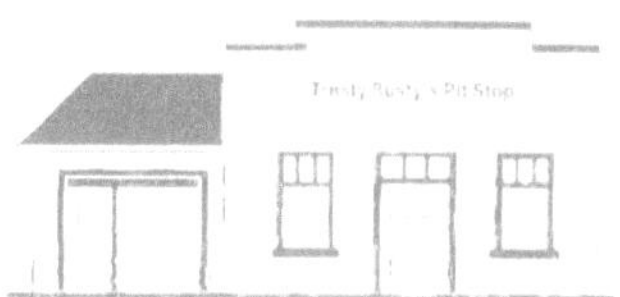

Wilma's close to outdoing herself, and as you well know by now, that's a tall order. This current obsession isn't driving me nearly as bonkers as the others though. I guess I might be the only other person even half as excited as Wilma is to see the Munch Box back in business, so we both have been a little silly.

Since the opening three days ago, she's been doing a countdown to Halloween that involves a "spooky daily special." Rusty and I have been given strict orders to consume said special every day as a way to advertise it to the other customers. I suggested that we should get these meals for free if we're being used as a marketing tool and she almost laughed me out of the restaurant for it.

This afternoon Rusty inhaled his lunch, anxious to get back to the theater. Incredibly, he found time between bites to regale me with a boring and tedious account of the wiring he's doing in the projector room.

It's not that I don't care about Palmer's progress, mind you. It's that I don't care about wiring.

So, I'm alone with the last couple bites of my Not Your Mummy's Grilled Cheese, my second crossword of the day open before me on the table.

"Do you want to play fetch?" says a tin-canned version of Wilma's voice. I look down at Maggie, poised at the end of my booth, nubby tail wagging. Dan has rigged up a travel kit of sorts so she can carry a set of five talking buttons around with her. If I live another thirty years, I don't know if I'll see anything to compare to a talking dog.

"Thanks, Maggie, but no. My shoulder and all, you know," I reply. My shoulder isn't bothering me anymore, but as much as Maggie and I have become friends I still can't abide the thought of touching a slimy, Maggie-slobbered tennis ball with my bare hands.

She scrutinizes me before slapping another button. "Are you sure?"

She knows I'm lying. "Let's make a deal. You can have a sleep over tonight with Mable and Wiggles if I don't have to play fetch."

Without hesitation she pushes the button for yes, gives me her paw for a handshake, takes her talking kit and moves on.

The joke's on Wilma, because I didn't specify which household would be hosting this sleepover. The Harpers might do well with a reminder of what it's like to deal with Mable's middle of the night excursions into the yard to potty.

"Got room for us?" Lee asks as he and Val take over Rusty's abandoned side of the booth.

"I do," I remark dryly, putting the crossword aside.

"You're not spending the day with Hart?" Val asks.

"It's an Ido day," I answer. "That means Joe and Jewels are at work, Palmer and Rusty are at the theater, Sally's at school and here I sit, bored to tears."

They exchange a glance. "You're bored," Lee states with a dubious gape.

"Yes. I'm bored," I grunt. Do they really not understand what being bored means?

"But isn't this your kind of day? Peace and quiet while you're eating, seventeen across the only problem facing you?" Lee asks, laughter bubbling just behind his words.

"Yes, Lee, I like to have measured amounts of peace and quiet," I bark. "I have had that all day, however, and am now on my second crossword as a result of all this peace and quiet. Can't a man enjoy a little variety in his day without getting the third degree?"

Lee and Val both laugh outright, but I'm not seeing the humor in any of this. How I feel is how I feel, and there's no comedic twist to it that I can see.

"Thomas, we aren't really making fun of you or anything. It's just that your reasoning is quite the paradox," Val placates me.

I roll my eyes at them. "We are now all done discussing my daily habits. What's driven you two neanderthals out of your caves?"

"You're not going to believe it," Val chuckles.

"Entertain me," I invite.

"Bob's called an emergency quarterly ministerial meeting," Lee says, bemused. "He wants to convert his building into a community center."

"You know how he's been sharing his facility after the tornado?" Val asks, and I nod. "He loves it and has decided he wants to expand the whole idea permanently."

Lee shows me a key card. "He's serious about it, too. He's already installed those contraptions like on a hotel door and handed these cards out to a few of us. He means to give more of them out at the meeting and take suggestions for what else we might do with the space."

"I'm not surprised. He's really done a one-eighty because of Joe. It's almost like he's determined to do a good deed every day to make up for lost time," I say. "He's a lot easier to stomach after his transformation, that's for dang sure."

"I almost forgot!" Val practically chokes. "Weren't you there when he confronted Frank?"

"I sure was," I snort, remembering Frank's fury in the face of Bob's composure. "It was a sight to see."

"Did you hear that some of Frank's parishioners have asked Bob if it would be okay for them to attend his church services?" Lee's eyes are open so wide his wrinkles have almost disappeared.

"No kidding?" I say. "I wonder if it was some of the people who were there for the so-called march? Bob put a spotlight on a few of them for their bad behavior, especially toward Joe and Kenny. I kind of saw it as a good telling off, but Rusty called it 'having church.'"

They laugh at Rusty's description. "Well, whatever it was, it worked. I'm not one to just go along with running someone out of town, but Frank's negativity was getting to be a lot to handle for everyone," Lee says.

"Bob didn't run him out of town at all! He gave him multiple chances to make peace, but Frank wouldn't have it. It was Frank who threatened to leave town unless his followers came back to his way of seeing things, but no one did. By the time Bob was done, there were only two people still standing with Frank." I explain. "Honestly, Bob tried to make amends."

"Interesting." Lee says. "I'm glad you told us this, actually, just in case we catch wind of any gossip floating around town. I'd hate to see Bob get a bad reputation for what happened."

"You both know we parted ways because I couldn't agree with his fear-based views on God," Val says, "but I'm telling you, Frank's morphed into something else entirely this last year."

"Unlike a fine wine, he definitely didn't age well, did he?" I laugh.

"More like a moldy hunk of bread," Val murmurs.

I'm about to ask them if Bob is going to take in the churchless when Wilma scuttles up to our table looking harried and hot. "Sorry for the delay," she says. "I've been dealing with a server crisis." She puts two glasses of ice water in front of Val and Lee.

"Nothing serious, I hope?" Val asks.

"Nothing a good swift spanking wouldn't fix," Wilma says, tucking a strand of loose hair violently behind an ear. "Course, that's illegal, so I had to make do with a writeup."

"You could always force them to listen to one of your conspiracy stories, Wilma. That's about as bad as a spanking," I suggest.

"Beating the bush that buries the hatchet, I see," she snaps.

And with that gem, I'm laughing even harder.

Lee gets her mind off of me, soothing her into a smile with talk of food. "Can we both have the spooky special, and afterwards we need to make a pie order for the quarterly meeting."

"Ok, hon," Wilma says sweetly to him, huffing at me as she leaves.

"One of these days she's going to start spitting in your biscuits and gravy," Val chuckles.

"Nonsense. She likes a good argument just as much as I do," I say.

"What's the spooky special, by the way?" Lee asks, checking out the scattered remains of my plate.

"Not Your Mummy's Grilled Cheese." I answer. "Delicious as usual."

Wilma rushes back to our table, brows drawn tightly, ringing her hands together. "Tommy, I need you to come with me," she says, a catch in her voice. "You guys, too."

I stand up, instantly worried. Wilma's always going on about something, but her countenance is so serious it's glaringly apparent this isn't one of her schemes. "Okay, Wilma."

We follow her to the back of the diner, solemnly giving one another questioning looks. Whatever it is, it must be bad. As we pass Scott at the grill, his expression is so full of regret my heart skips a beat.

What in the world has happened?

She stops outside the small office, turning to face us, tears gathering in her eyes.

Val immediately circles her with an arm, squeezing her shoulder. "What's happened, Wilma?" he asks gently.

"Oh, Tommy, it's horrible," she starts, tears now falling. "Palmer just called Scott. There's been an accident at the theater."

"Is he okay?" I ask, a hard lump forming in my throat.

"Palmer's fine," she stumbles over her words, a sob escaping her, before plunging on. "It's Rusty who's not alright."

The lump travels from my throat to my stomach. "What," I croak, clear my throat, and try again. "What happened to Rusty?"

"It's bad. We need to get to the hospital right away."

Chapter 47

I stumble down the steps, following Wilma.

My thoughts are fractured.

I'm having a hard time getting enough air into my lungs.

Rusty had been injured is what she said.

"I'll drive, Thomas," Val says quietly, taking my elbow. "My car is just here."

"To see Rusty?" I ask.

"Yes," he says simply. "I'll drive us all to the hospital."

"Alright," I nod.

Wilma said it's bad.

Lee and I pile silently into the back seat, Wilma up front with Val.

As the engine turns over, I remember Rusty told me once that Val's car purrs like a kitten. He was right.

I look out the window, allowing snatches of their conversation to float in and out of my awareness. I'm careful not to listen too closely. It's better to only let the information in a little at a time.

We pass a house with men on the roof, hammering.

Next door to them, another group of people are repairing a fence.

Wilma says something about scaffolding.

Lee asks where Palmer is meeting us.

They've almost finished the repairs on the laundry mat, I notice. We're going too fast to read the sign, but I think I saw the words *opening soon.*

Val stops at a red light. The turn signal goes click-click, over and over. The normalcy of it is out of place.

Wilma blows her nose.

Val turns onto the main road that goes right through the middle of Cardinal Creek. It's the road that passes all the necessary places a town needs, like the post office and Ido's Market.

Necessary places, like the hospital.

I remember when Bea and I first moved here, it was spring. The whole town was coming to life, splashes of green taking over the dull browns of wintertime. Spring has always been her favorite season, but for some reason she especially loved spending those weeks here in Cardinal Creek.

She still felt up to getting out of the house a few times a week that spring, but we had to be creative in how she did it. Her favorite thing was for me to drive her around town with the windows open so she could see what everyone was doing in their yards.

"Oh Thomas, just look at that glorious bed of hostas," she'd said on one drive.

"My gosh, I'm crazy about that darling, clever bird feeder!" she'd exclaimed over repurposed teacups and saucers.

"Oh, dear, let's see about doing something to spruce up that equipment" was another comment as we passed a public playground.

We ran out of time before we could give the playground a facelift.

We drove on this main road probably a hundred times during her last few months of life.

We're passing Juniper Lane, her absolute favorite street because several of the houses have those stone ducks that wear clothes. I guess it's a neighborhood thing. She gushed with childlike enthusiasm over their outfits, particularly the holiday ones.

Today, I see one witch duck and one ghost duck. She would've lost it over these outfits.

Bea was too sick for leisurely drives by the time fall rolled around.

I know she saw the ducks dressed for the fourth of July, but I think that's the last holiday themed outfits she had a chance to see.

I know for sure she didn't see the Halloween costumes they have on today.

The last time Bea was with me on this road, her window was up. She was slumped in the seat, blue eyes closed, her sweet features overwhelmed by the pain consuming her body.

We were going to the hospital that day, too.

Chapter 48

Val turns off the engine. We're in the parking garage of the hospital.

I've been in this garage countless times. I hated it then, and I hate it now.

Lee gets out of the car. So do Wilma and Val.

They watch me through the window.

I'm paralyzed. I can't make myself touch the door handle.

Eventually, it's Wilma who opens my door and holds her hand out to me. I take it, shocked by her vitality. My mind has a hard time reconciling vitality and the hospital.

"Come on now," she says softly, but firmly. "Let's go inside."

I let her lead me up to the automatic doors.

The familiar antiseptic odors seep into my nostrils and mouth.

I gag, fighting back the urge to vomit.

"Tommy," she says, still soft but firm. "Are you okay?"

I can only look at her blankly. I'm not okay at all.

"How about you two go on ahead and find Palmer. Thomas and I will be along in just a few minutes," Lee says. "Come this way, Thomas. We'll collect our thoughts and fortify ourselves before we talk to Palmer."

I have no confidence that I'm capable of fortifying myself, but I nod and allow him to lead me off to a couple chairs in a hallway outside the ER waiting room.

"This brings back some tough memories, I would imagine," Lee says.

I gulp. I have to. There's a literal ball of something hot and sinister in my throat.

"I'm as old as you are, Thomas, but I've never lost a wife. I won't try to speak to it as if I understand what you're going through, because I don't. Here. Sit down," he guides me into a chair. "I do understand some things about grief though, and I know it feels like you're suffering, too. Grief hurts something awful."

He's got that right.

I stare blankly at the wall next to me. A landscape painting hangs a foot above my head. It's the ugliest landscape I've ever seen in my entire life.

"Just look at this ugly painting. Trees aren't shaped like that." I make a sound of disapproval. "Bea would've hated this picture."

He looks over my head at the painting. "You're right. It is ugly."

"Plus, it stinks in here," I add, quietly.

"Yeah," he agrees.

I scowl at the dingy, off-white walls.

"They haven't changed the colors or anything since Bea was here," I say.

"No?" he asks.

"We thought it was very drab. She was always joking about donating money in my name so they could paint the whole place yellow. Something sunny and cheerful, like she wanted our house to be," a heavy smile briefly lifts the edges of my mouth. "Can you imagine? My name on a plaque, boasting about my generosity." I try to laugh, but all that comes out is a hoarse whisper. "She was the generous one. She knew all her nurses' names and what their private lives were like. We hauled boatloads of cookies and cupcakes, smelly lotions and bath salts, and god knows what else up here so she could give it to the people who took care of her."

Lee is smiling. "You probably never knew about the goodies she had me, Val, and Mike bring up, did you?"

"Oh, I did," I chuckle. "I acted like I didn't, but I knew. She had you three wrapped around her little finger."

"She had *everyone* wrapped around her little finger," he corrects me, smiling fondly.

I laugh. It evolves into a lonesome, sorrow-filled sob.

Lee places one hand firmly on my arm, and the tears start to fall.

I hate this.

I hate crying.

I hate, hate, *hate* this.

It feels like an eternity before my wailing dwindles down to a few tears, and hours until it finally dries up altogether. Lee has handed me several tissues that are wadded in a soggy heap in my lap.

"Whew," I blow out a huge breath.

"Better?" he asks.

"Not at all," I answer grimly.

"We can sit here some more," he offers. "Or maybe you'd want to go wash your face in the bathroom?"

"Bathroom," I say, standing shakily to my feet. "I'll be back."

"I'll be here," he assures me gently.

I can't look at him for fear the crying will start up again.

"Do you know where the bathroom is?" he calls after me, but I can't speak anymore right now. I wave a hand behind me and keep shuffling that way.

Naturally I know where the bathroom is. I know every stinking inch of this hellhole by heart.

I shove the door open to the family bathroom because I know in here I can have privacy. I turn the lock on the door and walk to the sink.

Now that I'm alone I stop fighting the tears.

Visions of Bea as she was those last days crowd into my mind, haunting me. Thin and frail, a light sheen of sweat on her face, her cancer-ravaged frame propped up in a too-big bed.

My love, my friend, my tether to sanity, faded away as I watched.

I was frozen in a hopeless void back then. I couldn't throw a check for thousands of dollars at her cancer and make it disappear. I couldn't give her my own organs to use. I couldn't say magic words to make things all better.

I couldn't fix her, and I couldn't stop how much her dying hurt my heart.

The hurt seared right through all my logic and reason. It throbbed relentlessly, so much so that I wanted to die right along with her. My physical body lived, but there's more than one way a man can die.

With time, I learned how to dampen the hurt from a raging boil to a steady simmer. I kept it buried just beneath the surface where I could control it.

I started enjoying food again. Rusty made me laugh a few times. I doubled up on crosswords.

I wouldn't say life was wonderful, or amazing. It certainly wasn't whole.

At best, I enjoyed some peace and quiet, and that soon became the most precious thing in my life.

All that hardship and turmoil was because what I loved the most, Bea, was taken from me unexpectedly. I remember vividly the moment I fully understood the truth of what happens when you let yourself love.

You get hurt.

I tweaked Bea's version of the Code to make sure nothing triggered that hurt again, and as long as I was careful, I could limp along through my days with minimal emotions.

Today, I've lost that control.

Chapter 49

I've finally stopped crying.

I blow my nose and splash water onto my face.

I walk slowly back to Lee. He stands when he sees me, asking if I'm better now.

I'm not, but I can't find a way to say this. He won't understand. No one could.

I give him a weary nod, and we walk together to the waiting room.

I've known Rusty since we were small children. The first time I went along with my dad to the Pit Stop to have the family car tuned up, I might've been all of eight. Rusty's dad ran the shop back then, and it was quite a bit smaller. Rusty and I exchanged the typical words of young boys who've been put together by adults. I like that toy you have there. Wanna try my candy? Let's race to the barn and back!

Rusty inherited the Pit Stop a handful of years after I made it big and started touring. I didn't have a reason in those days to drop in at the Pit Stop when I came home to visit my parents, but I'd still see him around town at one event or another. We'd always say hello, how ya been, that sort of thing.

We became friendlier when Bea and I ran into him and his new wife Hildy at one of the many town festivals. Bea and Hildy chatted away like long lost pals with Rusty and I sitting beside them cracking jokes. Our lifestyles couldn't have been more different, but the four of us became close anyway. Over the years, Bea and I made sure Rusty and Hildy were a consistent part of our visits back home, and our friendship grew stronger.

Hildy left us roughly two years earlier than Bea. We came back to Cardinal Creek for her funeral and stayed around for a week or so afterward. Rusty handled all that her death entailed better than I did when I lost Bea. He handles everything in life better than I do.

For most of Hildy's funeral I hid in a back corner, clueless about what I should be doing and saying.

But Bea knew.

"You can *say* anything out loud to another human, Thomas, but that doesn't mean it's the right thing. We *have* to say something in times like this, because saying something makes *us* feel better. And don't get me started on how useless it is to say 'she's in a better place now.' That phrase only magnifies the fact that we've been left behind in the 'not better place.'"

That made good sense to me because I've always been better at actions.

"Rusty doesn't need a lot of fancy words. He needs someone to do whatever it is he wants to do. Someone to simply be present for him."

So, that's what I did.

The day after the funeral, I called him up and asked him what he wanted to do. He hadn't eaten yet, so we met at the diner. That one meal turned into two, then five, and before long it was a ritual.

At first, we mostly sat in silence.

Then, one afternoon I told him a terrible joke I'd heard on the radio, and when he laughed I felt like I'd just won the world series or something. After that, things slowly started to sort themselves out.

The diner became ours, and before long our meals turned into two-hour hangout sessions. We both had known Wilma, of course, but only in that passing way you have with a familiar cashier or something. After Hildy's death is when Wilma really took an interest in us. Spending several hours in the space of a week listening to her conspiracy theories was a fast-track indoctrination into her world, and by the end of that week she'd gone from acquaintance to little sister.

Eventually, I had to get back to my busy life, but I told Bea we needed to make sure Rusty didn't get lost in the shuffle. The way my performance schedule worked, I usually had downtime in the middle of the week, so I made my way back to Cardinal Creek every Tuesday. Some weeks it was both of us, some weeks I came alone, but for the next several months I had at least three or four meals a week with Rusty at the Munch Box.

He still brings it up sometimes, bragging on me for being so self-sacrificing.

I've never felt like I sacrificed anything. Traveling home once a week for a few months was a piece of cake compared to how he was learning how to live without his wife.

Two years later, when tragedy struck my life, it was Rusty who took care of me. The rest of our friends fussed a lot over Bea, and I was happy they were around to do it. Unlike me, she needed to be surrounded with people because that's what kept her full and happy.

It was Rusty who figured out exactly what it was I needed though, and then did it.

He got me out of the house for a few minutes every day, even if all we did was walk around the block. When Wilma would come to see Bea, we'd make a game out of sneaking over to the bistro for cinnamon rolls. He bought a book of classical music crossword puzzles and made me do one a day over pie at the diner, a habit I still cling to now. Hard to imagine I laughed at all during Bea's last weeks but the few times I can recall it happening, Rusty was almost always involved.

Rusty became more to me than a friend when Bea died, but I didn't realize it until it was too late to stop it from happening. And now here I am—horrified that because of this accident, he's going to leave me.

I've never said the words "I love you" to anyone outside of my parents and Bea.

Not to Rusty, or Palmer, or Ido.

Not to the Harpers, or Olive and Taffy.

Not to Mike, Lee, or Val.

Not to Joe, Jewels, Sally, or Hart.

But, of course, you know as well as I do that I love all of them.

I tried not to. I had a Code to protect me.

But it happened anyway.

I love Rusty, and when I love someone and they leave me… even if they don't want to… well, you know what happens.

It just about destroys me.

CHAPTER 50

Lee and I walk into the waiting room.

Palmer is surrounded by many of the people I love.

As soon as I see their tear-streaked faces, I stumble.

Lee steadies me.

I search for something to focus on. Anything.

The painting on the wall behind Palmer is hideous. The artist used the same muted colors for everything so it's hard to tell what each image is supposed to be.

We join the group. I stand behind Joe. Hide behind him, really.

He touches my arm in acknowledgement, but thankfully I'm not seen by the others yet.

"...so, they will know more once they get him into surgery," Palmer is saying.

I focus my eyes on the painting. It could be a farmhouse, if you squint.

Sally is saying, "Ido said he would keep Hart as long as I need him to..."

The farmhouse is surrounded by fields of something tall and skinny.

"His nephew is closing up the shop. He'll be here shortly," Palmer says, his voice strained and nasally from crying. I make the mistake of looking at his face. His sadness breaks my heart.

I force my gaze over to the painting again. If it was a cornfield, there'd be ears of corn, I would imagine. There's nothing like that on these stalks, so it must be a wheat field.

"...surgeon said it will take several hours, since they have to find the source of the internal bleeding..." Wilma is saying.

I scream inwardly. I can't handle words like surgeon and internal bleeding right now.

I push their voices out of my head and focus more closely on the painting.

There are blobs in the sky. Hot air balloons maybe?

Charlotte and Denise join the group.

"...nothing fatal, but still very serious..." Scott is saying to Denise.

Nothing fatal. He said nothing fatal.

I can handle nothing fatal.

Wilma starts talking again, and I don't like these words either. "... wall caved in... scaffolding collapsed... unconscious..."

Nothing fatal is enough information for right now. I get back to the painting. The blobs are most certainly clouds, I decide, based on the shape.

"...long wait, why don't we sit down..." someone else says.

As they move to find seats, they notice me.

Sally and Jewels come to hug me... Wilma asking me if I feel better... Palmer's eyes tear up again as he moves toward me...

A ringing starts in my ears.

My chest tightens.

I can't take in enough air.

I have to get out of here.

"Take me home. Now." I say in clipped, struggling words to Joe.

"Are you okay, Thomas?" he asks.

I shake my head no. "I have to get out of here. Now. Right now." I grab him roughly by the arm and propel him toward the door.

Voices call after us, confused, worried, but I can't stop now.

In seconds we are out of the waiting room, and this brings me a sliver of relief.

By the time I get to the hall, I can breathe again.

Once the automatic doors close behind me, my ears stop ringing.

When I'm securely seated in Joe's truck, I sigh.

I need this time to do some thinking.

By the time Joe turns onto our street, I feel almost like myself again.

Chapter 51

Joe follows me into the house.

I go straight to the kitchen, open the fridge, and take out a bottle of water. "All that crying made me thirsty," I say, upending the bottle. It only takes me a few seconds to drain it. "Welp, I killed that one in a hurry," I show him the empty bottle with a grin, and go back for a second one.

Mable and Wiggles wake up and rush to us, demanding pets. "Hello, Missy. Have you been good?" I scoop Mable up and give her scratches on her plump belly.

Joe watches me carefully, like I'm an escapee from a psych ward.

I understand why. I didn't say a word on the drive home, and now all of a sudden I'm a chatty Cathy.

The answer to my problems was obvious once I cleared my head. I've formulated a plan, and now that I know what I'm going to do I feel like I'm walking on clouds.

I put Mable back on the floor and down the second bottle of water in a few thirsty gulps.

"Good gravy," I show Joe my empty bottle. "I must be super dehydrated!"

I grab a third water and head to my bedroom. He follows me, his expression cautious. I cast a bright smile his way, hoping to ease his mind.

Everything is going to be just fine, and I want him to know it.

The dogs follow us with their chew toys, and I wish Joe could take a page out of their book. They aren't worried about anything, and he shouldn't be either.

Unfortunately, when I haul a suitcase out of my closet and lay it open on the bed, it's too much for him. "Going somewhere?"

"I am," I answer lightly.

"I didn't know you had a trip planned," he says.

"Well, I don't exactly have it planned," I say, opening the closet. I sort through shirts and slacks, grabbing a few of each.

"Okay," he says, hesitantly. "Can I ask what *is* going on exactly?"

I toss four outfits into the suitcase before turning my full attention to him. "I need to leave."

He takes this in. "You *need* to leave?"

"Yes. I need to leave." I answer self-confidently as I head back to the closet. I rummage through sweaters and cardigans and suit coats, choosing one of each.

"Thomas," he says, and I look at him. "Why do you *need* to leave?"

I fold the sweater and cardigan before adding them to the suitcase. "Because I can't stay here with all of... this." I make a swirling motion with one hand.

"This... what?" he asks. "Sadness?"

"Sadness is a good word for it. I'm not cut out for this emotional stuff, Joe. You know that." I reply, heading back to the closet for a garment bag. Bea would scold me for cramming a suit jacket into a suitcase.

"But, buddy," he falters.

I hand him the garment bag to hold while I wrangle the suit jacket into it. "I'm sure that's hard for someone like you to understand. You thrive in this kind of situation, and that's nifty. It really is." I zip the garment bag, and lay it on the bed, looking around the room for whatever else I might need. "Ah, yes," I say, going to the dresser. "However, I do not thrive in these kinds of situations. Finding a way to survive

Bea's death took all I had. That's it. I used up all of my... whatever it is you have that lets you deal with hard stuff."

"But Rusty's not dying, Thomas. He's got some serious injuries, but nothing that can't be fixed with surgery and time," Joe says.

"Not dying *yet*," I correct him, taking an armful of socks, tee shirts, and underwear to the suitcase. "You're missing that one tiny key word. *Yet*. Even if he survives this accident, he could still very well die before me. I would have to watch disease kill him, and try to survive the funeral, and the weeks and months and years afterward without him." I maneuver my underthings into the pouch on the lid of the suitcase. "I mean, if he makes it out of surgery. We aren't even considering the fact that he could die from complications with the anesthesia, or bleed out on the table, or from an infection that sets in forty-eight hours later."

He listens. He thinks about it. He processes.

I smile reassuringly at him.

"I..." he sits cross legged on my bed, gathering his thoughts. I finish my third bottle of water, letting him have the time he needs. "Would you consider that you're in shock? Maybe it's not a good time to make a big decision right now."

"That's a fair question. I was in shock back at the hospital. Oh boy, was I ever. Had a bit of a panic attack, too, for good measure," I readily admit. "I'm all better now that I have a plan. Fully aware of what I'm doing, and entirely sure it's the right thing."

"Okay, well, what about us? We need you, Thomas. Sally and Hart, me and Jewels, all of us," he tries to reason. "Rusty will need you the most as he recovers."

"*If* he recovers," I correct him, but gently. "And I wouldn't ever leave without providing for you guys. I'll call my accountant and have the house put in Sally's name. The four of you can stay here forever if you want to." I go back to the dresser, dig around inside the bottom drawer, and pull out a fat envelope. "Take this. I think there's about five thousand here, maybe a little more. It should get you through a month, and by that time my lawyer will have a trust fund set up for Sally and another bank account to manage the household bills." He makes as if he's going to refuse, so I toss the envelope onto his lap. "What everyone says is true, you know. I *do* have enough money to buy Cardinal Creek if I wanted to, so please just take the money."

"It's not your *money* we need—it's *you*," he insists.

"Well, I can't help that," I say kindly. I'm not mad at him for trying. It's who he is.

Another thought occurs to me. I snap my fingers. "Rusty isn't wealthy, so I'll set up an account to cover his medical bills, rehab, and whatever else," I say, pleased with this idea.

"*If* he recovers," Joe throws my own words back at me, but it doesn't have the effect on me he wants.

"Yes, *if*. I'm glad you understand," I nod. "If he doesn't make it, give the money to Mike. In fact, I better make an account for the shelter, too."

"So, let me get this straight," he says. "You're leaving for good, and we will just be dudes who talk on the phone once a week?"

"Oh, sorry, but there won't be phone calls," I patiently explain to him. "My version of the Code works if I follow it. I got myself into hot water when I let Bea talk me into altering it. Can't do that again, so there won't be any phone calls or letters, or yearly Christmas cards. I need a clean break."

"Thomas, please," he stands up, the envelope fluttering to the floor unnoticed. "Please, please don't do this. Life *is* hard, but that makes relationships all the more important. You said you don't have the same 'thing' I have that lets me deal with hard stuff, but you're wrong. It's the relationships I have that get me through everything! You have the support and love of all of us, so you'll be able to get through whatever happens with Rusty," he pleads. "If you leave, you'll have to face the rest of your life completely alone!"

I sigh, turning to pick the envelope up. I put it on the bed and look at him. He's just not getting it.

"Yes, Joe, I do have relationships, friends, all of that. You're missing the point. What you see as the *answer* is what I see as the *problem*." I place a hand on each of his shoulders, squeezing. "I'm going to let you in on a little secret. I love you, Joe. I love you and

Jewels a lot. I love Sally, little Hart, Wilma… I love the whole lot of you. That's why I'm going to so much trouble to make sure you all have everything you need." I release his shoulders and shrug. "Possibly, I love Rusty the most. But when someone I love goes away, it hurts. That hurt is so hard, you see, so terrible, I just can't stand it. Rusty getting hurt made me realize I can't face losing *any* of you."

"You love me?" his voice is breathy, as if he's trying to reconcile some great mystery.

"Yes. I love you." I reply.

"You love all of us?" he asks.

"Every last one of you. I know I always say I don't love anyone but Bea, but that's because I don't know how to balance a bunch of emotional stuff. Now that I've told you the truth, I hope you can understand why reinstating the Code is the only option I have."

He stands up a little straighter, smiling easier. "Yeah, I get it now. I get the whole picture, dude," he stuffs his hands into his overall pockets, rocking back on the balls of his feet.

"You do?" I ask.

"Yep, everything is crystal clear. Hey, you better get your toothbrush and stuff," he points out.

What an abrupt change of attitude. Have I broken Joe Tackett's brain, maybe?

"I was just about to grab that," I reply, looking him over. He seems to be actually happy.

He follows me to my bathroom, leaning on the doorway to watch as I fill my toiletry bag. "So, I guess Mable will live with Sally and Hart," he comments.

"That's how I had it figured," I reply. "You know Hart needs her more than I do anyway."

"Is, uh," he looks around, "is Bea going with you?"

"I would imagine," I reply. I haven't actually talked to Bea about this decision for obvious reasons, but I don't want to draw his attention to that.

He grins, saying, "Cool."

"Alright, I guess that's it," I zip the bag.

"Well, let's get your car loaded up," he says cheerfully.

Again, I pause, puzzled by this abrupt shift.

I toss my bag on the bed and give Mable a long, satisfying scratch. "You grow up to be smart like Maggie, you hear? And watch over Hart." She wriggles against me, licking my face, and I allow it, since it's the last time ever.

"Ready?" he asks.

"Ready," I say, picking up my garment and toiletry bags.

"I'll grab this bad boy," he picks up my suitcase.

He walks me to my car, we load up the trunk, and he sticks out a hand for me to shake. "I can give everyone a message if you have one."

"No message, aside from letting them know my lawyer will take care of everything," I answer.

"Sweet," he sticks his fist out to me, and I return the expected bump.

I get in the car and turn the key, smiling at him through the open window. "Take it easy, Joe," I say.

"You too, dude," he replies smoothly.

As odd as I find his behavior, I guess this version of a goodbye is better for us both than him hanging onto my legs, begging me to stay.

I back out of the drive, then suddenly stop the car. I lean my head out the window and call his name. "Hey, Joe?"

He turns back to me. "Yeah?"

"The water heater acts up sometimes, so you might need to get a new one soon," I call out.

"Noted," he yells, tucking his hands into the straps of his ridiculous overalls.

I ease off the brake and back out of the drive. I'm glad this is the last image of him I'll ever see. It's fitting somehow.

Chapter 52

For the millionth time this morning, I mutter to myself about my deplorable hotel. "This place stinks."

Not in an olfactory way, like baby goats.

Indulge me, if you don't mind, and I'll tell you all about my stay thus far in the nicest hotel this area has to offer.

The lady at the front desk recognized me when I checked in. You know how I feel about that. She had the nerve to ask me if I would autograph something for her and then produced the blank side of a used envelope for me to sign.

This is what I have been reduced to. Signing trash so a stranger can show it off to her book club before selling it on eBay for twenty-nine dollars and ninety-nine cents.

The bed is lumpy. The bedspread is thin, ugly, and has a weird texture that gives me the willies if I accidentally touch it. I instructed the cleaning staff to leave it off the lumpy bed but replacing it each afternoon is the only thing they've consistently done.

The bathroom is too small, and its windows are too big. I'm forced to ricochet around in a child-sized area while the whole neighborhood watches me like a specimen in an ant farm.

The remote to the TV is missing the volume button, so I have to listen to everything on a six. What makes it extra interesting is that all the commercials are ten times louder than the shows, regardless of the remote deficiencies. Half the time I can't hear a thing and the other half I have to cover my ears for fear of going deaf.

The front desk is manned during the graveyard shift by a barely human nitwit with less people skills than Frank Norris. I couldn't sleep my first night here and thought perhaps a crossword puzzle might help, foolishly coming downstairs to ask the front desk for help. Not only was he asleep at his post, but when I woke him up he had the audacity to be snippy with me! I explained how it's quite commonplace for the guests at a hotel to expect good customer service around the clock since that is, in fact, what we have paid for. He wasn't fazed at all by my ethics speech, and I went back to my room without a crossword.

You're probably thinking that's a lot to deal with, aren't you? Well, hang onto your hat because there's more.

Oh yes, don't let me forget about the cleaning service.

Twice they've come while I was out foraging for food—more on that fruitless challenge in a minute—and left without doing anything that actually matters. To my knowledge, they have yet to scour the shower or tub, and there's been a smudge of something unidentifiable on the dresser mirror since the day I checked in. They've only changed one of the three trash can liners in my suite, and the faraway sounds of the vacuum cleaner has yet to cross the threshold of my door.

I asked politely if they would give me a fresh bath mat every day, and they said that wasn't the policy. I've had the same one for my whole stay, and its level of disgustingness fluctuates depending on the time of day. For the first couple hours immediately following a shower, the fibers of the mat seep water steadily onto the floor. Half a day later, the mat has dried out as much as it ever will, lending itself to the consistency of soggy cereal.

The towels are rough like the scouring side of a dish sponge. Trust me, these towels are terrible, yet when I ask for more than two at a time they look at me as if I'm some kind of a cockroach with devious plans.

Speaking of cockroaches, let me tell you about the dining establishments around this hotel. I drove north for close to three hours, thinking I'd have an enormous choice of excellent restaurants so near to Chicago.

I found a diner just a few blocks from my hotel but didn't end up eating there. I sat down excitedly, opening the trifold menu with visions of open-faced roast beef sandwiches flashing before me, only to have a dark, shiny, multilegged bug scurry out of it and across the table.

I've kept to the nicer eating establishments after that, and while there haven't been any more cockroach sightings, they've still been awful. There's only so much bland food and room temperature water a man can stand. Why ritzy places think tepid water is a delicacy will always stump me.

No one around here makes a decent pie. No one. It's all fancy pastries with names I can't pronounce.

I've not been able to locate an edible hamburger, properly brewed cup of coffee, or digestible platter of biscuits and gravy even after visiting seven different restaurants.

I'm miserable.

"This whole town really, really stinks," I say again to the empty room.

CHAPTER 53

I twist around in the tangled sheet to look at the clock on the nightstand. It's three-sixteen in the morning. I sigh in frustration, kicking the sheet off with so much force it flutters halfway to the floor.

The room is pitch black, like my mood.

These last four days have shown me that I'm a self-made, miserable old man.

This hotel room isn't my house.

The restaurants around me aren't the Munch Box or the Bistro.

The grocery stores are all the big, dumb chain kinds.

Those are the mechanical, if you will, aspects of my new life that I find terrible.

The largest problem – the one that haunts my every waking moment – is going to shock you. There's no community for me to be a part of. In fact, here are several things I now realize I genuinely love about community.

1. Hart's bug drawings covering the front of the fridge.

2. A fiery redhead bellowing about this and that, and her ever-faithful family.

3. Eating most of my meals across from Rusty's grizzled black face.

4. Poker games with three non-nutjob pastors.
5. Talking, intelligent dogs.
6. Inside jokes and witty banter with Ido and Palmer.
7. Belly laughs with Olive and Taffy.
8. Slobbery kisses and stranglehold hugs from Jewels and Sally.
9. An abundance of positivity, overalls, and being called dude.

Loneliness has taken up permanent residence in me.

I tried to talk myself out of it. I've been going over and over why I left Cardinal Creek. I think about crying in the hospital bathroom earlier this week. The panic attack. The hopeless sorrow. The fear. I rehash all of that, but the reasons I had for reinstating the Code don't make sense anymore.

The truth is, I don't feel scared, sad, or fearful. There's just loneliness. I'm hollow without the people I love, and it's *this* truth that brings on the tears.

"Honey?" I say to the dark room.

I haven't talked to Bea since I got here. The first couple days I was too busy being mad at my surroundings. The rest of the time I've just been too embarrassed and ashamed of myself.

"I'm here," Bea answers.

"I think I've ruined everything," I say, choking on emotion.

"No, sweet husband, you haven't," she says with confidence.

"I left home because I didn't think I could handle losing Rusty unexpectedly," I say, sobs punctuating my words. "Losing *you* unexpectedly was the single most horrible thing I've ever experienced, and I didn't think I could handle it happening all over again with him. Now look at what I've done."

She smiles patiently.

"I chose the time, place, and even the way I'd lose Rusty, thinking that would solve all my problems if I took control of things. It's been far harder to do it this way than if I would have stuck it out there," I say remorsefully.

"I see," she responds softly.

"So I guess you heard I've admitted to loving them," I say quietly.

"Yes, I heard all of that," she answers.

"Leave it to me to wait until I leave to tell anyone. So stupid," I shake my head, furious with myself. "I'm a self-made miserably lonely old man."

"My poor Thomas," she mumbles sympathetically.

"I want to go home, Bea," I whisper.

"I think it's time," she agrees.

I lay quietly in my lumpy bed.

There's something else I've been thinking about. Something that scares me more than the thought of losing Rusty. After a few painful minutes, I gather up enough courage to tell her.

"Bea, I left town when my best friend was on an operating table," I say mournfully. "What kind of a monster does something like that?"

"Monster?" she scoffs. "That's being a bit dramatic, isn't it?"

"It feels authentic," I admit. "I'm so ashamed of myself, Bea."

"Ashamed of what?" she asks gently.

"Ashamed of leaving my friends, ashamed of putting my own selfish feelings ahead of theirs, ashamed of running away when they needed me," I whisper in anguish.

"Having genuine fear and anxiety doesn't make you a selfish man, Thomas," she says. "It's perfectly normal to run away from things that terrify us. The good news is that there is a way to deal with that fear and anxiety so it doesn't have control of you."

"Like another Code?" I ask hopefully. I could sink my teeth into a new Code, especially if it gets me back home.

"No, honey, you don't need Codes anymore. You've grown up this summer," she says. "There are people you can talk to who've gone through a lot of the same things you have. They survived, got healthy, and know how to live their lives unencumbered. Now their victories can be your wise counsel."

"Therapy," I say glumly.

"It's not a dirty word, love," she laughs. "Tell me something. If a member of your orchestra came to you and said he was struggling to get his part nailed down, what would you do?"

"I'd work with him one on one until he was up to speed with everyone else," I say.

"Would you make fun of him for coming to you?" she asks.

I laugh softly. "I see what you're doing."

"Then it should be easy to answer my questions," she says.

"No, Bea, I would never make fun of someone for needing my help." I know I'm digging my own grave, but maybe she's right. Maybe I do need to bury my fear and anxiety once and for all.

"And if the other members of the orchestra found out he asked for help, would they make fun of him?" she asks.

I roll my eyes. "How is it you always make so much sense?"

She laughs lovingly. "Life doesn't come with a handbook. We go through each day doing what we do. Sometimes we make mistakes and have to say we're sorry. That makes us humans, not monsters," she says.

"I've mastered being human then," I say.

"And," she continues as if I hadn't said a word, "sometimes we do the right thing and can be proud of ourselves. Some days are uneventful and we're grateful for the little things that make us happy. Some days are so hard we think it will be the end of us," she pauses, laughing again. "Usually it's not though. Doesn't matter which one of these days you're having though, honey, because all of them are just regular old human days."

"Are you just saying all that to make me feel less like a monster?" I ask.

"Well, sure I am, but it all happens to be true." Her laugh echoes in the dark hotel room.

"So, I've grown up and I'm good at being a human. Hooray for me." I pause, still not entirely convinced. "But, maybe there's no excusing how I left, human or not. I let down a lot of people, not just Rusty. How about little Hart, who can't understand the complex adult behavior of numbskulls like me. Leaving her might be the worst thing I've ever done in my whole life," my voice thickens with tears. "I abandoned Sally, who's been depending on me for a lot more than money. I left Joe and Jewels, who've become family. I left Dan and Scott to deal with Wilma all on their own, and I left Wilma," my throat hurts from stifled tears, and I pause.

"Oh, Thomas," she says softly.

"I don't think they'll want me back," I whisper, fearful that saying it out loud might give it some kind of power. "I wouldn't welcome a jerk like me home after the stunt I just pulled."

"You're on dangerous ground when you assume you know the minds of your friends," she cautions. "If you want to know where you stand with them, you have to tell them exactly what you're feeling and then listen while they do the same. It's as simple as that."

"They might yell at me," I say.

"They might forgive you," she counters.

"What if they look at me differently?" I ask.

"You *are* different, honey, but different doesn't mean bad. What if your differences make life even better than before?" she comes back with sincerity. "The hard part is over. You've revamped your whole belief system in a handful of months. That is vastly harder than sharing your heart with people who love you."

I want to believe her with every fiber of my being. I do.

I just don't know if I have the guts to test her theory.

Chapter 54

"Five days," I tell my haggard reflection. "You've been gone for five days."

I spent all of yesterday trying to muster up the gumption to call home. I cycled through every person I could think of, imagining their reaction to hearing my side of the story. It was awful. None of the conversations ended up with me being welcomed home.

So, I flopped down in the lumpy hotel bed for another sleepless night, depressed and lonely.

It's just past noon on my fifth day of purgatory. I'm not even hungry. I stare listlessly at the wall.

A light rap on the door gets me out of the chair. It's time for the cleaning people to invade my room and do everything but clean. I'll go down to the lobby, I decide. I can't stand the thought of watching them pretend to clean my room one more time.

I turn the knob and swing the door open. A rotund, brown torpedo shoots through the air and knocks me to the ground, her slobbery tongue wetting my whole face.

"Gawd's nightgown, Tommy, you look like the cat's cradle that fell over the moon," Wilma says, stepping over me.

"Maggie?" I gasp, astonished. "Wilma?"

"Well, it ain't the tooth fairy and the Easter bunny," she snorts.

She's really here, standing above me with her hands on her hips, emerald eyes blazing. She opens the closet, pulls out my suitcase, and throws it open onto the bed. "Go get your stuff from the bathroom while I start packing your clothes," she orders.

Maggie lets me sit up. I reach up to scratch behind one of her floppy ears, and the next thing I know I'm sobbing like a baby.

I sob, and sob, and sob some more. I can't quite handle the joy at having Wilma Harper here in my room.

Wilma sits next to us on the floor, takes one of my hands in hers, and holds onto it until I stop blubbering.

I sheepishly peek at her.

"Now then," she says, patting my hand with finality.

I sniff. "Now then what?"

"Now then, if you're all done crying let's get you packed up and go home," she answers with a smile. A tender, sisterly smile.

"Wilma," I'm flabbergasted that she's here. "Aren't you mad at me?"

"Mad at you?" she asks, absently scratching Maggie's neck. "For what?"

"For being a coward and running away," I grimace in shame.

She studies me. "Is that why you've been sitting in this hotel room for five days? Because you're afraid I think you're a coward?"

"Well, yes," I nod. "At least for the last two days."

"What were you doing the rest of the time?" she asks with a slight grin.

"Hating this town mostly," I say. "And realizing just how big of a mess I've made out of my life."

She mulls this over. "You mean the mess you've made of it since you left, right?" she says. "Because back home in Cardinal Creek I'd say you have a fantastic life."

I sigh. "My life is over the top fantastic back in Cardinal Creek," I agree.

"Okay, then let's get going," she starts to stand up.

"Wilma, you didn't answer me," I say, laying a hand on her arm to stop her. "*Are* you mad at me? Do you think I'm a coward?"

"No, Tommy, I'm not mad at you, and no one else is either. And no one thinks you're a coward," she pats me with her free hand. "What we do think is that you have no idea how to manage the love you feel for all of us."

I smile weakly at her. "Are you being serious?"

"As serious as a one-inch nail," she replies, crossing her heart.

I throw my head back, laughter billowing out of me and, man, does it feel good. Maggie barks, running around us in a circle, and Wilma pulls herself to her feet. "Come on now, we've got to get on the road. It's getting late."

"Okay!" I jump up, feeling twenty years younger. We rush around, haphazardly grabbing my things. In the bathroom, a thought crosses my mind. "Wilma, how did you know where to find me?"

"Oh, that," she cackles. "Easy. You started carrying your cell everywhere after the tornado," she pulls her phone out and shows me the screen. "I had Joe turn that thing on so that my phone would always know where your phone was," she points to a red dot above a map of the area my hotel is in. "See here, that's you."

I look at her, amazed. "If that don't beat all."

"I wanted to be sure I could find you if there was another emergency," she chuckles. "I didn't know I'd have to try it out so soon though."

We finish packing and head down to the parking lot where her car waits. "Throw your stuff in the back," she says.

"I can't just leave my car here," I protest.

The Wilma we are all afraid of emerges. "Tommy Sanders, get your rear into this car. Some of those young kids Joe hangs out with can come back tomorrow and fetch your vehicle." She throws the tailgate open and glares at me, hands on her hips.

I could almost kiss her.

"Okay, okay, you don't have to get hostile about it," I surrender, thumping my suitcase into the back. Maggie woofs, pushing at my legs with her head until I walk around to the passenger door.

Wilma talks almost the whole three hours it takes us to get back to Cardinal Creek. She's not had my ear for five days and is sitting on quite a buildup of town gossip. I lean back, stretching my legs out, and listen to her with contentment.

She starts off with an update on Rusty. He's doing way better than anyone expected. He's going from the hospital to a rehab facility in a few days, but that stay should only be minimal. Palmer's going to move in with him permanently for now, she says, to help him manage his crutches and therapies. I cut her off when she starts to talk about his injuries though.

For now, it's enough to know he's doing great.

Sally's taken on more hours at Rusty's shop, and to hear Wilma tell it, she's probably saving him from certain bankruptcy at the hands of his inept nephew. Hart has been trying to teach Mable to read, which is hilarious because that's one thing Hart can't do yet. Palmer and Charlotte have hired contractors to finish up the remodel of the theater. Yes, they are still together, and yes, I'm still expected to be nice to her.

Olive and Taffy are about a month away from their reopening. They've decided to make room for a salad bar while they have the chance to reconfigure the layout of the bistro. "Since I don't have any intentions of ever having one at the diner, I think it's a fine idea for them to have one," she says generously.

Scott and Denise have set a date, she informs me, and next week there's an official meeting of the Harpers and the Brothens to decide who will handle what aspects of the wedding planning. Although she's been ordered to coexist with Edda Mae or else, Wilma tells me in confidence that she's going to ask Sheriff Ryan to be on standby that night, just in case.

"In case of what?" I ask.

"Tommy, don't be naïve," she scolds. "In case of anything! She might try to slip arsenic into my drink, or seduce Dan, or argue about Maggie being the ring bearer."

I don't even know what to say to that.

Joe's kept busy this week while I've been gone, she tells me. When I ask in what ways, she just says, "You'll see in a few minutes. We're almost home."

I look out the window. A warm feeling wells up in me at the sight of my hometown.

Chapter 55

Wilma turns off of the main road that leads to my house, directing us toward the only part of town that was completely untouched by the tornado. When I ask where we're going, she merely grins at me.

She rounds the bend on a county road and pulls into the entrance of the largest of our two public parks. The parking lot is so packed it takes her a minute to find a spot.

"What's all this?" I ask.

"Honestly, Tommy, do you even know what day it is?" she demands.

"Saturday, maybe?" I ask. "Sunday?"

"Oh, for the love of pumpkin spice!" she cries. "Today is Halloween!"

"It is?" I ask, bewildered that this detail has escaped me. After Hart's excessive discussions over the past few days about how much candy she plans on collecting, I can't believe I forgot.

"It is. Joe and Jewels put this big party together for the whole town. Many people don't have an actual house right now, so trick or treating won't be right at all. They figured this was a way for all the kids to have a good Halloween," she explains.

I follow her slowly, taking in all the sights. There's a hand-lettered sign with arrows pointing out different events. Bobbing for apples is by the bouncy house, Trunk-or-Treating is in the east parking lot, pumpkin decorating and the costume contest are to my right. "This is enormous! It must have taken Joe a lot of persuading to get the town to pay for it," I comment.

Wilma's laugh is full-bodied. "The town didn't spend a penny on this."

"Oh really?" I ask. "He got people to donate?"

"Not people," she grins, pulling a bag out of the back of her car. "Person, as in one old sugar daddy who handed him an envelope with five grand in it."

My mouth drops open.

"Here, this is yours," she thrusts something made of cloth into my hands.

"Wait," I say, trying to understand. "Are you saying Joe used my money to pay for this? How did he know he wouldn't need it for the bills?"

"He just knew," she replies distractedly. She's fussing with a folded rectangle of cloth. She shakes it out, draping it over Maggie's back. It's a costume that resembles a certain orange dog from Hart's favorite cartoon.

"But what made Joe…" I stammer, but she's not having it.

"He just knew!" she snaps. "Now get your costume on!"

My costume is a tee shirt with the grandpa character from Hart's dog cartoon printed on the front. Wilma takes off her cardigan, revealing her shirt has the grandma character.

I'd bet everything I know who's dressed as the littlest blue dog from the show.

Suddenly, my curiosity at Joe's free spending disintegrates. I pull my tee shirt over my head, eager to see Hart.

Wilma inspects me, pulling at my collar. "Looks like I got the size right," she says.

Impulsively, I cover her hands with mine. "I'm so glad you did weirdo spy stuff to my phone so you could always find me. Thank you for bringing me home."

She turns her hands upside down, grasping mine firmly. "You're welcome," she smiles. "However, I'm not a woman with tons of free time on my hands, so don't run away again. Got it?"

"Got it," I gladly agree. We start out across the park in the direction of the bouncy house, Maggie trotting along beside us.

I hear her before I see her, and my heart swells with so much love I almost explode. A blue streak shoots down the bouncy house slide and into my arms. The small human wraps herself around my neck, the motion so familiar and so wonderful I have to bite the inside of my lip to stop happy tears from falling.

"Gramps!" she screams. "Gramps, look at my costume! We match!" she points back and forth between my shirt and hers.

"Let me get a look at you," I tilt her to one side. She's wearing a little suit almost like pajamas that looks just like her beloved blue cartoon dog. I'm pretty sure she's grown an inch and gained ten pounds since I've been gone. "I see now. We do match."

"So does Eema!" she yells, pointing to Wilma. "I have a head hat, but it makes my hairs sweaty, and I don't like it." She keeps talking. "Mommy said you went on a bacation, but you forgot me and Mable. Next time you gots to 'member us, okay?"

"I won't ever go on vacation again without you," I promise.

At the mention of her name, Mable romps toward us, leash trailing behind her and Sally trailing behind the leash. "Welcome home, Gramps."

I accept the kiss she places on my cheek with a big smile. "It's good to be back," I reply.

I put Hart down and pick up my puppy, laughing as Mable whines and licks and squirms with joy. I missed her, too.

"You and I don't need to have a big, long talk about it. Just know we're glad you're home, and we will kill you if you go off like that again," she whispers to me. I touch her shoulder, smiling the warmest smile I can.

"I think he's learned his lesson," Wilma tells her.

"Come on, Gramps," Hart says, pulling my hand. "I wanna swim for apples."

"Catch up to you later at the food truck?" Wilma asks, and I nod.

Me, Sally, and Hart follow Mable. Mike, Val, and Lee are gathered around the apple bobbing stations, trying to keep some semblance of order among the throngs of small humans milling around the barrels. When they notice me, there are lots of hugs. I hug them right back.

"Look at you," Val says, tapping my shirt.

"Nice to have you back," Mike says.

"Wait," Lee sizes me up with a grin. "Have you been gone?"

I give him an especially hard hug, saying, "Thanks for, you know, all of it."

"I didn't mind a bit," he smiles.

Too antsy to wait in line, I leave Sally and Hart to "swim" for apples.

"Okay," Sally says, "see you over at the food truck?"

"You bet," I say.

I find Ido at the pumpkin decorating station. His bushy brows raise in surprise at my sudden appearance and he grabs me in a burly embrace. "Hi, moron," he says. "Glad to see your old face."

"Good to see you, too, you big idiot," I reply.

Bob and Neil are a ways down from us at another decorating table, but when they hear Ido's cries of surprise they wave at me as well.

"Hey, Thomas, good to see you!" Bob yells.

"You too, Bob," I yell back.

"I'll be tied up here for a while longer, but I'll see you over at the food truck later," Ido says.

"Yeah, sounds good," I say.

The food truck seems to be where it's at, so Mable and I follow the signs past the costume contest, spotting the truck in the east parking lot.

Several cars have formed a loose ring around Olive and Taffy's food truck. The back end of each car is facing inward, adults positioned at the decorated, open trunks with buckets and bowls of candy.

Costumed kids are clamoring around each trunk, bags held out and cries of "trick or treat!" echoing around the lot.

I scan the cars, my heart leaping with joy at the sight of Rusty's pickup flanking the food truck. Rusty's sitting inside a miniature version of a black convertible, eyes crinkled from smiling at the kids.

For a moment, fear floods my brain again. What if he's not willing or ready to forgive me?

My fears are short lived because he notices me too and waves me over with a warm smile. I raise my hand so he knows I see him and tell my feet to start walking.

"You ain't gettin' no candy without a proper bag to put it in, I don't care how much you beg," he greets me.

My response doesn't leave my lips because, up close now, I see his convertible has been built around the wheelchair he's sitting in.

I stare at him, eyes wide, emotions rising.

"Hey," he says, snapping his fingers.

I pull myself together, saying shakily, "Hey."

"This is just for show. Don't get hung up on it," he says, tapping the wheelchair. "Besides, it's not all that bad," he moves the front of the cardboard car away from his wheelchair. Only one leg is in a cast. "See? Not a big deal at all."

"So, uh, you're okay then?" I murmur.

"Right as rain," he grins. "How about you? Feeling okay now?"

"I feel like a coward," I confess.

"Aww, Thomas, that's malarky. A coward wouldn't have faced down a tornado to save Peggy," he says. "You're a bit stunted emotionally. Fragile like a delicate flower maybe, and thick headed like a Neanderthal, but you're no coward."

"Yeah," I say, looking up into the sky. I kick at the gravel. "Okay, I guess, but still, I feel awfully bad about leaving like that."

"Don't. If I'd been conscious, I'd have sent you away for a week anyway. I know how hard that hospital is on you," he says. I look back down at him, he grins back up at me, and I see he's the same old Rusty. "Come on, now. We've been through too much over the years for you to feel bad about leaving. I'm serious."

"I don't know why you still want to be my friend. I don't think I deserve you," I blow out a breath. "I'll tell you one thing though. I love you."

"I know you do, Thomas," he says. "I love you right back."

"Alright then," I say, relief sweeping through me.

A group of kids walk between us, and Rusty tosses handfuls of candy into their outstretched bags. Another group follows them, and then a little boy and his dog come up. Mable and the dog exchange butt sniffs, and when my eyes meet Rusty's over the heads of the kids we bust out laughing.

I'm starting to feel normal.

When the kids are gone, Rusty says, "Did you have any fun up in Chicago?"

"It was the worst place on earth," I reply. "But I had a lot of time to get some thinking done. I made a decision that's probably going to be a good thing for all of us."

"Oh yeah? What's that?" he asks.

"I'm going to ask Mike to, you know, help me find someone to talk with me about my, uh, issues," I say.

He squints in surprise. "Therapy, you mean?"

"Blah," I make a face. "Can't we just say I'm talking to someone?"

He laughs. "I guess you *did* do some thinking."

"Bea's kind of thinking mostly," I say.

"I reckon her way of thinking is always a fine way to approach life. *Talking* about how you feel will do you some good," he says.

"I think so too," I reply.

"Uh oh, here comes the happy brigade. I should warn you; he's been a little bonkers ever since Wilma called to say she was bringing you home," Rusty aims his gaze over my right shoulder. I don't have to guess who he's talking about because the cry of "My dude!" tells me.

Joe, Jewels, Kenny, and Palmer bum-rush me, the force of their hugs practically knocking me to the ground. I'm kissed on the cheek. I'm pounded on the back. I'm hugged, and hugged, and hugged some more. They're all talking at once, and I let it wash over me like a tidal wave.

It feels incredible.

"Oh, Thomas, you big goof," Jewels says, smothering me with affection.

"I knew Wilma wouldn't take no for an answer," Palmer grins.

"Hey, hey, Sanders," Kenny says. He's wearing a pirate costume, shirt and all.

"Kenny, I don't know if I've ever seen you in a shirt before," I remark.

"Don't get used to it," he says, eyes twinkling. "Halloween is a once-a-year event."

Finally, I turn to Joe. "My main man," he says, eyes glossy.

"I thought you might have outgrown those overalls while I was gone," I say, swiping at my own wet eyes.

"No way, man," he protests. "No way."

"We've got a little welcome home party arranged for tonight," Jewels says. "Everybody's meeting at the diner."

"Who's everybody?" I ask.

"Everybody. Olive and Taffy, Kenny, the Harpers, of course, Peggy… everybody," Palmer says.

"What about…" I cough, clearing my throat, "will there be any local nitwits there?" I ask, winking at Palmer.

"Well, sure," Palmer replies. "After all, the party is for you, you nitwit."

I would've been happy to carry on bantering with them for hours, but another horde of kids cram themselves in between us and Rusty, their voices screaming for candy, and that's mostly how the rest of the afternoon goes.

I'm home. It's chaotic, loud, and emotional, but that's okay.

Because I'm home.

Chapter 56

The sun sinks down into the treetops, casting my neighborhood in yellow and red hues. Peggy's house is in shadows but glowing from the inside. I happen to know she's baking pies tonight, and if I play my cards right I might get a slice or two tomorrow.

I've brought a glass of iced tea out to the porch, the old rocking chair Bea favored fitting my tall, lanky frame just right. I rock back and forth, rhythmically, waving occasionally when people walk past my yard. It's been in the high seventies all day, which is warm for November, but as the sun sets I know it'll cool off quickly.

Last night me and all my closest friends (even Charlotte Davens) stayed at the park until it got too late to see. Then we moved the food truck and our private party to the diner, and that segment of the celebration lasted until almost eleven. There was food, and laughter, and more food, and pie. There were a lot of hugs, too, and I can now say I've had my fill of hugs for a while.

By that, I mean at *least* until tomorrow morning.

Once everyone decided to call it a night, I asked Joe to walk home with me.

I described Bea's last months of life, the good and the bad, and the hell I went through those first weeks after she died. We talked about

Rusty becoming my new tether to sanity even though I was too dull to really grasp that until now.

I shared with him in depth about the mental gymnastics I've experienced since we heard about Rusty's injury, frankly explaining how the agony of my days away progressed until Wilma showed up at my door.

I was only two or three sentences into my speech when I realized just how easy it was to be brutally honest with him—as easy as it has always been with Bea. He listened quietly while I talked, taking it all in, just like she would have. Just like she did every time.

"Without Rusty's friendship, I would have done a lot more than tweak Bea's Code," I acknowledged. "I would've become so afraid of having any feelings, I think I would have holed up in my house like a recluse and that would've been the end of me."

"Love and relationship will always win out over fear," he nodded emphatically. "Remember when you started packing and I was flipping out, begging you to stay and all?"

Cringing, I said, "I do."

"I was afraid of losing you, too, and that fear had me almost paralyzed. I couldn't think of anything to say that would convince you to stay, or imagine how we would all live without you," he said. "I get it, dude. I get what you were feeling."

"I was out of my mind that day," I said.

"You were in hyperdrive, that's for sure." He agreed. "When you were trying to convince me that having relationships was the problem, I told myself it was over. We were all going to lose you."

"Ugh," I said, my voice full of regret.

He clapped me on the shoulder. "As soon as you dropped the L-bomb, I settled down. Love is a powerful force when it's finally set free to do its thing," he tapped my arm, chuckling. "You might've thought you needed to leave, but the second you admitted out loud how you really felt about us all, I knew right then you'd never be able to stay away. Everything in the whole world comes down to love, and you were overflowing with it, man."

"You're cocky when you're right, aren't you?" I remarked.

"Maybe a little," he said, his Joe Tackett patented grin taking up his whole face. "Or maybe I'm just a smart guy."

"Well, smart guy, *this* is all your fault, you know," I said, patting my chest.

"What's my fault?" he asked.

"Whatever it is that's happening to me. This emotional evolution I'm having. That day you showed up in town with your little brown package, you set the wheels in motion that changed my life. Because of you, I did and said and felt things this summer I never would have if left to my own devices," I said.

"You think?" That gigantic Joe Tackett grin was still lit up.

"I *know*. Rusty still would've gotten hurt, and I guarantee you I would've run away from that at top speed." I shook my head incredulously. "But without your influence, there's nothing on this planet that would've gotten me to come back here to face all that emotion, not even Wilma."

He considered this for a block or so.

"The emotional evolution of Thomas Sanders…" he said thoughtfully, "was all my fault."

"Yep, that's how I see it," I replied.

"That's pretty dang cool," he said, wonder in his voice.

"Before your head swells with too much pride, let me make it clear that an emotional evolution does not mean I'm going to believe in your fairy tale god, or drop the L-bomb willy-nilly, or let the girls kiss me without putting up a little bit of a fight," I warned. "I won't ever be *that* emotionally evolutionized."

He tucked his thumbs into the straps of his overalls, threw his head back, and laughed long and hard. "Alright, dude, alright."

"And while we're confessing our deepest secrets to each other, don't you have anything to say to me?" I asked.

"Um," he hesitated.

"Maybe about how you blew through the money I gave you to pay the bills with?" I supplied, trying not to smile.

"Oh, dude, I mean, I did feel a little touch of guilt over that," he laughed, adding, "but not much. You did tell me you're rich enough to buy the whole town, after all. I figured a Halloween party was chump change compared to a whole town."

"Yeah, yeah, I see how it is. Old Thomas looks away for five minutes and you got yourself a financial coup," I joked.

It's that one tiny snippet of our conversation that has me out here on the porch tonight. The phrase "emotional evolution" has reminded me of something Bea said back in that hotel room. An early stirring of an idea that's now turned into a full-blown understanding.

"Honey, are you here?" I say.

"I'm here," she answers, her voice soft and satiny.

"I've been thinking about the first time I got close enough to you to see how blue your eyes are," I say wistfully. "They reminded me of the skies over the ocean."

"You were so shy that day," she smiles. "It made you cuter."

I chuckle. "I was terrified by how much I liked you. I think you were the first thing I had ever truly wanted that didn't have anything to do with music. I had no idea if I could win you over. No confidence at all. But I had to try. I remember thinking it would have devastated me if I didn't get you."

"You did get me," she says, giggling. "Although I wasn't going to let you leave the room without giving me your phone number."

"You never told me that before," I laugh with her. "We were together for, what, almost fifty years?" I ask.

"Fifty-one," she says, eyes beaming. "Fifty-one lovely years."

My eyes trace the dark silhouette of the trees against the fiery sky.

Today's sunset is moments from being over. There will never be another sunset exactly the same as the one that happened on this November first. I am in awe of the distinctiveness, the unique raw glamor of the special, gorgeous sunset that belongs only to this specific day. I soak it all up, appreciating how the colors in the sky shift and swirl in their final moments.

Here's the neat thing I've learned. Tomorrow when I wake up, I won't grieve that tonight's colorful sunset had to give way to the dark. I will see hundreds or thousands more sunsets in my lifetime. While they won't be exactly like this one, they will be similar enough to conjure up these same wonderful feelings.

Contentment, peace, amazement, and even joy.

Feelings of home.

"Back in that horrible hotel, you said I grew up over the summer and don't need a Code anymore," I remind Bea.

"That's right, sweetie. You don't need it," she answers. "I'm so, so proud of you."

I sit there, quietly, taking in the last beautiful bursts of pinks, oranges, yellows.

When it's completely dark and the sliver of the moon is the brightest thing in the sky, I reply. "I think I'm proud of me, too."

"You should be. You've done an amazing thing this summer," she says.

"That's what got me thinking that maybe it's time I let you go. It's not that I would love anyone else the same way I love you, but I'm surrounded by humans who act like you, talk like you, love like you." I say. "How could I feel alone with all these people around?"

She gasps, her tearful smile warming my heart. "You won't."

"So, you think it's time for me to let you go, too," I say, the words feeling bittersweet.

"I'd say it's about finding yourself more than it is about letting me go, Thomas. You're ready for that," she says.

My voice catches, and I swallow hard. "If I let you go tonight but need you in a few months or years, will you still be there?"

"I don't see that happening," she answers, adding, "but where else would I be?"

And that's all the answer I need.

"Good night, Bea," I say, and head into the house to see what my family is up to.

Ponderings on The Emotional Evolution of Thomas Sanders

"It's fine, I suppose—if you like Tommy's watered-down point of view. If I were telling the story, you'd understand the seriousness of the criminal activity we're facing in Cardinal Creek."

— Wilma Harper, Munch Box Diner

"Thomas wrote a book? I wasn't aware of that. Does it mention my, uh, daughter's vocal skills, by any chance?"

— Charlotte Davens, Cardinal Creek Resident

"I know Palmer thought it was a bit on the dull side, but personally, I was on the edge of my seat until the very last word."

— Rusty Burdine, Trusty Rusty's Pit Stop

"Oh, Rusty said that, did he? Well now, what kind of man has to slap "Trusty" onto his own name just to lure folks in?"

— Palmer Rawlings, Starstruck Theater

"Dude, I'm so stoked—this town's an outstanding subject for a book. I mean, who wouldn't want to read about relationships all woven together by love?"

— Joe Tackett, Optimistic friend of Thomas

"A wholesome story rooted in the raw reality of everyday life."

— Bea Sanders, Thomas' tether to sanity

"If you sniffed this book all the way to the end then you've found yourself some good friends."

— Maggie the Boxer

www.ingramcontent.com/pod-product-compliance
Lightning Source LLC
Chambersburg PA
CBHW020458310726
48979CB00016B/2704/J
* 9 7 8 1 9 6 1 6 0 5 8 5 5 *